Series: Small Town Happiness
Title: Hank's Widow
Location: Belgrade NE

Hank's Widow

By Linda (NMI) Joy

Dedication:

To John, who always supports me,
To my mother, whose efforts have encouraged me.

© 2021 by Trudy V Myers

Print 1 - July 2021

MoonPhaze LLC, 613 del Pilar Dr., Groveland FL, 34736
MoonPhaze.com

Cover designed by:
https.//selfpubbookcovers.com/DesignzbyDanlelle

Table of Contents

Table of Contents (cont.)

Table of Contents (cont.)

Prologue
May 15

The sky was overcast, the air saturated with mist, as if the entire universe found this day as sad and miserable as the humans who lived through it.

In a tiny town in Nebraska, a glistening red car pulled off the graveled street and into the driveway of a small house that had seen better days, stopped close behind the ancient sedan parked in front of the garage.

The lawn was overgrown, but the driver of the sports car ignored the drops the grass deposited on his black suit legs and polished shoes. He opened the front door and climbed the 3 steps to the enclosed front porch, then walked into the house's front door, into the living room. He walked forward, faced the sofa, and considered the picture frames on that wall. Each frame held a number of photos of people; some trimmed down to show only one person. He was well familiar with these frames and their contents, although some of the faces he didn't know personally.

The final frame held his attention. Large and crowded, it held all the grandchildren. Most of them had spouses, too. Gram had been toying with the idea of getting a larger frame for the grandchildren, and to use this frame to start a collection of great-grandchildren. But she hadn't gotten around to it.

His gaze landed on the last 4 grandchild entries, and his eyes stung. Way back when those pictures had been of babies, they had looked like quadruplets, although they weren't. As they grew, they had each slowly developed their own look, until they looked like brothers, and not the cousins that they actually were. The 2 in the middle of those 4 were still high school graduation photos. The outside 2 were wedding pictures; one of Lyle and his extremely pregnant bride; Lyle looking bored and Gloria looking… scared.

But the picture he stared at was the other wedding photo, a snapshot of a blissfully happy couple on the steps of a large courthouse.

"Forgive me, Gram," he muttered, then removed that frame from the wall, pulled the happy couple from the collection. In another moment, the frame was back in place and he slipped the photo into the inside pocket of his suit jacket.

Just in time.

He turned as the outside door opened and another black-suited man stepped onto the porch, paused to wipe his shoes on the welcome mat. The 2 men could have easily been mistaken for brothers. The first man stepped forward and opened the door to the porch. "What are you doing here?"

The other man held up 2 bottles of beer. "Thought we could both use one of these."

A brilliant flash of light and deafening thunder left them momentarily dazed. Then the sky opened and rain fell in sheets. In Nebraska, a hard rain might last a few minutes or several days. They unbuttoned their suit jackets and moved forward to sit at the dining room table, unscrewed the caps from their beers.

"Got any plans for this place?" asked the recent arrival.

The first man took a pull from his drink and watched the rain through the windows. "I only half own it. So, no, not without talking with Hank. Keep it from falling down, I guess."

"Well, here's what I think."

"You've started thinking?" the first man teased. "That will sure surprise your old teachers."

The other man grinned in acknowledgement of the teasing, then let it fade. "I was thinking you should at least lock it up tight. Otherwise, Lyle's likely to move in. And even if he didn't, he'd probably sell everything off, piece by piece."

"He doesn't own it."

"Would that stop him?"

The first one sighed. "No. Probably not." He stood up. "Well, turn off the utilities… I can call the companies tomorrow and get them officially turned off, but I can turn things off here today. You want to check the doors and windows? And I'll lock the front door as we go out. Once the rain settles down."

"Sure. I'll start with the garage and work my way back here."

They both entered the kitchen, turned right through the washroom, out to the enclosed breezeway between the house and garage. The first man halted at the hot water heater, while the second headed to the other end of the breezeway.

The first man cleared his throat. "Bob, Lyle's got his family at the old Jessup place."

Bob stopped halfway down the breezeway, but didn't turn. "I know."

"I could ask Hank about letting them live here."

Bob sighed. "I won't ask you to. He has to grow up. I can't condone bailing him out any more, Chuck."

"You sure?"

Bob continued up the breezeway to the garage door.

Chapter 1
February 2 (3 Years Later)

When the doorbell rang, Wanda dropped her soup spoon in surprise. Glancing at the kitchen clock, she pulled a tissue from a near-by box, dried her eyes and blew her nose. Then she headed for the apartment door, tossing her unfinished bowl of soup in the frig along the way.

Two men stood in the hallway, one with a batch of flowers and the other with a six-pack of beer. She opened the door. "If you've come a-courting, I'm not in the mood," she jibbed, or tried to. It was so hard to be brave, after these past few weeks.

"We have come bearing gifts," Greg stated, "in hopes of cheering you up."

"Thank you," she said sincerely. "Come in."

They knew their way around the apartment, like old friends do, but they demurely followed her into the living room. Wanda plopped into an easy chair, wondering how quickly she could get rid of them. Then guilt set in, for they were Hank's friends, and therefore her friends, and she had been pushing them away since the funeral, unable to pull herself out of her grief long enough to accept any of the help they had so generously offered.

Eyes stinging, Wanda leaned forward and grabbed the box of tissues off the coffee table. "Sorry I've been so distant, guys. I just... I haven't been able to think or... do much of anything."

Jack was the first to respond. He always seemed to know what to say. "That's understandable, Wanda. You needed some time, maybe still need time. We just wanted to stop by, make sure you were okay, see if there's anything we can do, any way we can help." He sat down on the closer end of the sofa.

Greg was seldom at a loss for words, but he merely stepped forward and handed her the bouquet before he sat next to Jack.

For a moment, Wanda stared at the flowers. When the tears started flowing down her cheeks, she pulled a tissue from the box and set the flowers haphazardly on the side table. "They're lovely, Greg. But please don't bring me any more flowers. All they do is remind me of the hospital, and of the funeral."

"Sorry, Wanda," he muttered.

"Have you been eating?" Jack asked. "Sleeping?"

"Not much," she admitted, and blew her nose into the damp tissue before she tossed it into a wastebasket. "And not well."

"That's what I thought. I brought beer because it's a good soporific." He opened a bottle with a practiced twist and offered it to her.

She accepted it without thinking. It seemed to be the only way she got anything done these days, without thinking. If she had to think, she simply broke into tears and couldn't function.

It was how she had managed to pay the monthly bills a few days back. She hoped there was money in the bank to cover them. Hank used to take care of that.

Feeling tears welling in her eyes again, she raised the bottle of beer and took a large swallow, then grimaced at the taste.

"You don't like beer," Jack realized.

"No, I don't," she agreed. "It's why we always brought rum and cola to game nights."

"Do you have any of that?" Greg asked.

"I don't know. I haven't looked."

"Well, you don't have to drink the beer," Jack told her. "Sorry, I didn't think. The furthest my thoughts got was that you might need some help sleeping."

"I do," she agreed. "I've been raging at myself for not sleeping. So I'll drink the beer and hope it works. I just ask for one favor."

"Anything," Greg promised rashly, which was the way he did things.

"When I start nodding off, don't put me to bed, just get me onto the sofa. There's a spare key near the door; lock up when you leave, and bring it back in a couple days." She took another drink, not quite so large, because she knew the awful taste now.

"We'll do it," Jack agreed.

She felt a touch of dizziness already, and wondered just how much of that bowl of soup she had managed to eat before their arrival. She'd lost track of how many times she had reheated that same bowl of soup and tried to eat. Obviously, she didn't have much food in her stomach to soften the effects of alcohol.

She considered the two men sitting on her couch, Greg and Jack. But where was— "Where's Lee?"

"Well, we haven't seen much of him, either, since the... accident," Greg stated.

Lee had been Hank's roommate, his best friend, despite having studied completely different fields in college. "Have you checked on him?" She hoped he wasn't having as hard a time adjusting to a world without Hank as she was.

"We call him once or twice a week. He always seems to be busy with work. Even on the weekends. But maybe things are loosening up a little; we got together for supper a couple nights back. He's awfully worried about you."

"I just have to... get through this rough patch and get used to the way things are now."

"We're all having to get used to that."

She started to raise the beer to her mouth again, stopped as her stomach objected to the idea. "Jack."

"Yes."

"I want to lay down now."

Both men stood up, and Greg carefully removed the beer from her grip, helped her stand and make her way the 2 or 3 steps to the couch. He even found a throw pillow and placed it under her head, while Jack draped the afghan over her.

She thought she would probably cry, as was usually what happened when she tried to sleep, but she was out before her friends turned the lights off.

Chapter 2
Wednesday, April 15, 3:05 PM

So much for the Midwest being flat. These hills might not be tall, but they're still— As her car topped the latest hill, Wanda slammed on the brakes. She breathed in relief when she realized the blacktop road did not suddenly end at the bottom of what was—in comparison to all the others—a very large hill. In fact, the blacktop made a sharp right turn to run into a small village.

As she approached that sharp turn, she realized a dirt road wandered from the corner to the left. But the blacktop led into town, and it was the town she wanted, so she slowed almost to a stop to make the sharp turn.

Two residential blocks had a trailer house and several old houses, some of them looking abandoned. Then 2 blocks of businesses, which seemed to consist of 2 gas stations—neither open, but one of them obviously out of date and defunct—two bars directly across the street from each other, a couple unused buildings, a small post office and a fire station.

The fire station was on her left. She stopped to consider it, for it was one of the landmarks she'd been given. It was on a corner where a side street crossed the blacktop. She considered the grassy area directly across the side street and saw some pieces of playground equipment. That was evidently her 2nd landmark, the city park. She turned left onto the dirt side street.

One block, another left, and the house is on the right— ***Oh!***

The house on her right was an old-fashioned 2-story, made of wood with a porch across the front. But the roof had fallen in, the porch was barely still there, and the entire thing leaned precariously.

All her hopes fell into her belly, leaving her feeling sick and hopeless. Her eyes stung, and her foot slipped off the brake, allowing the car to move forward before she got her foot back in place. That movement brought the car further along, almost to the overgrown hedge along the dilapidated house. She thought she saw something beyond the hedge, and she let the car move further forward.

This house was only a single story, also wooden, once painted white, with 3 cement steps leading up to an enclosed porch. Between this 2nd house and the hedge was a driveway that led to a garage. Was she being irrational, to hope that this was the house she had inherited? At least it wasn't falling down, even if the grounds did look over-grown.

She threw the transmission into park, grabbed her phone and the card she'd gotten from the real estate agent in Fullerton, the county seat. "Mr. Parkins, this is Wanda Davis. We just met about an hour ago."

"Yes, Wanda. I'm surprised to hear from you. Did you get yourself lost in tiny little Belgrade?"

"I am confused. I followed your instructions, and I found 2 houses on this block, on either side of an overgrown hedge."

"What? 2 houses? There can't be. You must be lost."

"Oh, you old fool," a woman's voice came over the phone at a distance. "I told you the old Egger house hasn't fallen down yet. I imagine all the junk stored inside is what's holding it up. But following your instructions, she would have seen the Egger house first!"

"Wanda, does one of the houses look ready to fall down?"

"Yes, definitely," Wanda confirmed. "Any second."

"Well, that would give you a fright, if you thought you had bought that place, wouldn't it?"

"It certainly did."

"I never intended to scare you like that. Remember, I told you the house isn't a palace, but it is livable. So, the 2nd house, with the garage and an enclosed front porch."

Wanda sighed in relief. "That's good. Thanks. And it has furniture, too?"

"The way I understand it, it holds all the possessions of your friend's late grandmother-in-law. It could take you some time to go through and clean it all out. At least, I'm not aware of any of the family doing that. The house and everything in it when she died went to 2 of her grandsons. But one of them already had a house of his own, so he signed it over to the other."

This is getting to be a habit. First, cleaning out all my father's possessions when he left us. Then all my mom's when she died. Then Hank's stuff, when I decided I had to move here, that I couldn't afford to live in Chicago anymore. And now all of Hank's grandmother's stuff. "I can handle that. Thank you, Mr Parkins."

She parked in the driveway, close to the garage. She doubted many people would notice her SUV unless they actually drove by. Taking her purse and laptop, she went to the front door and tried the key. It worked.

She hurriedly stepped onto the porch, almost afraid someone would stop her. There was a sofa against the old windows of the house. Straight ahead was the front door, with another window into the house to the right of the door. A rocking chair stood in front of that single window.

The same key unlocked the original front door. She stepped into a stifling hot, large room. The top of a former wall denoted where it had once been 2 rooms. There was an upright piano in the near left corner, a dining table and chairs against the windows of the left wall, a big heating stove in the far left corner. On the right wall was a large curtained doorway, then a sofa, and 2 doorways in the far right corner. The door on the right wall was closed; the open doorway in the far wall looked like it led to the kitchen.

Everything was covered in dust. When she pushed the curtains aside to look inside the room on the right, dust enveloped her, inducing a coughing fit. She staggered across the room and opened a window, then another and finally the 3rd. Slumping into a dining room chair, she gulped in fresh air several times.

"I need to be more careful until I get a chance to clean," she told herself.

This time, there wasn't a great billow when she moved the curtain, but still enough to irritate her nose. A quick look revealed a built-in closet on the left, a window to the driveway straight ahead, a hospital bed along the right wall, and the window to the porch at the foot of the bed. She carefully lowered the curtain and headed for the closed door in the other right-hand corner of the living room.

This door opened onto another small bedroom; closet door and a bureau on the left, double bed on the right, window out to the driveway in the far right corner.

The open doorway did lead to the kitchen, which had a frig, cupboards, sink, stove and 2 more doorways. She moved straight ahead, squeezed past the cooking stove to the next room, which was 2 steps down.

This room was as large as the living room, but it was, again, a bedroom. It had 1 old-fashioned dresser in the far right corner, a double bed in both the near right and far left corners, and a small heating stove in the near left corner. And there was another door across from this one. She walked over to open it.

It opened to the back yard. *Oh, I have enough to do today to look through the house. Save the back yard for another day.*

She closed and re-locked the back door, opened all the high little windows in this back bedroom, and returned to the kitchen. Going to the side through the next doorway, and down 1 step, she found herself in a utility room, with 2 sinks on the near wall, a washer and dryer on the far left corner. Straight ahead and on the right were doors. She checked the right door first, and finally found a bathroom.

It was tiny, with maybe 2 square feet of open area to stand in, but it had a sink, a shower stall and a toilet. She could live with it.

The other door was thick and heavy, hard to open. Beyond it was the clapboard side of the garage, 3 steps down, a cement floor of a narrow, enclosed 'breezeway' between the house and the garage.

Okay, that's enough exploring for today, I guess. Wait a minute. She carefully placed a hand on the side of the water heater. *Cold. Well, I suppose they turned it off when they realized the house would be empty for a while. Oh!*

Wanda stepped back into the utility room, tried to turn on the faucet in one sink. Nothing happened, so she tried the sink in the kitchen. Ditto on the nothing. Without thinking, she opened the refrigerator. Somebody had cleaned it out, so it wasn't full of mold and stench. It also wasn't cold, and the interior light hadn't come on.

Closing that, she tried the light switch by the door, but the kitchen light didn't come on.

Great. No water. No electricity. Even if I find stuff to clean with, I can't.

Wonder who I call to get the utilities turned on?

Back in the living room, she noticed an old fashioned landline on the wall near the heating stove. Searching the room, she found a thin telephone book in the drawer of an end table sitting against the wall. Oh, no, it's years old, almost a decade. Well, how often does a utility change its phone number? At least one of them has to have the same number.

Ignoring the gathered dust, she sat down at the dining table, pulled out her cell phone and called the first utility. In the space of half an hour, she had made appointments for the water, electricity and gas to be turned on. Nobody could arrive before tomorrow. And no matter how hard she studied the old phone book, she couldn't find a listing for any cable company or an internet provider.

Her stomach growled with hunger, and she tossed the phone book away. Guess I've done as much as I can do today. Looks like I go back to Fullerton, find a place to eat and a motel room. How long a trip is that? Twelve miles, according to Parkins, but it seemed so much longer.

She stared at the sofa, thought of all the beds this small house held. Why would 1 old woman need so many beds? Did she have a lot of company? Are they hold-overs from when she was raising a family?

Well I won't need this many beds, but they are here now, and it seems silly to go looking for another. Which leaves food. And bars often serve food. So before I spend the gas to drive all the way to Fullerton, maybe I should try for something local.

She paused outside in the shade, grateful for a slight breeze that cooled her off a bit and cleared her head. If she understood the layout of this town correctly, she should find both bars by going to the end of this block, and then turning left for a block. She made sure she had her purse and had locked her car and the house, then set off on foot.

The open area on the same side of the block as her house was mostly grass, with a few large trees scattered about. Hedge bushes did their best to designate the inner corner where two sidewalks met, but like the grass, the bushes were overgrown. She could see where the sidewalk should be, but found herself walking more and more on encroaching weeds as she got to the corner and turned to head for the main road through town.

There was a corrugated steel building on the left corner as she crossed the gravel street. It looked like a giant tin can laying on its side and half buried in the dirt. She couldn't imagine what it was used for, but she had a vague memory of another such building someplace along the main road.

Across the street from the half-buried can—katty-corner from the overgrown emptiness—was a blue house with various flowers in pots dotting its porch and walls. She wondered who might live there, taking such particular care of their home.

As she approached the alley halfway along the block, her sense of smell was assaulted. The back end of a bar reached the alley, and behind it, several garbage pails were overflowing, their lids either on at a canter or missing completely.

She glanced across the street, where the other bar also reached the alley. Those garbage pails were in a neat line, and the lids were on tight, or seemed to be. She found herself crossing the street, having suddenly decided to try the other bar first.

Somehow, the sidewalk on this side of the street, on this half of the block, was about 3 feet above the street, and without declining, this difference disappeared by the corner sidewalk. As she walked forward, she passed a metal staircase leading to the 2nd floor. When she approached the front of the bar, she saw a teen-aged boy sweeping the sidewalk, sending dirt and dust over the curb.

"Good afternoon," she greeted the boy as she approached. "Is this bar open at this time?"

"Um, yeah," he answered so softly she barely heard him.

"Good. And does it serve food?"

"Uh huh."

"Wonderful. Thank you for the information." She turned to look at the store front. The windows were clean, and several potted plants on display looked healthy and happy. She stepped up onto the small indented porch and stepped inside.

She froze in the sudden coolness of the bar, but the temperature wasn't the reason. She found herself staring at a man who looked almost like Hank's twin.

The man who looked so much like her dead husband stood behind the bar, writing. He looked up, put his pen down and gave her a close copy of Hank's smile. "Hello, stranger."

Of course it's not Hank. Hank is dead. And he did tell me one time that everybody in this town is related to him. I should have thought about that before I came. But there's no going back. I have to make a new life for myself. Here.

She managed an uncertain smile. "I wasn't sure you were open." She glanced around the bar, which was devoid of any customers. "Must be too early for the crowd to come in."

"Not much crowd on Wednesdays," the bartender stated. "Mostly I open up because that's the day my supplies are delivered. How can I help you?"

She walked over to the bar and sat. "I'm looking for food."

He put his crossword puzzle book away and gave her a menu. "Want to start with a drink?"

"Oh, I think I'd kill for an iced tea, if you have it."

"I do. And you don't have to get rough to get some. You look the menu over, I'll be right back."

She ordered deep fried mushrooms, a grilled cheese and fries, and commented that his menu didn't have any desserts, not even ice cream.

"Not a lot of call for desserts here," he answered. "Weekends, I bring in a couple pies or a cake, if you're still here. You in town visiting?"

"No, I'm moving in."

He seemed surprised. "We seldom get people moving into Belgrade. What house?"

She couldn't remember the address, the street number wasn't even on the house, as far as she remembered. The house had belonged to Hank's grandmother before Hank had inherited it. "Davis. The old Davis house."

He stared at her for a long moment. "Okay, this is serious. It's not called the old Davis house. It's called the old LaFlamme house. Gram was abandoned by her first husband, Davis, and left with 5 kids to raise by herself. Once she'd done that, she married LaFlamme, and they had a great marriage; he welcomed all the kids to the home like they were his own, and all the grandkids as well. So it's called the LaFlamme house."

"Why is that important?"

"Because if you call it the Davis house, everyone will know you must be an outsider. Nobody here would have ever called it the Davis house. Maybe you heard it referred to as Gram's house. Or even Hank's house."

"Mr Parkins kept calling it my house," Wanda whispered.

"Ah." The man gave a short nod. "Then you must be Hank's wife, Wanda. I thought you looked like her."

"How do you know what I look like?"

"Hank sent a wedding photo to Gram. But it wasn't a big photo, so I wasn't sure it was you. You might have been anyone. So, what are you doing all the way from Chicago?"

"Moving in," she repeated. "My job can be done anywhere, so why pay rent in expensive Chicago if I own a house here?"

"I see." He glanced out the bar's windows, then at the big clock on the wall behind him. "Well, I suggest you use your maiden name, and don't tell anybody you even knew Hank. Let them think you bought the house from Hank's widow. And while you're at it, stay away from the rest of the 4 cousins."

"What 4 cousins?"

"Gram's last 4 grandchildren were boys, all born within a month, and they all have tarnished reputations, especially when it comes to women. Hank was the oldest, and he went away to es-

cape his reputation. Probably the smartest one of us. So do yourself a favor and stay away from the rest of the cousins."

"How can I stay away from someone when I don't know
who they are?"

He sighed. "Well, we all look like Hank. Like twins, practically."

"So… you are one of the cousins that you're warning me to
stay away from?"

"Right."

"Doesn't that strike you as strange?"

"Not in Belgrade," he answered, and gave a slow smile.
"Some of us grew out of the behavior that tarnished our reputations. But Belgrade has a long memory."

"That must be hard to live with."

"It's hard enough."

An old car with a peeling paint job drove past outside,
flipped a u-turn in the intersection and parked in front of the bar.
"Here comes my Wednesday crowd," the barkeep stated.

Two teenage girls got out of the front of the car, and 2 simi-
larly-aged boys from the back seat. They were joined by the
young sidewalk sweeper.

"Teenagers?"

"Nieces, nephews and cousins," the bartender said. "They
come in on Wednesdays—which, as you guessed, is not a busy
day for me—to play pool, listen to the juke box, and just generally have a couple hours to themselves.

The barkeep offered his hand. "By the way, I'm Bob Nichols, the next to youngest of the 4 cousins."

She completed the handshake. "Wanda, um, Sinclair. Glad
to meet you. How much do I owe you for lunch?"

The teens entered, making enough noise with just 5 of them
to drown out any effort to talk. The girls headed for the juke box;
the boys selected pool cues.

Bob held up a finger to ask Wanda to be patient, then gave a
shrill whistle. "Okay, kids, you know the rules. One free can of
pop each. Come and collect them, just as soon as I've settled
with Tommy. Come on, Tom."

Bob went to the cash register, opened it up and took out 2 checks, which he laid out on the bar, along with a pen. The sidewalk sweeper signed the backs of both checks, and Bob laid out some money on the bar, returned the checks to the cash register. Tommy shoved one bill of the cash across the bar toward Bob and pocketed the rest of the money.

The rest of the kids moved forward, and Bob gave them each a can of soda. They turned back to their chosen entertainment, but they had noticed Bob's paying customer, and were quieter about enjoying themselves.

Bob came back to stand before Wanda. "Tommy does a variety of chores for me, I pay him, he sends most of the money to Fullerton with me, where I deposit it in his college savings account.

"Now, let's see. Burger, fries, mushrooms, drink, tax. That's $17.52."

Wanda placed a $20 bill on the bar. "Keep the change. And I hope you can help me with a problem."

"Depends on the problem."

"Well, I found an old telephone book, and I've made arrangements for my utilities to be started tomorrow. But I wasn't able to find the local cable company or internet provider. I'm particularly worried about internet. I can work anyplace that has electricity, but without internet, I'm out of touch with my editor. Among others."

"Well, that is a problem. Hang on a minute." He pulled a rotary phone and a skinny phone book from under the bar. Then he opened the phone book and started dialing.

"Hello, Wilma. This is Bob Nichols in Belgrade… Yeah, it has been a while, but you know where I work, and it's open to the public… Yeah, I know how that goes… Listen, there's a new family moving in here in Belgrade, and they need to get cable and internet hooked up… That would be 12 North B Street, right here in Belgrade… Hang on." He put a hand over the receiver and asked Wanda, "Sorry, what was the last name?"

"Sinclair," she answered. It felt strange to use her maiden name again.

He turned back to the phone. "Last name is Sinclair… No, it's never had either one hooked up. Maybe the houses on the back side of that house. Or across the street. This used to be my grandmother's house… Of course it's still standing. I think you're thinking of the Eggers house, not the LaFlamme house… Is that the earliest you can do?... Okay, I'll let them know. Thanks, Wilma."

He hung up and turned to Wanda. "They can't get to it until Friday afternoon. Something about having to splice into the wires at whatever is the closest point the current wires get to your house. But they're fairly sure they can get you hooked up in time for the weekend."

"Wonderful! Thank you so much, Bob. I was so afraid I would have to drive to Fullerton and just start asking questions."

"Well, just the neighborhood barkeep being helpful," Bob told her. "Anything else you need?"

"Well, I could use some help moving furniture, washing things, sorting through things. I never knew your grandmother. Her belongings won't mean anything to me; they might to some of the people who live here. On the other hand, useful items like towels and sheets I'm likely to keep, but I need to figure out where they are."

"How do you feel about teenagers?"

She smiled and glanced at the teens. "I'm not much older than they are."

"Okay, then." He gave a whistle and addressed the 5 teens. "Kids, this is Wanda Sinclair. She's bought Gram's old house, and she'd like some help cleaning it up, moving furniture, stuff like that. Anybody up for that?"

The sidewalk sweeper put up his hand right away. The others agreed a little slower.

"Well, thank you all," Wanda told them. "I wasn't expecting quite so many helpers, but that just means the work will go that much faster, right? Now, I don't even have water yet, so I'm thinking we can get started on Friday. About noon?"

"No," one of the girls said. "We don't get home from school until almost 4."

"Okay, I'll just get started without you, and you guys show up when you can. I can swing $10 an hour for each of you, so we'll look at 2 or 3 hours on Friday and see how far we get, okay?"

That met with their approval. "Good. So, I'm going to Fullerton Friday morning to lay in some groceries. What kind of snacks and drinks should I bring back for you guys? I've heard teens are always hungry."

They all started talking at once—even Tommy—and Bob gave another shrill whistle to quiet them down.

"I know what you can get for them," Bob said. "Any kind of chips, cookies or candy. And to make it simple, regular and diet cola. They'll all drink one of those." He turned to the kids. "Get back to enjoying yourselves, before I send you home to study."

One of the girls stuck out her tongue. "School's almost over, cousin."

"Then you've got finals to study for, papers to finish," he returned. "Maybe I should send you all home to start doing all that, so us grown-ups can talk."

The teens reacted with raspberries and groans and returned to their pool and juke box dancing.

Bob grinned and softly explained, "They hate being told they aren't grown up. Now, anything else I can do for you?"

"I don't think so. I doubt if you serve breakfast here."

"Nope. Don't open until 11. Some days, even that seems too early."

"Well, as soon as my utilities get turned on tomorrow, I'll be here, looking for something to eat. See you then."

"Yeah, I'll be here," he promised.

"Thanks for everything." She left the bar and walked back to her new home.

Chapter 3
Thursday, April 16, 8:05 AM

Wanda had just dumped the bedding from the 2nd bed into the cement double sinks in the laundry room, when she heard pounding from the front of the house. She stepped into the doorway between the kitchen and the living room, saw Bob standing on her front steps. He held up a brown paper bag.

She walked across the room, unlocked the inner door, stepped onto the porch, unlocked the outer door and opened it. "What are you doing here?"

"Welcome Wagon." He bounced the bag up and down. "Bacon and egg sandwich for breakfast, ham sandwich for lunch, a unit of blue ice to keep things cool. Thermos of coffee, a couple bottles of tea and a couple of water. Thought you could use help to get you through all your appointments today."

"Come in!" she invited, and they moved to the table in the living room. "You are a life saver. I was already feeling hungry. How much do I owe you?"

"Nothing. The welcome wagon doesn't charge for their welcome basket."

"Then I definitely owe you a big favor."

"Be careful saying that around here. You never know what the person you say it to might demand in return."

Wanda munched her first bite of the bacon and egg sandwich and poured herself a thermos-cap full of coffee. "You keep warning me not to trust you. But you haven't done anything to warrant my distrust."

"So far," he added. "And now I'd like to talk about something I've told you not to talk about here in Belgrade. Call me curious. You and Hank never even came back to visit before he... passed. Why did you decide to move here?"

"Because rent in Chicago is expensive." She blew on the hot coffee and went on. "I get a bit of survivor's pension, and I make a bit with my work, but my income is thin and… unpredictable. Why pay rent when I've inherited a house?" She dared to take a sip, blew on it some more. "Hank used to say he came from the middle of nowhere. I don't think I realized just how far into the middle of nowhere I was moving."

"Well, it has some good points," Bob said and grinned. "Give me enough time and I'll think of one."

"Oh, come on!" Wanda told him. "If you really felt that way, you wouldn't still live here."

"You're right. Belgrade is probably a whole lot quieter than Chicago, so maybe that will help you work. And if you're worried about money—"

"Not currently."

"Let me finish. I drive to Fullerton every Monday morning. I go to the bank, do errands and get groceries. Now, that's just part of my life, it's already figured into my budget. So if you want, you could ride with me, run any errands you have, get your own groceries. That way, it's a trip to Fullerton that you don't have to pay for gas."

"That doesn't seem very fair to you." She held up a finger to stop him from protesting. "So when I'm feeling fairly flush, you must allow me to pay you a few dollars toward the gas you use." She took another bite of her sandwich.

"Well, I'm reluctant, but I agree, because I suspect it means a great deal to you, to be able to stand on your own 2 feet."

"You're right," she agreed. "I wasn't sure anybody would ever catch onto that idea as quickly as Hank did. You only took a tiny bit longer than he did."

"Hank was a good man. I'm happy he found himself a level-headed woman." He gave a deep sigh. "And now, let's not talk about him again. I don't think you'll be happy with the results if people here discover you're his wife." He glanced at his watch. "I'd better take off, before somebody realizes I'm here. Remember, you don't want to be friends with any of the Four Cousins."

"I'm not sure why, but I assume you know the community."

"Okay. Come to the bar this afternoon, and I'll let you buy your own supper. After all, I have to make a living."

She grinned. "You've got a deal. And thanks again."

* * *

9:10 AM

Wanda had finished both her breakfast and stripping the beds. Since the bedding filled the large sinks in the wash room, it seemed a depressing amount of laundry. Rather than tackle any of the closets or dressers, she turned to unloading her car. Not having any place ready to receive her computer, books or note-books, she stacked most of it in front of the old piano, with stuff that was more easily replaced on the front porch sofa.

She was in the midst of unloading her car when the first ser-viceman arrived. She was thrilled to hear he was there to turn on her water, but she wouldn't have any hot water until after the gas man had arrived and the water heater had time to heat up. But cold water could start washing away the dust that covered every-thing.

As she waited for the receipt for her deposit, the service-man—he'd said his name was Xak, if she understood him right—asked, "You said you moved here from Chicago?"

"Yes."

"You renting this place from the owner?"

Not really. But Bob said... "Yes."

"Excuse my nosiness, but how are you going to support yourself all the way out here? It's not like there's any jobs here."

"I have a job," she answered. "I just need access to the in-ternet to turn in my product, and that arrives tomorrow after-noon."

"Oh, one of those inner-net jobs, huh? I'll probably never understand how those work. Still, why all the way out here?"

"Because living in Chicago is expensive."

"Hope you know what you're doing," he said, handing over the receipt. "If the pipes start banging, let the water run for a while, it should work itself out."

She smiled as they both stood up. "I've dealt with air in pipes a time or two."

21

"Well, good luck," Xak said as he left.

Wanda followed him out and finished unloading her car. Then she went to the kitchen and found a large plastic basin and a washcloth. In the living room, she climbed on chairs to reach the cobwebs up by the ceiling.

Cleaning up all this dirt and grime was a dirty job, with lots of trips to the kitchen to get fresh water. It was a small price to pay for a new life.

* * *

5:43 PM

There were 3 or 4 people–adults, this time–already in Bob's Bar when Wanda entered. Bob turned from talking to one of his patrons and smiled at her. "Looks like you've been busy."

She looked down, saw her t-shirt and jeans smudged with dust and grime. She grimaced and sat at the bar. "I think I've taken the top layer off in the living room. I'd love to take a good vacuum to that sofa. Or shove it into the washing machine."

Bob barked with laughter. "That might be what it needs, at that. Well, anybody that's worked that hard is probably hungry. Do you know what you want, or would you like to see a menu?"

"You're right, I'm hungry. Cheeseburger, fries, fried mushrooms, one of those bags of chips–the blue bags–and a cola."

"Coming right up." He was back in a few minutes with her drink and the chips, placed a beer on the bar for a newcomer, and shortly after that, he brought her food.

As Wanda ate, another 2 men came in, looking sweaty, disheveled and dusty. Bob looked surprised to see them, but served them each a beer without asking what they wanted. He did ask one of them, "Is your boss coming in?"

"No, he went to St Ed to bid on a roofing job."

"You guys that far along on the Zimmerman house?"

"No," the worker answered. "But it may be a matter of, you know, cash flow problems. The house is our biggest job ever."

"Yeah, that's for sure."

Wanda finished her meal and ordered another cola, paid her bill. "Thanks, Bob. That really hit the spot. Now I'm going to go home and call it a night."

"Worked that hard? Well, some days are like that. See ya."

As Wanda turned for the door, Bob turned back to his customers, all of them regulars, she was sure. As she walked home, she wondered how long it would be before she was a regular, too. She didn't drink much, but like the teens, she might look for companionship, as she struggled to make friends in this totally alien place.

Chapter 4
Friday, April 17, 7:59 AM

As Wanda drove down the main business street of Fullerton, she found an open spot directly in front of the Dew Drop Inn café and pulled in. *Wonderful. I can have breakfast first, and by then, maybe every place else I want to visit will be open.*

She stifled a yawn. The hospital bed had been more comfortable than the sofa had been the first night. But she had just spread out a freshly laundered blanket to sleep on. And despite going to bed so early, she was still tired from all the work she had done the day before.

Grabbing her purse, she climbed out of her car and headed for the café door. Several men emerged as she approached, all laughing. "You just want us in a good mood," one of them said.

She skirted around them until she got right up to the door, where one of them had stopped short and now blocked her progress. She looked up and… *Hank! No, not Hank. Of course not Hank. The hair is too light, the eyes not the right green. Another relative, no doubt.* "Excuse me."

"Sorry, stranger," the man replied. "You surprised me." He stepped out of her way and the entire incident was over.

Wanda entered the café and sat, ordered pancakes and eggs.

Pulling a small notebook from her purse, Wanda added 'alarm clock' to today's shopping list. Like most everything else in the apartment back in Chicago, the alarm clock that had awakened Hank every weekday had been given away or sold. Happily, this house was furnished, and she hadn't noticed many things that she would need to replace immediately. But she'd get an alarm clock today. For Mondays, when she'd need to be up and ready to leave. She didn't want to make Bob wait for her. It would be a poor way to repay his generosity.

* * *

12:21 pm

Most of the groceries went into the refrigerator, but a few things she left on the counter. Part of moving in was to take everything out of the cupboards, discard some things, wash everything she was keeping, and figure out how she wanted things arranged. There were cup hooks under the cupboard to the left of the sink, and she'd spotted dishes and bowls inside it. It made sense to store those things there, she supposed… easy to put them away as they were dried. But the old cupboard to the right, she hadn't even peeked inside that. Maybe her cans and boxes would go in there. Or, maybe in the built-in wall cupboard she'd finally noticed along the doorway from the living room.

Too many variables to make many decisions right now. The living room would be the living room. One of the side rooms from that would be her office, and the other would be her bedroom. That was as far as her decisions had progressed.

Later, Wanda finished folding the bedding from all 4 beds and stacked them on the couch on the front porch, where they would be out of the way. Later, she would need to find a place to store it all. Or get rid of it, which also applied to the beds. Except the hospital bed, which she was going to use as hers.

She was going to ask the boys to take the other beds apart. She would need a place to store them. Possibly the big back room, she supposed, but they'd be an eyesore. That would be her exercise room, and she'd prefer not to have to look at extra beds that would never be used because she didn't have any friends who would ever come visit her in this middle-of-nowhere.

She sighed and pushed away her self-pity. If not in the back room, she'd better find a place to store them. The only places she hadn't considered yet were the breezeway and the garage.

The breezeway might be a possibility, if she moved a couple chairs out of the way. The chairs were dirty and wobbly, and she wasn't sure they were worth keeping. Behind the chairs, she was surprised to find the frames and mattresses of 2 cribs. Cribs? How old was this lady? Well, old enough for grandchildren, evidently.

25

At first glance, the garage seemed full. *Tables, chairs, lamps, tools, even a lawn mower. Maybe. It's too dark in here to really be sure what it holds. The only windows are on the west side, and it doesn't look like they've been washed – or even just dusted – in decades. Maybe if I...*

The garage door was 'locked' with 2 hooks latched into eyes, and a board that fit into a pair of wooden supports. By trial and error, she discovered she needed to remove the board first, and then undo the hooks. Even then, the door wouldn't open all the way, because her car was pulled too close. But the partially open doors allowed her to see there were 2 lawn mowers in storage, both old, but one very old.

What a find! Because the lawn has definitely gone wild. But I didn't get any gas today, so it will have to wait until Monday, at the earliest.

*   *   *

3:37 pm

The kids showed up almost a full half hour before she expected them, and just as the cable/internet guy left. She stopped pulling clothes out of the dresser in the front bedroom to 'sign them in for the day'. Then she started explaining some of the chores she needed help with.

"I want all the full-sized beds taken apart. I'm thinking they might fit in the breezeway, where the cribs are already stored. I don't know if the chairs in the breezeway are any good, but they can go in the back room. Now, I saw a couple lawn mowers in the garage, but I don't have any gas, so the lawn will have to wait until Monday, or even later."

"Anything with plants, Tommy is your guy," the blond boy stated.

The blond girl—Wanda suspected they were brother and sister—seemed to bristle at that pronouncement. "And if the mowers need any service—which seems likely, after sitting for so long—then Zita is who you need!"

"Well, I need to know what kind of gas to get," Wanda stated. "Then if you could come back Monday afternoon and take a look at one of the mowers, Zita, we'll go from there. Oh, and could you all please leave your phone numbers this evening? I might come up with more chores after this weekend.

"Now. If 2 or 3 of you want to get started on the beds, the rest of us can start cleaning out the front bedroom. I'm hoping to get those curtains down from the doorway and throw them in the washer, where I expect they will completely dissolve and go down the drain, since all the fibers seem to have been replaced by dirt!" They smirked at that idea. "I so firmly believe that, I think those curtains should be a load all by themselves. I've got a load of towels and washcloths that's ready to fold. All the fabric items in the dresser and closet also need to be washed. We can stack those in the utility room sinks until it's their turn. Otherwise, I'd like cobwebs taken down, dusty woodwork and the windows washed. It's all grimy grunt work, and I truly appreciate your help."

The boys—en masse—went off to tackle the beds, and at some point, she heard them hammering on something metal, which seemed odd, but she and the girls were busy. "It's no worse than spring cleaning at home," Zita stated.

"Except this time, we're getting paid for it," replied the blond girl, whose name, Wanda gathered, was Ella.

"Perhaps you girls can give me some advice," Wanda suggested. "I'm trying to decide if I should make this room my bedroom or my office."

"I'd make it an office," Ella stated at once. "This room has avenues to let light in. And if you move the rocking chair on the front porch, you can look through that window and see who's at the door, decide if you want to stop working or not."

"Very good points," Wanda stated.

"Yeah," Zita agreed. "You have to remember that—way back when—this room was probably intended as the parlor. Gram had 5 kids. Therefore, a house with only 4 rooms was pretty cramped. There wasn't room to have a fancy parlor. Probably not enough need for one, either. So, by using it as an office, it gets a little closer to its original purpose."

"You're quite right," Wanda agreed. "I hadn't thought of any of that at all."

"Well, you aren't family," Ella stated. "We can't expect you to know the family tales."

Wanda realized the girl had raised her voice to be heard over some horrible noise that seemed to be approaching the house. "What can that noise be? I was told this was a quiet town."

"It's just a tractor," Zita stated. "They don't come into town very often."

"It could be Cousin Chuck," Ella suggested. "The grass has gotten pretty tall."

The noise suddenly stopped. "That's enough to give a person a headache," Wanda muttered. She caught a glimpse of someone moving up the driveway toward the garage. "Do you know him?" she asked in sudden alarm.

Ella leaned against the window for a better look. "It's Cousin Chuck. Oh, get out there, Zita, he's gone right for the lawn mowers."

"Oh, I left the garage doors open," Wanda remembered, but the girls had both dashed outside. She hurried after them.

'Cousin Chuck' was the man who had temporarily blocked her entrance into the café that morning. He was squatting just inside the garage, listening as Zita launched into a litany of things that needed to be done to the lawn mowers. He had a little smile on his face as he listened… until he looked up and saw Wanda.

He stood up abruptly. "I should have known."

"Hello," Wanda greeted him with a tentative smile. "I'm Wanda D—Sinclair. I'm just moving in here, and was hoping I could get the lawn mowed sometime in the next few days."

"Yeah, that could happen," he stated, then pointed to the lawn mowers. "But not with those."

"I can get them ready!" Zita exclaimed.

"I know you can," Cousin Chuck told her. "I'm the one who got them ready for storage, and pretty much all you need to do is clean and gap the spark plug.

"But the grass is too tall, too thick for a regular lawn mower." He pointed to the end of the driveway, where a tractor— silent right now, thankfully—stood at the edge of the gravel street. "I'll knock down most of it, and then Tommy—or whoever—can nibble at the rest of it once Zita gets the plugs gapped." He moved forward, closed one of the garage doors so he could move out past Wanda's Toyota and the old car she assumed the kids had arrived in. "Get back to work, kids. Don't make City Girl regret having you help her."

"They've been doing a great job. I won't regret paying them at all," Wanda told him, incensed by his casual assumption they weren't working well.

"Good," he answered, but kept moving toward the tractor. "I wouldn't want you to get any bad ideas about country folk."

He climbed up onto the tractor and sat down. Wanda—fearful of how loud the noise would be outside the house—made a beeline past the girls and Tommy, into the breezeway, where the other 2 boys were stacking up pieces of beds along one wall. A loud noise started up outside.

"That's good, boys. Are you about ready for a snack?"

"Always," one of them said.

"Felix is always hungry," the other explained. "We'll just finish getting these things arranged and then we'll be in. Oh, and what did you want to do with those 2 chairs? There's no room for them here anymore."

"Put them in the back room. They're dirty and wobbly, but maybe I can—I don't know—fix them. Somehow."

"Yeah, it wouldn't take much," he answered.

Wanda set out 2 packages of cookies, hoping the teens would like them. If not, she had 3 flavors of chips for them to choose from. That was when she remembered she hadn't yet washed any glasses for them to drink from, and then found it hardly mattered, because the ice maker had not made any ice.

That was disappointing. Happily, she had placed the soda pop in the refrigerator when she got back from Fullerton, and they routinely drank straight from the cans, according to what she'd seen in Bob's Bar on Wednesday.

The boys came in from the breezeway and crowded around the kitchen sink to wash their hands. Hearing them, the girls emerged from the front side room and joined in washing up.

Wanda heard a lot of put-down teasing from 4 different voices.

As she waited for the kids in the living room, she puttered with laying out paper napkins when movement outside the windows caught her attention.

The tractor was no longer on the street, but was now driving through the overgrown grass in the wide swath between her house and the old hedge at the end of the block. It pulled a contraption behind that chopped off the grass in a line as wide as the back tires of the tractor. Cousin Chuck drove it straight back to the alley, where he turned around and drove back again.

He said he'd knock down most of the grass. Does this mean… She swallowed in a sudden fit of fear. *Do I own all that land, from this house to the end of the block?*

Cousin Chuck was doing her a great favor. The least she could do was invite him in for… soda pop and cookies. As soon as he turned the tractor off, she'd go out and invite him in. There was no way he'd hear a word she said if she tried to talk to him while the tractor was on.

The kids came from the kitchen. Someone had gotten a towel, and they passed it back and forth as they dried their hands. They each picked a chair at the table, and when Wanda explained that she had no ice, Felix and Ella went back to the kitchen to get cans of pop for everyone.

The kids ate hungrily as they talked about school and what they would be doing once school was out for the summer. None of them mentioned having a job lined up.

Felix—as Wanda had thought—was Ella's younger brother. And the final young man answered to the name of Rusty. Other than the one set of siblings, they were all cousins of each other.

"So, Rusty, you don't think it would take much to fix those 2 chairs?"

"Naw, I've helped my folks fix up chairs in worse shape."

"Well, I haven't got any idea how to start. Other than to wash them down. Which won't make them wobble any less. At least, I don't think it would. Could I hire your parents to fix them?"

"You can try," he returned. "I'm not sure when they could

fit it in, though. I heard them put off a sofa job for a month, and that was just a couple days ago." He cleared his throat. "But if you want to trust me with the job, I'll only charge half as much. Plus, if I run across any difficulties, my folks will help."

"Are you sure this would be okay with your parents?"

"They've been suggesting me for a couple years now, when they're booked up and the job isn't too difficult. It's how my sis got started, and she's got her own shop now, down in Shelton."

Wanda didn't know where Shelton was, nor how big a town it was. She supposed having a shop meant the sister was able to support herself from proceeds from that shop.

"Wanda?"

She looked up from her ruminations in surprise, saw Ella holding her phone halfway to her ear. "Bob wants to talk to you." She handed her phone to the older woman.

"Wanda? Bob here. Look, I normally have 2 servers on Friday and Saturday nights, but one of them just called in sick. I was wondering if you could help me out. Things get pretty hectic here around 8. Start settling down around midnight. I'll pay you my regular pay for servers and you keep all your tips."

"Bob, it's been years since I've done any waitressing."

"Great! I didn't know if you had any experience at all!"

"What do you usually do when a server calls in ill?"

"Draft my mother and then hear about it for about 6 months. I'd really like to avoid that, at least once."

"Alright," she gave in. "When do you need me and what should I wear?"

"Jeans and t-shirt is fine. 8 to midnight, if that's all you've got; earlier if you can do it."

"Okay. Let me plan with the kids, and expect me by 7."

"Great! See you then!"

Wanda gave the phone back to Ella. "Well, we need to end this a little early. Are you all okay with doing some more tomorrow? I don't want to get you up too early on a weekend…"

"Gotta mow," Tommy stated, and glanced at the others. "Maybe noon?"

"Don't kill yourself, Tommy," Ella told him. "Fact is, Wanda, we all have household duties we do on the weekends. We could be here about 1, stay till 5 or 6. If that's okay with you."

"That sounds good," Wanda agreed, and was glad she had 'over-bought' snacks. "Now, being so new in town, I have some questions. Maybe you can answer them. I've never had to hook up my own computer before, not for years. I made notes before I took it apart, but if I have any trouble getting it back together, is there somebody you suggest I contact for help?"

Felix blushed and hung his head. His sister Ella studiously kept her mouth shut. But Zita said, "Felix is the local computer guru. If you have any problems, he can help you."

"Wonderful. Felix, you and I can work on that tomorrow, once I find some kind of desk for it, and we get the front side room cleaned out. Now, the guy who turned on my gas lit the pilot light on the water heater, told me I wouldn't need a pilot light on the heating stoves until the weather turns cold in the fall. Is there someone who can help with that? I confess I know nothing about heating stoves like this house has."

"Well, we all know how. But you should be taught the right way," Ella stated reluctantly.

"Oh, one other thing," Wanda broke in. "The ice maker in my refrigerator doesn't make ice. That seems to be more important right now than adding heat to this house."

Ella seemed to consider what to say, turned to Zita for advice. "She's already met him," Zita stated.

"Yes, you're right," Ella agreed, and turned back to Wanda. "The best handyman in town is Cousin Chuck."

At this sudden reminder of the man using a tractor to cut off waist-high grass, Wanda realized she no longer heard that tractor. "Oh! I don't hear him anymore! Certainly he's not done!"

"I heard the tractor move to the back yard," Felix stated. "That was about the time we started snacking. The back yard wouldn't have take much more than a couple swipes, and when he got done, he would have used the alley to head home."

"Oh, I meant to invite him in for a cold soda. It is hot today, after all."

"Don't worry about Chuck. He does a lot of work outside

during the summer, so he's used to it." Zita seemed pretty sure of her statement.

"So come back tomorrow around 1-ish and see how much we can get done?" Ella asked.

"Yes. And what I want to get done is get that hospital bed moved to the other bedroom, get ready for this front room to be my office. Anything more than that is pure gravy."

"I'll take one of the chairs home with me tonight," Rusty stated. "Have an estimate ready for you tomorrow."

"That sounds good," Wanda told him. "We can throw it in the back of my car and I can drive you home."

"Naw, home's only a couple blocks away. And a chair isn't that heavy."

"Well, if you're sure. Then I'd better let you all go so I can get ready to go help Bob."

* * *

6:59 PM

It was straight up 7 o'clock when Wanda walked into Bob's Bar. Five men were ranged around the pool table in the back, and almost all the seating places were full. "Hey, Wanda! Thanks for coming in on short notice. Down at the end of the bar, Helen will set you up with an apron and all you need to get started."

Helen was a middle-aged brownette whose mouth twisted in a moue of disapproval as Wanda approached her. "Some of these guys are likely to take that as a challenge," she stated, and tossed the apron over Wanda's head so its bodice semi-covered the word 'Taken' that embellished the front of Wanda's pink t-shirt. The hem nearly reached the floor, but Helen folded and tied it to form a pocket, to hold a waitress pad and pen.

"Bob will fill orders from the bar and us. Pick up is here at the end of the bar. You handle the pool table and the 2 tables nearest the pool table, and I'll handle all the rest. But if you need help, ask."

"Sounds good," Wanda agreed readily. "But tell me, please, who are the men playing pool?"

"Oh, that's Chuck and his crew," Helen answered. "Mostly harmless, as long as they're here in the bar. I don't expect they'll stay much longer. I heard they're working an extra day tomorrow. They must have fallen behind on the Zimmerman house."

Wanda would have asked more questions, but Helen moved away. Wanda checked her 2 tables to see if they were ready for more drinks. Mostly they were, and she jotted them down on the pad, then glanced at the pool players. Chuck was taking aim at the 8 ball, so Wanda approached a blond man who stood nearby, holding a pool cue and a beer bottle. "Good evening. I'm Wanda, your waitress for this evening. Are you and your friends ready for more drinks?"

"Hello, Wanda. I'm Steve. Yes, we are. Say, have we met somewhere?"

She nearly rolled her eyes. "Not officially. What is everybody having?" He showed her the label on his beer. "All 5 of you are drinking the same?"

"It's 6. Dick's outside, having a fight with his girl friend."

Wanda remembered a car at the side of the bar, the windows steamed up and the car rocking rhythmically. "Um, I don't think they're fighting anymore."

"Well, bring him one. Somebody will drink it, if he doesn't come back in."

"Okay. I'll be back in a moment."

By the time she returned, Steve was aiming, so she approached Chuck, handed him a bottle.

"Put it on my tab," Chuck told her, his attention on the table. "All of them on my tab."

"Yours is paid for," Wanda told him. His head jerked around to stare at her. "I wasn't quick enough to invite you in for a cold soda after you mowed." She turned away to deliver the rest of the bottles.

"That's not a good idea, City Girl." Chuck told her quietly. "You don't want me in your house."

"So I've been told," she responded. "On the other hand, I need someone to fix my refrigerator, and your name came up."

His brow puckered. "What's wrong with it?"

"The ice maker doesn't make ice. I found some ice trays in a cupboard, but like all spoiled city girls, I expect refrigerators that have an ice maker to make ice."

His lips started to curl, then he frowned instead. "I never called you a **spoiled** city girl."

"It's implied in the term."

"Then what's implied by the term 'country boy'?"

This was too close to flirting, Wanda realized, and resolved to nip that idea right in the bud. "That you're male and live in the country," she responded briskly. "If you aren't interested in fixing my ice maker—I understand your crew has fallen behind in a big job—then perhaps you could suggest somebody else."

"Oh, I'll do it," he told her. "If you don't mind my showing up tomorrow, about noon." He was whispering now.

How many people are wondering what we're whispering about? There's no reason for whispers. "Fine," she stated in her normal voice and turned away, gave the rest of the beers to the men with him, the one called Dick having come in through the door near the pool table.

When she returned to the end of the bar, Bob quietly asked, "What was that about?"

Now he's being secretive! What's with the men in this village? "He asked me to put that round of drinks on his tab."

"Oh. Sure. Chuck's tab. 6 beers. No problem."

Great. I never got a chance to tell him I was paying for Chuck's beer. Guess I still owe Chuck a cold drink. She set that thought aside and continued to work her tables.

By 9, Chuck and all his friends had finished their beers and left. A couple of older women left their booth and claimed the pool table. From the sounds of balls falling into pockets, they were both decent players. Wanda approached to see if they needed refills.

"What was your name?" asked the brown-haired woman she approached. "Wanda, wasn't it?"

"Yes, that's right."

"Moved into Gram's house," the woman went on. "Well, I'm Vallie. Bob's mother. And that's Alice, Helen's mother."

"Ella's my granddaughter," Alice offered.

"That's right, you've got the teens working for you, cleaning the house up, don't you? They're all excited about it, and don't quite know what to make of you. I think it's because you treat them like responsible people, and not like the little kids we still tend to think of them as."

"Well, I see them as kids, but not little kids," Wanda stated. "They aren't that much younger than I am. They just aren't out on their own yet."

"True," Alice agreed. "But that's getting closer every day, and all we can do is hope we've done a good job of raising them." She had missed her latest attempt, and Vallie was now aiming her shot. "Val takes a beer, and I'd like a tequila sunrise." She held out a ten.

Wanda took it. "I'll be back shortly."

Eventually, Helen met Wanda at the end of the bar. "You ready to call it a night?"

"Um, does the other girl usually leave before closing?"

"We take turns if it gets this slow," Helen stated.

"Well, if you're sure it's okay."

"You ready for your after-work drink?" Bob asked from behind the bar as Wanda started to untie her apron.

She was so surprised, she almost forgot to collect her tips from her apron and transfer them to her jeans pocket. "What?"

"It's a tradition here," Helen stated. "It gives us girls a chance to get off our feet for a while before we head home. And it helps us fall asleep when we do get home. Plus, it's on the house."

Wanda considered the state of her feet. They were painful, since she had given up waitressing several years ago. She thankfully sat on the empty seat at the end of the bar.

"What'll it be?" Bob asked.

"Sloe gin and coke," Wanda answered.

"You got it," he told her.

Wanda took a big gulp, then reminded herself to drink it slowly. She still needed to get home. And to bed. She wasn't fond of drunk people, and did her best to avoid getting drunk. There were only a few instances of drunkenness in her history, and those had been deliberate decisions. Most notably her wedding night, and one night a few weeks after Hank's funeral, when she hadn't been able to fall asleep on her own. Hadn't been able to sleep since the accident.

She didn't have either kind of reason for getting drunk right now, just some tired feet that would get her home with a little effort on her part. Helen had been right; letting them rest for a few minutes before she left would be a good thing.

Chapter 5
Saturday, April 18, 10:04 AM

Wanda paused after putting a 3rd load of laundry in the washing machine and the 2nd load in the dryer, to consider the state of her house and what she would have the kids do when they arrived that afternoon.

The dresser and closet in the front bedroom had been emptied, the contents partially washed and dried. What was done was folded and stacked on the couch on the front porch. She wondered if there was a thrift store where she could donate the old clothes. To be perfectly frugal, there were a couple shirts and a sweater she would keep for herself, but the vast majority would be of no use to her. She hadn't even started on the dresser and closet in what would be her bedroom, nor the dresser in the big back room.

I'm procrastinating, she realized. *I've had these thoughts every day since arriving in Belgrade.*

It was probably the shock of the move, of finding just how much her life had changed with this one choice she had made. She needed a bit of a pick-me-up, something she enjoyed, before the kids arrived this afternoon.

It didn't take her long to start a batch of bread. As it raised for the first time, she found herself humming as she brought in the rest of her stuff from the car. She had unconsciously been worried about its safety, even locked in her car, which was snuggled up close to the house and garage. It was a relief to toss back the old quilt she had spread over it and find her computer pieces and other items right where she had left them. She carried them inside and all the way to the back room. It was bare now, except for the 2nd wobbly chair and the dresser that was stuffed with she-didn't-yet-know-what. Sooner or later, she would need to find places for all her things, but it made her feel better to have those things in her house. Especially her computer. That needed to be set up soon, so that she could get some work done.

She only found 1 loaf pan in the kitchen, so she used a cake pan to hold the other 2 loaves of dough. Those 2 would be flatter, but it didn't matter, they would taste fine. With the loaves rising, she started a pot of potato soup. A simple meal, but one she and Hank had enjoyed many times. Her mother had taught her to make it way back when, before her father had left.

She invaded her boxes of personal stuff to find a notebook and started a list of things she needed to get on Monday. More yeast and flour. She had picked them up automatically on Friday, and already used most of what she had gotten.

Fans, several. Even without baking bread, even with all the windows open, the house got hot fairly quickly during the days, and it wasn't even summer yet.

Shorts. Most of what she owned was t-shirts and jeans. Jeans were fine in Chicago, where she was mostly inside. In the air conditioning during the summer.

Frozen pizza and TV dinners, for those days when she forgot to stop working to cook supper and she came out of her office half starved. Woops. She'd need a microwave, too. Now, where was she going to put that?

She went to the kitchen to look it over. *Maybe on that cupboard next to the old chimney. Or on this table next to the frig.*

Her gaze landed on the rising bread, which was threatening to overflow the pans. *Just another indication how warm this house is already.* She lit the oven and tossed the bread in. She knew how to bake bread without preheating the oven.

She went back to her list of needed items and added 'timer'. Something to remind her she had something going on. She had a habit of getting engrossed in her work, so a timer was a must.

Laundry detergent. Already. Peanut butter. She put down bread, because she knew how long a batch would last her, and she wouldn't want to bake another batch quite that soon.

She searched the kitchen for a potato masher and found an old one that looked like one her mother had once had. It would take a lot of work to make mashed potatoes, but thankfully, she wasn't doing that. She plunged the masher into the soup pot 3 times, and then another 3 for good measure. Some people, she understood, ran their potato soup through a blender, but she only partially mashed the soup; it gave the broth some body, but left chunks of potatoes and onion to provide some flavorful satisfaction for the consumers. After that, she stirred the soup to—

Someone knocked on the front door.

She walked through the house, realized it was Chuck. He was unshaven, possibly hung over, but when she opened the porch door, she realized he was wearing a tool belt. "Chuck's Odd Jobs, here to fix your ice maker," he greeted her blandly.

"Well, it's back in the kitchen, of course."

"I know," he answered, and stopped as they entered the kitchen. "Is that… bread baking?"

"Yes," she admitted. *So many of my friends think I'm a little weird for making bread by hand.* "I do that. Occasionally."

"My mom used to bake bread."

Why say it like that? "Used to?"

"We lost her a decade ago."

Woops. Just put my foot in my mouth. "I'm sorry to hear it."

"Thank you," he said simply, then crouched down and began fiddling under the kitchen sink.

Confused, Wanda reminded him, "The ice maker is in the freezer section of the refrigerator."

"I'd be a poor handyman if I didn't know that. I know what's wrong because I installed this refrigerator when the old one died. Gram always used ice trays to make ice, and wouldn't let me connect the new-fangled ice maker to a water supply. But the supply line is ready. Won't take but a couple minutes."

"That was nice of you, to install a new refrigerator in her hour of need. I lost my grandmother when I was very young. Well, of course I had 2 grandmothers, like everyone, but I hardly ever saw the other one."

"One of the advantages of living in a small town," he said as he continued to work, now in the corner between the sink and refrigerator. "Everybody helps. Well, for the most part."

She wasn't sure what the last of that meant. "Well, maybe you wouldn't mind telling me something." It seemed best to phrase her question as if she were clueless. "The servicemen warned me to stay away from the 4 Cousins. I got the impression they weren't fit company for women. And I think Bob claimed to be one, but I find that hard to believe; he's always been nice and respectful to me. Anyway, I'm wondering who these cousins are and how I will know them, being new in the area."

He stood up and pulled the frig away from the wall, began to work behind it. "The 4 Cousins got their reputation for being a little wild as kids. They were all born within a month of each other, and hung out together all through high school, where they seemed to make a game of stealing each other's girl friends. That part of the reputation has still stuck around.

"You needn't worry about Hank. He moved away, got married." He sighed. "And died in a car accident last winter."

"Oh," was all Wanda could think to say, and stirred her soup to hide her unease.

"Bob and I have grown up. I don't think Bob's had a date in over 5 years, and I don't think he's been looking. Pretty much the same with me. The one you still have to worry about is Lyle. He's married and has a kid, but that hasn't slowed him down any. As for knowing him, he looks a lot like Bob and me, but he's shorter and thinner. And often drunk. But drunk or sober, you'd do best to stay away from him."

"If you're grown up and hardly date anymore, why say I shouldn't invite you into my house?"

"Like I said, the reputation hasn't died." He pushed the refrigerator back against the wall, opened the freezer and flipped a switch. "There, your ice maker should be working. Anyway, because of that reputation, the gossips keep expecting Bob and me to behave like Lyle. Which is why I shouldn't have come alone, and should get out of here now. Tongues will still wag."

"Too bad you're in a hurry; I was going to invite you to have some lunch, simple as it is. I still owe you for using your tractor on my lawn. But if you must hurry off, then what do I owe you for fixing the ice maker?"

"Nothing." She pulled a loaf of bread from the oven. He followed her to the living room, where she emptied the bread pan onto a towel atop the heating stove in the corner. "I should have hooked it up after Gram's death, but… I wasn't thinking."

"Understandable. But I'm a new customer, and you did it for me, so I feel you should be paid." She returned to the kitchen for the other 2 loaves of bread. She thankfully turned the oven off before bringing them out to join their sibling on the towel. "If you don't want to accept money, how about a bowl of soup and some fresh bread? The soup is ready, and—"

Someone knocked at the front door. Chuck swore under his breath. "Your truck is out front," she pointed out. "Maybe someone else needs your help."

She went to answer the summons, waved Tommy in. "Come in. I was sitting down for potato soup and fresh bread for lunch. Would you like some?" Tommy sniffed the air, evidently catching the kitchen smells and nodded. Wanda turned to Chuck. "If Tommy can accept a friendly bite of lunch, you can accept, too. I may need a handyman for something else, some day."

"Well…" He glanced at his watch. "I have to get back to work, so I'd have to eat fast."

"Good enough. Bowls are in the cupboard. Spoons and knives in the drawer."

"Knives?" Tommy asked.

"For the margarine, if you want any. The bread is too hot to cut; we'll have to tear it into pieces."

"Just a moment." Chuck stepped into the tiny bathroom and washed his hands, stepped back out. "Your turn, Tommy. How'd mowing go this morning?"

"Quick," Tommy answered and began washing his hands.

Wanda got a ladle and put soup into bowls while Chuck moved the silverware and margarine to the dining room table. Wanda turned the flame down under her soup pot–there was still plenty left–and soon they were sitting at the table, sipping hot soup and passing hot pieces of bread around.

Surprisingly, Wanda felt like the3rd wheel in her own home. Chuck's questions were all directed to Tommy, who only seemed able—or willing—to give mono-syllabic answers. Actually, that suited her fine; potato soup and fresh bread was not only her favorite meal, it had been Hank's, too, and the memories it aroused were nearly overwhelming.

Another knock. Wanda started for the door, was met on the porch by Ella and her brother. Ella greeted her with, "If you don't want people just walking in, you'd best keep your doors locked."

Not a thought Wanda had had before; she had merely locked the door from habit. "Good to know. We're having soup and fresh bread, if you want some."

"We had lun— Chuck, I thought you were at work today!"

Chuck glanced at his watch again and his mouth became a thin line. "Gotta go." But he took the time to take his bowl and silverware to the kitchen sink.

Wanda grabbed a clean dish towel and wrapped it around one of the untouched loaves of bread, caught up with Chuck on the porch. "Wait!" He turned, and she shoved the bread into his arms. "You seemed to like it, so this is a gift, a friendly gift, nothing more. I'm not looking for a boy friend or even a date."

"You'll let me know when you change your mind on that, right?"

Surprised, she couldn't read his face. "No," she decided, because once again, they were too close to flirting. "Now go, before your boss gets mad." His sudden little grin made her wonder, but then he was gone, and Rusty was coming up the sidewalk.

"Did you fix her ice maker?" Rusty asked.

"Why I'm here," Chuck replied. His truck started and rolled away.

Wanda greeted the young boy and went back to finish her lunch. "There's hot potato soup on the kitchen stove, if any of you want some," she announced. A few minutes later, Zita arrived, and Wanda repeated the offer, broke a piece off the final loaf of bread so the kids knew it was fair game.

After lunch, the kids took the utensils to the kitchen sink and everyone gathered around the table. Wanda noted their 'start time' for the day. "Okay, I need that twin bed moved from the front bedroom to the next bedroom today. I don't know if you can do that without taking it apart, but I hope you can get it moved. And I want to continue cleaning out the closets and the dressers, because eventually, I want to put my own clothes away, instead of living out a suitcase. Once the bed is out of that front room, I need to find some furniture to make that room an office. Maybe I'll move that desk from in front of the windows."

"That?" Zita asked, pointing to what looked to Wanda like a small desk. She shrugged. "I guess you could use it as a desk, but it's actually a sewing machine."

"Really?" Wanda felt her cheeks go pink. "I don't sew, but maybe I can find something more suitable in the garage. Which reminds me. Rusty, do you have an estimate for that chair?"

"Sure thing. $10 to remove the wobble; $15 if you want it refinished, too. Same prices for the 2nd chair."

"That seems… extremely reasonable. Are you sure?"

He shrugged. "You're hiring a student. I'm adding to my experience and hopefully my client list."

Wanda laughed. "Sounds good. I accept. Both chairs, then."

"Did you want them refinished?"

"Sure."

"What color?" At her blank stare, he went on." I can paint them any color you like. Or I can stain them to bring out the wood texture, anything from black to blonde."

Wanda looked around her living room. The dining chairs ranged from dark brown to black, but the solidly built table was a rich golden brown. "Can you get close to the color of this table?"

"Sure, that's a honey blonde."

"That sounds good. Felix, I'd like to get my computer set up and connected to the internet today. I've fallen behind with my work, and my editor will be unhappy with me."

"Oh, are you a writer?" Ella asked. "Like a journalist? Or a magazine writer?"

"I am a writer, but I write novels," Wanda stated.

"Anything we might have read?" Zita asked.

Not likely. Everybody here seems very pragmatic and down to earth. Not the type of people to read about dragons and elves. "Probably not."

"Too bad," Felix stated. "Summer's coming, and I've read all the science fiction the library has."

"And fantasy," Ella added.

"Westerns," Rusty stated.

"Mysteries," Zita proclaimed.

"Well, we won't get much done if we sit around talking about books," Felix stated. "Come on, Rusty, let's take a look at that bed."

Before Wanda quite knew what was happening, the kids had all disappeared. She went to the kitchen to wash up, but found Tommy there, already doing that. She put what was left of the soup in a clean bowl and set it in the refrigerator. There was no bread left to worry about. "Tommy, would you be able to come over after school on Monday and mow my lawn?"

He shook his head, said only, "Test."

"You have a test on Tuesday?" He nodded, and she felt good at having figured out what he'd meant. "Maybe you could come on Tuesday, then?"

"Think so," he answered.

"Good. Hope to see you then. Now, if anybody has questions, I'll be in the garage, looking for some office furniture."

* * *

7:53 PM

Wanda washed up from her supper of left-over potato soup, dried the items and put them away. She filled a glass with ice–mentally thanking Chuck again for coming so promptly and not making her wait–and took a can of soda into the living room to watch some TV.

It had been a productive day. The twin bed was in the bedroom now. The dresser and closet in the office were completely empty, although some of the larger items were in the back room. The dresser in her bedroom was half empty, though they hadn't started on the closet there yet. They had opened the door and been overtaken by the stench of stale cigarette odor.

45

"Ugh! That must be Great Aunt Ruby's stuff!" Ella declared and firmly closed the door again.

"Has to be!" Zita agreed. "Gram didn't smoke. And neither did Popper."

"Popper?" Wanda asked.

"He was Gram's 2nd husband, Eli," Ella explained. "All the kids were grown up when they got married, so they didn't call him 'dad'. But all the grandkids called him Pops or Popper."

"Sounds like a good man."

"He was," Zita declared.

"Great Aunt Ruby and her husband were both chain smokers," Ella went on. "We may have to just burn everything in that closet, cause we'll never get that smell out of it so that somebody could use them."

"Well, we'll see," Wanda said. "I have a couple ideas I can try. But not the supplies I need, so leave them for now." Which was why she had added to her list, '12 cans tomato juice'.

The office had shaped up well, except the curtains had come out of the wash badly frayed. Zita had opened up the sewing machine, fiddled with it for a time and did some sewing to try to keep the curtains from fraying any more. They looked pretty sad, once they were back on the pole. "If you want to get some fabric, it would be simple to make new ones," Zita told her.

"I do need to replace them," Wanda agreed. "But I know nothing about fabric, how much to get, what kind to get, how to make it into curtains. I'm completely clueless."

"Well, either Ella or I can help you with that. You can search on line for a fabric you like, or look in the department store in Fullerton." She told Wanda how much fabric to get based on how wide the fabric was.

Wanda dutifully wrote that information on her shopping list. "Well, I'll take a look," she stated, startled by how long her list was getting. "But those old curtains may have to wait a while before I can actually retire them."

"No hurry on my part. I'd charge $10 to make the curtains on your machine. $12 if you want to watch and get an idea how it's done."

46

"And that sounds downright cheap, so I just need to find the fabric."

As for furniture for the office, the sewing machine was currently serving as a desk and held her computer monitor and keyboard. The stereo equipment was set up on top of the dresser. A small bookcase and an octagonal occasion table had also been moved from the garage, washed down and moved into the office.

She decided to place her bills on top the piano. She didn't want to keep her bills in her office, for fear their presence would distract her from her writing. They could be a source of worry for her, because she no longer had Hank's full paycheck coming in, only a small survivor's pension, and the savings that she had supplemented before leaving Chicago by selling off everything she could.

Hank's best college friend, Lee, had been Hank's financial advisor. He had been surprised when she told him she would be moving away from Chicago. But once she had explained that Hank owned a house in Nebraska free and clear, he had understood, and had done what he could to make things easier for her, including buying some of what she had to sell. He had met her at the bank and helped her get $900 in traveler's checks, a cashier's check for $5,000 that she could deposit at a new bank when she reached Nebraska. He—along with 2 other close friends, Greg and Jack—had urged her to keep in touch, and to let them know if she needed anything.

She should probably send notes to them to let them know she had arrived and was settling in.

She'd do that tomorrow. She'd also go through all the money she'd spent so far, including how much she'd paid the kids, as well as what she had agreed to pay them for future work, like the chairs Rusty was working on, the curtains and the mowing.

She also needed to email Paula, let her know that she was settling in and getting ready to get back to work.

Popcorn. And a popcorn popper. She missed the butter-dripping popcorn Hank used to make.

Chapter 6
Monday, April 20, 8:10 AM

As soon as Bob knocked on the porch door, Wanda put down her hairbrush and headed that way. She wore her belly bag; she liked the way the belly bag left her arms and hands free. This morning, she carried her notebook with her shopping list. And hidden between the pages of her notebook was the cashier's check for $5000; she hadn't found the local bank yet.

"Bob," she greeted him as she locked her front door. "I've got a lot of stuff to buy today. I think we should take my Rav."

"Oh." She must have surprised him with that request. "Okay. Why don't you follow me home, and I'll leave my car there, then?"

"Thanks."

Bob pulled his beat-up Chevy out of the driveway, pulled down the street halfway to the corner, and waited for her to catch up. They turned the corner toward the main street, crossed the asphalt and started up the hill. Halfway up the first block, Bob pulled into the driveway of a small house on the left. He locked his car and retrieved a Styrofoam ice chest from his trunk, which he put in the back seat of Wanda's Rav before he climbed in beside her. "Nice car."

"Thanks. I got it used after—"

"After the accident," Bob finished for her.

"Yes. We'd had a Rav for several years. So I'm used to it."

"Go back down to the main corner and turn left."

"I think I remember how to get to Fullerton," she stated. "Once we get there, you may have to direct me where to go."

"Okay." Once they were starting up the 'big hill' that had startled Wanda when she had first come to Belgrade, Bob asked, "How are the kids working out for you?"

"Very well," she answered. "They take direction well, wash up after we've eaten without being asked to, and it pretty much seems like if I need something done, at least one of them knows how to do it."

"Tommy knows plants," Bob nodded.

"And Felix knows computers, Rusty knows furniture repair, Zita and Ella know how to sew. I've got a whole team of specialists right there in those 5 kids. What more could I want? Well, actually, Bob, where is the bank in Belgrade?"

"Oh, Belgrade hasn't had a bank in… probably half a century. You'd have to do your banking in Fullerton, Cedar Rapids or Albion."

"Where are Cedar Rapids and Albion?"

"Cedar Rapids is 10 or 12 miles north and a little west of Belgrade. Albion is about 20 miles north and slightly east. Most people in Belgrade bank in Fullerton."

"Well, that's good, since we'll be going to Fullerton every week anyway."

"You don't object to my beat-up old Chevy?"

She smiled at the thought. "You should have seen the old jalopy I learned how to drive in!" She gave him a quick look. "I really do have a lot of things to buy, like a kitchen full of food and a dozen fans."

"Fans?"

"I don't handle heat very well; I've lived my life with air conditioning. As much of it as I remember, anyway."

"Did you try opening the windows?"

"Yes. And that helps. But we haven't even gotten to summer yet."

"That's true," he conceded. "Well, try getting oscillating fans. I think they move the air around more, and you might get by with 3 or 4 fans."

"I was probably exaggerating," she admitted with a smile of embarrassment.

"If you're getting a lot of food, you might want to get an ice chest. I use it for cold things, because 12 miles in the middle of summer can suck the goodness right out of that stuff."

"Good idea. So the grocery store is the last place for us to visit. Where do you suggest I look for fans and an ice chest?"

"The department store."

"What if I want some clothes, like shorts?"

"The department store."

"And I need to look at fabric. The girls are going to make a new set of curtains for my office."

"The department store. Although they don't have a huge selection, so you might want to try the internet as well."

"Sounds like the first place I should visit is the department store."

"Would you mind dropping me off at the bank?" Bob asked. "That's the first place I visit. Every Monday."

"Then that's where I'll start this morning." After a moment, she added, "You're very helpful, Bob. I wonder if I could impose upon you to go with me to the department store. From what I remember of the place, I wouldn't have any idea where to find anything in there."

"It is a jumble inside," he stated. "They keep adding new things as people come in looking for them, but they haven't added any floor space in… decades. Maybe a century."

"Wow."

"What?" he asked.

"People in Chicago don't nonchalantly talk about things in terms of decades, half centuries and centuries," she answered.

"Yeah, I imagine not. You'll get used to it. Things move so slowly here, you have to think in terms of decades, not weeks or months."

They reached the corner where highway 52 met highway 14, and turned south. Fullerton was only 4 miles, now. "Oh, don't let me forget to get some gasoline for my lawn mower. I can't remember if I put that on my shopping list. Zita is supposed to come by this afternoon and prepare one of the lawn mowers. Tommy has a test tomorrow, so he won't be over to mow until after that."

"Well, get a gas can at the department store. It'll be cheaper than getting one at the gas station."

She laughed. "Thank you. You're a fountain of information. So, there's this dinky little shed in the backyard. All the yard equipment is in the garage, so what is the shed for?"

"Oh, that's the outhouse."

Wanda blinked in surprise. She hadn't thought anybody used outhouses any more. "The bathroom inside seems perfectly fine."

"The outhouse isn't functional any more. It was filled in when Gram had the indoor bathroom built. I think, since then, the part above ground has been filled with boxes full of canning jars. Gram didn't do much canning in her later years."

"She seems to have been a very frugal woman," Wanda observed. "I'm still not sure how she managed to raise 5 children in a 4-room house. Or had the kitchen been added by then?"

Bob stopped to think for a moment. "I don't know. I don't remember anybody mentioning when the different sections were added." He smiled. "I'll have to ask her kids next weekend when most of them are in the bar. They always like to talk about the old days. And they rarely remember things the same, so between that and wandering off onto tangents, it's usually a night of good conversation. I never know what I might learn about the family."

"Sounds like fun."

"Well, come on over, if you want. Mom and Alice would be glad to see you."

She sighed. "Maybe I will. If I remember. My editor sent me a ton of corrections for my manuscript. Once I get started on that…" She sighed. "She made it sound more of a rough draft than a finished manuscript. So once I really get into it, I'm likely to forget."

"Ahh, work. Okay, if you don't make it, I'll take notes to satisfy your curiosity."

"Thank you, Bob. I'm sure it will be fascinating."

Chapter 7
Tuesday, April 21, 6:27 PM

A knock startled Wanda out of the world of Ilyacore, scattering her thoughts about the imaginary place like autumn leaves in a cold breeze. She blinked as she looked around, wondering where she was. Another knock—rather than a doorbell—reminded her of her recent move to an old house in Nebraska, and she got up from the desk to see who had disturbed her work.

"Tommy? Oh, gosh, is this Tuesday, already?" The boy nodded, and she let him onto the porch. "Zita was here yesterday and worked on one of the lawn mowers, but I'm not sure which one. Let's go out to the garage and see if we can figure it out."

He followed her to the garage and they opened the doors to look at the lawn mowers. Zita had made it plain which one was to be used; one had a chair and an old stool stacked atop it, while the other had the can of gasoline sitting right next to it.

"Well, I think that's pretty clear, don't you?" she asked. When Tommy nodded, she went on. "I won't keep you standing here talking. I've got work to do myself. So, put the lawn mower back and close up the garage when you get done. I've got cold pop and goodies in the kitchen you can raid whenever you need a break. When you do get done, remind me to lock the door behind you; I get tunnel vision when I'm working. And don't let me forget to pay you!"

Somebody honked, startling her, and she turned to see a pickup driving by. Tommy raised a hand and waved, but she didn't see who it was.

He nodded, and she retraced her steps, back to her office and the 400 pages of fantasy she was working on.

Back to Ilyacore.

Chapter 8
Saturday, April 25, 7:25 PM

"Hey!"

Wanda jumped and whirled from her computer to stare at Chuck, who was turning from her audio player, which had suddenly stopped playing the pounding music that had kept her working. "What are you doing here?" she demanded.

"Wondering if you're okay," he returned. "That music has been blaring, over and over, for several days, and nobody's seen you since Tuesday."

"Well, it's only Wednesday," she protested, and rubbed her suddenly tired eyes.

"Try again."

She frowned and caught sight of a couple discarded glasses and a dish next to her keyboard. "Thursday?" Then she saw the collection of glasses and dishes stacked on the floor, vaguely remembered sleeping on the couch a time or two. Okay," she conceded, "I lost track. What day is it?"

"Saturday. Evening. People got worried when you didn't come to Bob's bar tonight."

"Why would I?" she wondered. "I don't drink that much, and right now, I'm on a deadline. My editor wanted some rewriting done. Plus she's moved up my publication date." She collected as many of the dirty dishes and glasses as she could carry and started for the kitchen. Now that her thoughts had been interrupted, she discovered she was hungry.

Chuck followed and put the rest of the dirty dishes in the kitchen sink atop what she had already placed there. "Well, none of us knew that. Zita said you were preoccupied when she was here Monday, and Tommy said you were 'worse' when he saw you on Tuesday. Anyway, it's just what's done in Belgrade; you come to Bob's place, either on Friday or Saturday, for some social interaction. Call it an unwritten rule. You don't have to stay long, and Bob serves pop and tea, even water, if you don't want alcohol. Showing up lets everybody know you're okay."

"That must get in the way of people's love lives," Wanda stated, opening her refrigerator. "Where's my lunch meat?" She turned to the cupboard. "All my chips and bread are gone, too."

"I expect that's what you've been living on this past week."

She sighed, glanced at the dishes piled in the sink. "Probably. Since nobody was here to heat me up a can of soup or tell me it was time to sleep."

"I don't think he's got any soup, but Bob's got a grill he knows how to use. Come on, I'll pay for your supper."

She gave him a quizzical look, wondering at his sudden offer. "I can pay for my own supper, thank you. But eating out tonight does sound good."

"I'll give you a lift; my truck's outside."

"It's only 2 blocks away!"

"A little less, actually, but it's raining heavily."

"It is?" She turned to stare out the kitchen window and could hardly see the hedge at the end of the block for all the water coming down. "Let me get my purse and put on my shoes. And I have to save my work and turn the computer off."

* * *

8:05 PM

Despite getting a ride, by the time Wanda walked into Bob's Bar, she felt soggy. She was surprised as she worked her wet and wind-blown hair out of her face, to see Alice and Val waving at her to join them. It wasn't until she slid in next to Vallie that she realized Chuck had taken a seat at the bar. *Don't know how much that will work to keep 'tongues from wagging' when he came to my house to get me and drove me here, just because of an unwritten rule that I was supposed to come here of a weekend night. A rule nobody bothered to tell me about!*

"We were getting worried about you," Alice told her. The kids said you weren't your usual self when they saw you on Monday and Tuesday, and nobody's seen you since then."

54

"I was working," Wanda explained yet again. "I could have sworn I told... somebody that I get... tunnel vision when I'm working against a deadline. I guess whoever I told either didn't understand what I meant or didn't think to spread the word."

Helen approached with a menu in her hand. "Chuck says you want a menu."

"Ugh, my eyes are too tired to look at it. Give me a grilled ham and cheese, fried mushrooms, french fries, ice tea. Are those pies I see on the counter?"

"They are," Helen answered. "You've got your choice of cherry or peach."

"Two of my favorite pies," Wanda stated. "Well, I'll have to see if I have room for any after I eat."

"I'll be right back with your tea," Helen promised.

"Ella said you write novels," Alice stated.

"Oh! Anything we might have read?" Vallie asked eagerly.

"Val always has her nose in a book," Alice teased.

"Well, I pretty much doubt it. My publisher is a small company, and I doubt if she has any outlets this far from Chicago."

"A small press?" Vallie stated. "That doesn't seem to be a way to make much money. Why not go with a real publisher?"

Wanda's face reddened. "Well, none of the big publishers wanted to take me on, which is often the case with new writers. More and more of us are having to go with small publishers—or self-publish—in order to get published at all. But my publisher and I have worked hard to get my books noticed. My royalty checks have grown. Of course, this is my 4th book, and she says the more books I have available, the more people will find me."

"Well. Maybe I should dust off the old novels I wrote decades ago and see if I can get them published that way. I couldn't get my foot in the door back then, either," Val confided.

"First, you'd have to type them up," Alice told her. "And you'd probably have to modernize them. Most people just don't chain smoke anymore."

"I know how to type," Vallie reminded her friend. "It's a little different on a computer than an old typewriter, but not that different. And it's a lot easier to correct typos."

"Oh, it sure is," Alice agreed. "Back in high school, when Mr Overton wanted our papers turned in typed with no mistakes... I thought I'd never get done! Must have used more than 100 sheets of paper for a 5-page report!"

As the 2 older ladies chuckled, Helen returned with the ice tea, and also set a piece of pie on the table. "Bob said you'd better take the peach pie, as this is the only piece of it we've got left. And if I don't bring it now, it'll be gone for sure."

"Ahh, thank you," Wanda told her, but wondered why it was so important that she have the last piece of peach pie. She would have been just as happy with the cherry. If she even had room for it after eating all she had ordered.

On the other hand, she was super hungry. Just when had she last eaten? She had no way of knowing, her tunnel vision had been so focused on her rewrite. "Life is short," Wanda muttered, pulled the pie closer and started eating.

"Haven't been eating regularly?" Alice asked.

"I've been eating," Wanda replied. "I have a sink full of dishes and a bare cupboard to prove it. But I've been so focused on my work, I couldn't tell you **when** I've eaten."

"Yep, I know people like that, unaware of anything else, once they get started on a project."

"So, ladies, I've been wondering about Gram's house," Wanda stated. "It obviously started as a 4-room house, and it's been added onto several times. There's still an outhouse in the backyard, which has apparently been filled in some time ago. Can you tell me when all the different changes to the house were made?" It seemed a safe subject to get them started on, and might keep them from asking too many questions about herself.

"I'll leave that question for Val to answer," Alice told her. "I married into the family, I didn't live there."

That started Val on a treatise of the various changes that had been made to the house, from indoor plumbing to the back room and all points in between. Wanda had no trouble keeping her focus on the tale, even after her food had arrived and she started to eat. The 2 women squabbled a bit over details from time to time, but that just made the tale more interesting.

Alice and Vallie were still talking about yesteryear when Wanda finished her meal. Helen came and cleared off the dirty dishes, and brought a fresh ice tea. "Oh, bring the check, Helen, so I can settle my bill. Now that I've eaten, I'm super tired and want to go home."

"Have it for you in a tick," Helen answered.

A moment after that, there was a brilliant flash of light and then a horrendous clap of thunder. Wanda groaned as she remembered, "It's still raining."

"Cats and dogs," Alice agreed. "Probably will be most of the night."

There came a strangely long and steady flash that seemed to shine right in the bar's front windows. "Is that—" someone asked of nobody in particular.

"He's going to come in right through my front wall, one of these nights," Bob stated.

After another bright flash and crash of thunder, the front door opened, and in stumbled another Bob. Or a Chuck. Only shorter and slimmer, with black hair. Remembering Chuck's description, this could only be...

"Lyle," Bob greeted the newcomer. "Didn't know if you'd be out tonight. Thought you might be home with the wife."

Lyle stopped in the middle of the collection of tables and turned to face the barkeep. "Stay away from my wife, Bob." Then he swayed where he stood, looking around the bar until his eyes landed on the booth where Wanda sat with Val and Alice. He lurched forward and plopped down next to Alice, across from Wanda. "Hello, mom. Who's your beautiful new friend?"

Alice had hurriedly moved as far from Lyle as the booth would let her. "For crying out loud, Lyle, you're soaking wet and getting me all wet. You may not care if you catch a cold, but I don't want to!"

"Sorry, mom, I forgot it was raining. Guess I forgot when I saw your beautiful friend."

Alice rolled her eyes. "Well, he's not going to shut up about it until I introduce you. Wanda, this is one of my sons, Lyle. Do yourself a favor and try hard to avoid him."

"Mom! Is that any way to talk about your favorite son?"

"You're not my favorite son. I don't have favorites, and you're darn hard to tolerate, sometimes."

He seemed on the verge of saying something in response when Helen showed up with a colorful mixed drink and set it down in front of him.

"Here you go, Lyle."

The drunk man frowned. "What's this?"

"That's your drink," Helen answered. "You ordered it when you came in."

"I did?" He didn't appear to remember ordering. Wanda didn't remember him doing it, either.

"Well, drink it up," Alice told him. "That's what you're here for, isn't it?"

"I came... I came because I heard there was a beautiful new woman moving into Gram's old house."

"That's what I figured. Well, she's moved in already, and there's nothing you can do about it."

Lyle emptied about a third of his glass and returned it to the table with a dull thud. "I'm not here to make any trouble," he told his mother carefully. "I just... I just wanted to meet her, that's all."

"Don't you think that's something you should do when you're sober?"

"Who says I'm not?" he demanded and took another drink. "Anyway, you know I don't get into town during the week. I've got too much to do."

Wanda had been around drunks before, and this was the type she liked the least; loud and full of himself. She waved at Helen, trying to remind the waitress that she wanted her bill so she could pay it and go home. Helen saw her wave, but solemnly shook her head slightly. Confused, wondering if Chuck or Bob had already paid her bill, she turned back to ask Val if she knew what was going on.

"Well, this is her," Alice told her son coldly, waving a hand at Wanda. "Her name's Wanda, and I don't know why I bother, because tomorrow you won't remember having met her."

"Shure I will." His slur was definitely more pronounced, but some people could drink until they were absolutely unintelligible, and still make trouble. "And you know why?" He took another drink, started to set his glass down, and took another drink. "Ya know wy?"

His mother sighed. "Why?"

"Becosh Wendy ish too butiful ta fergit." He turned to face Wanda. "Ya know dat, Wendy? Ya are too butiful ta fer—" His head lowered until his chin rested on his chest. After a long moment, he started to lean sideways until he rested against his mother. After another moment, he started to snore.

Alice sighed in relief. "Okay, Jim, let's get him home."

It seemed to Wanda that the bar customers—who had been a frozen tableau only seconds before—now took on life and movement. A tall lanky middle-aged man got up from a near-by table to come forward, followed by Chuck from his stool at the bar. The 2 men pried Lyle from his position in the booth, Alice got out and headed for the door, her car keys and an umbrella in her hands. As she left, Chuck and Jim slowly carried Lyle toward the front door. By the time they got there, headlights showed that a car had pulled up as close to the door as it could get. Helen held the bar door open, and the 2 men moved outside with their burden.

Helen watched them for a moment before she came to the booth, picked up Lyle's nearly empty glass and put Wanda's check down. "Sorry for the delay, but you did not want to leave before he passed out."

"Even if I weren't so tired, I'd still want to leave, to get away from him," Wanda muttered.

"Yes," Val told her. "But he would have offered to take you home, and if you refused, he'd have gotten mean about it. If you had agreed, you'd probably have to fight him off. Best to get him passed out. And now, since it's still raining, I will take you home."

"Thank you," Wanda told her gratefully. She went to the bar and paid for her supper, and the 2 of them made a dash for a ford parked just around the corner.

"The problem is," Val told her as she started the engine, "is that you never know when Lyle's going to show up at Bob's. There can be weeks when he doesn't show up in Belgrade at all, and others when he's underfoot all the time. And if he's awake, he's probably drunk, or working on it." She pulled out of her parking spot and turned left onto the paved highway.

"I don't understand how any of you could have known he'd pass out with only one more drink."

"Well, I wasn't sure. But Bob asked about his wife—which is normal—and Lyle got belligerent. Meant he was pretty far gone. And the drink Bob made was probably extra strong." She turned left again, between the fire department and the playground. "But don't repeat that to anyone. If Lyle ever finds out..." She left the sentence unfinished and turned left again, backed into Wanda's driveway so she wouldn't have to walk far in the rain. "Lock your house up tight, Wanda," Val instructed.

"I usually do, but... why do you mention it?"

"Because you never know with Lyle. He's passed out, and probably won't wake up before noon, but he still thinks he's irresistible to women, believes they say no to make the sex spicier."

"That's... awful."

"Someday he'll probably wind up in prison, and then I don't know what will happen to his wife and kid. But in the meantime... there's no reason for you to go through any of that."

"Thank you," Wanda told her. "I appreciate the warning." She hesitated. "What about the other cousins?"

"As in the 4 cousins?" Val asked. "Well, Chuck pretty much gave up dating shortly after Hank moved away, and Bob, too. I think you might be fairly safe with either of them, but I may be prejudiced. One bad apple in the family is enough."

"Thanks for everything, Val. You've been a real friend. Good night."

"Sleep tight. Get a fresh start on your work in the morning."

"I will." Wanda hurried to the door, which unlocked normally, so she was fairly wet by the time she got onto the porch. She turned around and locked it again, went into the living room and locked that door as well.

She felt a pang of *deja vu* at locking the doors, but then remembered clearly that she had done the exact same thing after paying Tommy for mowing her lawn. But if her house had been locked up, as she remembered, how had Chuck gotten in this evening?

It was enough to send a cold chill down her spine, and she resolved to get lock-bolts for all the doors on Monday, during her trip to Fullerton with Bob.

Chapter 9
Monday, April 27, 8:08 AM

This time, Bob drove his old Chevy. After picking up Wanda, he drove past his bar and up the hill past his own house. At the top of the hill, where he had to turn one way or another, and he turned right. The gravel street followed the hilltop for another block or two, then veered downhill to the left, and Bob was driving on a gravel road between fields of... something.

Corn? That's what they grow in Nebraska, isn't it? Do they grow anything else? She didn't know, and couldn't be sure that what she saw growing was corn.

Bob followed the road through several intersections, in a pattern only he knew, and soon he slowed the car to a crawl as they drove past a farm house that looked nearly as bad as the house next to Wanda's. The roof hadn't yet caved in, and the porch was still intact, but there was no way to tell what color the house had been painted, or if it had ever been painted at all.

While they crawled past that house, Bob stared at it intently, almost as if he could see through the wall and see what was happening inside. Eventually, the house fell behind them, and Bob sped up until the dry road sent billows of dust into the air to mark their passing. "Who lives there?" Wanda asked.

Bob gave her a quick glance. "Gloria and Sammy."

"I don't think I've met them yet."

"No, they don't get into town," he answered, and cleared his throat. "Gloria is Lyle's wife. Sammy is his son."

"Then... doesn't Lyle live there, too?"

Bob frowned as he stared at the road ahead. "You wouldn't know it from following him around."

Shortly, they turned another corner. Wanda looked back. The house looked completely unlived in.

"Something's been bothering me, Bob. It's got me so spooked, I need to get a bunch of slide bolts, just to make sure my house really is locked up tight."

Surprised, he turned to look at her, then quickly turned his attention back to the road. "What did mom say when she took you home Saturday that spooked you that much?"

"Well, apparently, she wouldn't be surprised if Lyle showed up to rape me."

"Well, no. She doesn't think much of him."

"But what really got to me was when I was locking up my front door, I distinctly remembered locking the house up after Tommy mowed my lawn last Tuesday. I wasn't expecting any-body after that, and I didn't want to be disturbed."

"Good idea. A lot of people just walk in and think nothing of it. The whole town's related to each other, you know."

"Well, if my doors were locked, then how did Chuck get in on Saturday?"

"What do you mean? Didn't he pound on the door until you answered?"

"No. He came in the house somehow, came into my office, yelled at me to get my attention over the music, and then turned the music off. I should have asked him how he got in, but my brain was only half working and I never thought of it. After all the stories you two have told me about the 4 Cousins, and then he does that!"

"Oh." He turned another corner. "Yeah, that would be enough to put you on edge, I'm sure." He sighed. "But there's an easy explanation."

"Easy! Well, what is it, because I sure haven't figured it out!"

"Chuck has a key."

"What? How did he get a key? That house was left to Hank!"

"No, actually, that house was left to Chuck and Hank," Bob corrected. "I think Gram hoped that co-owning it might bring them back together. Chuck never figured it would, so he signed his half over to Hank. But he kept a key so that he could get in and do whatever repairs might need to be done. He's been taking care of that house, even without any instructions from Hank."

Wanda sat back in her seat, confusion overruling her anger and fear. "Why would he do that?"

Bob broadened his explanation. "First, it was Gram's house. And don't ever think anybody in Belgrade didn't love her. Especially Chuck. As soon as he was old enough to do odd jobs, he took over keeping that house running.

"Gram died and left the house to the 2 of them. Chuck didn't need it; he already had had his farmstead. But he did miss Hank, and he blamed himself for making Hank so mad he went away. So he gave Hank his half of the house, hoping that someday Hank would forgive him, and maybe even come back. He'd have a place to live. But only if it didn't deteriorate in the meantime. So he's been seeing to the upkeep all this time.

"And that's why Chuck has a key to your house."

Wanda frowned at the grocery list in her lap and thought about her decision to move to tiny Belgrade. It had seemed such a simple decision when she made it: claim the house Hank owned, and live in relative contentment out in the middle of nowhere. How could she possibly foresee that there would be unwritten 'rules' like people being expected to spend time at a bar once a weekend, or that a self-proclaimed womanizer had a key to her house, and another man who—apparently—was not above rape.

"How do I get my key away from him?" she wondered.

"I'll talk to him," Bob promised. "I'm sure he didn't mean to scare you on Saturday. People really were worried about you, especially after hearing the same music play so loudly over and over for days on end."

"Hard rock," she identified it. "It's what I listen to when I'm not sure I'm going to make my deadline."

"And did you?"

"Did I what?"

"Make your deadline?"

She smiled at his assumption. "Not yet, but I've still got time. Waking up well rested on Sunday helped me see that I was over-complicating the rewrite. A snip here, add a few words there... It's going much faster now."

"Good. Now I don't feel so guilty about making you come to the bar on Saturday."

"You?" she asked. "Chuck made it sound like the entire town expected me to be there. To ease their minds over my well-being, or something."

"Well, it did do that," he responded, and cleared his throat. "Unfortunately, it also introduced you to Lyle."

Wanda took a deep breath. "That was bound to happen sooner or later."

Before much longer, they crossed an asphalt road, and then another a few minutes later. They entered a town on gravel, and it wasn't until Bob parked at the bank that Wanda realized this was Fullerton. Why take such a long route here? Did he find the drive on the highways boring, since he drove it every week?

Bob paused with his hand on the door handle. "Do you have a lot of errands to run today?"

"Not really. I'll stop at the department store for a few things, but I won't need anywhere else but the grocery store."

"Well, it's about 8:30. Why don't we meet at the Dew Drop around 10 for coffee and pie, and then do groceries afterwards?"

"You want us to meet where?"

"At the Dew Drop Inn. A cafe about a block up the street."

Now she remembered the place, although not the name. "That sounds good. If I get lost, can I call you?"

He grinned. "Sure, but the town isn't that big."

"Says the man who's lived here his entire life," she retorted, and started off to explore the department store again. Even with the windows open wide and the fans to blow air around, the summer was heating up, and she really needed some shorts to wear instead of jeans.

* * *

10:08 AM

Bob was hanging up his cell phone when Wanda shoved her sack into the booth and sat down. "I am really ready for a glass of tea and a piece of pie," she told him across the table.

65

"That's what I suggested," he returned, and waved at the waitress. "Unless you'd rather have cake."

"Oo, choices," Wanda stated in surprise. The waitress arrived and refreshed Bob's coffee. "I'd like an iced tea," she ordered. "And Bob says you have both pie and cake to choose from. What flavors do you have?"

"For cake, we have German Chocolate or Angle Food with strawberries. For pie, we have chocolate banana, cherry and coconut."

"They all sound delicious," Wanda decided. "Bring me a piece of chocolate pie."

"Chocolate banana," the waitress corrected. "Still want it?"

"Chocolate banana?" Wanda had never heard of that flavor.

"It's a banana pie made with chocolate pudding instead of banana or vanilla," Bob explained. "I'll take a piece of that, Uma."

"You got it," the middle-aged woman responded. "And your lady friend?"

"Hmm, I like chocolate and bananas, so I'll take a piece of that, too," Wanda decided. "Oh, and separate checks, if you wouldn't mind, Uma."

"Not a problem." The waitress moved off.

"So, how was your shopping this morning?"

"Not too bad," she answered. "I found some shorts for these hot summer days, but only 3 pair in my size. Good thing I have my own washer and dryer."

"I think the Fullerton stores are probably waiting to put out the warmer stuff for fall and winter. You might have to go to Columbus to find more shorts, if you want more than that."

"Or I can order some on line," she returned. "Shouldn't take that long to get a couple more delivered. Oh, that reminds me, do you think we can make it home by 2? Some stuff that wouldn't fit in my car is being delivered this afternoon."

"Shouldn't be a problem. All I've got left is groceries."

"Me, too."

"Scoot over." Suddenly Chuck was standing next to their booth, shoving himself in next to his look-alike cousin. Wanda looked at him in wonder, because Bob hadn't said anything about Chuck joining them.

Chuck reached into his shirt pocket and placed a key on the table, pushed it across the table at her. "I should have returned it to you before this. My apologies. I wasn't thinking."

She took the key and slipped it into her belly bag. "I probably over-reacted when I found out about it. I didn't realize there was another key to the house until Bob told me you had one."

"Well, all's well that—" He stopped when Uma returned with a glass of tea and 2 pieces of pie.

"Ain't you got a job to be at?" Uma asked Chuck sourly.

"Taking a coffee break," he returned. "So bring me some coffee. And what is that, lumpy mud pie? Bring me a slice, too."

She moved off again, muttering something about he should be trying to finish that house, not frittering his time something...

Chuck gave his cousin a baleful look. "Am I frittering my time?"

"Yes," Bob stated.

"Okay, yes, I am. But I'm not frittering it the way she thinks I am."

Bob gave him a serious look. "I hope not." He leaned forward and lowered his voice. "I bet you made it home and back again in record time."

"I did, and was lucky the cops didn't catch me at it. My own fault for not getting it back to her before now."

"You drove home to get the key?" she asked. "Why not just wait and bring it to me this evening?"

"Nope, couldn't do that," he stated at once. "First, I didn't want you worrying about it all the rest of the day. And 2nd, if you were working again and I had to use it to get in to give it to you... well, it just didn't seem like a good idea."

"No, probably not," she agreed. "Although I will be working this evening, I won't be so intensely involved in it as I was last week. I'll be polishing instead of rewriting."

Both men stared at her in confusion. Bob cleared his throat. "You'll have to explain the difference. I mean, I thought you were working that hard because you had a deadline."

"Yes, I still have the same deadline. But polishing is easier than rewriting. Basically, I'm looking for grammar mistakes. Mostly."

"Oh, I always hated having to look for grammar mistakes," Chuck stated, and thanked Uma, who had arrived with his coffee and pie.

"You never knew when to use a semi-colon," Bob stated.

"I still don't," Chuck agreed. "Happily, there's no call for them in invoices. I don't think there is."

"Probably not," Wanda agreed, and watched in surprise as Chuck gulped down his pie and hot coffee. "You'll give yourself a stomach ache, eating like that," she chided.

"If I do, I have a first aid kit," he returned. "And I really do need to get back to work and stop frittering." He stood up and took a bill from his wallet, walked over to the counter to hand it to Uma. "Keep the change, Beautiful." And then he was out the door and gone.

Wanda turned to Bob, feeling guilty for having pulled Chuck away from his job. "Bob, you said you would talk to him. I never expected—"

Bob held up his hands in surrender. "Hey, I told him you were uneasy having an extra key out in the world. He said he'd take care of it. Like you, I expected he'd bring it to you this evening. Then the next thing I knew, he called me back asking where he could find us. Or you, if we weren't together."

"So it wasn't your idea?"

"No. I was ready to tell you to expect him to get it to you to-night."

She took another bite of her pie. "What did he call this? Lumpy mud pie? That doesn't sound very appetizing."

"It's from his sister. She decided she wanted a banana pie. But the only pudding mix in the house was chocolate, so she used that. She loved the flavor combination, she didn't want to share it, so she called it lumpy mud pie. Then she started making chocolate banana pie for every pot luck event she was invited to, so now the whole county knows about it. And lots of people make it."

"It's very good," Wanda told him. "But I'm glad the wait-ress didn't call it lumpy mud pie before I ordered it."

He laughed. "Everybody likes it, but Queenie got mad that everybody 'stole' her idea, so she wouldn't even talk about it."

Wanda pulled her billfold from her belly bag. "Now, if we could get our checks, we should probably go get our groceries. They aren't going to buy themselves."

"Well, they never have," Bob agreed, and called out to the waitress, "Hey, Uma, checks, please."

* * *

1:04 PM

Bob drove around the corner and saw a man climbing into the driver's seat of a delivery truck parked in the wide ditch in front of Wanda's house. "Woops," he said. "He's early."

"That figures," Wanda breathed.

Bob pulled to the wrong side of the gravel street and rolled his window down as he approached the truck's position. "Hey, are you delivering at this house?"

"Well, I was, but nobody's home," the driver answered.

"She is now," Bob told him. "Just give her a second to un-lock the door." He pulled behind the truck and into the driveway, then got out to talk to the driver while Wanda unlocked her door. Wanda walked over to join them.

"Sure, I could help you get it inside. A couple filing cabi-nets? Let's make sure where she wants them before we try wres-tling them up the front steps."

"It should be 2 filing cabinets and an exercise bike," Wanda clarified, wondering if the bike had been misplaced.

The driver nodded. "That's right, but the bike doesn't weigh that much. Not like the file cabinets. I was really hoping you might want those in the garage or something."

"Not the garage, but the back room of the house," she an-swered, and thought about the narrow opening between the kitchen and that back room, where the cooking stove protruded several inches into the doorway. "Bob, I think he's going to have to bring them in through the back door. The doorway between thc kitchen and the back room—"

69

"You're right. And that will make things easier," Bob agreed. "There's only 1 step up to get to the back room from the patio. That room isn't raised off the ground like the body of the house is. So, tell you what, drive to the corner, turn for half a block and come up the alley. Meanwhile, we'll unlock the back door and I'll meet you in the back yard. This will be a piece of cake, compared to trying to take them through the house."

"Drive into the back yard?" the driver asked. "I can't be responsible for any damage I might do to your lawn."

"What kind of damage?" Wanda asked Bob.

"It depends how wet the ground is," Bob answered. "If it's soft, his tires could sink and create ruts, maybe tear some of the grass up. It did rain pretty good on Saturday, but that's mostly dried up by now. I mean, the ground might still be damp, but not squishy. If it was me, I'd have him back right up to the patio, and if there is any damage, Tommy can fix it. In fact, I can pay for Tommy to fix it, since you're relying on my advice."

"Let's see how much damage is or is not done first," she told him. "I'll unlock the back door and start taking my groceries in while you 2 work, okay?"

They agreed, and she grabbed a couple sacks to take inside with her on her way to unlock the back door. She was a little surprised when she turned around in the kitchen and found Bob had brought in her cooler of frozen and refrigerated items.

Bob put the cooler down near the sink and jerked a thumb toward the door to the back room. "You're right, we'd never get a file cabinet through that doorway. Well, do you know where you want the items he's delivering?" he asked as he stepped into the back room and headed for the opposite door.

She stepped over to the doorway and considered the room's layout. There were windows on the south and west walls, but they were half-sized and located near the ceiling. The floor was tiled, except for a large rug taking up most of the space on the south side that covered a wooden door, probably to the basement. Wanda hadn't bothered to explore that yet. "Well, I'd like the file drawers in the southwest corner, I guess. And the exercise bike in the northeast area."

"Sounds good." He unlocked the inner door and slipped the hook and eye lock on the screen door. "Just leave it to us."

"Okay. I think most of my stuff made it inside. I'll just go out and get the rest of it."

By the time Wanda had her groceries put away, the two file cabinets were in the corner, and the men were bringing in the exercise bike. Wanda stood in the doorway between the kitchen and the back room, to make sure she didn't get in their way.

"Hello, beautiful."

Wanda bolted into the back room, away from the grasping hands and oily voice that could only belong to— "Lyle! How did you get in?"

His shrug matched his smirk as he came down the 2 steps into the back room. "The front door wasn't locked. Here, that's a clear invitation to come visiting."

The back screen door was tossed open as Bob started to back into the house holding the front half of the exercise bike. Wanda walked over and reached around the door jamb to help hold the screen door open. "Is there anything Lyle can do to help you guys?"

Bob's head jerked around, though he didn't stop moving in. "Lyle! What are you doing here?"

"I could ask you the same thing, cuz."

"I'm helping Xeck deliver some heavy items for Wanda."

"And how did you get suckered into that?"

"I was driving past to go do Chuck's bookkeeping, and they were arguing how to get these things into her house."

"So naturally you volunteered," Lyle added. "Trying to beat my time with her, Bob? You'll have a hard time of it. Our conversation the other night was both cozy and... intimate."

"No, it was awkward and... disjointed," Wanda corrected. "You spent more time talking with your mother than with me, which suited me fine." She turned her attention to Bob and Xeck, the delivery guy, as they set the bike down in the northeast area of the room. "Thank you so much, both of you, for working so hard on such a hot day. Can I get you a glass of tea or lemonade before you go?"

"Sorry," Xeck returned. "Company policy keeps me moving. Lots of deliveries to make yet."

"Then what about a can of pop to take with you? It's cold." And she listed the flavors she had in the refrigerator.

"Thank you. I would like a cola. And I hope my truck didn't do too much damage to the back yard."

She shrugged. "Before I moved in, the grass was routinely cut by a tractor, is my understanding. If it can put up with that, I doubt if you've done much to it. I'll be right back." She hurried past Lyle to get the cola Xeck had wanted.

"Isn't it time you were headed for work, Lyle?" Bob asked, probably to keep his cousin from following her.

"I've got plenty of time," was the answer. "Speaking of jobs, I hear Chuck's fallen behind on his latest project. I thought he was reaching too high. Knowing Old Man Zimmerman, there'll be a stiff penalty if he doesn't get done on time."

"It's rained more than Chuck anticipated it would, and that's put him a little behind."

"Thanks again, Xeck," Wanda told the delivery man as she handed him the can of pop and let him out the back door. She waved as the delivery truck pulled back across the yard and onto the alleyway, then locked the screen door and closed and locked the inside door. She turned to face the two cousins, who had been silent, apparently having run out of casual conversation. "What about you, Bob, did you want something to drink?"

"What about me?" Lyle asked. "Don't I deserve an offer?"

"You haven't been moving heavy objects," she returned tartly. "Well, Bob?"

"No, that's okay. Chuck keeps a well-stocked refrigerator," Bob returned, and with Lyle there, Wanda couldn't ask what he was going to do with his groceries. "So, I'll just go, and let you get back to your work."

"Work? Where did you find work in tiny little Belgrade?" Lyle asked with another smirk.

"I do computer work from home," Wanda said. "For a company based in a Chicago suburb. And I am working under a deadline, so I'm not available for a 'visit'. Even if I had invited you to come around, which I didn't. Therefore, I must insist that you leave."

"But I just got here," Lyle protested.

"Come on, Lyle," Bob said, urging his cousin towards the front door. "Just because she works at home doesn't mean she doesn't have to put the hours in. Can't imagine your employer would think well of you if you paused in the middle of your shift to have a nice visit with someone."

Lyle glanced back over his shoulder as Wanda followed them through the house. "Well, all work and no play... What about Saturday, Wendy? We can go see a movie."

"First, I don't date married men. And second, I'm not interested in dating anybody. Please do not ask again."

"That's not fair! To me, let alone boring for you."

"There's nothing that says life has to be fair," she answered. "And it's my life; I'll live it the way I want. Thanks once again for your help, Bob. Now both of you go away and don't come back." As soon as they both were down the steps from the porch, she closed the porch door and shot the deadbolt. Then she crossed back into the main house, closed and locked the inner door as well.

If the two men argued in the front yard, she wasn't aware of it. She ducked into her office, turned on a series of classical symphonies—nice and loud—and let the rhythmic tones wash over her for a minute before she returned to refining her novel.

Chapter 10
Saturday, May 2, 4:17 PM

Wanda hit the 'send' button and watched her computer screen as her large file was sent to Paula, her editor and friend. *There. Practically at the last minute, but that's okay. I don't want her thinking she can give me impossible deadlines and that I'll meet them. Paula's a good editor and a wonderful friend, but sometimes she doesn't realize just what she's expecting from me. And probably from every other writer she works with.*

She leaned back in her chair and stretched, then went to the back room for a good hard ride on her bike. The ride wasn't as long as she would have liked, as she hadn't been using her bike lately.

All that grieving has gotten me out of shape. Well, it's not like there's a lot of other stuff to keep me distracted in this tiny town. Not until Paula gives me another rush deadline, at least. What do people here do for entertainment? Lyle suggested a movie, but there sure isn't a theater here in Belgrade. Just 2 bars and a gas station that may or may not be open. Even the school was closed up years ago. Well, I worked up a sweat; a hot shower would feel good.

* * *

5:33 PM

After her shower, Wanda got dressed and wrapped her hair in a dry towel, then tossed her used clothes and damp towels into the sinks in the wash room. Stepping into her kitchen, she took a TV dinner from her freezer and tossed it into the brand new microwave atop the refrigerator, then went to the living room to see what she could find on the TV.

This is Saturday, she realized. *I haven't been back to Bob's Bar since last Saturday. Well, I have been busy. But did Chuck really mean it when he said it was an unwritten expectation for everybody to appear at Bob's at least once a week? Why would I go? I'm not made out of money; I can't fritter it away at a bar every week. I've still got 2 weeks before my next survivor's check from Hank's job comes, and that's if I got my new address to them in time.*

She pulled out her cell phone and dialed.

"Bob's Bar."

"Hey, Bob, it's Wanda."

"Hello, stranger. What's up?"

"Last week, Chuck said I was supposed to come to your bar at some point on the weekend. Every weekend. Is that really an... unwritten rule around here?"

"I assume he thought he had to say something to get your attention, since you were busy at the time."

"I was, and this week has also been busy, although not as intense. I've managed to change my music. Several times. I've stopped and had actual meals. I mean, if you can call a TV dinner a meal. And I've even managed to go outside a few evenings and walk around the house, tried to imagine flower beds."

"I believe I have heard some folks say they've seen you out in your yard," he answered.

Was it Chuck who had told Bob? Twice this week, she'd been out in the yard when Chuck had driven past in his work truck, turned left at the corner to the north and headed out of town. "Well, I'm kind of tired tonight, and was hoping nobody was expecting me to put in an appearance. I just want to take the night off and relax, now that I've sent my finished manuscript to my publisher."

"That sounds like fun," he responded. "Oh, Ella and Zita say they've got your sewing done. If you're done working for the day, maybe they could stop by with it?"

"Sure, that sounds great," she agreed, and wondered at her enthusiasm to see the local high school girls. *Well, let's face it, I haven't seen anybody... well, haven't talked to anybody since Monday. I may not be an extrovert, but I'm not a hermit, either.* "Oh, but if they can't make it by 8, it will wait until tomorrow.

It's been a rough couple weeks."

"Okay, I'll let them know. Have a good evening, Wanda."

In the kitchen, the microwave dinged. She retrieved her supper and watched some news while she ate. The news didn't seem much different here than in Chicago; most of it was bad. The weather report was aimed at farmers, and then the sports, surprisingly, was full of local high school scores. *What do they talk about when school is out for the summer?* she wondered.

She tossed out her dinner tray, washed her silverware , wiped out the microwave, then sat down in front of the TV with a cup of tea, started flipping through the local channels. *There only seem to be 3, and I haven't really seen much on them that I would watch.* She started going up into the cable channels, but still wasn't having a lot of luck finding something to watch.

Someone knocked on the porch door, startling her. Maybe it's the girls. She walked out onto the porch, but only saw one shadow. Lyle stood just outside the porch door.

She didn't unlock the door, but stepped to the open window, spoke to him through the screen. "What are you doing here?"

He grinned, as if the answer was obvious. "I've come for our date."

"I told you; No. I never agreed to go out with you, and I never will. Stop wasting my time—and yours—and go away."

"I thought we could go for a movie and pizza," he stated as if she hadn't spoken. "It's a really good movie. The latest Star Wars, in fact."

The latest Star Wars movie was released before Hank's accident, almost 6 months ago. "I've already seen it. It isn't quite as good as the rest of the series. But you go ahead, I'm sure you'll like it."

"Wendy, I was saving it to see with someone special. You."

"I'm not going anywhere with you," she stated. "So just move on along. Find someone else to go with you. Maybe your wife would like to go."

"No, she never leaves the house."

Wanda didn't know what to say to that. *Never? I'm pretty close to a hermit when I'm writing. Or rewriting. But I seldom went a full week without leaving the apartment. Groceries, game nights, date nights... They all came regularly and I seldom passed one up. Does this woman suffer from agoraphobia?*

"I'm so lonely," Lyle complained. "Please, Wendy, I just need some company."

There it was, one of the many forms of 'my wife doesn't understand me'. Such lines had never worked on Wanda, but she wasn't sure how to get Lyle to go away, short of calling the police. *And what would I tell them is wrong? A man has asked me for a date and won't go away? I've never heard of that being something the police can handle.*

A car came up the street and pulled into the broad gutter between the sidewalk and street. Ella and Zita got out and started for the door. "What are you doing here, cousin?" Ella asked.

"Taking Wendy to the movies," he answered sullenly.

"You must have misunderstood," the teen responded. "We made arrangements to bring her curtains to her tonight, and then we're going to talk. I hear there's all sorts of colleges around Chicago."

Wanda moved over and unlocked the door to let the girls in, but Lyle followed them in before she could get the door closed and locked again. With a frustrated sigh, she led the group into the living room, then turned around and glared at her unwanted suitor.

"Well, if you're going to be here," Zita told him, "then make yourself useful and take down the curtains."

Lyle glanced around the living room, but all the windows were standing wide open, their shades drawn up. "What curtains?"

"Oh, for crying out loud," Zita muttered, and put the new curtains on the end of the couch, then reached up to pull down the rod holding the curtains in the office doorway.

Lyle stared at the faded and frayed green cloth that she and Ella were taking down. "What happened to Gram's curtains?"

"They got old," Ella told him sourly. "And then got washed, probably the first time in at least a decade, so as you can see, they have barely held themselves together while we made some new ones. Why? Do you want them? Maybe Gloria could make herself a new outfit with them."

"She'd need a needle and thread," Zita stated.

"Well, that's true," Ella agreed. "I'm pretty sure she hasn't got anything like that."

During this tart exchange, Wanda was vaguely aware of a pickup stopping in the street for a few minutes before continuing on its way. As the old worn curtains slid off the rod and into a pile on the floor, the porch door opened and the 3 teen boys walked in, two of them carrying a chair apiece.

"Hey, I got your chairs done," Rusty stated as he and Felix carried the items in. They sat them down between the dining table and the sofa. "Look them over, make sure you're happy with the job."

"Wow, those really look nice," Ella stated, She leaned the curtain rod in the corner of the room and moved past Lyle to give the chairs a closer look. "They actually look like they match the table."

"Well, now that I see them with the table, the color is a little off. The table's got just a hint more red to it. Maybe someday I can re-finish the table and get it to match these 2 chairs."

"They look great," Wanda stated, and then, because she didn't know how else to judge his workmanship, she sat in each chair to see how badly they wobbled. Neither one did. "Very good."

"Putting up the new curtains, huh?" Felix asked as he picked up one of the new ones and shook it out. "Well, this will be different. Fresh."

"Rather garish, if you ask me," Lyle stated.

Wanda stood up straight and glared at him again. "I didn't ask. These are my curtains, in my house, and I liked the fabric!"

"Better give up any dreams you might have of taking her to the movies," Ella told her cousin. "You just made her mad, calling her taste garish just because these ugly green curtains have been in this doorway since the beginning of time. I can't blame Gram for being frugal, but this fabric will bring a fresh bit of color to this room."

Lyle turned puppy-dog eyes to Wanda. "Wendy, please. That isn't what I meant."

"It's what you said," she told him firmly. "Go away. I never agreed to go out with you. I never will go out with you. Don't bother me again!"

"But—"

She turned her attention to the boys. "Could you take those to the back room, please? And then I think I've got some cookies and pop left if you want a snack while I settle up with Rusty and Zita. After that, the girls wanted to talk about colleges in the Chicago area. You're welcome to stay for that, if you want."

She heard the porch door slam shut, and by the time she turned around, Zita was returning from the porch. "I locked the door behind him, so he can't get back in," Zita revealed.

"Thank you!" Wanda took a deep breath and released the tension that had been growing in her. "He can't even get my name right," she muttered to herself.

The boys moved off towards the back room with the 2 chairs. The girls resumed hanging the new curtains. Wanda took another relaxing breath, went to the bedroom to remove the now-damp towel and drag a comb through her hair. Taking the towel to the wash room, she paused in the kitchen. Tommy was pulling a couple partial packages of cookies from the cupboard, and Felix... it looked like Felix was putting a box of pop into her refrigerator? A sound from the back room caught her attention and she gave a short scream of surprise as a large figure emerged from the darkness.

"Sorry," Chuck said softly. "Didn't mean to startle you."

"How did you get in?" she demanded. "This time?"

"The boys had instructions to unlock the back door, either once Lyle had left or if it looked like he was losing his temper. I figured if you were going to entertain the kids tonight—to keep Lyle at bay—then you might need more pop, which I was taking home. Plus some chips and dip." He held up 2 bags and a container of dip.

She gave him a suspicious look. "That almost seems like you planned this."

"Not exactly, more like problem-solved," he answered. "I noticed Lyle's car here as I was headed home, and I knew that wasn't good. Called the kids, found the girls were already on their way over, that Rusty had the chairs done, so he could bring them over. Lyle finds the teens irritating—it's mutual—so I facilitated that get-together."

"Complete with pop, chips and dip?"

"No, I really was taking them home with me. Fact is, I've been under some stress lately, and haven't been eating as well as I should."

Felix came in from the living room and took the chips from Chuck. "All the shades are pulled down," he said.

"Down?" Wanda said, puzzled. "The house will get hot. Er."

"We can direct your fans to help keep us cool. The heat should break soon, anyway. Look, I haven't even been home to take a shower. Could I at least use your bathroom to wash my hands?"

*　*　*

7:04 PM

"What do you think of the new office curtains, Chuck?" Zita asked as she fished another chip from the nearest bag.

For the first time since his arrival, Chuck turned to look at the curtains. "Well, that's different," he stated.

"You don't like my roses," Wanda guessed.

"No, they're fine," he returned. "Pretty. But they are obviously new, colorful. That makes the rest of the room look..." He couldn't seem to come up with the right descriptive word.

"Shabby," Wanda offered. "I don't mind that too much. The nails holding some of the tiles in place on the floor tell me your grandmother didn't have a lot of money to spend on keeping the place up."

"Gram couldn't afford replacement tiles, so nails was all she'd let me do."

"You could paint the walls in here," Ella suggested. "A pale lilac would look nice with the purple roses and wouldn't overpower everything."

"First, I'd have to finish washing the walls. Taking down the

80

cobwebs left streaks, so now I need to take off at least the top layer of dirt. But it's something to think about," Wanda replied. "If I find a few extra bucks. Of course, then I'd want to do something with the floor, too, and I haven't got a clue how much that would cost."

All the kids turned to look at Chuck, as if expecting him to say something. Eventually, he cleared his throat. "Right now, I'm behind on my current project. I could give you a ballpark figure, but I can't take on any more jobs for at least a month."

"Oh, I'm not even ready for a ball-park figure," Wanda assured him. "It usually takes me a long time to decide to change something. First I have to get things cleaned up and rearranged and... just live in it for a while."

Chuck cleared his throat. "Well, I see you've changed Gram's photos for some artwork." He nodded toward the wall over the sofa, where frames full of small photos had been.

The kids all turned to look, and Ella's mouth dropped open. "Dragons, unicorns and mermaids!"

"Yes, I've always had an interest in fantasy," Wanda stated. "I've picked up a few pieces at various science fiction conventions I've attended."

"What do you know, Ella. Maybe your paintings aren't so weird," Felix told his sister.

"Weird?" Chuck asked. "I thought you painted landscapes."

"Still is," Felix answered. "Only she's been putting fairies and gnomes into them."

Her face pink, Ella stated, "It just takes a little imagination."

Wanda chuckled. "Sounds like your artwork might fit right in at convention art shows. Maybe you could bring a couple over and I could give you some advice. I mean, if you have any interest in doing that."

"Well, maybe after school is out," Ella stated. I still have finals and prom to get through. Anyway—" she glanced at the artwork again, "—I didn't figur there would be any money in it."

"Oh, I've never spent a lot of money on any art I've bought, but they're prints, not originals. Still, if you get $20 per print, and you sell 500 prints, that's... $10,000. Not all at once, but it adds up. Especially if you get asked to do book covers. So, whenever you want, we can talk about that, but it's a big subject and not all of us at the table would be interested. I've been meaning to ask, and now that I've sent my book to my publisher, this is a need-to-know thing. What do people here do for fun?"

"Do you mean, like on dates?" Zita asked.

"No, just as a general thing. I'm not any good at yard work, but I need to get out of the house from time to time, or else I'm likely to try to write 12 hours a day, 7 days a week. I can do that for a week or two but then my writing deteriorates. I don't see a library in town. Are there any book clubs I could join? Or just what is there to do?"

"Believe me, we've been wondering that our entire lives," Zita answered.

"Well, you've got a bike in the back room. You can always ride that around town," Rusty offered.

"That's a stationary bike, for exercising. It doesn't move," she told him with a smile.

"Hike," Tommy suggested.

Rusty told him, "Farmers won't like people hiking through their fields. But you could go down to the river and have a picnic, or just watch the water go by. It's just half a mile from here. You go west on the way to Chuck's place, but when you get to the railroad tracks, turn south. The river's just 100 yards along the railroad tracks."

"And as I've warned these kids many times, it's not safe to walk on the railroad tracks," Chuck piped up. "And don't try swimming in the river, because the bottom is ever changing, as are the currents." Having squashed that idea, perhaps he offered alternatives. "There are libraries; Cedar Rapids, Albion, St Edward, Fullerton. There's a movie theater in Albion; the next closest is Columbus. I'm not aware of any book clubs, maybe the libraries would know. Once in a while a bunch of the local ladies will gather at one house for what they call a 'stitch and bitch', where they all bring their knitting, crocheting or embroidery and just talk while they each work on their own project. Or if someone has a quilt to be finished, they'll have a quilting bee. Otherwise, people will go to someone else's house and they'll have coffee and talk."

"Or play cards," Ella added.

"Bridge?" Wanda asked.

"Pinochle, pitch or spades."

"Oh, I don't know how to play any of those games," Wanda stated. "It's too bad, it was beginning to sound a little like the game nights we would have in Chicago. Every Friday night, a group of friends would get together and play dungeons."

"You play dungeons?" Chuck asked.

Wanda rolled her eyes. "I hope that doesn't mean the local priest will want to run me out of town."

Chuck grinned. "No churches in Belgrade, so you're safe. Anyway, Hank would get a bunch of us playing in the bar whenever he was home from school. I've thought about teaching the kids how to play, but I don't know how to be a dungeon lord."

"It sounds like a fun game," Felix stated.

"Yeah, I even bought a bunch of the books, but I couldn't make any sense out of where to start. I remember everybody had to roll up a character, but not how to do it."

Wanda looked around at everybody. "Do you want to learn how to play?" They assured her they did. "Okay, hold on a minute."

She went to the back room, and paused, remembering that Chuck had come in through the back door. Happily, somebody had thought to relock the door. Relieved, she opened the 2nd drawer of the right-hand file cabinet and got out her dungeon books, assorted papers and the dice. These had all been Hank's when they'd married, and they were very nearly all she had left of him.

She deposited the books at her place at the table, placed the forms and dice in the middle of the table. "Everybody take one of these forms. I'll get some pencils. Each of you find six 6-sided die and we'll get some characters rolled up."

The kids were fun to be with. She could and probably would eventually learn to play one of those card games and start hanging with the older citizens of Belgrade, but for now, having a group to play dungeons with might be just the thing she needed.

She briefly considered the artwork that had replaced the frames of generational photos. One frame had had a bare spot, a spot she thought might have been intended for a photo of Hank, but it wasn't there. *Would they know what had happened to it?* But she got busy explaining how to roll up characters, and forgot to ask.

* * *

10:48 PM

Chuck stood up and stretched. "Cripes, where did the time go? Okay, kids, time to clean up and head for home."

"But we just got our characters created!" Ella complained. "I want to play!"

"Creating characters takes time," Chuck told her. "Playing a game can take days, and your folks won't be happy if you start staying out past your curfews. Besides, some of us have had a hard week and need to get some sleep."

"Well, when do people want to get together to start your first dungeon?" Wanda asked. "School nights aren't a good idea, so that leaves Friday or Saturday evening."

Zita grunted as she gathered the dice and put them back in their leather bag. "I'm ready to say both, but I've still got a paper to finish for history, so we'd probably better make it just one."

"Prom is Friday night in a few weeks," Ella stated. "So if we pick Saturdays, we avoid the whole problem of what to do that week."

"Plus, some of us are working a full day on Saturdays, so staying up late on Fridays doesn't sound very appealing," Chuck said.

"Are you planning to join us?" Wanda asked. He had created a character as well, but she thought maybe he was just 'leading the way' for the kids.

He paused in stacking the papers. "Do you want me not to?"

"I just thought it might get in the way. If you had a date or something."

"I told you, I haven't dated in... a good long while." He slid the papers into the file folder. "If I do start dating—once this job

84

is done—I'd still have Friday evenings available."

"So you would. Saturdays about 6? Or whenever everybody gets here, but it's best if we have 4 or 5 hours of time to play. As for cleaning up tonight, I can..." She looked down, saw the books and papers neatly stacked, the empty containers removed from the table and she could hear water running in the kitchen, and assumed somebody was washing the glasses. "Well, it seems to be done." She grinned. "You guys can keep coming over, if you're going to clean up before you go."

"See?" Chuck told Rusty and Felix as they emerged from the kitchen. "It's always appreciated when you help the hostess clean up after a gathering."

Zita stuck her head in from the kitchen. "I think we should make it a pot luck. All of us take turns bringing chips, sweets, stuff like that."

"I volunteer to bring the pop," Chuck stated. "Every week."

"And I volunteer to make some actual food," Wanda added. "So that you kids aren't eating just junk food all evening. Although, 'food' might consist of spaghetti."

"What brand of spaghetti sauce do you use?" Zita asked.

"Home made! It simmers in the crock pot all day long!"

"I'll want the recipe. I don't like the brand mom gets."

Wanda smiled. "Of course. It's not a big secret; I found it in my mother's old cookbook."

"Where did you get the recipe for bread?" Ella asked.

"Same book." She looked around at the youngsters, all gathered around the front door, while Chuck headed for the kitchen. "Didn't you boys come with Chuck?"

"Yeah, but he doesn't want people to know he spent the evening, so Ella will run everybody home," Felix answered. "I can hardly wait until next Saturday!"

"Chuck parked out back, so that's the door he'll go out," Rusty added.

"Don't forget to lock the door behind us," Ella told her as she started across the porch and out the front door.

"I'm right behind you," Wanda responded. "Good night!" she called as the teens climbed into Ella's car, then she closed the door and locked it. When she entered the living room, she paused to lock that door, too. She opened the window shades, letting in a night breeze, then headed for the back room, assuming Chuck had left and the back door needed to be locked.

"Ready to let me out?" Chuck asked as she entered the kitchen, and she jumped in surprise.

"I thought you'd already left," she told him.

"Not and leave the door unlocked," he answered. "It isn't likely Lyle's still around, or still sober enough this late to be functional, but I don't want to risk it."

"Okay." She reached for the light switch for the back room.

"Leave the light off," he told her. "No need in advertising that somebody is leaving by your back door."

"What about the people across the alley?" she asked. "Aren't you afraid they'll get curious if they see you sneaking in and out?"

"Nobody lives in that trailer house; it's been empty about 7 years, since Great Aunt Edna passed away. The big house on the corner, to the south of it, those people are nosey enough to wonder, but they can't see anything through the trees." He unlocked the door, then opened the screen door and stepped out. "Good night, Wanda. Thanks for being so kind to the kids."

"They seem—" she started, but stopped, because he was already headed for a pickup parked in the deep shade of a stand of trees behind the house next door, the only other house on this side of the alley. She heard the high-pitched bzz of a mosquito and quickly closed the screen door, hoping it hadn't gotten in.

In a moment, she had the back door locked and headed for her bedroom. But sleep didn't come easily.

What am I doing? I haven't been living in Belgrade a full month! But here I am, friendly with 2 of Hank's cousins—who are apparently Belgrade's only available bachelors—and I am now seeing both of them regularly. Not on dates, at least, but everybody around here warned me to stay away from them! Including them! But here I am, driving to Fullerton with Bob on Mondays to buy groceries. And now I'll be spending Saturday evenings with Chuck—and a handful of teens—playing dun-

geons.

At least the players won't be drinking alcohol while they play. I never really liked that about our game nights back in Chicago.

87

Chapter 11
Saturday, May 9, 5:42 PM

Wanda finished folding the last of her laundry and turned her attention to Ella and Zita, who had arrived an hour early, their arms full of Ella's artwork. "Okay, I need to put my clothes away. Could one of you stir the chili? And I need the oven lit and the skillets of corn bread put in, please."

"Sure," the two girls agreed, and headed for the kitchen, leaving the artwork scattered across the table.

"Where's the chili?" Ella called from the kitchen.

"In the crockpot," Wanda answered from her bedroom as she placed her clothes in the drawers. She started for the kitchen, but got distracted by a knock at the front door. She let the young boys in. Each of them carried something; a cake pan, a big bag of candy and 2 bags of chips. "Where's your uncle?" she asked.

"Whichever one you're asking about is probably at the bar," Felix answered on his way inside. "Or about to go there."

"I think she means Cousin Chuck," Rusty stated as he placed his chips on the corner heating stove. While Wanda locked the front porch door, Tommy placed his bag of candy on the table and started pulling down all the shades in the room.

"I did mean Chuck, yes," she admitted.

"He's probably at the back door." Rusty headed through the kitchen.

Felix followed him into the kitchen, the cake pan still in his hand. "Ella, you forgot to bring your cake."

"Oh. Thank you, Felix. I don't care what anybody says, once in a while, you're a good little brother."

"Well, don't get all mushy about it," Felix returned. "Mom said to put it in the frig until we're ready to eat it, because you had to have cream cheese frosting."

"Yeah, I forgot that, too," Ella agreed.

"Hang on," Rusty called as the refrigerator door was opened. "Let's put the pop in first."

That must mean that Chuck had been at the back door with tonight's donation of sodas. Wanda didn't need to imagine the congestion in her kitchen as everybody jostled to get around everybody else. "Okay, if you don't need to be in the kitchen, please come out."

Ella was the first. "The chili really smells good."

Next came Zita. "I put both skillets in, Wanda, but they won't get done at the same time."

"I know, but I didn't have 2 big skillets, which wouldn't have fit anyway."

"Why skillets? Why not a cake pan?"

Hank had asked something similar, once, and she gave the same answer now. "I don't know. I've just always used an iron skillet for cornbread."

Felix and Rusty finished putting the boxes of pop in the refrigerator, and then found room for the cake. As they emerged from the kitchen, Chuck came from the still-darkened back room. Wanda was dismayed to see he carried a small cooler, but she tried to put a smile on her face. "Beer?" she asked.

"Ice," he answered, and set the cooler in the kitchen sink. "We ran out last week," he reminded her.

She nodded. "And it's even hotter this week."

"Are the shades pulled down?"

Wanda glanced around the living room. "Yes, all of them." The house would be stifling in short order, and they'd need all the ice they could find to make it tolerable.

Tommy, having finished with the shades, was now looking at Ella's artwork. "Cool," he opined.

"Thanks," Ella muttered, and started to pull the artwork into one stack.

"Wait, wait," Chuck told her, picking up the top piece for a look. "Wow. I knew you had talent, Ella, but these are great."

"Well, I have taken every art course school offers," Ella replied, and started to lay out the various pieces so everyone could look at them. "Now it's just me and a couple others getting personal lessons from Ms Daniels. She's been wanting us to sign up for Saturday classes at the community college in Columbus, but I don't know where I'd get the money for that."

"How much would it take?" Chuck asked.

Ella grimaced. "I haven't even checked into it."

"You'll never come up with enough money if you don't know how much you need. Check into it. Maybe there's some financial aid you qualify for. Ask your relatives to brainstorm about it. Maybe you can do odd jobs for people other than Wanda. Maybe someone knows of a summer job for you. Or maybe enough of us can chip in $5 apiece to get you into that class."

"It's awful late for any of that," Ella moaned.

"Then you should have done some of this before now," Zita chided her. "Talk to Ms Daniels on Monday. Or maybe even call her tomorrow. Enlist her help. Is it too late? How much does it cost? Are there any other costs associated with it? How soon would you need the money? Check the college website. Don't just dismiss the idea. You know if I had any, I'd give it to you."

"Ella and I were talking about a way to make money off the paintings she's already done, but I'm afraid it will take time and some front money for her to get started," Wanda offered.

"What do you mean?" Chuck asked.

"I suggested she make prints of her paintings, mat them and send them to various science fiction conventions. She could send her originals, but without any name recognition, she'd probably be lucky to sell them for $50 each. However, if she did a limited print run—say, 100 copies—she could price them at $15 or $20 apiece. I can't make any promises. "It could take several years to sell all 100 copies. On the other hand, it's possible that 2 or more people will be determined to buy the same print at some convention, and the price might be bid up to$75 or $100, just for that print."

"You mean silk-screen prints? Those are work," Ella said.

"I don't think so," Wanda agreed. "I have artist friends who have been doing it for years. I could ask them to give you some guidance. It might take some graphic arts knowledge."

Wanda took a step toward the kitchen for a sniff. "Woops! The cornbread." She hurried to pull the small skillet from the oven. The edges were just a little more brown than she liked. "Ella, why don't you put your artwork away so we don't get any chili spilled on it? And could somebody help me set the table?"

All of the boys—including Chuck—came into the kitchen to grab bowls, silverware, glasses & ice, margarine, and the crock pot full of chili. Wanda followed with the small skillet of cornbread, which she cut into pie slices. "It's a little overdone, but I think it's still edible," she offered. "I'll keep a closer watch on the larger skillet."

* * *

9:22 pm

Wanda stopped describing the room the dungeon party was entering as a loud siren suddenly started and didn't seem like it would stop. "I can understand—sort of—" she started, but stopped when she realized all the kids were staring at Chuck.

"Wanda, do you have any flashlights?"

"Flashlights?" she repeated in confusion. "I think I saw one in that wall cabinet going into the kitchen. Why?"

"Tommy, you look," he instructed. "Girls, do you have any flashlights in your bags?"

"Out in my car," Ella offered.

"No time for that. Wanda, any candles?"

"There's one in my bedroom."

"Rusty," he dispatched the next boy. "The rest of you kids gather the books, papers, dice. Get it all together and let's head downstairs."

None of this made any sense, and the unrelenting siren was giving Wanda a pounding headache. "I don't have a downstairs," she shouted, trying to make sure he could hear her over the noise from outside. He came around the table and pulled her out of her seat by her upper arm. "I don't have a downstairs!" she repeated.

"You just don't know about it yet," he stated, and hurried the kids ahead of them as they headed through the kitchen and into the back room.

Tommy had tossed aside the large rug that sat lopsidedly in

91

the back room, revealing the wooden door in the tiled floor. He reached for the flush metal handle.

A cacophony of cell phone ring tones all went off at once. Chuck cursed and let go of Wanda as he fished his phone from his pocket. Papers and dice were hitting the floor as others were trying to get to theirs.

"Bob?" Chuck practically yelled into his phone. "Make this announcement: We're all headed for the basement. Bye." He stepped forward and jerked the door open. Rusty took hold of it from the bottom and held it open. Ella started down the stairs the door had hidden, with Zita behind her.

Tommy waggled the flashlight he'd found. "Dead."

"Figured," Chuck acknowledged. "Ella, when you get to the bottom step, reach to your left, there should be a light switch."

"Got it." A dim light revealed cobwebs and dirt walls.

Felix was stepping forward to go down the steps. "Wanda, you go down right after Felix," Chuck instructed.

"Down there?" She didn't like spiders. Or snakes.

But Chuck had turned his attention to the descending Felix. "Look under the seats of the benches down there. There should be blankets, candles, matches, flashlights and batteries."

Wanda heard thumps from down below, and soon the dim light was augmented. Not that it made the cobwebs, the dirt walls and floor any more inviting. "Chuck, I can't—" Chuck was gone.

The siren finally stopped, leaving her ears throbbing in the sudden silence. Rusty opened the door a little wider. "Wanda, we need to go downstairs."

"Why?" She rubbed her ears, trying to stop the throbbing.

"Because that was the tornado siren," Rusty answered.

Suddenly the house was dark, and Wanda yelped in surprise, then realized there was still the dim light from below. "What happened to the lights?" she asked in mounting panic.

"Chuck turned them off," Felix called up the short stairway. "Come on, Wanda, get down here so we can all get settled in."

"But Chuck—"

"Be there in a second," his voice called from the kitchen, or possibly from further into the house. "Get downstairs."

"Come on, Wanda," Ella urged from the dimly lit hole.

"Yeah, don't make Chuck carry you down," Zita added. "Cause he will."

Wanda knew a moment of indignation, and then determination that she wasn't going to be **that** kind of woman. This hole had been under her house all along. That she now knew it was there didn't change anything. She hadn't noticed large numbers of spiders, had never given a thought to snakes until now. The kids were acting as if all this was normal; she was the only one hesitating to follow Chuck's lead.

Stiffening her resolve, she stepped onto the staircase and woodenly made her way down, scuttled over to the end of the narrow tunnel and sat on one of the blanket-draped wood-backed benches. There were 3 benches; the girls had the one on the end, and Felix sat opposite Wanda.

"Do tornadoes happen often?" Wanda managed to ask.

Zita shrugged. "Oh, every 5 or 6 years, one might get close enough to send people to their basements. Rotten luck for you that one happened so soon after you move here."

On the contrary, Wanda thought to herself, *my good luck that it happened when my house was full of visitors who could guide me through it.*

Tommy and Rusty had come down after her, taking a seat on the bench next to Felix, and then Chuck clattered down the steps and the door slammed shut, disgorging a cloud of dust. Chuck paused to slam 2 bolts into place, then observed how people had arranged themselves.

Wanda hadn't noticed how low the tunnel's ceiling was; she and the kids had stood up with no problem, but Chuck was bent over and occasionally brushed his shoulders on the ceiling.

"Wanda?"

It took her a moment to realize Chuck had spoken. "What?"

"Do you mind if I sit with you?" he asked.

She considered the bench she sat on, moved to one end of it and studied what was left of the sitting area. "Will you fit?"

"I hope so. I made the benches to suit Gram. And any visitors she had." He glanced at the kids. "What got left upstairs?"

"My artwork," Emma stated, her voice strained.

"I'm not sure I got all the dice picked up, when they got dropped in the back room," Felix stated. "But I'm pretty sure we have all the books and paperwork."

"Okay," Chuck acknowledged and half disappeared into a side tunnel Wanda hadn't noticed. After a moment, he was back with boards or something. It took Wanda a moment to realize it was a folding table. Somehow, over the next few minutes, he got the table legs down, himself seated on the bench next to Wanda, and the small table situated over everybody's knees.

"Emma, I'm sorry I didn't think of your artwork," he told the young girl softly. "It's just one more reason to hope we aren't hit."

Emma nodded and sniffed. "Yeah, I know."

"Well, I don't know about the rest of you, but I hate the idea of sitting down here for who knows how long with nothing to do but worry about why we're down here," Chuck stated. "I propose we continue our game while we wait for the all clear."

"You want to keep playing?" Wanda asked in disbelief.

"It'll make the time go by faster."

"Why? How long do we have to stay down here?"

"That depends on how long it takes for the storm to move on," Zita answered.

Wanda had heard it start raining, but hadn't thought rain meant tornados. "How would we know that it's moved on?"

"I knew I forgot something," Chuck said. "Rusty, take a flashlight and look in that side tunnel. Should be a radio on the second shelf. Wind it up and stick it on the table so we can listen to the alerts. Meanwhile, the rest of you sort the papers and put the dice in a pile in the middle so we can share them."

* * *

11:14 pm

"Okay, I'm done," Chuck announced. "What have I found?" Wanda wrote some figures on a sticky note and handed it to him. He glanced at it. "Nice."

"What was that?" Ella asked.

"What have you been doing?" Wanda asked her. "Weren't

94

you getting an arrow pulled out of your leg, and then getting it bandaged?"

"Yes."

"Then you were in too much pain to see what he was doing," Wanda returned.

"Chuck," Rusty said, "they just went through all the alerts again, and Nance County is off the list."

Despite the distraction offered by the game, they all relaxed at the news. "It's over?" Wanda asked.

"Just a minute," Chuck returned. "What about Cedar Rapids, Albion or St Ed?"

"Nope," Felix replied. "Just a line going between Humphrey and Columbus, headed northeast."

"Then we seem to be in the clear," Chuck stated, and started to collect papers together, placed them in one of the gaming books. "Rusty, please put the radio back where you found it. Tommy, once it's cleared, can you fold the table up? The blankets should be folded and—"

"No, I'll want to wash them first, so just take them upstairs and put them in the washroom."

"Okay, let me go up and get the utilities turned back on." Chuck pulled a small flashlight from a back pocket and made his way to the bottom of the steps. Wanda heard a couple of thunks as the locking bolts were pulled back, and then smelled fresh air as the door was opened. Chuck disappeared up the stairway and into darkness.

"Felix, give me a flashlight," Ella requested. "I'll bring it right back." And then Ella was headed upstairs, a blanket in one hand and the flashlight in the other.

Tommy gave the folded table to Rusty, who put it in the cross tunnel. Zita picked up the books, papers and dice bag, all nicely stacked up, and then headed upstairs.

Felix and Tommy stood at the bottom of the stairs, looking up, waiting for the lights to go on upstairs.

Wanda watched Rusty carefully take the flashlights apart, one by one, and put tape over the contacts. Then each battery and flashlight body went into a separate plastic bags, which all had a small bag inside.

"What's the paper inside the baggies?" Wanda asked.

"Those are desiccant. So the battery posts and flashlight posts don't get rusty while they're waiting to be used again."

"Very smart."

"Chuck tries to think of everything." He waved at the storage benches. "The story goes, Gram and two visitors her own age spent an afternoon down here with no place to sit, no light source, and no radio to tell them when they could come out again." The next day, Chuck was here, building benches and storing flashlights and batteries."

"He cared a great deal about her."

"Well, Chuck's an action kind of guy."

"Lights," Tommy stated, and started up the stairs.

"What's wrong?" Wanda heard Chuck's distant call.

"It rained in," Ella called back.

Wanda climbed up the stairs and entered the kitchen, where she found Tommy and Zita retrieving the dusty blankets from the wash room to take them to the living room. "How bad is it?" Wanda asked. "Ella, it didn't get your artwork, did it?"

"No, I don't think so," Ella replied. "That was atop the piano, and that part of the floor is still dry, but there's a big puddle under the table. It's a good thing we took the books and papers with us, or they'd be a mess."

"Move the chairs out of the way, and we'll put the blanket down," Zita suggested. "Rusty!"

"I think he's still putting flashlights away," Wanda told her.

"Wanda, could you bring a couple towels?" Zita asked. "There's water in the window sills."

Wanda headed back, ran into Chuck as she turned the corner headed for the bathroom. "The artwork?" he asked quietly.

"Appears to be okay," she answered. "Right now they're putting down blankets to soak up Dining Room Bay. And I'm getting towels to deal with the Window Sill Lakes."

He smiled. "I like your sense of humor." Then he was past her, headed to see for himself. "Where's Rusty?"

Wanda ducked into the bathroom and pulled a couple towels off the cabinet above the toilet, headed back. She was startled by a sudden whump! from the back room. "Rusty?" she called.

"Yeah," he answered, and mounted the steps into the kitchen. "Sorry for the noise, the door is kind of heavy and hard to control once gravity gets hold of it."

"As long as you're okay," Wanda told him. "Everything under the table is wet. The window sills are full of water. I have some clean-up to do."

"Wanda, where are those—" Chuck appeared in the dining room doorway. "Ah, there they are." He pulled the towels from her hands. "Rusty, why don't you start washing up the supper dishes?"

"Not now!" Wanda objected. "The kids should have already been home by now! I can take care of things in the morning!"

"But that isn't fair to you," Rusty interjected. "Making you clean up after us."

"I don't want anybody's parents to not let them play anymore. Believe me, cleaning up is much preferable."

Chuck handed the towels to the teen. "Take these and see how those window sills are doing, okay? Meanwhile, I'll start calling parents."

"Okay, Chuck."

Chuck pulled out his phone from the holster on his belt and punched a button. He leaned against the refrigerator as he waited for an answer. "Hi, Helen, can you talk for a minute?"

"Of course I can." Wanda plainly heard the waitress over the phone. "How are the kids?"

Chuck smiled. "All the kids came through the scare just fine. We just realized a few minutes ago we could come out of the basement."

"And you're calling because..."

"Because Wanda's worried that it's past time for the kids to go home and they haven't yet. And we haven't had a chance to clean up the supper dishes, but the real point is that the living room is a big puddle where the rain came in the open windows. I'd kind of like to take a swipe at that before we call it a night."

"Go ahead. I assume Wanda's got buckets and a mop and stuff. You said the kids came though okay. How's Wanda?"

"Well, now that you mention it, she's looking a little pale."

Wanda had started for the living room to see if any more towels were needed, but at that pronouncement, she stopped short and gave him an indignant glare. He held up one finger asking her to stay silent. Pantomiming biting her tongue, she went to check on the kids.

Someone had found the plastic bucket she kept in the washroom. Tommy and Felix were taking turns wringing out water-laden towels into it. Meanwhile, Ella and Zita were slowly walking across the blankets spread over the floor, encouraging the water to soak into the blankets. Rusty gathered together an armful of wet, half-empty pop cans and headed for the kitchen.

"That's a lot of water," Wanda remarked. "I'll get the mop."

"It's already in here," Zita told her. That made sense. Wanda left the mop standing in the bucket, so the 2 items would have been together.

"What can I do to help?" Wanda asked.

"Check and see how wet the sofa is. We may have to borrow a wet/dry vacuum in the morning."

Wanda stepped forward and felt the sofa in several places. "No, it doesn't even seem damp."

"Oh." Zita seemed embarrassed. "I meant the sofa on the front porch. All those windows were open, too, and it's a lot smaller area than this room."

Wanda hurried out to the front porch, started feeling that sofa. The middle of it was damp; the south end was soaked. Then she realized she was standing in a pool of water. "Oh, shoot," she muttered, went back inside and entered her office to check conditions there. The window sill felt damp, but everything else was fine. It was the same in her bedroom. *Good. I won't have to remake my bed before I can climb into it.*

She returned to the washroom, passing Chuck, who was still on the phone. This time, she couldn't hear the person on the other end. She pulled the 3rd blanket from the cement sinks and headed for the front porch.

Chuck was dialing again, but paused to ask, "Where are you going with that?"

"There's a puddle on the front porch, and the south side of the sofa is soaked. I think I'm going to have to borrow a wet-dry vacuum from someone."

"I've got one. I'll bring it over in the morning."

"Won't that be too late?" she asked, not having any idea how long water could be allowed to sit inside a sofa.

"It'll be okay," he assured her blandly and continued with his phone call.

Miffed, she hurried for the front porch, nearly slipped on the edge of the wet blankets soaking up 'Dining Room Bay', so proceeded more carefully to the porch.

Once she got as much water absorbed into the blanket as she could, and stuffed part of the not-completely-soaked blanket under the sofa, in case water dripped out, she shivered in the cool dank breeze coming in through the open windows and went back inside the main house.

Chuck had emerged from the kitchen. The teens were done with the emergency portion of their clean-up, it seemed. The table top was dry and Ella was gingerly spreading out her artwork, looking for any damage. She sighed in relief. "It all seems dry."

"Good," Chuck told her, and glanced around at everyone. "Okay, I've spoken to your parents. They understand why you did not make curfew. And, in light of this having been Wanda's first tornado scare, they've agreed to let Ella and Zita sleep over on the click clack."

"On the what?" Wanda asked.

"The sofa," he answered, pointing to the sofa Wanda had earlier deemed dry. "In addition, the boys can come to my place for the night. That way, we can all come back tomorrow morning to finish the clean up, rather than leaving it for Wanda to deal with. And, I will provide brunch."

All the teens perked up. "Waffles?" Tommy asked.

Chuck grinned. "The only thing I can cook indoors."

All the teens seemed to approve of that idea, and Wanda couldn't bring herself to disapprove. After all, Chuck was teaching the youngsters to be kind to others, to help when others have a problem, and he was rewarding them for doing it, apparently. Anyway, despite her indignation at his presumption that she was too frail to handle a 'tornado scare' when she was surrounded by so many who took it in stride, the fact was that she had had some fear, and now that she faced all those stalwart friends leaving her all alone in the house, she could almost feel a bit of panic welling up inside her. As long as they didn't mind both sleeping on one sofa...

Chuck bent down, grabbed the front of the sofa and pulled it up. The back slid down and the seat slid up until the sofa was facing the other wall. He pushed the seat even closer to the wall.

"Wait a minute. Let us get the blankets and pillows out," Zita told him. Most of the teens reached down and pulled out either a blanket or a pillow, until the storage chamber under the sofa was bare. Chuck started to lower the seat, but the back started to slide back up against the wall. He pulled the seat up again, then pushed it further until everybody could hear the 'click'. This time when he lowered the seat, the back stayed down, and soon the sofa resembled a bed. Two blankets and two pillows were tossed on top.

"Well, I think that's about all we can do tonight," Chuck stated. "Are you girls going to be okay? Ella, where is your artwork?"

"In a plastic bag on top of the piano," she stated, and pointed vaguely in that direction.

"Good. Okay, there's nothing to be worried about." He included Wanda in the group he was reassuring. "The storm has gone by, and there isn't likely to be another one tonight. But—just in case—you remember where to go and what we did, right?"

Ella and Zita nodded, but Wanda spoke up. "All except turning off the utilities."

"Well, don't worry about that tonight. Just turn off lights as you head downstairs. **If** anything happens, which it won't. But if you get worried, just remember, you're only a phone call away from your parents."

"My parents are dead," Wanda muttered, but it came out louder than she expected.

Chuck's mouth worked, as if he couldn't decide whether to make some smart-aleck remark or treat the statement seriously. "Well, you might have to borrow one of the girls' parents, then."

"We can handle it, Chuck," Ella told him.

"Okay. Tommy, come lock the back door behind me. I'll pull around and into the driveway so you boys don't have to traipse through the mud."

Felix and Rusty moved to the front porch. "Ella, your car's drowned!" Felix called back through the house.

"What?" Wanda followed Tommy, and soon they were all standing on the porch, their shoes squishing over the blanket on the floor as they stared out at Ella's car, now sitting in a huge puddle between the sidewalk and the gravel street.

"Oh, no!" Ella exclaimed. "I worried so much about my artwork, and never gave my car a thought! Everything in it will be ruined!"

"No, now listen," Zita told her. "It's fine. The water isn't up to the door jambs, so it won't have any water inside. Just be glad it's not Chuck's car. His rides 6 inches lower than yours, so it'd be a swimming pool inside. We'll just have to deal with getting it out of the puddle tomorrow."

"You're sure it's okay?"

"I'm sure, Ella. Anyway, it'll be easier to see what we're doing in the daylight."

"There's Chuck," Rusty stated as a big pickup paused in the street and then backed into Wanda's driveway. The boys said good-bye and trooped out to pile into the pickup. Wanda locked the porch door and then the inside door as she and the girls moved back into the living room.

"Well, tonight was more excitement than I expected," Wanda quipped. "I think I need a drink. What about you girls?"

"Wanda, we aren't old enough to drink," Ella pointed out.

"Not even chocolate milk?"

"I've seen inside your refrigerator, and I don't remember any chocolate milk."

"No, but I've got milk and I've got chocolate syrup."

"That sounds real good," Zita said as she headed for the kitchen. "Is there any of that cake left?"

"If there is, I want a piece, too," Ella stated.

There was half a bag of chips and two pieces of cake left, plus the bag of candy. Wanda put the candy away for the next Saturday, then she mixed chocolate syrup into mugs of milk, and they split the chips and cake for a nice snack before going to bed.

Chapter 12
Sunday, May 10, 7:04 AM

Despite going to bed rather late, Wanda woke up at her usual time of 7 the next morning. She was about to start water for a shower when she thought better of it. Best to wait until she'd dealt with those soppy wet towels and blankets and mopped up what water still remained. So she dressed in some old clothes and got started, emptied the bucket of last-night's water and put the towels in it for another quick trip to the double sinks in the wash room.

Ella and Zita were still asleep, and she didn't want to wake them, so she went to the front porch to start mopping up water that had overwhelmed the blanket. She was just squeezing out the water into the pail for the 4th or 5th time when a sudden noise made her jump. Looking around, she saw Chuck and the boys waiting to be let in, each with some kind of box in his hands. She unlocked the door to let them in. "You're here early."

Chuck returned, "It doesn't look like we woke you."

"No, but the girls are still asleep. I thought I'd get started out here and let them sleep a little longer. It took us a little while to settle down last night. You might have thought we were having a slumber party."

"Yeah, the boys were antsy, too," Chuck stated, then stepped aside to let the boys get by. "Take everything into the kitchen, gentlemen, and see if you can—gently—wake the girls. We need to get things cleaned up before I can make waffles."

The boys all nodded, but as Felix walked past the sofa/bed, he loudly said, "Ella! Chuck says it's time to get up!"

"Alright, alright!" Ella groused as she sat up. "I swear I just got to sleep! I kept thinking about calling Ms Daniels. And then a whirlwind blew me and one of my paintings to another planet, where everybody loved my one painting, and I had to keep painting it again and again because I didn't know how to make prints, and nobody wanted me to paint anything else."

"That sounds like a dream," Zita commented as she rolled over and rubbed her eyes.

"Does it?" Ella asked as she tossed her blanket aside and crawled over to the edge of the sofa to look for her shoes. "Yeah, I guess it does."

"Well, before you call Ms Daniels and get whisked off to another planet, let's help Wanda get her house set to rights and then have some waffles."

"Yes, Chuck," Ella agreed, having found her shoes.

Chuck laid a huge metal bowl on the porch floor. "Here, let me get that blanket into this bucket, and I'll take it to the washroom." The blanket was thoroughly soaked, and Chuck was half soaked by the time he got it nestled into the metal bowl. Wanda had gotten a few drops of water on her, too, but she smiled at how much wetter he had gotten. "I think I should have brought another set of clothes with me," he muttered to himself.

Wanda thought of all of Hank's clothes, all sold or given to charity long ago. "Sorry, I don't think I've got anything that would fit you."

"Oh, a little dirt and water never hurt anyone," he answered, and started for the washroom.

Wanda continued to mop, easier now that the blanket was out of the way, but she wondered if she was making any progress. She was vaguely aware of Rusty going outside, and then he was back again, struggling to carry a huge round... vacuum cleaner?

"Chuck says take the mop and pail into the house, and let me work out here with the wet vac."

"Is that what that is? I'm not sure where you can plug it in."

"There's an outlet inside, just on the other side of these windows."

"That's right. Where the sewing machine used to be. Will it actually do any good on the sofa, or just the floor?"

"Both," Rusty answered. "Slower going on the sofa, because

it'll have to pull the water out through the stuffing, however deep the water got. The floor will be fast in comparison."

"Well, I'll let you get to it," she told him, and took her tools inside, only to see Chuck disappearing into the kitchen with yet another blanket in his metal bowl. She started mopping up excess water from around the lone blanket that remained.

Water was running in the kitchen. Felix emerged with a wet cloth and washed the top of the table off. Apparently, he and Tommy were washing up last night's dishes.

Chuck came back. "Hey, girls, there's an old wringer attached to the washroom sinks. Do you know how to use it?"

"Yes," Zita answered. She finished tying her shoes and stood up. "Come on, Ella, let's start washing the blankets."

"Wait for me," Wanda told them. "I've never used a wringer before. I'd like to see how it's done." She finished squeezing the sponge and set the mop aside, hurried after the 2 girls.

The wet stuff had been deposited in the first sink, the one closest to the kitchen. The wringer sat between the 2 sinks, its crank outside the sinks. Zita already had 2 neighboring corners of one blanket together. Once Wanda arrived, she continued, explaining its operation to Ella as well. "The trick is to not get your fingers caught. This one has a pressure release, but you could still do a nasty job with a fingertip, if you aren't careful.

"Put the edge of the fabric up against the rollers, with your hand back a few inches, but close enough you can hold it in place while you get started. Turn the crank just enough to get the cloth started through, then take your hand away and let the rollers pull the fabric through. Blankets are bulky, and you need to fold them up a bit as they go through so that you don't get a big pressure point. If you get one of those..." She seemed to be waiting for something, and a moment later, the wringer sprang apart, making both Wanda and Ella cry out.

"What's wrong?" Chuck asked, coming in with the final blanket in his bucket.

"Showing them what happens if two much fabric tries to go through at once," Zita told him. She put the mechanism back together, and continued her explanation. "Toss that one in the washing machine, Ella, and I'll crank the next one." She turned her attention to Wanda. "I think 2 blankets will fill the washing machine, don't you?"

"Yes," Wanda agreed. "Thank you for the lesson, Zita. I'm going back to mopping."

She returned to the living room, to find a very wet Chuck already at work with the mop. She smiled at the sight, for he seemed to be pushing the water around faster than the sponge could soak it up. He looked up. "What's so funny?"

"You are very wet," she observed.

He looked down at himself and struck a pose. "I'm thinking of entering a wet t-shirt contest."

She chortled in amusement. "Those are usually for women to compete in."

"I should be treated equally." He struck another pose. "I think I could win. Don't you?"

It suddenly dawned on Wanda that this conversation was very close to flirting. *And I'm not ready for flirting. With anybody.* "That would no doubt depend on who was judging."

His look held a touch of puzzlement, and he went back to mopping.

"I think you'll pick up more water if you don't chase it so aggressively," she suggested. "And don't bear down on the mop so much."

He stopped and watched the mop's sponge proceed to soak up water. He gave her a quick half smile. "When I mop, I don't usually have this much water on the floor."

"No, me neither," she agreed. "But since there is a lot of water, the sponge seems to work better if you go slow."

"I will proceed to go slow," he told her, squishing the water from the sponge into the pail. "Tell you what, why don't you go in the back room and see if you can get the cellar door open on your own?"

She hesitated, wondering why she needed to open it. "Is there a trick to it?"

"No, just grab the ring and pull up."

"Why do you want me to open it?"

He stopped mopping again. "To make sure you can. The cellar does you no good if you can't get into it."

"Oh." The thought was chilling.

"Plus, I'd like to make sure everything is put back where it belongs, and that you know where that is. How to get the flashlights working, how to change the battery on the ceiling light, if you need to. And, of course, we'll need to put the blankets away."

He made it sound so... common-place. And yet, someday her life might depend on those things. "Okay, I'll give it a try."

It took her several tries for her to get the cellar door half open. The first 3 times, gravity pulled it back down before she got it up more than a few inches. Then she got a pot holder from the kitchen to stuff through the metal ring so it wouldn't bite into her fingers so hard, but the thick cloth made it hard to grip, and she barely got it up 1 inch that time. Finally, she got it up about a foot, but couldn't get it any further, her fingers jammed into the metal ring, her other hand helping to hold the door open, but both arms starting to shake with the effort. Worse, she had stepped a bit forward, and if she could get her fingers out of the ring or somehow let go of the door, she was afraid it would smash her toes before she could get them out of the way.

"Tommy!" she called, for he was doing something at the cook stove and she could see him.

In a flash, the teen was at her side, held the door steady with one hand while he helped her extricate her fingers from the ring. With a sob, Wanda stepped back, and Tommy lowered the door to the floor. *I can't do it.*

"What happened?" Chuck asked from the kitchen doorway.

Wanda wiped tears from her face, but more followed them. "I can't get it open," she told him.

"Four fingers," Tommy offered, which made no sense to Wanda. Of course she had used 4 fingers; she had to get a good grip on the ring.

Chuck stepped down into the room, then stopped and folded his arms over his chest. "Don't worry about it. We'll try again later. There's things we can do to make it easier if you're here alone.”

Wanda hoped so, but she was still embarrassed. The door hadn’t been too much for an old woman—Chuck’s grandmother—to handle. How could it be too much for her?

Chuck turned back for the kitchen. “Okay, the dishes are washed, dried and put away. The mopping, I’m afraid, is not quite done. How is the wringing coming, Zita?”

“All done,” she answered, and passed her towel to Ella, who had just washed her hands in the bathroom. “You want us to finish the mopping?”

“No, I thought you could help me start preparing breakfast. Tommy, can you see how Rusty’s doing on the front porch? Maybe there’s something you can do to help him. And Felix and Wanda, if you would finish the mopping, please.”

* * *

8:46 AM

“Anybody need another waffle?” Chuck asked, looking around the dining room table.

“Not me,” Wanda told him. “I probably won’t eat another thing all day. When you said you were going to make waffles, I never expected so much stuff!”

Despite nobody wanting any more waffles, Chuck poured more batter into the waffle iron and closed it. “When I decide to cook, I tend to go overboard,” he admitted. “I didn’t know what type of juice people would want, so I brought 3 kinds. Ingredients for the batter. Some berries and fruit from the freezer. Butter and syrup, of course. And I wouldn’t forget whipped cream.”

“Why are you still cooking waffles when everybody's full?”

“To use up the batter. I’ll take the leftover waffles home, put them in the freezer, and I’ll have instant breakfast for a couple days.”

Wanda smiled. “I could almost think you took a class in home economics. Except ‘economics’ never came up when I took that class.”

“No, one of my aunts probably suggested it when I was feeding a herd of kids and started to throw out leftover batter.”

“I think we are all going to sit here and watch you cook up

108

the rest of that batter, because I—for one—am too full to even think about getting up and starting the dishes."

"Fine with me," he told her. "We've got plenty of time. The kids don't need to be home until noon." Wanda saw Ella and Zita exchange glances at the mention of a time when they needed to be home. It took the boys a little longer to start wondering why they had a daytime curfew. "So, Zita, didn't you say you had a history paper to finish? How are you coming with that?"

He asked all the kids questions about their school work while he finished cooking. Then he unplugged the waffle iron and set it aside to cool, but continued asking questions. Finally he glanced at the clock on the wall and asked, "Any of you kids got a summer job lined up?"

All of them shook their heads, except Tommy, who cleared his throat and said, "Usual. And... more garden."

"Garden?" Chuck asked. "Your own garden?" Tommy nodded, and Chuck asked, "You got a place in mind for it?"

Tommy pointed out the window where he sat.

"Behind the old house, huh?" Chuck reached for the tub that had held the whipped cream topping and proceeded to eat the last dollop of it. "You should have said something when I mowed; I could have plowed it for you that weekend. It's getting kind of late to plant a garden, isn't it?"

"Almost," Tommy agreed.

"Well, let's get this show on the road, then. I've got a patch to plow this afternoon." He stood up.

"How much?" Tommy asked.

"Oh, it's going to be like that, is it?" Chuck returned. "Alright. 10 bucks. But you can pay me in produce, whatever you grow that I can eat without having to cook."

"Deal," Tommy agreed, grinned and stood up to start gathering dirty dishes.

"Girls, I believe it's your turn to wash dishes," Chuck stated. "Rusty, how is that sofa coming on the front porch?"

"I'd like to empty the tank and take another stab at it, see if I've got all the water out."

"Sounds good. Girls, how are those blankets from downstairs coming?"

Ella was quick to answer. "The first 2 are dry, folded and sitting in the back room on the file cabinets. The flashlight I brought up last night is out there, too. The other blanket probably has another 10 to 20 minutes in the dryer."

"Okay. Tommy, Felix, as the table gets cleared off, bring those boxes in here. As soon as my bowls and stuff get washed and dried, start packing things away. In the meantime, put the juices in the frig. Those are Wanda's containers, and need to stay here. And you, Wanda, let's go see if we can figure out how you can open that door."

Wanda grimaced as she stood up. *My arm's sore from the last time I tried. But I need to figure out how to do it.* In the backroom, Wanda reached down and forced her fingers into the metal ring that served as a handle—

"Stop," Chuck told her. "Don't use all 4 fingers. Try using 3, or even just 2."

"I need to get a good grip on the ring," she protested.

"You need to wrap a finger or two around it and keep them like that," he explained. "Your little finger won't add any strength, only volume. I can't even get 3 fingers into that ring, I just use one."

"You have muscles." She nearly bit her tongue once it was out. He would no doubt think she was flirting.

But all he said was, "You do, too, you just haven't been using them every day. Now, get a grip, give a strong pull. Not a jerk, but put some effort into it."

Wanda hesitated, afraid she'd embarrass herself. Then she took a couple deep breaths and pulled, grabbed the edge of the door before it could slam shut again. "Ugh! It's heavy!"

He bent a leg, and his knee slid under the edge of the door, taking the weight off her arms. "Good, you got it halfway open."

Wanda frowned. "That's only a quarter open," she refuted.

"That's halfway to being perpendicular to the floor. Any more than that, and you'd have to get it perpendicular again before you could close it. So until you get more muscles in your arms, shoot for perpendicular, or as close as you can. Now, what

110

do you think, could you crawl through that opening and go down the stairs? While holding the door up?"

"No."

"Okay." He looked around the room. "Bring me one of those chairs." He had her place one of her newly finished chairs over the bottom edge of the doorway, so that 2 legs were inside the hole, resting on the top step, while the other 2 feet were on the tiled floor of the back room. While she held the chair in place, he lowered the cellar door to rest on the seat. "Okay, now see if you can raise it to perpendicular."

Her first try didn't manage much. "Why does it feel like all the weight is on the other end of the door?"

"It's physics," he answered. "Or geometry. It feels that way because you're trying to pick it up from one end instead of in the middle. Once again, no jerking, just some muscle. Let's see how far you can get it."

She got it up not quite perpendicular, and was startled when the chair toppled inside and down the steps. "My chair!"

"So what?" he asked bluntly. "So what if the chair got battered, or even broken? It's a chair. It can be replaced. You can't."

She swallowed and struggled to keep the door up as far as she had gotten it. "You're right."

He reached out and steadied the door, then came to take her place and opened the door as far as it would go. It wouldn't lay flat on the floor, but rested against the small heating stove in the corner of the room.

"Okay, let's go down so I can show you where everything is and how it works."

She thought he would go first, since he was the most familiar with it, but he indicated he would follow her. When she got about halfway down, he said, "There's a battery-powered light. Do you remember where the switch is?"

She thought back to the night before, when he had been giving everybody instructions. The switch was higher than she expected, but wasn't hard to find. The bulb hardly added any illumination to the cellar. She picked up the chair that had fallen in and placed it at the end of a bench, where it would be out of the way. She turned to face him, found him sitting down on one of the steps. "I think you said the blankets were inside the benches. And that's where Rusty was putting the flashlights and batteries. How do you keep the mice out of them?"

"By keeping mice out of the house," he answered. "Plus the benches are lined with sheet metal." He pointed to a dark alcove halfway between the stairs and the benches. "That's the root cellar that this place started as. Shelves along the walls where Gram kept the stuff she home-canned. There's a light in there, operated by a pull chain, but it's attached to the house electricity, so it wasn't working last night."

Wanda stepped into it, found the pull chain and turned on the light. The shelves were all covered in a thick layer of dust. but she saw the emergency radio right away. When she stepped forward to see what the plastic package was beside it, her foot struck the folding table leaning against the shelves and she had to set it right again. "Okay, I found the table and the radio. What's in the plastic bag next to the radio?"

"A spare battery for the light out here," he answered. "Let me show you how to change it."

The light at the bottom of the stairs went out, and the place definitely got dimmer, but that was because Chuck blocked most of the light coming from above. Changing the battery seemed easy enough. Although they didn't actually do it, the explanation was simple.

"I don't see any canned goods in here," Wanda observed.

"No, Gram didn't do much canning the last few decades of her life. Either she used it all or it spoiled." He went back to the shelter tunnel. "Let's go back up and I'll show you how to turn off the utilities," he suggested. "The electricity is in the washroom, but the gas and water are in the breezeway."

I know that. It's been less than a month since I watched the servicemen turn on the utilities.

She followed him to the breezeway and watched carefully as he explained how to turn off the gas and water. "If you have any damage to the house, don't turn the utilities back on," he cautioned. "Go to the fire station, which should be manned for several hours after a severe weather warning. They can give you a cup a coffee, a cot to sleep on, and find somebody to check out your house and make sure it's safe to turn things back on."

"A wet floor isn't a reason to not turn the utilities on?"

"Depends on why it's wet," he answered. "The windows were open to the rain, it's probably safe. Half the roof is gone, don't chance it. And of course, you don't want to be standing in water when you turn the electricity on."

She shook her head as she turned back for the washroom. "There's an awful lot to remember."

"You have a good brain. Now that I've explained things to you, I'm sure you'll do fine."

"I hope I never have to."

"Well, there is that. I hope you don't have to, either." He paused and pointed to the electric box on the wall of the washroom. "Do you know how to use that?"

She reached up and opened it. "Well, I think if I push this big red lever to the opposite side, it shuts everything off. If that doesn't work, I suppose I move all the individual levers to the other side."

"Yes, but the big red lever will work," he told her. "Remember, you're trying to get to the cellar in a hurry, so don't dawdle. Especially if you hear a big noise, like a train coming."

She looked at him with her brow puckered in confusion. "I don't remember hearing anything like that last night."

"That's because the tornado didn't get close enough that you could hear it."

She swallowed, but had to ask. "How close is it, if you can hear it?"

"Too close," he answered shortly. "If you can hear it, forget about turning anything off, just get downstairs." He turned to the kitchen. "How are the dishes coming, girls?"

"Zita is drying the last of them now," Ella answered as she wiped down the front of the refrigerator. "I was just going to go get that last blanket out of the dryer and fold it up."

"Good." He moved on. "Boys, how's the packing and the

front porch coming?"

"I've gotten all the water I can get out of the sofa," Rusty reported. "So I emptied the tank and put the machine in your truck."

"And all the food stuff is packed," Felix said. "You're taking a lot less home than you brought."

"That's right, because teenagers have bottomless stomachs," he teased. "Rusty, when you put the machine away, did you bring in the cleaning supplies?"

"Yes."

"Okay, then, let's get downstairs and start cleaning."

"Cleaning?" Wanda asked. "It's a hole in the ground, how to do you expect to clean it?"

Chuck turned to face her and guided her to the side so he could re-enter the kitchen. "You'll see," he promised.

The boys—and Wanda—followed him into the back room, where Ella and Zita were folding the last blanket. "Okay, you boys scoot downstairs, and the first thing I want you to do is hand the chair back up to me. It took a tumble a little earlier." The boys clattered downstairs, and soon the wayward chair was being handed up. Chuck set it aside. "Okay, boys, safety first. That sack holds goggles and masks. Put them on."

"What do they need those for?" Ella asked. "We didn't wear anything like that last night."

"Because I don't want them getting a lot of dust in their lungs. Or their eyes."

"Okay, we got them on," came a muffled voice from below. "I assume these whisk brooms are for sweeping."

"Sweeping a dirt floor?" Wanda asked. "That doesn't make sense."

"It's been done," Chuck told her, but I don't expect it. Boys, I want the shelves swept off, as well as the benches and the stairs. Long, slow sweeps. Too fast, and you'll kick up all sorts of dust and those masks will clog in no time. Plus the dust will just settle and need to be swept up again. You decide who does what, and I'll be back."

Wanda stopped him on his way to the kitchen. "What should

114

I do?"

"Your part comes later." He entered the kitchen, then the washroom, and came back with her plastic pail, which he handed to Tommy, who was sweeping the steps. He had them sweep the dust from the various surfaces into the pail.

Ella and Zita finished the blanket and sat in the 2 chairs that Rusty had returned the previous weekend. Wanda got tired of standing around, not knowing what was going on, and went to the living room to add a few items to her shopping list.

It wasn't long before Ella came to find her. "Chuck's ready for us to do our share now."

"Oh." She got up and followed the girl to the back room. "And what is our share of this cleaning process?"

"Putting the blankets away," Chuck answered. "Boys, go wash up and then please put the cleaning supplies back in the pickup." He turned his attention to Wanda, who was picking up the last blanket from atop the file cabinets. "This way, you can see exactly where everything is kept." He picked up the flashlight and handed it to her. "You should put that away, too."

She took the flashlight, but put it back atop the files. "I'm keeping that one up here for now. The one that was up here was dead last night, so I'll need to get new batteries, at least. Maybe just a whole new flashlight."

"Oh." He smiled. "Well, it would be a rash of bad luck to have another tornado scare so soon, but it's good that you're thinking about being prepared for it, whenever it comes."

Wanda followed the girls down the steps, and they soon had the blankets put away, with plastic baggies of flashlight bodies and their batteries nested atop each blanket. They turned to head back up.

"Wanda, stay down there a minute, there's something else you need to practice."

She frowned a little, remembering he had talked about her having to practice opening the cellar door. "What?"

"Come about halfway up," he told her, and pulled the cellar door perpendicular to the floor. "Take hold of the door. Just raise your arms and place your hands flat against it. Try not to slide them, you might get a sliver. Okay, walk down the stairs until it's closed. Don't worry, I'm going to hold onto it and steady it for you."

For all that Chuck was 'steadying' the door for her, the lower it got, it seemed the heavier it was. When she reached the next-to-the-bottom step, she stopped. "Let go, Chuck."

"Are you down yet?"

"Let go, Chuck!"

Without her moving, the door got heavier. "Okay, clear."

Wanda took a deep breath and suddenly sat down on the previous step, folding her arms around her lowered head. The door thumped into place, and she felt a cloud of dust sprinkle down around her. She moved further in the tunnel for a deep breath, and then returned to the stairs. "Okay, it's down," she called up through the wooden door. "Can I come out now?"

"The door is down," Chuck agreed. "But it isn't locked. It won't protect you if it isn't locked. There's a bolt mechanism about half-way up the stairs and another near the battery-operated light."

Will this game of his never end? I am thoroughly sick of his big, strong, protective male posturing. "I see the one next to the light." She shot it shut, and then crawled up the stairs to do the other one. "Anything else?"

The door creaked a bit as it moved ever so slightly. *He tried to open it, to be sure I actually locked it! He didn't believe me!*

"Okay, unlock it and come out," he told her.

The bolts were easier to disengage than they had been to lock. Perhaps her slow-burning anger lent some extra strength to her tired muscles. She reached up and started pushing the door open as she climbed the stairs. It was heavy, but went up fairly easily, and she was soon standing at the top of the stairs, holding the door perpendicular to the floor. "Ella, would you please hold the door upright so I can go back down and turn off the lights?"

"Sure."

Wanda didn't look at Chuck during her trip back down and then up again. She wasn't sure she could look at him and not give him a blistering piece of her mind. When she had lowered the door into its closed position—she let it drop the last few inches, after making sure nobody's toes were in the way—she finally stood up straight and asked Chuck, "Are we done now?"

"I think you should practice opening the door from up here a time or two."

"My arm is sore and needs to recover," she answered firmly. *All these years of riding a bike for exercise has evidently left my arms weak.* "I'll recuperate tonight and try tomorrow."

He gave her a questioning look, but seemed to think better of whatever he was about to say. "Well, be careful. I wouldn't want you to take a tumble like that chair."

"I will be careful," she said evenly. "After all, I'm not a teenager." Even after she let the 2nd sentence slip out, she wasn't sure he got the idea. *Men can be so dense, sometimes.*

"Well, let's see, we've cleaned up from last night, had breakfast, cleaned up from that, put the cellar back to rights. Is there anything else you need us to do?"

"No, I don't think there is. And while I appreciate all the work the kids have done—work I didn't ask or expect them to do—I definitely feel the need for a hot shower and a chance to relax before I start my work week again tomorrow."

At the mention of a hot shower, Chuck's lips wriggled, as if he was about to make a suggestive remark, but she raised an eyebrow at the very idea. He gave a sigh, and turned for the kitchen. "Okay, kids, let's get my stuff out to the pickup and let the lady enjoy what's left of her weekend.

Wanda, glad that Chuck had finally taken the hint, but sorry if she'd made the kids feel guilty, made sure the back door was locked and followed the group to the front porch.

"Oh, my car!" Ella remembered as soon as she looked out the front windows. "It's still in a big puddle!"

Chuck stopped at the bottom of the porch steps. "I might have a board or two in my truck."

"No, never mind." Ella sat down on the porch sofa and rolled her jeans up to her knees. "I'll just wade out to it, and then I can drive it out of the puddle, and the others can get in. Zita, you bring my paintings. I for sure don't want to drop them into a pond of muddy water!”

“Are you sure?” Chuck asked. “Your shoes will get wet.”

“They’ll wash,” Ella answered easily. “They’ll get all wet anyway, unless you’ve got 12 by 12s in your truck.”

“Well, no,” he answered. He turned away, seeming reluctant to let Ella have her way. “Okay, did you get all my boxes in my truck?” he asked the boys.

“Yes,” Felix answered. “Are we going home with Ella, then?”

“Seems like it,” Chuck answered, and walked toward his pickup.

Ella turned to Wanda and quietly asked, “Are you okay, Wanda? How badly is your arm hurt?”

Surprised, Wanda blinked before she could answer. “It’s just sore.”

“Then put ice on it. Especially after your hot shower. Now, is it okay if we play dungeons again next week? Do you need time to think about it?”

So at least one of the kids had picked up on Wanda’s anger. She smiled at the teen. “I enjoy playing dungeons, Ella. I did get a little riled this morning, but that will be all done by next week-end. Long before that, I’m sure.”

Ella smiled back. “Well, I’m glad, because we really enjoy dungeons, too. But if you change your mind, just let me know, and I’ll make something up.”

She turned and walked briskly down the sidewalk, slowed to wade out to her car and got in carefully. Despite the size of the puddle, the top of the water was still 2 or 3 inches below the bottom of the door. She backed out onto the street before she closed her car door. Then she motioned for Chuck to move his pickup out of her way.

Wanda wasn’t sure why Chuck hadn’t pulled out, but he took the hint and drove north to the corner, where he turned west. Wanda knew by now that the tiny village only extended another block west of that corner. She wondered how far he had to go to get home.

With her car removed from the water, Ella pulled into the

driveway, the kids all piled in, waved good-bye and were gone.

Wanda locked the porch door, then the inner door as well as she went inside. She was alone in her own house, on a Sunday, and it wasn't even noon. What was she going to do with the rest of her day?

Well, yes, a hot shower to start, and some clean clothes, but she didn't have enough dirty clothes to do a load. Putting some ice on her arm was probably a good idea, just in case. She could work on her shopping list for tomorrow, and that meant planning what to fix for supper for the group for next Saturday.

And maybe, instead of writing, she would read the afternoon away.

Chapter 13
Monday, May 11, 10:07 AM

Wanda stared at Bob with a bite of the Dew Drop Inn's peach pie halfway to her mouth. "Every single one of them?"

"Every one," Bob confirmed. "He went to each house, sat down with their parents and them, told them exactly what he was expecting from them, and what they could expect from him. Every set of parents gave their approval, and every kid accepted. Which kind of surprised me, because I thought Tommy was pretty busy with mowing and gardens and stuff. Me, I kind of think Chuck's gone off the deep end, hiring half a dozen kids to help on a construction site."

"Only five kids," Chuck corrected as he approached their booth. "Scoot over, cuz." He looked for the waitress. "Uma, bring me a cup of coffee and a piece of pie, would you, please?"

"What kind of pie?"

"Surprise me." he returned and sat down next to Bob. "Besides, I tested them. As best as I could, given the situation."

"How did you test them?" Bob wondered. "Every single one of them was stunned when you asked them to work for you."

"Well, first, Wanda's had them working for her, and she's been happy with their work. Then, we all went to Wanda's Sunday morning to help her clean up from the rain getting in. I gave them some directions, but they followed through without any arguing and did a good job. Same with cleaning the cellar and putting it back to rights."

"Cleaning the—! How the devil do you clean a hole in the ground?" Bob demanded.

"That was what I wondered," Wanda agreed, and went on, "Apparently, you do it by using whisk brooms and moving them very slowly and carefully, so as not to kick up any dust."

"On anything made of wood," Chuck added. "I didn't ask them to sweep the floor. Although, seeing how much dust the door kicked out when it closed, maybe I should have had them sweep it down, too."

"I think I can manage that part," Wanda stated.

"I meant both sides. You'd have to open it."

Wanda felt a little bit of yesterday's anger return, and she coldly stated, "I'm adding arm and shoulder exercises to my workout routine."

Chuck considered her quietly while the waitress deposited his coffee, pie and silverware in front of him. Once she had left again, he lowered his eyes for a moment. "It seems I owe you an apology. You didn't know I was testing the kids. It must have seemed strange, my coming in and barking orders. It's just... that's the way I am on a job; I tell my men what to do, and I expect them to do it. But I wasn't on a job, we were in your house, and I should have, at the least, explained to you that I was testing the kids."

Actually, he didn't bark any orders out, not really. He asked the kids to do this or that. And they had accepted it, so it hadn't struck me as anything out of the ordinary. It was being treated like a teenager who needed to be tested that made me angry.

"Okay, then, go ahead," Bob told his cousin.

"What?"

"You said you owed her an apology, but you never actually gave her one."

Chuck blinked in surprise. Then he sat up straight to address Wanda. "I'm sorry for... Well, for the whole mess I made of the situation. I should have been more sensitive, especially of you."

Wanda knew that should be the end of it; she should accept his apology and let her anger fade away. But it didn't fade away, not really. It crawled deep inside her and went to sleep, but if he ever slighted her again, it would rise up in full force. She ate a bite of pie and washed it down with iced tea, to give her time to get her voice under control. "Well, that does sound like an apology. So I hope that's the end of it. On the other hand, you just, what, doubled your workforce?"

"If you don't count me, then yes," he agreed. "Except the kids are just part-time."

"How much is part-time?" Bob asked.

"The paperwork's on the desk in my office," Chuck said. "There's only a couple more weeks of school, so they can work up to 5 hours a week until school's out. They can either work an hour a day after school, or come to the site on Saturday and work the entire 5 hours then. They all opted to work next Saturday morning for this week. Which will give us a chance to actually get them doing something useful, rather than just getting started and have to stop. But don't tell them I said that. Saturday, they'll let me know what they plan to work the next week."

"So, training while they finish school, sounds like," Wanda summed up. "And once school is out, then what?"

"Twenty hours a week," he answered. "I told them I'd prefer they work weekday mornings, but we'll see. They might be better working in the afternoons or something else."

"When you said you were going to look for help, I thought you'd put an ad in the paper or something," Bob stated.

"I did that a month ago. Nance County, Boone County, even in Columbus and Grand Island. The only responses were from Kevin Oliver and Useless Young, 2 men I won't hire again."

"I can't blame you," Bob responded. "On the other hand, you fired Steve 6 times in the first 2 months he was with you."

"Steve knew how to use a hammer. And a saw. He didn't always know how to hop to it, or how to keep his mouth shut. It took us 2 months to get the rough edges smoothed out on each other. After all, I was used to working alone."

"Well, that's true."

"Anyway." Chuck turned his attention to Wanda. "I hope you got some relaxation yesterday, after all that excitement."

"I spent the day reading a novel," she answered, and smiled mischievously. "Until somebody showed up with his noisy tractor and tore up the ground practically in my backyard. I couldn't hear myself think."

"We all have to make some sacrifices when Tommy wants to plant a garden," Chuck told her.

"It's a little late to plant a garden, isn't it?" Bob asked.

Chuck shrugged. "Tommy doesn't think so. Maybe he's got fast growing seeds he wants to try out." He checked his watch and shoved the last bite of his pineapple pie in his mouth, swallowed the last of his coffee. "I got to get back to work." He stood up and headed for the cash register. "Uma, my check, please."

Bob watched his cousin pay and then leave the cafe. "Is that true, Wanda? The kids never argued or complained about what he had them do?"

"I haven't noticed that they ever argue or complain with him," she answered. "But I don't remember him barking orders, either. No, he asked them to do something, and they did it. It's like they knew all these things needed to be done, but they were kind of overwhelmed until he gave them a direction. I know I was."

"Well, we used to take them to the movies every month or two, the 2 of us and the 5 of them. At first, they were a noisy group of kids. It got on my nerves, but Chuck took it in stride. You're right, he never barked at them. He'd just ask them to use their inside voices, and then he'd drop his voice to a whisper." He shook his head. "I stopped going when I was in college and working. Took too much time to drive to Columbus or Grand Island, but I'm always happy to help them with their studies. And it just seems like they're looking for approval, they hardly ever need my help."

"You may have hit it on the nose," Wanda stated. "They like having Chuck's attention, and mine, too, I think. They're happy to have found something to do on Saturday evenings that includes us. I think they'd be thrilled if you could join us, too, but Saturday is probably your busiest day."

"Yes," Bob agreed, and sighed. "And I don't have anybody to take over to let me take even 6 hours off." He drank the last of his coffee and smiled. "Well, someday I'll hire another barkeep, but not this summer. Are you ready to go get groceries?"

"Before we get groceries, could we swing by the library? I need a new book to read."

"No, but we can do that after we get groceries. The library

doesn't open until noon. The hazards of living in small towns."

"Oh, I never considered... Then I guess that's the way we'll do it. If you don't mind."

"No, I could use a book, too."

They walked to the cash register. Uma looked at them from her seat sat at the counter. "Chuck paid for all of you."

"He did?" Bob asked. "Okay. Thanks. See you next week."

"You better watch him like a hawk, Bob. Well, you know that better than me."

"Maybe so," Bob replied. He turned and opened the door, let Wanda precede him out to the sidewalk. "That sneaky little weasel!" he declared.

"Why? What's wrong?"

"If he thinks he's going to butter me up by buying me a piece of pie and coffee—"

"What do you mean?"

"Remember when Chuck told me the paperwork was on his desk at his office?"

"Yes, so?"

"He was telling me to get the kids set up as employees. He doubled his workforce and doubled my work for his business!"

Somehow, that didn't seem to Wanda what Uma had been warning Bob about. "How in the world did you become his bookkeeper?" she wondered.

"That's what I studied in school. I'm his bookkeeper; he's my handyman."

"Well, I guess that's one way to keep it in the family."

He smiled. "Get used to it. I'm pretty much the bookkeeper for anybody who needs one in and around Belgrade. Or at least I teach them the basics, and help them with their taxes."

"That sounds like a lot of work."

"It can be. From time to time."

"I mean, and a more-than-full-time job running your bar. You need to hire some help and let yourself take some time off."

"Frankly, I wouldn't know what to do with myself if I did," he answered. They had reached the grocery store and walked in, each getting themselves a shopping cart. "So, what are you feeding the kids next Saturday?" Bob asked as they headed for the produce department.

"I just fed them chili and cornbread this past Saturday," she revealed. "I was thinking pasta alfredo. Or maybe meatloaf. Why?"

"I get tired of cooking for myself," he answered. "Not that I do a lot of cooking at home. I tend to rely on TV dinners. Anyway, I think the girls were hoping you'd make spaghetti. I don't think Ella likes the brand of sauce Helen buys. But apparently, you make your sauce from scratch."

"Not entirely. I use canned tomatoes. But okay, I'll make spaghetti. And I'll make sure the recipe is available for anybody who wants it."

"You'll spend your whole day cooking," he predicted.

"Nope," she refuted. "All the sauce ingredients go in the crock pot in the morning and simmer all day. I'll cook the meatballs Friday evening, and add them to the crock pot about 5. Now the spaghetti might take some time; I don't have a huge pot for it, so I'll have to do batches."

"If it was me, I'd just give them hot dogs and sauerkraut. Every Saturday."

Wanda laughed. "That probably would work, if they were younger. Oh, look, bananas. I want some of those."

Chapter 14
Friday, May 15, 5:49 PM

Wanda exited her office and walked to the back room, where she opened a file drawer and rummaged until she found the folder she needed. Going back to the living room, she opened the file folder and took out the 3 pieces of paper in it.

Only 3? Hank had a file for every convention we went to, packed with information on the convention, the hotel, how to get there, our pre-registration, the schedule, a list of what panels I was scheduled to be on, what each panel was about... anything we could possibly want to know about, he had in that file.

Well, that explains it. Hank always handled the details of going to cons. And in the aftermath of his accident, I completely forgot about some convention in Denver who had just asked me to be their Author Guest of Honor. So he had just started the file. And here's the beginnings of that normal mass of information; a print-out of their website, some information on the hotel, and some hand-written notes.

Her eyes filled with tears at the sight of the familiar hand-writing, and she got her box of tissues from the piano, and had a good cry. Then she dried her tears and got a notebook and pen, to take notes on what she needed to know.

Let's see, Hank's notes say the con was going to fly 2 of us out to Denver and provide transportation to and from the air-port. Well, it's only one of us, now, and they won't be flying me from Chicago, it'll be from... where? Omaha? That's half a state away in the wrong direction. Surely there's another city with an airport that's closer.

When they couldn't get hold of Hank, they called Paula. She reminded me I had promised to go. Maybe she's got some infor-mation she can share with me. I'll give her a call.

But the call to her publisher didn't really provide any answers. She took some notes on the vague information—or possibly only vague beliefs and assumptions—that Paula offered. The only real, concrete information that Paula could share was the name, number and email of the convention chairperson.

Wanda locked her front door as she left, and started down the sidewalk, reviewing the notes she'd taken during her frustrating conversation with her publisher. As usual, following the conversation had been rather like following a chicken that had had its head cut off; the trail led in a myriad of directions, with no rhyme or reason, until the listener finally gave up in sheer exhaustion. Consequently, her notes were scattered across a number of pages, and nearly incoherent. She was headed to Bob's for some supper, and she'd spend her time there trying to make sense of her notes.

A car horn bared quite close by, making her jump and drop her notebook. She looked up to see Chuck's pickup sitting in the broad gulley that the locals used as a parking area. "Sorry," he called out his driver's window. "It was supposed to be a polite, 'howdy' beep. Man, you were in a world all your own."

"Hello, Wanda," called the man sitting next to Chuck, and the one on the other side of the cab waved.

She realized she was close to the corner, and if he hadn't beeped, she would have walked into the street without realizing it. She picked up her notebook and pen, briefly held the notebook up for him to see. "My publisher gave me some info on a special assignment. I'm trying to make sense of it. But thanks for waking me up. I shouldn't be walking with my head in the clouds."

"Some people try to drive with their head in the clouds," stated the middle man.

"Or work," added the 3rd guy.

Another pickup went by and beeped as it headed west. "Oh, that's the rest of my crew," Chuck stated, and put his pickup into gear. "I'd better get home so these guys can get home and get some rest. Big day tomorrow."

"Oh, that's right. Training the new guys," Wanda said, and raised a hand in good-bye.

"Wait a minute," one of the passengers said as the truck slowly moved away. "What new guy?"

"No," said another voice. "Guys. I distinctly heard her say new guys. More than one." The voices faded away as the truck moved off, and Wanda quickened her pace.

It was Friday night, a busy night, but it was still a bit on the early side, and Wanda hurried to claim an empty seat at the bar. "Hey, Wanda," Bob greeted her. "Need a menu?"

"No, I know what I want, whenever you're ready." He was pouring drinks, and she didn't want to distract him.

"Go ahead and tell me," he invited.

"Grilled ham and cheese, with fries, and a sloe gin coke."

"Got an apple cobbler, if you want dessert," he offered.

"Oh, the kids bring all sorts of goodies for our Saturday night games, so I'd better not."

With that settled, Wanda opened her notebook and looked at the scribbles in dismay. Taking a deep breath, she found a clean sheet and made some decisions "1 is for transportation, 2 is for hotel information, 3 is for the convention schedule. And 4 will be for miscellaneous." She wrote those down on her clean sheet, then went back to her Paula notes, began circling batches of words and placing a number inside each circle.

By the time she was done with that, it was plain that she had next to no information on transportation. So when Bob brought her meal, she hurriedly asked, "Hey, Bob, maybe you know where the closest airfield is?"

"Fullerton," he answered at once.

Surprised, she wrote it down.

"No, don't put that down," said the man on her right. She thought his name was Quince, but she wasn't sure where he fit on the local family tree, if he did.

"Why not?" she asked.

"It's a private airfield, not even a real runway on it. Dr Upton flies himself in and out from there."

She sadly crossed out 'Fullerton'. "I should have asked for the closest airport. Someplace the airlines can be caught."

"Well, that's either going to be Grand Island or Lincoln.

And those will be small, so don't expect much choice in flights. You can either go east or west. Maybe south. Where you trying to get to?"

She had decided she wasn't going to say much about her upcoming trip. What would the locals know of science fiction conventions? Just like saying not much about what she wrote; these were people of the Earth, farm folk, a lot of them, and not given to flights of fantasy. Or of science fiction. But giving out her destination didn't seem too out of place. "Denver."

"Well, you'd probably want to go to Grand Island, then."

"Oh, what for?" the man on her left argued. "She could drive just 20 miles south of Fullerton, catch the interstate and be in Denver in 6 or 7 hours."

"Yantz, you mean, drive an hour south and west to Grand Island to catch the interstate, so she might as well catch a plane, while she's there," Quince returned over Wanda's head.

"Them plane's over-rated," Yantz declared. "Specially these days, with all the security measures ya gots ta go through. Ya gots ta get to the airport 4 hours before your plane takes off, or maybe more. So by the time she drives to Grand Island, finds the airport and gets her car situated, gets checked in, waits 4 hours, she's already used up 6 hours, at least, and she hasn't even gotten on the plane yet."

"That's just foolish talking," Quince shot back.

Bob sauntered over. "Aren't you the lucky one, to be caught in the middle of a Quince and Yantz argument."

"Not sure how I got it started," she said in a subdued tone.

"Oh, it wasn't nothing you said," Quince stated. "Yantz and I have been like this since we were kids. Do what you want, either fly or drive."

"Driving will be faster," Yantz inserted.

Quince grabbed his beer and turned around on his stool. "Come on, Yantz. Let's go claim the pool table before Chuck's crew gets off work and monopolizes it all night."

"Well, they won't," Yantz declared. "They're so far behind, they're working long days, 6 days a week. So when they do get off today, they'll come in for a bite and a drink, and then head home, just to do it again tomorrow."

The 2 men moved off, still arguing, and Wanda soon found herself wrapped in a pocket of relative quiet. "Thank you," she told Bob.

"What was Quince talking about? Either fly or drive?"

Oh, I've got a... special assignment, so I'll be taking a trip in mid-July. I was trying to figure out the best way to get to Denver. If I were still in Chicago, the best way would be flying, but Yantz was of the opinion that driving would be faster."

"I'm not sure Yantz has ever been outside the state. Let's ask someone who knows." He motioned to a man at the bar to Wanda's right. "Hey, Frank, you've hauled to Denver, right?"

"Yep," the man agreed.

"How long does it take to drive there?"

Frank pursed his lips while he thought about it, glanced at Wanda. "Car or semi?"

"Car," Bob answered.

"About 7 hours."

"There you go," Bob said, and moved off to refill an order.

Wanda made a note in her notebook, and then asked Frank, "I guess it takes longer in a semi, huh?"

Frank flashed her a dull grin. "Nope. You get that semi up to speed, and you just keep going till you get there. No stopping every couple hours to get a snack or whatever." That explained a lot of the behavior of big trucks during her drive from Chicago to Belgrade.

Frank turned the other direction to converse with that person, and Wanda ate as she tried to decipher her scribbles and transfer the information to the proper page.

She had finished eating the sandwich, almost finished the fries, and had just asked for a 2nd drink when somebody slid onto the stool on her left. "Hello, Wanda." She looked up, but didn't recognize the man, although he did look vaguely familiar. "I'm Dick," he told her and offered his hand.

She put her pen down, but hesitated before she took his hand. "Have we met?"

"Not officially," he answered. "I'm one of Chuck's crew."

Still she hesitated. She was trying to keep Chuck at arm's length, as best she could when he had so easily slipped into her life on a weekly basis. Did she really want to encourage any of his crew? Especially one who had a wolfish look about the eyes.

Steve came through the front door and placed a heavy hand on Dick's shoulder. She recognized Steve, from the night she had helped Bob out by waitressing for a few hours.

"Dick, if you're going to date Wilma, you'd best not try to get friendly with other women. Wilma's got a short temper, and she knows how to use her pa's guns."

Dick glared at the man. "This isn't any of your business."

"Well, it is, because we need every man we have ready and capable of working. And you heard Chuck; he's doubled the crew, so now I not only have to expect you to pull your weight, but to train your own shadow as well. Starting tomorrow."

"And I will! Now back off—"

"You won't be able to with a bullet through your kneecap."

This looked like it could become heated in half a minute, so Wanda broke in. "Dick, I'm not interested. Find someone else."

Dick was obviously surprised, if not offended. "But... you don't even know me! Don't listen to anything Steve says—"

"Apparently, you don't listen to anything Steve says. Nor did you listen to me, because when I say no, I mean no. I'm busy. I'm not interested. Go away."

"But—"

"Is there a problem here?" Bob asked as he walked down the back of the bar. "Good to see Chuck finally turned you guys loose for the day. You need menus? The pool table's taken, but there's a booth over there you could sit at."

Dick sighed in resignation and got up. "Fine, I'll sit in the booth." But he didn't sound happy about it.

Wanda pushed her dirty dishes out of her way, and worked on her notes some more, then looked up when someone sat down on her left side again. This time it was Vallie, who was brought a beer by Bob. "Bob, you gave our booth away," she complained.

Bob leaned forward and confided, "Dick was bothering Wanda. I had to give him someplace else to sit. Sorry, mom."

Val took a drink of her beer and looked over at the bank of booths for a moment. "Poor Steve. After working long hours with Chuck's crew, now he's stuck being chaperone for them."

"Why? Are they all like Dick?" Wanda asked.

Vallie took another look. "No, maybe not. Of course, the pool table is already taken by the Egger twins."

"Quince and Yantz are twins?"

Somebody sat down on her right side, and it was Chuck, who answered her question, "That's right. Nephews of Gram. Evening, Aunt Val."

"Wondered where you were," Vallie replied. "Most of your crew are over there sitting in our booth. Now poor Wanda is stuck with me sitting next to her, pestering her while she's trying to work. Wanda, it's Friday night, past time to put work away. All work and no play..."

"Well, normally, I would, but I just got this special assignment," Wanda not-quite lied. "I've done projects like this before, but always as part of a team. Someone else handled the details, but this time, I have to do all of that."

"And no doubt you're nervous, want to make a good impression, do a good job for your boss," Vallie sympathized. "But, um, that's not straight coke you're drinking, or the can would be sitting next to the glass. Mixing alcohol with work is not a good idea."

Wanda frowned down at her notebook and realized her notes were not making much more sense than her earlier scribbles. With a sigh, she closed her notebook. "Bob, could you bring me a plain cola and some of that cobbler?"

"Thought you were watching your figure," Bob commented.

"I've underestimated how much alcohol I've been drinking," she answered. "I have to be able to get home."

"So early?" Vallie asked.

"Well, no," Wanda allowed. "Now I have to wear off some of the alcohol in my system."

"Won't take long," Vallie stated. "You haven't had much."

"I don't know. I'm not used to more than one."

Chuck said to Bob, "Hey, how about a burger and fries?"

"And a beer?" Bob asked.

"No, tomorrow's going to be a hard day. Make it lemonade." He glanced at Wanda's notebook. "What kind of special assignment? If you don't mind my asking."

Again, she was daunted by trying to explain science fiction conventions. "Well, I'm being sent on a business trip in July. To Denver. I don't know whether to fly or drive."

"Well, ask Chuck," Vallie suggested. "He goes every year. Not to Denver, I don't think, but someplace out in the Rockies."

"Ahh, I drive," Chuck answered. "It's just a quick trip I take, be in the mountains for a few days."

"Why not fly?" Wanda asked.

"I'd still need a car—or some kind of vehicle—when I got there. And driving is about the same amount of time as flying, maybe a little less. Depending on how low I'm flying. When I'm driving."

Steve placed a hand on Chuck's shoulder to get his attention. "I can't believe you hired 5 new people and expect every one of us to train one of them, starting tomorrow."

"That's right," Chuck responded. "And I have to make sure you guys are training them right."

Steve looked surprised and then grinned. "That's right! Well, that's why you get paid the big bucks, I guess."

"Good night, Wanda," Dick called from the doorway.

"Shut up and go home," one of the other crew members told him and shoved him out the doorway.

"What was that about?" Chuck asked.

Steve rolled his eyes. "Oh, Dick forgets he's dating Wilma. But Wanda saw right through his malarkey and wasn't having any of it. Wish more women had that kind of sense. Would make things easier for the rest of us guys. See you in the morning, boss." He followed the others out.

Vallie watched the foreman walk out and head for his pickup, then turned to Chuck. "What's going on between Steve and his girl friend?"

"Fran? I don't know that anything is going on. Or not going on. We don't compare notes, you know."

"Well, of course you don't. You wouldn't have any notes to compare!"

Chuck's face reddened. "And if I did, you wouldn't be happy about that. He turned to eat the meal Bob placed in front of him.

"Well, now that there's a booth free, I'd better claim it," Vallie decided and moved with her drink to the empty booth.

"At first, I thought maybe Vallie was saying you attend some kind of construction convention in Denver," Wanda offered to Chuck.

"I'm not aware of any of those," he returned. "Is that what you're going to?"

"Oh, no!" she declared, and took a bite of her cobbler, washed it down with her drink. "So you go up into the mountains? Camping or hunting?"

"Sightseeing, actually," he answered. "I just take a long weekend and let somebody else handle the business while I'm gone." He frowned at his hamburger. "Might not be able to go, if we don't get caught up on this job."

"That would be a shame," She told him. "Bob was saying the other day he doesn't have anybody trained to take over for him so that he could take some time off."

"Well, I'd suggest he hire Useless, but I think his inventory would be sorely depleted by the time he got back."

Wanda giggled. "He was only pining for half a day off."

"Even so," Chuck returned. "There's a reason why everybody calls him Useless."

"Everybody?" She hadn't considered that it was a common nickname for the man. "How sad."

"It is," Chuck agreed. "But I swear, the man does his best to live up to it."

The door closed behind Wanda, and Alice was standing on her left. "Wanda! How good to see you! Oh, and you tried the cobbler. I hope you liked it."

"It's very... comforting," Wanda stated.

"Too sweet, is it?" Alice asked. "I used a recipe for rhubarb cobbler, but I didn't have any rhubarb, so I used frozen apples. I cut back on the sugar, but I think I still got a little too much in it. Perhaps I should have added a touch of vinegar.”

“In a cobbler?”

“Oh, you’d be surprised how much flavor a bit of apple vinegar can give a dish. Now, there’s no need for you to sit over here at the bar. Val’s got a booth, and there’s plenty of room for you in it!”

“Thank you, Alice. Val wasn’t here when I got here, or I would have joined her. I just came to have some supper and do some thinking. And then I was hoping to leave before Dick did, but that didn’t happen.”

“What does it matter when one of Chuck’s crew leaves?”

“I wanted to get home and get my door locked behind me.”

“Apparently, he came in and started flirting,” Chuck added.

“And he didn’t seem inclined to take ‘Leave me alone’ for an answer.”

“No wonder you aren’t too fond of this place; every time you come in, some man starts hassling you.”

“Not every time,” Wanda refuted, thinking of her first day in town, when she came in for food and information.

Alice was shaking her head. “Even when you were working that first Friday. Steve kept talking to you far longer than it takes to order a new round of drinks.”

“Steve!” Wanda stared at the older woman in surprise. “We were just talking, because I was new in town and didn’t know anybody.”

“If Steve Xanderson is talking to a pretty young woman like you, he’s flirting. Just like his father, that way.”

“Aunt Alice, the man has a girl friend,” Chuck protested.

Alice sniffed. “I’m sure it doesn’t keep him from looking. From what I hear, that romance is off more than it’s on. But I don’t expect you know anything about that, do you, Chuck?”

“I don’t poke my nose into his business.”

“No, it’s not,” she retorted. “The man is your best friend, and you can’t be bothered to be aware of it when he’s having problems. Men!” She smiled at Wanda, and her voice warmed. “Join us in our booth anytime, Wanda.”

"Thank you, Alice, but I think I'll be going home soon."

Chuck stood up and finished his lemonade. "Think I'd better get home and try to sleep, considering what tomorrow will probably be like." He caught Bob's attention and placed a bill under his plate, then turned and left.

Bob hurried over to clean the dirty dishes away and wipe down the bar for the next customer. "Say, Wanda, you wouldn't happen to have that recipe for spaghetti sauce with you, would you?"

"What? For you? No, I don't, Bob, but I can get a copy to you."

"And those meatballs you mentioned, are those just little balls of ground chuck, or is there a special way to make them?"

She gave him a slow smile. "Basically, I make meatloaf and shape it into little balls. I'll get you the recipe for those, too."

"Yeah, usually I just throw something in the oven, when I'm off. If I'm here, it's something off the grill, of course. But I been thinking all week about you making spaghetti and meatballs, and I just feel like I've got to have some. So if I can get those recipes by Monday, then I can lay in supplies and give it a try on Tuesday."

"I can do that," she agreed, and finished drinking her cola. "Let me pay my bill."

A few minutes later, she turned for the front door. "Wanda."

She turned back. "What?"

"You can use the back door."

She glanced at the 'Employees Only' door behind the bar.

"Not that one," Bob stated. "That one mostly just gets used for deliveries. I thought you might use the door by the pool table. It takes you out under the fire escape from the 2nd floor. Save you a few steps."

She looked back and saw the door he meant. She'd been semi-aware of it all along, but hadn't thought of using it. She adjusted her grip on her notebook and pen and started for the back door. "Thanks, Bob."

Outside, thick clouds had gathered and it was already going dark. The day hadn't cooled off at all, or else she was used to the air conditioning in Bob's Bar. The clouds had brought moisture with them, and the night was sultry, almost steamy. It wasn't going to be easy to sleep tonight. Even if there had been a breeze—and there wasn't—breezes never seemed to wander into her bedroom. Maybe she'd sleep on the couch tonight. The air seemed to move marginally easier in the living room.

She walked to the alleyway and started across the street at an angle. As she stepped up onto the sidewalk, she realized a pickup was parked on the lot with the giant half-buried can. She couldn't remember seeing a pickup parked there before, ever.

Frowning, she felt for her house key and gripped it firmly, the rough end sticking out between two fingers. Then she hurried to the corner, and crossed the next street at an angle again. As she approached her own yard, and was about to cut across the grass to the front door, there was a rustle in the bushes next to her driveway. She stopped on a dime and stared in dread at the bushes. Anything, anybody could be hiding there, waiting for her to come home. She thought of Lyle, of Dick, and even of Steve, now that Alice had put that thought in her mind.

After a frozen moment of terror, a cat fight broke out in the bushes, and a yellow tabby came running past Wanda's legs, followed closely by a calico. Wanda giggled in nervous relief and hurried to her front door, let herself in, then locked it behind her.

Taking a deep breath, then another, she told her heart to stop beating wildly and settle down; she had been scared by neighborhood cats. She turned on the light in the living room, doused the light on the porch, and locked the interior door.

Across the street, next to the giant half-buried tin can that she had been told was a storage shed for the county department of roads, the pickup turned on its lights, pulled onto her street and turned north. She didn't see which way it went at the corner.

She got her pillow from her bedroom, adjusted 2 fans to blow on the living room sofa and settled down to watch some TV. The fans weren't helping. It was going to be a long—and probably sleepless—night.

She had been frightened tonight, for the first time since she'd moved here. No, the tornado scare didn't count; there was nothing she could do about that except get a new flashlight to keep upstairs, and put the 'borrowed' one back downstairs, which she had done.

But those bushes had looked downright sinister, a black mass flanking her driveway that could hide anything and anybody. Tonight, it had been cats, but what if it had been Lyle? His own family had implied he was not above rape.

Restless, she got up and went to the kitchen, stole a piece of candy from the partial package she had put away last weekend. She got half a mug of orange juice, and went back to the sofa and TV.

At the next commercial, she again went to the kitchen, this time feeling like she'd forgotten something. But no, all the ingredients for her spaghetti sauce were on the counter, next to the crock pot, waiting for her to put them together in the morning. Her largest soup pot sat on the stove, so she wouldn't have to dig it out when it was time to cook the pasta. She opened the frig again and found nothing out of the ordinary. She went back to watch TV.

Five minutes later, she sat up. The meatballs! She hadn't cooked them, hadn't made them, hadn't even taken the ground beef out to thaw! She raced to the kitchen, pulled the 2-lb package of ground chuck from the freezer, and placed it in the refrigerator. Then, on 2nd thought, she put the 2-lb package back in the freezer and got out 2 1-lb packages instead.

Well, that messes things up, she thought as she returned once again to watch TV. *But not beyond fixing. Hopefully, the meat will thaw by morning. After I start the sauce, I'll make the meatballs and cook them. They only need to join the sauce during the last hour. No one needs to know I nearly forgot the protein of the meal!*

She got as comfortable as she could, but the night was uncommonly stifling. *I hope it cools off before I have to cook those meatballs. Of course, cooking them will just heat the house up.*

Chapter 15
Saturday, May 16, 4:20 PM

The day was unbearable, just as the night had been. Wanda had managed to get up in the early morning and had started her spaghetti sauce, made the meatballs and baked them in the oven, to avoid having to stand at the stove, because she was not at her best this morning. When they were done, she had carefully transferred them to a bowl and placed them in the refrigerator.

Then she did some research about getting to the convention, and had sent an email to the convention chairperson, apologizing for not being in touch earlier. Since Hank had passed, she explained, she would be handling the details for Linda Sinclair. That was the name she used for writing. She told them there would be no need for airline tickets, but she wasn't sure exactly how she would be getting there. She had asked about Linda's schedule, eating arrangements, hotel arrangements and so on.

Finally, she had taken a cold shower, trying to cool off. And then she had lay down on the sofa and tried to doze.

The day was just as stifling, as hot, as steamy as it had been the night before. Only worse, because somewhere up above, the sun was trying to break through the clouds, and although it wasn't managing it, the heat was coming through, just the same.

Somebody knocked on her door. She opened bleary eyes and checked her watch; too early for anybody to be here for the game. She had been dozing; maybe she had imagined it.

Another knock.

She didn't want to get up. She just wanted to lay here and melt, since that seemed to be her destiny.

At the 3rd knock, she rolled off the sofa and climbed to her feet. The room seemed woozy around her, and she kept a hand on the chair backs as she started for the door, faltered away from

the line she wanted to walk as she crossed the porch to tell
Chuck through the door, "You're early!"

"Are you okay?" he asked.

She fumbled with the lock, opened the door. "You're early."

He climbed the steps and put a chilly hand on her forehead.
"How do you feel?"

"I'm fine," she answered, then decided to sit down on the
porch sofa. "Why are you here?"

"We had a rough day working today," he answered, his hand
around her wrist. "I thought about you being in this house, in this
heat."

"It'll cool off eventually." She closed her eyes.

"You stay right there," Chuck told her. "I'll get you a cold
drink."

She heard him walk away, but it seemed to take him a long
time. Suddenly, her forehead felt cold and wet. She jerked upright, and a wet washcloth fell into her lap. Chuck handed her a
glass of ice water. "Drink up."

That seemed like a good idea, so she took it and drank nearly half of it in a few gulps. "Thank you."

"Drink the rest of it," he told her.

"You're bossy," she complained, but continued to drink. Her
forehead was the only part of her that felt... comfortable. She remembered hearing that the body looses most of its body heat
through the head, so she placed the wet washcloth atop her head.
Sweat started rolling down her scalp, but it actually felt cooling,
so she didn't mind.

Somewhere, somebody was sawing. What a strange thing to
be doing on such a hot day.

She handed the glass back to him, the ice sliding around in
the bottom. "There, is that better? Sir?" She tried to put a lot of
sarcasm in the last word, but wasn't sure she managed it.

"Much better," he answered, taking the glass from her.

The top of her head felt cold. She took the washcloth off, realized it was dripping with water, so maybe it wasn't sweat that
had rolled down her scalp.

"Here." Chuck took the cloth from her to wipe her face.

"Hey!" she yelped at this indignity and grabbed the cloth back. "I can do it myself!" she declared, and began wiping her face, moving the cloth down and around her neck.

Chuck breathed a sigh of relief. "Good, you're beginning to sound like yourself again"

"And just who do you think I sounded like before?"

"I don't know. Some helpless woman who didn't realize how close she was to heat exhaustion."

She had opened her mouth to protest his remark about a 'helpless woman', but his comment about heat exhaustion stopped her. "Are you sure?"

"Believe me, I know what to look for."

"And you guys were working in this heat all day. It must have been murder."

"It was slow going," he admitted. "Luckily, the shell is all up, and we all worked inside today, with lots of fans going, like you have. Still, every hour, we took a break in the vehicles with the AC going hard while we drank a bottle of cold water. I sent Ella to the store twice for more ice and water for the coolers."

"I should have gone to Bob's," she muttered. "That would have cooled me off."

"Or take a cold shower," Chuck suggested.

"It didn't help for very long.

Now she could hear somebody pounding. *Or am I having auditory hallucinations, like when I have a fever? But my hallu-cinations involve people roller skating back and forth, and some-times a lamp breaking. Sawing and pounding are new.*

"You want some more water?"

"I think I'd better."

"Keep using that cloth. I'll be right back."

She tried to follow his instructions, but her earlier lethargy soon had her stretched out on the sofa and trying to drift off. And then she *felt* someone standing over her and opened her eyes. It was Chuck, with a fresh glass of ice water and a quizzical look on his face. "I was reviewing my training, trying to decide if I should try to get the water in you or let you rest."

"You've had training in how to treat heat exhaustion?"

He nodded. "Yeah, I've some first aid training." He bent down and took her wrist again. "Well, your pulse is better, and you don't feel quite so hot."

"I'll drink the water," she decided, and forced herself to sit up again.

Chuck sat down on the edge of the couch next to her and while she drank, he took the wet cloth and ran it down her near arm several times. When she set the glass aside, with only 3 half-melted ice cube inside, she pushed the cloth away. "That doesn't feel as good as it used to."

"Let's try something, he suggested, and dumped the small ice cubes in the middle of the washcloth, then folded it around them and gently pressed the cloth against her arm.

"That's better," she stated and returned to wiping down her face, neck, arms, and even her legs. "I have to remember this."

"It's hard to think when you're on the brink of heat exhaustion."

She was surprised to hear footsteps inside her house, and turned to look just as Steve stepped onto the porch from the living room. "She okay?"

"She will be," Chuck answered. "Would have been a different story if we hadn't gotten here when we did."

"We're done in here. I'll check on the others." He turned to address someone behind him. "Come on, Ivan, and be careful with that ladder."

"I know enough to be careful with the ladder," said the man who followed him out of the house, holding a step ladder parallel to the floor as he crossed the porch and walked down the porch steps. Steve closed the door gently behind them.

Wanda realized she was staring at the door. *Those are Chuck's men; Chuck has some explaining to do.* "Why were they in my house? With a ladder? What were they doing?"

"They installed a couple ceiling fans in your living room."

She had to work to keep her temper in check. *Surely this is all a misunderstanding. He didn't just do this without asking me or anything.* "Why did they do that? I already have half a dozen fans scattered through the house. Why would more be better?"

"Ceiling fans move more air around than those little ones. And they're quieter, too. Less noise to get in the way while we're playing dungeons. Or when you're working."

"I don't remember us ever discussing ceiling fans."

"Well, we haven't," he admitted. "But if you had talked to me about fans before you bought all those other fans, I would have been happy to talk to you about ceiling fans instead."

"I was looking for fans I could afford—and use—immediately," she pointed out.

"I would have been happy to install them myself."

"But you're already working long hours."

"Still, this is one of those things I should have done for Gram, if she'd have let me. But she was a tough old bird who never let the heat get to her, and wouldn't let me do much to make her life easier."

"Maybe I want to be a tough old bird and not let the heat bother me."

"Well, then don't use them. Unless you absolutely need to. Like today."

"Today was rough," she conceded.

"I figured it would be, considering what we had to do in order to keep working today. I'm glad I came to check on you."

"But you came early," she remembered. "And you brought half your crew with you."

"Ah, actually, I brought all my crew with me."

"You left them outside?"

He seemed to think about that a moment. "I left a lot of stuff outside, including the pop and ice. If you don't mind, I'll bring those in now."

"Oh. Okay."

When Chuck went outside to bring things in, Wanda took the glass back to the kitchen. The two ceiling fans sent a steady breeze down to her as she walked through the living room. She thought about washing out the iron skillet she had used to bake the meatballs, but the breeze didn't reach the kitchen. She opted instead to get another glass of ice water and sit at the living room table.

She could hear voices from outside, probably from her driveway, if all of Chuck's crew were here, waiting for him to get done. *Get done with what? How long has he been here?* She checked her watch. It was 5:15. If she remembered correctly, Chuck—and his crew—had arrived about an hour ago. She considered the ceiling fans. *Those are done. If he's going to let them off early today, then they'll all help bring stuff in, and then they'll be gone, and I can add the meatballs to the sauce, and everything will be on track again.*

But Chuck was the only one who brought the game refreshments in, and he took 3 trips to do it, pausing at least once during each trip under each of the ceiling fans, as if to be sure they were sending down a steady breeze. *Or as if he's trying to cool off by standing there for a moment. Is he overheated? What does it look like when someone is approaching heat exhaustion? He seemed to know I had a problem just by looking at me, but I haven't got a clue what to look for.*

He came back from the kitchen for the 3rd time, having taken a cooler full of ice for the pop, which wouldn't have much time to cool before the kids arrived. He stood between the table and sofa, just watching her for a moment. "Um, Wanda?"

She turned her head from watching the ceiling fan on the other end of the living room. "What?"

"Do you need help making supper?"

She stared at him in surprise. "Are you volunteering? Don't you need to let your men go?" Which seemed to mean having them all go to his place, for some reason. Especially at the end of a week.

"Yeah, we'll be going in a couple minutes. But if there's something I can do to help with supper..."

He is volunteering. But I feel fine. I'm not a helpless female. Or is heat exhaustion more complicated than I think it is?

"There's not much left to do," she stated. "Just put the meatballs in the sauce and boil the pasta. It's too early to do the 2nd, and... well, yeah, I should do that." She started to stand up.

"Put meatballs in the sauce? I can do that. Just, uh, where are the meatballs?"

She finished standing up, feeling suspicious because of his over-protective attitude, and guilty for being suspicious of someone who was just trying to help. "I'll do it. There isn't much room left in the crock pot, and I doubt if they'll all fit."

"Are you sure you're up to it?" he asked, following her.

She paused to reverse the fan that sat atop the refrigerator, making it blow into the kitchen rather than obliquely into the living room. Then she pulled the meatballs from the frig and a spoon from the silverware drawer. Setting the bowl on the counter next to the crock pot, she started transferring the meatballs into the sauce. She only got about half of them in before the sauce threatened to overflow. "Well, that's all I can get in now. The rest will have to go in later, after the first batch of eaters take their sauce."

"What do you mean, the first batch of eaters?"

She replaced the lid and waved at the pot waiting on the stove. "I can't cook enough spaghetti for everybody to eat at once. I'll have to cook at least 2 batches."

"Oh. Then it won't matter if I'm a few minutes late getting back."

"No. How far is home from here, anyway? I had the impression it wasn't far."

"About a mile."

"Then if you leave now, you could be back in time."

"Ahh, I'd like to shower, get the stench of work off me."

"Well, I don't know how long that would take you."

Someone came in the front door. Wanda moved over to look into the living room, and saw Steve disappear into her bedroom. "Hey!" she protested, and moved to her bedroom door. "What do you think you're doing?"

Whatever he was doing, he was squashed between the foot of her bed and the window facing the driveway. He had an electrical cord in his hand, which came from a machine she had never seen before, now ensconced in her bedroom window. He plugged the cord into an outlet not far from the window and manipulated 2 buttons on the front of the machine. A new breeze entered the room.

145

Wanda turned slowly to face Chuck, who had only followed her part-way. "Now what have you done?"

"I had AC units I wasn't using, and you needed them."

"Bull!" she declared. "You have this habit of doing things and assuming that I'm just going to accept them as some kind of nice gesture! And don't try to give me any more bologna about it being something you should have done for your grandmother! Because the fact is, you didn't do it, and I am not your grandma! I am not a helpless female! I have limited funds, but that doesn't make me helpless! And it doesn't make me a charity case, either! Now you just take those gizmos back, put everything back the way it was, and then you and your crew get out of here!"

A loud thud drew her attention away from the person who had invoked her anger, and she saw they were now in the back room, that she must have chased Chuck through the kitchen and down the step as she walked forward, trying to impress him with how irate she was. Steve had just closed one of the windows in the back room, and now turned to face Chuck with a half-angry expression on his face. "You said you were going to tell her!"

"It hadn't come up yet," Chuck stated.

"And then you said she had said it was okay."

"I meant the ceiling fans."

"Those go, too!" Wanda declared.

Steve closed another window. "I never would have agreed to install these things if I thought she didn't want them."

"Well, I don't!" But a voice inside said she was lying.

"Steve, you saw her when we arrived! If we'd gotten here any later, I probably would have had to run her to the hospital."

Hospital? That made her hesitate.

Steve closed another window and this time turned to face her. "Well, there is that, Wanda. You definitely were in a bad way when we got here. I'm surprised all it took was a little cold water, inside and out. And we haven't even gotten to full-on summer yet. There's sure to be more days that are this bad or worse. Now, if you're worried about the bill,—"

"I wasn't—" Chuck started, but stopped as both Wanda and Steve glared at him.

"I hadn't even started worrying about the bill!" Wanda exclaimed. "Probably because of all the things he's already done, and refused to take any payment for! Well, I won't have it! I expect an itemized bill explaining just exactly what I'm paying for! But guess what! Don't expect any big payments on it, because my funds are limited, and you are not at the top of my list to get paid! Now get your men and get out of here!"

"Um, what's all the yelling about?" asked a new voice coming from the doorway to the kitchen. Wanda turned to see Ivan, who had formerly been carrying a ladder out of her house.

"Chuck never told her what we're doing," Steve answered.

"And she's mad about it?"

"She never approved any of it, because they never talked about the possibility, and she never got an estimate." Steve turned and closed the last window in the back room.

"Wow. Even I know better than that," Ivan stated, and turned away. "By the way, all the rest of the windows are closed, and the AC units are going full blast. Should start feeling it a little bit before too long."

Steve gave his boss a blistering look. "Even Ivan knows better than to keep a woman out of the loop when it comes to spending money."

"But we don't need the units or the fans," Chuck insisted.

Wanda snorted and stormed into the kitchen, started filling the big pot with water, then suddenly whirled to face them as the 2 men were walking through on their way to the front door. "I got a better idea! Steve, I want **you** to make up the bill! Since I can't trust Chuck to put real numbers in it."

"Me!" Steve seemed shocked. "I don't do the billing!"

"Then it's probably time you learn," she answered briskly, moving the filled pot to the stove and onto a burner. "You probably do everything else involved with the business when Chuck takes his sight-seeing trips to the Rockies, don't you?"

"Well, yeah. Everything except the bookkeeping."

"Maybe you should enlist the help of the bookkeeper, to teach you how to make up a bill." She realized something and frowned. "Oh, I've just piled more work onto Bob, haven't I?"

"He's used to it," Chuck said. "Come on, Steve, let's go."

Having made sure the burner lit when she turned it on, she raced into the living room after them. "Wait a minute, Steve!" They both turned. Chuck had pink flags in his cheeks, but she ignored him. "How much power do those AC units have? How many cubic feet will they cool?"

"Each one should cool the room it's in without any trouble. But not much further than that. So use the one in your office when you're working, the one in your bedroom when you're sleeping. In the evening, if you turn them both on, and aim their fans into the living room, it should help. Probably won't do much in the kitchen. Sorry."

"So it's definitely not going to help in the back room," she surmised.

"Hardly any. You'll have to continue using your floor fans in there."

"Well, I don't go out there much. So I'll close the door and not even try to cool it."

"That will help with your electricity bill," Steve offered.

Wanda rolled her eyes. "Another bill. Thank you, Steve. Oh, uh, Chuck."

"What?"

"Don't try to come in the back door tonight. The kitchen door will be closed, and if you pound loud enough for me to hear you, all the neighbors will likely hear you, too."

"Wasn't planning on it," he revealed. "After last weekend, everybody knows I spend Saturday nights here, so there isn't any need to use the back door anymore."

Still angry with him, Wanda retorted, "I didn't think there was in the first place."

Ella and Zita came in the front door and stopped short. "Chuck, what are you and your crew doing here?"

"We're done," Chuck said, and turned to leave. "I've gotta take the guys to their cars."

After the men left, the girls followed Wanda to the kitchen. "I feel we walked into the middle of something," Ella stated.

"Yeah, like a fight," Zita added.

"Oh, it was just the tail end of a fight," Wanda returned.

"Want to talk about it?" Ella asked.

"I'll set the table," Zita suggested, and disappeared into the living room with a load of plates.

"Chuck just has a way of setting me off by not thinking," Wanda stated. "Well, actually, he does think. He thinks he's doing me a big favor, but he doesn't consult with me on what he thinks would be a good idea, he just does it. I've told him I'm not looking for favors, I'm not looking for a boy friend... But he just keeps doing it!"

"Kind of sounds like he treats you more like a child than an adult," Ella stated.

"Well, that's how it comes across to me, too," Wanda agreed. "But when I calm down, I think that in his mind, he's just trying to be nice."

"Well, he can be generous," Ella stated. "So that's probably a good guess. What did he do today?"

"Oh, it's all this equipment he brought in and had his men install. He never talked to me about it, wasn't going to tell me about it until I regained my senses and demanded to know what they were doing."

Ella's brow furrowed. "What do you mean, you regained your senses?"

Wanda sighed, wished the water would start boiling so she could add the pasta to it. "Apparently, when they arrived to do all this work, I was on the verge of heat exhaustion, and not very cognizant of much of anything. Except that he was early for the game. I remember telling him that, several times."

"And he just had them do the work while you were out of it?" She hesitated. "All what work?"

"Installing 2 ceiling fans and 2 window air conditioners."

"Oh. Well, if you were in heat exhaustion, you need them. At least part of the time; it isn't even full summer yet."

"That's what Chuck said. Or was it Steve? But it doesn't change the fact that they came here ready to do all this work, and they didn't know I'd be in that condition when they got here! He just ignored my feelings until I lost my temper!"

"Yeah, I hate it when people do that."

Wanda gave her a wan smile. "Thanks, Ella. You're a good listener. Hey, can you cook the spaghetti? I want to look something up on the internet."

"Sure, I can handle that."

"Okay, good. I'm planning to cook both these boxes so that we have plenty. If there's any left, I'll package it up for meals later in the week. When the first box of pasta is cooked, just fish it out with this spaghetti ladle and put it in this big bowl. I should just be a minute or two." As she passed through the living room, she saw Zita sitting bleakly at the table, and the 3 boys were coming in as she approached her office. "Hi, boys. Zita started setting the table, but I think she got distracted. Could you take over?"

Her office felt chilly already. Not icy cold like Bob's place, but definitely cooler than she was used to. "Zita, could you come here for a minute?" When Zita stepped inside the curtains, Wanda asked, "Sweetie, I need to let the air conditioning get into the living room so we can all be more comfortable this evening. I know you made those adorable ties to pull the curtains apart, but I need to look something up on the internet before we start this evening. So could you tie the curtains back and let some of this cool air move on? Thank you."

A few minutes later, Wanda came out of the office with a little peace of mind, having looked up the going price for ceiling fans and window air conditioners. Maybe the bill wouldn't be too huge. "Okay, does everybody have drinks?" she asked on her way through the living room again. "Ella, how is the pasta doing?"

"The first box is almost done."

"Wonderful." She got pot holders and lifted the inner pot from the crock pot, then took it to the table. "Woops. I guess we need a ladle." She turned the crock pot off when she went back for the ladle, then looked at the kids seated around the table.

Wanda took a deep breath and let it out. "Okay, I'm going to say something and hope it doesn't ruin everybody's fun tonight. Chuck and I had a fight this afternoon. He thought he was being kind, thoughtful and generous, and I saw it as over-bearing and sticking his nose into my business. I may have over-reacted. But I let my feelings be known, and I hope that's the end of that particular fight. Now, we're going to have to eat in shifts tonight, because I didn't have room for all the meatballs in the sauce, and I could only cook the spaghetti one box at a time." She walked over to look into the kitchen. "When you get that box of pasta out of the water, bring the bowl in and you kids can start eating, okay, Ella?"

"I'm just stirring the 2nd box into the water now."

"Oh, good. I can take over."

"So Chuck isn't coming tonight?" Rusty asked.

Wanda blinked in surprise at the question. She glanced at the clock; it was after 6. "I don't have any reason to think he won't. In fact, the last thing we said was to determine that he'll come in the front door. He did say that he could be a little late, because he needed to take the guys to their cars, and he wanted to take a shower. He couldn't have left here before 5:45."

They all seemed to relax, and when Ella brought the bowl of spaghetti in, they took turns getting some. Wanda went to the kitchen and stirred the big pot, then took the rest of the meatballs and added them to the rest of the sauce, stirring it up so they would all be coated and could soak up some warmth from the sauce. In a few more minutes, she returned to get the pasta bowl to put the freshly cooked spaghetti into it. She had just gotten herself a serving when Chuck walked in.

For the sake of the kids, Wanda greeted him with a little smile. "You're just in time. The 2nd batch of spaghetti just hit the table a moment ago."

He had taken his shower, as indicated by his damp hair. It was slicked back and only mildly disheveled, rather than the spiky mop it had been earlier. He wore a button-down shirt and a clean pair of jeans. He sat in his usual chair on the other end of the table and lay down a handful of flowers he'd carried in. "Pass those to Wanda, would you please?" he asked Zita.

Zita passed them to Ella, who handed them to Wanda. The bouquet consisted of dandelions, lilies of the valley and several groups of tiny yellow flowers that formed long cones of yellow. And one red tulip. "I know it's not much of an apology, but there's no florist in Belgrade," Chuck stated.

"They're beautiful," Wanda stated. "Let me get some water for them." Once they were placed in a mug of water, she placed them on the table.

This argument seemed to be over. She hoped it would take a while before they had another one. Unfortunately, Chuck's attire tonight—so different from the t-shirt and scuffed jeans he usually wore—and his arrival with flowers of any kind, made her worry that he still hadn't listened to her when she said she wasn't looking for a boy friend. She spent the meal asking the kids about their day at work.

Wanda entered the bar through the back door and paused to soak up some of the coolness before she moved further in.

Bob looked up from his grill. "Wanda. Good to see ya."

Wanda looked around at the empty bar as she made her way to the bar stools. "Who are you cooking for, Bob?"

"Myself. Did you want something from the kitchen?"

She sighed. "Actually, I was kind of hoping I'd get here in time for you to have this for lunch." She placed the bowl on the bar in front of her, then pulled some folded paper from her back pocket. "And here's the recipes you asked for."

Brow furrowed, he glanced inside the bowl, saw the nest of spaghetti with sauce and 3 meatballs nestled inside. With a big grin, he asked, "Have you eaten yet?"

"Not yet. The morning kind of got away from me."

"I'll swap ya. You have my grilled cheese, and I'll eat spaghetti." He seemed eager to try her cooking rather than his own.

"Even swap?"

"I'll toss in a drink of your choosing."

She laughed. "Okay."

He hurried to the grill to dish up his lunch, bringing her just a grilled sandwich with a pickle spear. "I can throw in some fries, if you want. I try to avoid them, when I can."

"No, this is fine," she stated. "Even swap is what we agreed. Besides, I still have a piece of cake left over from last night in the frig at home."

"What do you want to drink?"

"Iced tea."

He placed the bowl in the microwave and turned it on while he got her tea, placed a 2nd tea at the bar stool next to her. Then he retrieved the bowl, got himself a fork and sat down to eat with her. "Ymm, this is great, Wanda. And you brought the recipe, too. I definitely want to make this on Tuesday."

"Those recipes make enough for 4 servings with 3 meatballs each. You can store leftovers for a couple days in the refrigerator, or a couple weeks in the freezer. Han— Husband and I had spaghetti almost every week."

"Believe it or not, I'm tired of fried foods. I really appreciate this."

"Well, I was hoping you would like it. I meant it as a kind of peace offering."

"Peace offering for what?"

"I kind of signed you up for some extra work."

"Really? How did you manage that?"

"Well, it all started when I fought with Chuck yesterday."

"What was it about?"

"He brought his crew over yesterday afternoon and had them install ceiling fans and window air conditioners."

"And that made you mad?"

"We had never had one discussion about either one."

"Oh."

"Plus, I was sure he wasn't planning to charge me for them, because he kept saying he had them and didn't need them."

"I still don't see where I fit in."

"I insisted on getting a bill. Then I decided I couldn't trust Chuck to make out a real bill, so I told Steve I wanted him to make up the bill."

"How did Steve react?"

"He sputtered that he didn't know how, so I suggested he enlist your aid."

"Ah! Now I see."

"Then I told Chuck that he shouldn't expect any hurry on my part to get that bill paid, because I'm on limited funds, and a bill I never agreed to was certainly not high on my list to get paid."

"Serves him right," Bob declared, and pushed the empty bowl away, pulled the iced tea closer. "You know what? It kind of sounds like you—on your own—came to a suitable solution. For both of you."

"Both of us! What do you mean?"

"If he truly didn't intend to charge you—and he can be very generous, when he wants to be—then he wouldn't have been expecting any payments from you. You let him know that you might only be making very small payments. That way, he doesn't feel bad about accepting a few bucks here and there, and you don't have to feel bad if that's all you can manage."

"You mean, I was so mad, I pretty much placed myself right in his trap."

Bob frowned. "Not a trap, Wanda. Chuck wouldn't be trying to trap you. He thought he was helping you. The summers here can be awful. But I bet he'll never remind you that you have a bill."

"So I've got to keep track of how much I've paid and when I've got it paid off. Okay. I can do that. Maybe when I make the last payment, I'll put a pretty bow on it. To indicate that it's the last payment so we can be friends again."

"Again?" Bob asked, but Wanda didn't know what else to say about it. "After all that, how did the game go last night?"

"Well, it started out stiff. But after half an hour, I had them in a pitched battle with a horde of goblins, and it was like the argument was forgotten."

"Goblins. Now are those the little ones, or the big ones?"

"Goblins are pretty small. Hobgoblins are big and nasty."

"That's right. I remember now."

"Do you know, he brought flowers as a kind of apology?"

"Flowers?"

"They looked like he picked them from his own yard. Or somebody's yard. There were dandelions, lilies of the valley, another flower I didn't recognize and 1 red tulip."

"You're right, those would be from his yard," Bob confirmed. "The lilies and tulip would have come from flower beds his mother planted before she passed. They've gone wild since."

"Oh. I wish I'd known last night. That means so much more than if he'd gone to a florist." That thought reminded her of how he had looked when he came in for the game. She frowned and took a deep drink of her tea.

"What's wrong?"

"I've told him I'm not looking for a boy friend," she stated, and stopped because she heard the door open.

Bob looked around. "Steve. Come to do your homework?"

"Oh, she told you?" Steve sat down next to Bob, then leaned forward to address Wanda. "Fran isn't too happy about me having homework on the only day I get off this week."

"Tell Fran I'm sorry. But I had to say something to get through to Chuck, to try and make him think about my side of things." She sighed and lowered her voice. "No telling if I managed it."

"Well, he was real quiet when we unloaded the pickups and washed out a week's worth of dirt. Not an angry kind of quiet. A thoughtful kind of quiet. There were times when we had to work around him. Got so bad, Dick sprayed him with the hose. Supposedly on accident. Even that didn't make him angry."

Wanda shrugged. "Well, he wanted to take a shower before the game." She finished her tea and reached for the bowl and its lid. "I should take off. That way, you guys can hash out that bill and Steve can go spend some time with Fran." She stood up and started for the back door. "Thanks for lunch, Bob."

"Yeah, same to you," Bob answered, and turned his attention to Steve. "How many ceiling fans and window units are we talking?"

Wanda turned back around. "Oh, I know the retail prices of those items now, you guys. Basically, it's the labor costs I'm worried about."

Steve turned to face her. "Chuck wants me to include a discount, Wanda."

She rolled the cue ball against the opposite bank of the pool table. "I made a big deal of paying the bill, I can't ask for a discount. But... if he has a discount that he routinely gives to, oh, angry women, or more likely, pains in the butt... I can be talked into accepting that." She turned for the door again. "See ya."

Chapter 17
Monday, May 18, 10:13 AM

"How did Steve's homework go yesterday?" Wanda asked as she stirred sweetener into her tea. She had opted not to have pie, and surprisingly, Bob had made the same decision.

"Only took about half an hour. Would have taken less time, but he was so uncertain of himself... Well, we got it done."

"Okay." She wanted to ask how much it had come to, but another part of her didn't want to know. Her first errand this morning had been to the bank to see how much money she still had in her account. She had tried to be frugal, but there had been expenses she hadn't expected. She still had a tidy sum in her savings account, but she worried she would have to dip into it to make ends meet. Where would she get any more money to replenish her savings? Or maybe the bills would settle down now and her survivor's pension would get her through most months. She decided to change the subject. "Have you heard how the kids did on Saturday? Did they live up to Chuck's expectations?"

"Chuck said they pulled their weight, for newbies who had to be trained how to do everything. Steve said... well." He seemed disinclined to go on.

"What did Steve say?"

Bob grimaced. "Steve said he was ready to quit when he saw who Chuck had hired. But then he decided he'd finish the day before he picked a fight with Chuck and get himself fired."

"What?"

"End of the work week. And he can claim unemployment faster if he gets fired. But it usually only takes a day or two before Chuck offers him his job back. These days."

Wanda stared at Bob as she considered what he'd said. "And then I picked a fight with Chuck and messed up Steve's plan?"

"No, by then, he'd changed his mind. He said the kids were good workers, ready to learn, and they weren't smart-alecky at all. The only problem he sees is having to keep Dick away from the girls."

"Dick does seem a bit like Lyle," Wanda observed.

"Not if they're together," Bob answered. "It's like if Dick sees what Lyle is like, he straightens up. But if Lyle isn't there, he doesn't make the connection between Lyle and himself."

"You men are so complicated," she stated.

"Did you want to hit the library after groceries?"

"Yes. I finished all 3 books I checked out last week. Oh, that reminds me, do you have any ideas where I could get my hair cut?"

"Steve's girl friend works at Studio Beautiful. Don't know if she can fit you in on short notice."

"No, not today, but maybe she can fit me in on a Monday morning not too far from now."

"It's west a couple blocks."

They were both startled when Wanda's phone rang. She looked at the screen. "Excuse me, Bob," she said as she answered. "Lee! So good to hear from you!"

"Wanda, where are you? Greg and Jack said you moved out of town a month ago. I've been calling and calling. Finally got your number from Jack. Turns out I had transposed 2 of the digits when I put your number in my phone. I never noticed before because I always called Hank."

Wanda giggled, pleased to hear from one of her dead husband's best friends. "Slow down, Lee. I have trouble hearing what you say when you're excited."

She heard him take a deep breath. "Okay. Jack says you moved out of town. Where are you living now?"

"In a tiny town called Belgrade, in Nebraska. I found a house I could afford to live in. No matter how I tried, I couldn't figure out how to afford that Chicago apartment any longer."

"You should have talked to me. Hank worked hard to make sure you were taken care of, in case something happened."

"Well, I know there was a nest egg that you were in charge

of investing, but I figured I would need that in my old age. Still, I should have called you before now, just to keep in touch, but... moving has kept me busy. Plus Paula moved up the publication date for my next book, and making corrections to the manuscript took me over a week. Almost 2 weeks.”

“Moving is a pain. How are you? Do you need any money?”

“No, I don’t think so. So far, the survivor’s benefits have stretched to cover things. Well, that and I sold pretty much everything in the apartment, as you know.”

“I would be remiss if I didn’t inform you how your nest egg is doing,” Lee told her. “Tell me your address so I can get a full statement sent out to you.” She told him her box number and zip code. “And your email address, so we can stay in touch. I’m sure I’ve interrupted your writing.”

Wanda smiled, then noticed both Chuck and Steve entering the cafe. “Actually, I’m on a shopping trip to Fullerton. I have to go to the county seat to get groceries, if you can imagine. Tell you what, when I get home this afternoon, I’ll email you. I stopped for an ice tea, and it’s time to head out for the rest of my errands. Is that okay? That lets you get back to your work.”

Lee laughed so hard, she had to put a little distance between her phone and her ear. “Always thinking of others! Yes. Alright. I’ll work on that report to get you caught up and get that sent to you within a week. But if I don’t get an email from you this afternoon, I’m going to call you again.”

“Anytime, Lee. It’s always good to hear from you. Thanks for reaching out. And I will email you this afternoon, I promise.”

“Good bye, Wanda.”

She hung up and wondered what was up with Chuck, since he hadn’t pushed Bob over so he could sit down in the booth.

“Boy friend?” Chuck asked.

“Just a friend of—” She stopped, remembering she wasn’t supposed to mention Hank. “A friend of mine,” she finished awkwardly. “You aren’t here for pie and coffee?”

“Not today,” Chuck answered. “Go ahead, Steve.”

Steve pulled a piece of paper from his back pocket and unfolded it to hand it to her. “There is the bill, as you requested.”

She glanced at it, saw the equipment—the fans and window units—were heavily discounted, but the labor came to a tidy sum, with 5 men working for 1.5 hours each. Still, it was under $1000. And right at the bottom, there was listed a 'Pain in the Butt discount of 10%'. "Okay," she agreed. "Once I pay my monthly bills, I'll see if I can make a payment."

"Don't be in any hurry on my account," Chuck told her with a smile. "Come on, Steve. Let's get back to work."

They headed for the door. "How come when I come along, there's no time for pie and coffee?" Steve complained.

"Because we've left the crew without a leader."

Once they were gone, and Bob and Wanda were preparing to leave, she confided, "It wasn't as bad as I was afraid. Before I looked up the retail prices, I was afraid the window units would be 5 or 6 hundred each, and the fans another 2 or 3 hundred each. And don't service people usually get $50 or $60 an hour?"

Bob hesitated. "Not around here. Besides, they weren't fixing; they were installing. What you see on that bill is Chuck's usual hourly fee per worker."

"Well, I still won't be paying it off soon. But it isn't as big as I thought it would be."

"So have you forgiven Chuck?"

She frowned and squirmed a bit as she climbed into his car. "I can't say I've completely forgiven him. I still think he was over-bearing to try to do all that without even talking to me first. I'll tell you, if he could stop treating me like a helpless female, I think we'd get along a lot better." And then she frowned again, wondering if it was a good idea to get along well with Chuck.

"Part of it may be because of his upbringing," Bob stated. "Before she passed, his mom battled a long illness, and she became pretty much helpless those last few years. Plus, in high school, and in college, if you wanted to catch a girl's attention, you had to impress them. Remember, he had 3 cousins he was competing with for girls."

"You said you guys had outgrown that."

"He and I have pretty much given up on girls."

"Then why would he be trying to impress me?"

"Because he doesn't know how to be friends with a girl. That's something we never figured out. Well, **he** never figured out. So in his mind, you're either helpless or you need to be impressed."

She gave a soft grunt. "I suppose it doesn't help that when he got there Saturday, I pretty much was helpless."

"How so?"

"On the verge of heat exhaustion. I remember I was pretty cotton-headed when he arrived."

"Which definitely would have made you seem like a helpless female. Cemented his desire to take care of you, I suppose. He was like that with his mother, and with Gram."

"I'm not either one," she retorted. "Why are we stopping here?"

"Because one door down is Studio Beautiful, and you wanted to make an appointment with Fran Zither."

"Yes, I did," she agreed, and stepped out of the car. "I'll be back in just a minute."

* * *

4:56 PM

Wanda got up from her desk and stretched before she stepped through the still-open curtains into the living room. She didn't get much work done today, but it felt so good to email Lee that she had emailed Jack and Greg as well. And then dropped a cheerful note to Paula and a couple other people she hadn't touched bases with lately.

She had also contacted the chairperson of the Denver convention that had invited her to be their author guest of honor, explaining that she (Wanda) would be driving their guest of honor (Linda Sinclair, her pen name) from the town of Belgrade, Nebraska. Since it was a long drive, they would like to arrive on Thursday and leave on Monday. She claimed she (Wanda) would be helping at Paula's dealer's table, so could they possibly find a liaison, somebody to help guide Linda around? In the past, Hank had acted as her 'handler' at other conventions, making sure she got where she needed to be on time, and keeping any drunks at bay. But Wanda couldn't do that for herself. As Linda Sinclair,

161

she wore a black wig and pale makeup, while Wanda would have to be there as herself.

So she didn't feel too bad that she hadn't gotten any writing done. Chances were she'd catch up by Friday afternoon, and if not, she could put in another couple hours on Saturday morning.

She turned on the fan atop the frig as she entered the kitchen to decide on something for supper. She reached in the cupboard for a glass, and saw Tommy working in his garden. His shirt had large sweat stains, and he kept wiping his forehead with a cloth from his back pocket.

The heat from the weekend had broken Sunday night when a rainstorm swept through, but the day was still warm, and Tommy was working in the full sunlight. When the sun got down further, trees on the neighbors' land would provide shade on some of his plot of land, but it hadn't reached that point yet.

She pulled a can of pop from the frig and put a foam sleeve on it to help it stay cool, then walked out into the back room, which was warm. She opened the back door to step out and found the evening slightly cooler than her back room. She walked over to where Tommy was working. "Hey, take a break and drink this," she offered. "I learned the hard way; you have to keep drinking in the heat."

He was kneeling in the dirt, and sat back to accept her offer. "Thanks." After a long draw on the can, he waved it at a red wagon sitting in the grass. "Brought water." A water cooler sat in the wagon, along with some tools and lots of seed packets.

"Water's good," she stated. "Look, this is a big patch, and you're going to be putting a lot of hours into it. If you ever need a drink, a bite to eat, or just to cool off, you come knock on my door. Better make it my front door as my back room has been closed off, now that I've got some AC."

"You'll be working."

She laughed. "Not as hard as you are! Now, I mean it, you've got to take care of yourself. I understand Chuck made you guys stop working every hour to cool off in the cars' AC and drink water on your first day. I want you to remember that while you work out here. Take a few minutes to cool off periodically rather than wind up in the hospital with heat exhaustion."

Tommy nodded in agreement. "What Chuck said."

Wanda walked over to the red wagon and browsed through the seed packets. There were a lot of carrots and radishes, of all sorts "Are you going to plant all these carrots and radishes?"

"Eventually." he answered, having gone back to work.

Seeds for tomatoes, beans, beets, cucumbers, squash, zucchini, sweet corn and popcorn were all in the red wagon, waiting for his attention. "What do you do with what you grow?" she asked, going back to kneel and pick up the empty pop can.

"Eat it. Sell it."

"Let me know when you're ready to start selling. There's a lot there I'd be interested in."

He stopped working to look her in the eyes. "Okay."

"You going to be out here much longer?"

"Til dark."

She stood up. "I'll let you get back to work."

The people in this town are fairly strange, she thought as she walked back to her house. *There's Bob, who's super friendly and generous and obliging, but none of that makes me worry that he's trying to ingratiate himself with me. It all suits him. He's just being... Bob.*

And then Tommy, who is still in high school for a few more days, but he's taken a summer job with Chuck, and he's planting a big garden, besides having people's yards to mow and all of that. Why does he work himself so hard? Why stay until dark to plant a garden? How long was he out there today? Since school let out? I wouldn't be surprised.

And then there's Chuck. I don't know what to make of him. Doesn't know how to have a friend who's a girl? Females are either helpless or to be impressed? That's gonna be a rocky road to navigate. I want to be friends, but that's all I want.

Chapter 18
Saturday, May 23, 6:05 PM

Everybody was sitting down to eat. Wanda had decided on soft tacos. "This is so easy," Zita said. "And the sour cream and guacamole make them dreamy delicious. We need to have these again, Wanda."

"These are good, but I vote for spaghetti again," Ella stated.

Wanda laughed. "I'm not ready to start repeating myself already. Oh, I understand prom was last night. How many of you went? Was it fun?"

"As seniors, Ella and I felt we had to go. Last chance, and all that. I was a little surprised to see Tommy there, but he was. Tommy, you looked really nice. The carnation in your jacket lapel was a nice touch. But you didn't bring a date, did you?"

Blushing, Tommy could only shake his head.

"Well, it was nice of you to dance with Zita and me," Ella stated. "Before that, you'd think we were lepers, the way the boys were avoiding us. And not just us, most of the junior girls were left sitting against the wall, too. What is up with high school boys, Chuck?"

"Uhh, it's been about 10 years since I've been one," Chuck stated.

"Well, after Tommy started dancing with any girl who wasn't already dancing—and him the shyest guy in the school—the other boys finally started asking girls to dance, too. So thank you for that, Tommy, and I think I probably speak for every girl who was there without a date."

"I think he danced every dance," Zita added. "So, did you get around to every unattached girl, Tommy?"

Still blushing, the boy managed a quiet, "Maybe."

"So, what hours did you work with Chuck this past week?"

"Zita and I worked 2 hours Friday morning, cause we had the day off from school. So we worked from 10 to 1 today, to get our 5 hours in."

"The boys went in at 8 with my crew today," Chuck offered. "They got done at 1 also, and rode home with Ella. Next week, as I understand it, everybody is working Monday through Friday, 8 to noon, right?" The kids all agreed that was the plan.

Wanda nodded. "So Ella and Zita have graduated?"

"Not officially until tomorrow evening," Ella stated. "Do you want to come?"

"You could ride with me," Chuck offered.

"I know where the high school is," she replied. "Is the event open to strangers?"

Zita snorted. "You aren't a stranger. You live in Belgrade, so that pretty much makes you family!"

"There's a parking lot across the street that you can use," Felix offered. "And I can wait for you at the front door."

"Yeah, I would have volunteered," Ella stated, "but they'll have us all sequestered, getting into our gowns and caps so we can make our grand entrance."

"That's part of the pomp and circumstance." Wanda said.

"And then there's the after party," Zita went on. "Which is happening at the fire station."

"In a fire station?" Wanda asked in surprise.

"Other than the bars, there's no other place in town to have it," Zita stated calmly.

"Well, I haven't seen the inside of the fire station yet," Wanda commented. "I suppose I'd better drop in. I won't be throwing off the count or anything, will I?"

"It's a party, not a wedding reception," Ella told her.

"I don't want to just drop in when I'm not expected."

"We'll tell our parents to expect you," Zita promised.

"Okay. And then what are your plans? You work the summer with Chuck, and then what?"

"I'm going to the community college in Columbus in the fall." Zita stated. "Want to get a certificate in auto mechanics."

"That's a good idea," Wanda told her.

"I'm still hoping to get accepted at UNO," Ella said.

"The University of New Orleans?" Wanda wondered.

"The University of Nebraska at Omaha," Ella explained. "Technically, I've been accepted, but the trouble is, I'd need some financial aid, and I got my paper work in late." She smeared a dab of guacamole around her plate, trying to get it back into her latest taco, and then looked up, excited again. "Oh! I forgot to say thank you last week, Wanda!"

"For what?"

"For introducing me to those artist friends of yours to learn how to make prints. Ms Daniels wasn't much help, as she thought I meant making silk-screen prints. We did that at one point in class, but I didn't think that was what you meant. Anyway, Lucy and Mitch have been super helpful, explaining exactly how to do it. Lots of tips and tricks. They've even sent me information on several science fiction conventions where I can send my prints. I'm hoping to get started with my first paycheck, which I think we get Monday. I never would have this art opportunity if not for you and your friends!"

"Well, it is an opportunity, but it's a bit of a gamble, too," Wanda told her. "Did they happen to mention WindyCon in Chicago in November?"

"Yes, they did. They said you would know about it."

"Yes, it has a big art show, and it isn't uncommon for a piece of work or a print to go into a bidding war, where the selling price can double or even triple. But not every piece goes to the art auction. If a piece only has 1 or 2 bids, it is sold to the last bidder for his bid. So don't put down super low prices on your prints. Make it a fair price, so if it goes for that amount, you can still make a little money, after you pay for shipping and printing and everything."

"Lucy and Mitch are teaching me all about those kinds of calculations."

"Good. I thought they would be good mentors for you. Okay, looks like we are out of meat and beans for the tacos, so let's move on to dessert. Looks like Rusty brought 2 pies. Peach and, uh, vanilla cream?"

"That's banana, with a layer of chocolate on the bottom. And you can keep the leftovers, Wanda. Mom didn't mind making them, but she's trying to diet."

"A common refrain for women, I'm afraid," Wanda answered. *And one I'm going to have to adopt, after all these goodies on Saturday nights.*

Chapter 19
Sunday, May 24, 8:46 PM

The graduation ceremony in Fullerton was about what Wanda remembered graduation ceremonies to be, except shorter, with less than 30 seniors to receive their diploma.

It was strange to get back to Belgrade and see Bob's Bar closed, but all the parking on main street taken. The front door of the Fire Station stood open, and the entire place was brightly lit. She opted to park her car at home, and walked through the alley to come out on the main street next to the post office, then walk the remaining half a block to the fire house. There were four big pictures on the wall above a banner that said, "Congrats!", indicating this was not just a party for Ella Swanson and Zita Craig. The two others were Shirley Campbell and John Bell, who apparently were farm kids in the Belgrade area.

A table under the banner held 4 different cakes—one for each kid—and bowls of chips, nuts and mints, plus glasses of punch. Other tables provided places for people to sit down to enjoy the refreshments. Wanda noticed a tiny kitchen off this room, where there were more bags of chips, nuts and mints, plus fixings for more punch.

The door to the engine floor was open, and people were in there as well, standing in groups and sitting at a couple card tables that had been set up. It seemed like all of Bob's usual customers were here tonight, plus another group just as large, including old people who didn't get out much, and children, possibly younger siblings of the 4 who had graduated tonight.

"You ever figure out how to get to Denver?" She turned to see one of the Eggers brothers—she wasn't sure if it was Quince or Yantz—was waiting for her answer.

She swallowed the half-melted mint she had in her mouth.
"Yes, I did. Thank you for your input."

"You gonna fly or drive?"

That didn't help her. Which way had this brother leaned? "I decided it would be cheaper to drive."

"Well, that's all right, then. But it's a long drive, and you never know, something might happen, like a flat tire or something, so you'd better leave yourself plenty of time."

"Yes, that was my thought," she started to say, but his brother joined them.

"What are you doing?" the newcomer asked his brother. "First you tell her she should drive, and now you're trying to talk her out of it? Leave the poor girl alone. She'll have a lot better time talking to just about anybody but you." The 2 brothers moved off, still arguing.

Wanda took a bite of the chocolate cake that was for Ella, having had her name on it, and looked around. Through the shifting crowd, she caught glimpses of a young woman sitting alone in a corner with a child in her lap. The boy was eating a hot dog, and the woman a sandwich, though Wanda hadn't seen any of that kind of food in the kitchen or the party area.

"I'm really glad you could make it," Zita told Wanda. "You don't get out of the house much, and I was beginning to think you might be a hermit."

Wanda smiled. "A hermit who lets her house be invaded once a week for the sake of a game. But I get out from time to time. You just don't see me. For instance, I go to the post office 3 times a week."

"Well, you kind of have to, if you want to get your mail."

"Unfortunately, some trips to the post office are less than fruitful. Most of the time it's just bills and junk mail."

"Mom says the same thing. But once in a while, she gets a letter from a pen pal. She's had 3 or 4 since high school."

"Pen pals. I hadn't thought of that."

Ella joined them. "It's your turn, Zita. Fill her up with cake and chips; she needs the calories. And if they want more meat, that's in the refrigerator."

"I still think we should have invited her parents."

"I did," Ella stated. "I mailed them an invite to the party myself. They probably just though I was after a graduation gift."

"Who are you filling up with chips and cake, Ella?" Wanda asked as Zita hurried away.

"Lyle's wife," Ella answered.

Wanda knew a moment of abject fear and looked around nervously. "Lyle's here?"

"No, he should be at work. Mom stopped by and picked up Gloria and Sammy and brought them here for the party." The girl paused, took a deep breath and pasted a smile on her face. "Now, this isn't the time to talk about the failures of some of my relatives. I have succeeded in getting through high school, and that's a reason to celebrate."

"It is. It's a lovely party, Ella. The cake is delicious. Did all the graduates' parents get together to organize the party?"

"No, the only thing the parents have to do is provide a dessert for their child, and a picture for the wall. The party itself is organized by the Belgrade Fire Brigade."

"The fire brigade?"

"Well, it's more than a fire brigade, but they worked hard to raise the money to build this station and buy some used fire engines. They raise money every year, and some of it is used to educate members of the volunteer fire department, and some of it is used to have parties for important milestones, like kids who graduate from high school!"

"So it sounds like it started as an organization to get a fire brigade started, and now it does other things too, but it hasn't changed its name."

"That's right. Oh! There's Shirley. I should go tell her how great her mother's banana walnut cake is."

Finding it difficult to eat while balancing a plate and a glass, Wanda found an empty end of a table and sat down. This made eating much easier, but it wasn't long before Bob sat down with her. "Are you enjoying the party?"

"I am," she declared. "I'm glad I let the girls talk me into coming. I was afraid I would be an outsider."

"Hardly. You're just the new gal in town."

"In some places, even if you've lived there 20 years, you're still considered an outsider."

"Well, I'm glad that's not the case here."

Chuck sat down opposite Bob. "Well, I've decided to do it."

"Do what?" Bob asked.

"I'm going to suggest I pay for shipping Ella's prints to that convention she's talking about in Denver. It'll be $10 or $20 she won't have to lay out, and I won't feel it. It'll be my little contribution towards her raising money for college in Omaha."

"How come you make suggestions to Ella, but you come to my place and do things you've never even mentioned before?" Wanda heard herself ask. "Oh, criminy, did I just say that? Has the punch here been spiked?"

"No," Bob answered. "Believe me, I could tell if it had."

"You keep up that attitude, and I might have to give you another 'pain in the butt' discount," Chuck told her.

"No, she responded. "I'm not agreeing to any more discounts."

"So, how is the equipment working out?" he asked. "Of course, the weather hasn't been as hot as it was last weekend."

"It's kept me comfortable," she reported. "Now I just need to see how my electric bill handles it."

Chuck nodded. "The bills for July and August will be the worst."

"I just paid the first bill. It was for half a month. Hardly amounted to anything." She caught a glimpse of the woman and child again, didn't see what they were eating this time. "I guess that's Lyle's wife in the corner. Will one of you introduce me?"

"Nope," they both said together.

She looked from one to the other in surprise. "Why not?"

Chuck sighed and kept his voice low. "He's never gotten past the '4 cousins' mentality. Now, we're hoping he never hears about her being brought to this party, but if somebody slips up and mentions seeing one of us talking to her, even just to introduce another woman..."

"I'm afraid he'd take it out on her. Them," Bob ended.

Wanda lowered her gaze to her empty plate. "I didn't realize it was possible to dislike him any more than I already did."

"Yeah, he's a downer," Chuck agreed. "You need some more to eat. Bob, you get her another glass of punch, and I'll get her another piece of cake. Looks like you had some of Ella's devil's food cake, so how about some of Zita's angel cake?"

She didn't feel like arguing, so she laughed. "Yes, okay."

The 2 men had just moved off when Wanda realized Lyle's wife had suddenly moved to Bob's chair. "Somebody ought to warn you to be careful. With the cousins."

"We're just friends," Wanda told her.

"Yeah, sure. Until you're all alone with them some night in the middle of nowhere." She got up suddenly and walked over to a nearby knot of people that included Helen. "Helen, I wonder if you could take me home now?"

"So early?" Helen responded. "Lyle's at work and won't be home before 1 am, you know that. We hardly ever get to see you and Sammy."

"I know, but Sammy's eaten a lot, and he's not used to so many people being around, so he's getting cranky. And tired. I should take him home and put him to bed."

"Okay, I understand. Do you want any cake or anything to take home with you?"

"No, I— It all tastes wonderful, but I can't."

"Okay. Let me get my purse and my keys, and we'll go."

Bob placed a fresh glass of punch in front of Wanda and sat down with his own. "So you got to meet Gloria after all."

"Hmm, not officially. We didn't exchange names. She just warned me against being friendly with you two."

"So she finally smartened up," Chuck said softly as he sat down again. He placed a plate in front of Wanda, and another plate in front of himself.

Wanda decided to change the subject. "I've been wondering which of the Egger brothers owns the house next to mine."

"Quince," Bob said. "Why?"

"Well, actually, I've been wondering if the hedge between my driveway and that house is his or mine."

"It's yours," Chuck stated. "Gram had me plant it when she got tired of looking at that old eyesore. What about it?"

"Well, it's kind of scary at night. Not all the time. Most nights I'm safe inside with the door locked. But if I come home after dark—granted, that's not often—then I find myself imagining someone is hiding behind it, waiting for me. And before you laugh, that was a reasonable assumption to make in Chicago!"

"I'm not laughing," Chuck told her.

"Me, neither," Bob added.

"Gram never thought of things like that, but she spent her life in small towns," Chuck commented. He seemed to hesitate before asking, "Would you like me to chop them down?"

"I've already got one bill with you to settle," she pointed out. "Let's not get me too far into your debt."

"Maybe Tommy could tackle it for you," Bob suggested.

"I don't know. Tommy's pretty busy," Chuck stated. "Working mornings for me, then lawns to mow, and that big garden over by Wanda. Plus his parents' garden."

"And mine," Bob added."

"You planted a garden?"

"I'm letting Tommy use my garden patch. You know I love my tomatoes and corn. So he keeps me stocked in those, and the rest he can sell."

"Whose idea was that?"

"His, actually."

"That young man may be trying to do more than he can."

"He's been in that patch by me until dark, ever since he started it. I never see him arrive, but it's been dark every time he heads home. Well, he wasn't there Friday, because he was at the prom. And not last night, because of the game. But I expect he's there tonight."

"He's probably rushing to get it planted," Bob guessed. "It won't be quite as much work when it's down to hoeing out the weeds and watering. But then it'll be time to harvest, and he'll be working his butt off again."

"If he wants to go to college, why not get financial aid?"

"Probably doesn't trust the system," Chuck stated.

Bob piped in. "I think part of his motivation is just to get out of the house. Let's just say it's not a happy house and leave it at that."

Wanda finished the last bite of angel food cake and then finished her punch. "Well, that cake was delicious. Now, don't suggest any more cake, because I'm stuffed. I've spoken to the girls, I think I've congratulated both of them. I really think—What's wrong, Bob?"

"Gloria's parents just arrived."

Wanda turned to see a middle-aged couple standing in the doorway, looking ill at ease. Ella was moving towards them, a big smile on her face.

White-faced, Bob decided, "I'll go tell them they've missed her."

"No, you know how they feel about you," Chuck told him. "I'll go tell them."

"I know she's going to be super glad to see you," Ella told the couple as she brought them across the room towards the corner where Gloria had been sitting. "That's strange, she was right here in this chair. Perhaps she's in the rest room. I'll go check."

Chuck walked over and put a hand on the girl's shoulder. "No, Ella, she's not in the rest room. I'm sorry, Mr and Mrs Thompson. Gloria isn't here anymore. Sammy was getting tired and fussy, and she asked my cousin to take her home. She'll be devastated to know she missed you." The woman looked on the verge of tears. "I'm sure if she had realized you were coming, she would have waited for you. I know this is a big disappointment, and I promise to make it up to you. Could you come to Belgrade for a 4th of July get-together? I'll make sure Gloria is there, and you can spend an entire day with her, instead of just a few minutes."

"We don't want any favors from you, Robert Nichols!" the woman declared.

"Now, honey," her husband tried to comfort her with an arm around her shoulders.

"Oh. Let me apologize again. I should have started by introducing myself. I'm not Bob. That's Bob over there." He waved vaguely in Wanda's direction. "I'm his cousin, Chuck Applegit, of Chuck's Construction."

"You're the one building the new Zimmerman house," Mr Thompson realized.

"I am," Chuck agreed. "Now, don't answer me right away about the 4th of July. Think about it. Any other family members who'd like to come and spend time with Gloria, they'd be welcome, too. I seem to remember Gloria has a sister and a brother. Please feel free to bring them all and make it a family event."

"I suppose Lyle will be there." The lady's tongue must be dripping with venom, but having met Lyle, Wanda could hardly blame her.

"If he is, I'll make sure he's on his best behavior. But whether he's there or not, I'll make sure Gloria is there. She is part of our family, as well as yours."

"Thank you for the invitation, Mr Applegit. We don't generally make plans for July 4th so early. It's usually just a quiet day with the kids."

"But no Gloria!" Mrs Thompson whispered in dismay.

"Now, I know you're disappointed about this evening, honey," Mr Thompson said quietly. "I am, too. There's nothing we can do about it but go home and think about July 4th. Come on, let's go."

"They should have told her we were coming!"

"I'm so sorry!" Ella declared.

Mr Thompson looked up at the tears on Ella's face. "Thanks for the invitation. Your heart was in the right place. Oh, and congrats on graduating!"

The party was almost silent as the Thompsons walked out. Once people heard the car start up and move off, Chuck raised his voice and announced, "Looks like we're having a family event on 4th of July this year."

After the pronouncement, people cheered, and then laughed, and the party went on.

Ella threw herself into the chair Chuck had used earlier. "What an idiot I am! I should have told Gloria her parents were coming!"

"Wait a minute," Wanda said, putting a hand over hers. "I heard you talking to Zita earlier, and it didn't seem like you knew for sure that they were."

"No, I wasn't. Well, I mailed the invitation last week, and although I included my phone number, they never called."

"Then it's not entirely your fault," Bob told her. "Anyway, thanks to Chuck's quick thinking, now the Thompsons have a chance to spend the better part of a day with Gloria."

"Yeah, and all he has to do is host a huge event," Ella stated. "Man, I owe him something fierce."

"I'm glad you realize it," Chuck said, taking the seat next to her with a fresh glass of punch. "I hope my place is big enough. And since you kind of accidentally got me roped into throwing this party, I think you should act as hostess."

"Oh." Her brow furrowed. "What does a hostess do?

"Act as the point of contact. Call family members and tell them about it, try to get a feel for whether or not they'll come. It'll be pot luck, so try to guide them into what to bring. I will provide the meat. So, side dishes and desserts. And don't be afraid to double up on dishes like potato salad, because this will be one huge party, even if only local family members come."

Wanda looked up in surprise. "As big as this one?"

"Oh, sure," Ella stated. "Everyone here is related to us, and this doesn't include family members from Columbus or Albion, let alone those from further afield." She thought for a moment, and then sighed. "I'm going to need a notebook. I know! I'll finish using up some from school!"

"And anybody who wants beer has to bring their own," Bob suggested.

"Yes, definitely," Chuck agreed. "Neither of us is going to be responsible for people getting drunk."

Wanda laughed. "Sounds like you guys plan parties all the time. But I think I should go home before it gets totally dark and that hedge gets creepy."

"You need somebody to walk you home?" Bob asked. She gave him a surprised look, and he went on, "I can ask Quince or Yantz for you."

She gave him a lop-sided smile. "I think I'll forgo that pleasure. It's not totally dark yet. I'm sure I'll be fine."

"I can ask Felix and Rusty. They're probably pretty bored."

"Well, we didn't want to say it, but we are," Felix piped up from behind Bob. "Come on, Rusty, let's walk Wanda home."

"Okay," Rusty agreed from a little further away.

Wanda said her good-byes to the graduates, and she and the 2 boys left, walked past the post office and started through the block to get to her house. "It's not a long distance," Rusty observed. "And you don't have any trouble walking, so why do you need an escort?"

"Oh, I think Bob was teasing me," she responded. "I may have made a mistake by admitting that when I come home after dark, the hedge seems like a natural place for somebody to ambush me. A real concern in Chicago, but maybe not here."

"You want us to chop them down?" Felix asked.

"Chuck already offered. I don't know if I can afford it. Besides, now that school's out, you'll be working for Chuck. Won't that keep you busy?"

"Only half days," Rusty answered. "I saw some bow saws in your garage. I don't know if they need sharpening, but they'd get the job done. Even if we only did 1 bush a day, we'd have the whole thing chopped down in a couple weeks."

"But then you'd want to do something with the stumps," Felix countered. "They could be dangerous in the dark."

"This is far more complicated than I thought it would be," Wanda stated. "I'll think about it some more." She pulled out her keys to unlock her front door. "Do you want to come in and have a pop, or are you filled up on cake and punch?"

"Punch is nice, but I prefer pop," Felix stated.

"I want to go out to the patch and see how Tommy's doing with getting it planted," Rusty decided. "I saw him still working on it when we crossed the street."

"Yes, he's been working till full dark most nights," Wanda agreed as she held the door open. "Well, come in, get yourselves a pop, and take one out to him. He brings water when he's working, but I think he appreciates the sugar."

177

Chapter 20
Saturday, May 30, 5:53 PM

In the living room, Ella hung up her phone, made a final note in her notebook and closed it. "This is a lot more work than I expected," she announced to Zita and Wanda, who were in the kitchen. "At this rate, I think Chuck owes me. Now I need to figure out what to ask for."

"She loves it," Zita whispered to Wanda as she stirred the melted cheese into a giant pot of macaroni. Wanda had sprung for a huge new pot on Monday, and it was already handy. "She likes feeling important. And having Chuck owe her."

"Is that normal in Belgrade? People keep track of favors they've done for others and expect some payment in return?"

"Not really. I suspect she'll ask for a night at the movies with all the trimmings."

"Trimmings?"

"You know. Popcorn and pop. Maybe candy. Or pizza afterwards. Just like when we were younger. It's a wonder they didn't give it up after the first time they took us all to Columbus for a movie. We were so excited, we were all brats."

"You make it sound like it hasn't happened recently."

"Not since last fall. Thanksgiving weekend, I think." She grinned. "Ella caught sight of this cute blond boy there with his friends, and she suddenly started calling Chuck 'cousin' all the time, so the blond wouldn't think she was there with him. I mean, like on a date."

"Thanks for the ride, Ella!" Felix's voice came through the house, announcing the arrival of all 3 boys.

"I told you I was leaving," she retorted.

"Yeah, as you were walking out the door. I was putting my shoes on, and you couldn't even wait that long."

"You get a ride to work every morning, and a ride home at noon. What are you going to do when I go to Columbus after work instead of coming straight home?"

"Guess we'll have to go with you," Rusty suggested.

"Well, you'll all be bored to tears. I'm just going to a printer to see about getting prints made."

"And the school," Zita called from the kitchen. "You said we could stop by the college."

"If there's time," Ella returned.

"Time for what?" asked a deeper masculine voice. Chuck had arrived.

"Ella's going to abandon us boys in Fullerton when we get done working Monday so that she and Zita can go to Columbus."

"I need to get some prints made!" Ella declared.

"And I need to get enrolled at the community college," Zita added.

"Maybe it's time for Tommy to get a car," Chuck suggested.

"Ha!" Tommy's tone made it plain it wasn't likely to happen, and certainly not by Monday.

"Well, let's think about options, then," Chuck told them as he sat down at his usual place.

Wanda came in with plates, noted with satisfaction that a package of cookies and a package of candy had been added to the chips and dip on the heating stove. The kids were keeping up their end of the bargain. On the other hand, they never quite finished all that was brought, and she was developing quite a cache of candy in her cupboard, the only thing that would last from one Saturday to the next. "Can anybody's parent pick the boys up?" Wanda asked.

"They're all either working or sleeping because they work the night shift," Chuck answered. He didn't look at Tommy, but the boy looked uneasy at the statement. "I suppose I could drive them home, this time. Order some burgers from the Dew Drop to go, and eat while I'm driving."

"That doesn't sound very safe," Wanda opined. "Here's another idea. Why not ask Bob for a lift? We'll be in Fullerton anyway. I'm sure we can fit all our groceries in the trunk, which would leave the back seat for the boys."

Chuck gave her a calculating, half-smug look. "Are you volunteering Bob's services again?"

"No," she refuted. "I suggested they ask him."

"Okay, here comes supper!" Zita called out, and brought the huge pot of macaroni in, placed it on the pot holder that Ella had put on the table before she got distracted by a phone call.

"Hey, boys, one of you call Bob and ask," Chuck instructed. "The others need to finish setting the table so we can eat."

Felix was the one who called, and it didn't take long for him to announce, "Okay! We got a ride home." With that settled, the group settled in for a filling supper and a fun game.

Chapter 21
Saturday, June 6, 5:28 PM

Wanda opened the door to let the kids in. She had called to ask Ella and Zita to show up a little early to help her get supper ready, and the boys had apparently elected to come early also.

Ella tossed her now ever-present notebook to the couch. "What did you need for us to do, Wanda?"

"Hello, kids." She started back for the kitchen. "I've just started frying the hamburgers. I've got some potatoes cooking that will need to be mashed, beans that will need to be stirred, and once the hamburgers are done, I'll make a big skillet full of milk gravy."

"Hamburgers and gravy?" Rusty asked, and went to the cupboard to get plates.

"Not just hamburgers," Wanda replied. "Although if you don't want gravy, you can do yours that way, I guess. What I plan is to put a slice of bread on the plate, a hamburger, another slice of bread, and then gravy over that and the potatoes. I call it a hot hamburger sandwich."

"Kind of like a hot beef sandwich," Zita stated.

"That's right. But I use milk gravy because... well, I like it."

They got busy with handling the cooking, then. While Wanda was stirring the gravy, and Zita was mashing the potatoes, they heard Chuck come in and greet the boys in the living room, had them help him bring in the pop and the cooler full of ice. When the first boy tried to enter the kitchen to put the drinks away, Wanda warned him away. "Not now. The kitchen is full. Do it later. Stack them up in the living room for now."

"It smells good," Chuck stated.

"It's just simple food, which is all I ever promised, I hope."

"Milk gravy," Chuck identified it. "But it doesn't smell like you fried chicken."

"Nope, not chicken," she answered. "Ella, we're going to need, um, three pot holders on the table, and at least one loaf of bread."

"Margarine?" Felix asked, reaching for the frig door.

"I don't think so," Wanda returned. "You guys go ahead and sit down. I don't want to spill anything on you when we start bringing the food in."

"But the pop..." Chuck protested.

"They usually have it over ice anyway. We can sort it out later." Soon the food was all on the table. Wanda repeated her instructions for making a 'hot hamburger sandwich,' and they began building them.

After a moment, Ella commented, "The plans for the reunion are coming along, Chuck."

"That's good to hear. I haven't made much progress getting the houses ready."

The mention of plural houses caught Wanda's attention. "What houses?"

"Mine. The old farmhouse and the new house."

"What do you need to do to get those ready? I mean, you're living in one of them, I presume. The other might be a little dusty."

"I haven't had time for house cleaning," Chuck answered. "So they're both dusty. Plus I need to check for creaky floorboards, make sure the plumbing works in the farmhouse. Usually when I expect visitors who might use the farmhouse, I live in it for a few days, see what needs to be done. But working 10 hour days, 6 days a week..." he shook his head to indicate any such excursion to the farmhouse would not be happening soon. "That reminds me, we missed you kids today."

"The flattery is nice, but don't think for a moment we believe it," Zita told him.

"No, I mean it. I took a look around at noon and wondered why we hadn't gotten any more work done. Steve said because you kids weren't there to keep us from jaw-jacking all morning."

"As if!" Ella declared. "You guys are talking all the time!"

"That's what I said," Chuck told her. "So then he admitted that you kids actually do some work."

"That's more like it," Ella stated. "And thank you for noticing." She turned her attention to Wanda. "I haven't had a chance to talk to you yet about what you'll be bringing to the 4th of July reunion. I was hoping I could talk you into baking bread for it."

Wanda had wondered if this was going to happen, and now that it had, how was she going to handle it? She put her fork down and wiped her mouth with a paper napkin, then cleared her throat. "I wasn't planning to be there, Ella. So, no, I'm sorry."

"Why not?" Chuck asked. Almost demanded.

"It's a family event," she reminded him. "I'm not family, and I don't want to intrude."

"Everybody in Belgrade knows they're invited to any family event we have. Most of them are relatives, in some way or another, and you're—" He stopped short, and she wondered what he had been going to say.

Surely he didn't, he couldn't... "I'm what?" She asked softly.

"You're living here in Gram's house. Everybody who's lived in this house since Gram moved in has been family. That's close enough to family to suit me."

"No," Wanda returned. "It's a family reunion. How would you introduce me to all those people you're expecting from out of town? As the woman now living in Gram's house? I think they'd be appalled."

"We aren't stuck up," Felix stated.

"No, I don't mean that. My welcome here—to the town— has been wonderful, despite an occasional rocky bit here and there. But it's one thing to welcome me to the town and quite another to invite me to participate in something that's intended for family members."

"I don't like that answer," Chuck stated flatly, then sighed. "So I've got to see if I can change your mind." He ate a forkful of beans, and turned to Ella. "Do you remember what Steve said he and Fran would bring?"

"Steve wanted to bring deviled eggs. But thinking about how many people would be there, and her probably working the day before, I didn't know if that was feasible, so I called her. She decided to bring a carrot salad."

Steve and Fran will be at the party? No, Wanda decided, *I'm not going to question it. I made my feelings known, and I'll just have to resist all Chuck's conniving.*

Little did she realize how hard that would be.

Chapter 22
Monday, June 8, 8:18 AM

It amazed Wanda how many ways Bob knew to get to Fullerton via back country roads. Meaning gravel roads, so there was no possibility of opening the windows. Good thing his air conditioning in his old car still worked.

And she wasn't sure why he took a different route every Monday to Fullerton. After all, when they headed home after all their errands, they always took the same way to Belgrade, and it was blacktop. She'd asked once, and he'd shrugged, said something about the stage coach robbers and indians couldn't steal anything if they didn't know what route he took. She had asked about indians in this part of the country. But there were none. There were a couple reservations in the northeast part of the state, but he wasn't aware of any indians in the middle.

Today, he seemed to have something else he wanted to talk about. "Chuck says you're determined not to attend his party on July 4th."

"Well, that makes it sound like I have something against him," she started.

"I can see where you would," Bob said. "But he did ask if you wanted your bushes cut down. And I haven't heard anything about his coming along and cutting them down anyway, even though you told him no."

"Yes, I know that," she answered. "And since we've reached a tentative accord about the bill for the cooling machines, which I am enjoying immensely, I don't particularly have any bad feelings about him."

"But you refused an invite to the party."

She sighed. "As I explained, it is a family party, and I am not family."

"Technically, you are," Bob reminded her.

"But you are the only one who knows that," she returned. "And you were the one who told me not to let anybody else know who my husband was."

"That's true," he agreed with a frown. "Maybe I made a mistake, telling you that."

"Well, it's too late now. What am I going to do, stand in the middle of your bar and announce, 'Hey, everybody. I've been lying to you all along. I'm not Wanda Sinclair, I'm Wanda Davis, and Hank was my husband.'? How would that look? Nobody would ever trust me again."

"It wouldn't have to be that... forward."

"Well, make up your mind, Bob. Why did you think I shouldn't let people know who I am in the first place?"

"At the time, I thought it would make you that much more a target, as far as Lyle and Chuck were concerned."

"Obviously, I'm not safe around Lyle, no matter who I am."

"That's true."

"And I've told Chuck I'm not interested in a boy friend."

"Really?" Bob cast a quick glance at her before returning his attention to the road ahead. "What did he say?"

She rolled her eyes, tired of this conversation. "He asked me to let him know when I change my mind."

"As simple as that, huh?" After a moment, he asked, "And how did you answer?"

"I told him no! Jeepers, Bob, what is it about 'I'm not interested,' that guys just can't wrap your heads around?"

"Sorry. Sorry. It's just not something we're used to hearing. Even me."

"What do you mean, 'even you'?"

"I was the slow cousin," he answered. "Always the last one to ask a girl out." His jaw tightened and he added, "Usually."

"Yeah, well, you've given all that up, remember? You and Chuck both, according to what you told me. Or was it Chuck who said it?"

"Well, that's true," he agreed, and turned left at the next junction. "So why not go to the party?"

"Bob! I'm not part of the family!"

"Depends on your definition of family," he returned. "All of Chuck's crew is invited."

"Half of Chuck's crew **is** family," she reminded him. "And that's fine, if he wants to invite the rest. Maybe the Thompsons won't feel quite so out of place if there are other non-family people there."

"That's another reason why you should go."

"No, Bob, I'm not going. I'm not family. I'm not an employee. I'm only an outsider who very recently moved into town. And tell Chuck I don't appreciate him having others plead his case for him. If he can't make me change my mind, then he should just honor my wishes."

"Chuck didn't ask me to plead with you," Bob told her, and turned onto a blacktop highway, headed east, according to the shadows. "He just mentioned you'd decided not to go, and I could tell he was bummed out about it."

"He'll get over it." She looked ahead to where she could see buildings on a hill. "Is that Fullerton?"

"Yeah. Thought I'd take you past the house Chuck and his crew have been working on."

Before long, they were pulling up to the curb across from a large house that looked done on the outside, except for the landscaping. "Man, it's big," she declared.

"Mr Zimmerman probably wanted the biggest house in town," Bob remarked.

Two pickups with 'Chuck's Construction' on the doors turned into the house's driveway, while Ella parked across from Bob.

"Thanks again, Bob!" Ella called across the street, and then hurried up the driveway to join Chuck and the rest of his crew.

"Tommy," Bob called as that lad climbed out of Ella's back seat. "Remember, we'll pick you guys up about noon. If we're a little bit late, just chill. If you get worried that we've forgotten you, one of you can call me. But we won't forget."

"Okay," Tommy agreed, and trotted after the others. Bob started his car and pulled away from the curb.

"We're taking the boys home again today?" Wanda asked. It hadn't been an issue brought up at Saturday night's game.

"Yes. Ella's picking up her prints and getting some mat board to start framing them. And Zita has paperwork to take back to the community college."

"Will you take them to Chuck's while you do the books?"

"Possibly. Not sure Tommy will go. He might be about ready to start harvesting some of the veggies from his gardens."

"I was going to say, I don't see much growing in the patch near my place. But then, I wouldn't know a weed from something he planted."

"He comes over and waters it, right?"

"Just about every evening, unless it's rained. Sometimes he brings a hoe and breaks the ground up before he waters. Or maybe he's taking out weeds. I don't know."

"He still staying until dark?"

"No, not recently."

"Probably spends time with Felix or Rusty, then. That's good. Everybody needs to socialize from time to time."

"If that's another dig to get me to the party—"

"No, it's not." He pulled his car into the closest empty spot near the bank, but didn't seem in a hurry to get out. "It's a little dig for not coming to the bar from time to time. It's nice to have somebody new to talk to. And you are still new, with new topics of conversation. Like where to catch a plane to Denver."

"I'm not taking a plane. I'm going to drive."

"Which is what I would have suggested, had I known you were trying to get to Denver."

"Well, in that you agree with Quince. Or was it Yantz?"

"Doesn't matter. The other one always disagrees. Well, I've got to go make my deposit. Remember, your appointment with Fran is for 9. Shall we meet at the Dew Drop around 10?"

"Yes, that's fine. But first, I need the bank, too. I need to make sure my monthly check has been deposited, and if so, I need some cash." And if her check had not yet been deposited, then she needed to transfer some money from her savings to cover the bills.

Chapter 23
Saturday, June 13, 4:34 PM

Wanda was pulling the last few presumed weeds from the small flower beds on either side of her front porch steps when she heard a pickup suddenly slow down and then pull into her driveway. "Hello, Wanda!"

She sighed, pulled the last 2 green stalks and shoved them into the plastic bucket with the others. *At least it isn't Lyle.* She turned and saw Chuck sitting in the driver's seat of his truck, staring at her hedge. *Or rather, at what remains of the hedge.* She brushed off her knees and walked over to ask, "Did you need something, Chuck?"

He finally turned his head to look at her. "Who did you get to take out your hedge?"

"Nobody," she answered. "I'm doing it myself. One plant per weekday. Still gives me plenty of time for working."

"What are you doing with what you chop down?"

"Well, I'm a little stumped on that. I've cut them into lengths and put them in a trash can to be picked up, but they didn't get taken. All the house trash got taken, but not the hedge pieces."

"No," he agreed. "Hedge pieces would be yard waste, and the garbage men don't take that. It's assumed you'll chop it up fine and make it into mulch. Or compost."

"Well, that's a bummer. I don't know anything about mulch or compost." Her nose itched, and she rubbed it with the back of a dirty hand. "Is that all you wanted? To ask about my hedge?"

"Ah, no, I thought I'd drop off the pop and ice for tonight, rather than take it home and then bring it back again."

"Okay. Go ahead, the door is open. I'd help, but my hands are all muddy."

She turned and walked inside, leaving the bucket of weeds on the front porch, while she went to the bathroom to wash up. She heard a number of footsteps enter the house and make their way to the kitchen.

"Hey, Wanda?"

She grabbed a towel and dried her hands as she stepped out into the wash room. "What?"

"Hello, Wanda," Dick greeted her again with a big grin.

"If you don't have anything else to do with the hedge pieces you've chopped down, I'll buy them from you," Chuck offered.

She frowned, wondering what Chuck was up to. "Do you mulch or compost?"

"No," Dick stated, his grin even bigger.

"Then I don't understand. Why do you want them?"

"I've got a lot of hamburgers and hot dogs to cook in a couple weeks."

"Isn't that usually done with charcoal?"

"People have cooked over wood fires for millions of years."

Well, that was true. All her characters ate food cooked with wood, even when they lived in a castle. "How much?"

"I don't know. 5 dollars?"

She thought about all the hard work she had put into sawing down the hedge plants, and then sawing them into pieces that would fit in her garbage pails. It seemed like a lot more than $5 worth of work. On the other hand, she had chopped them down for her own benefit, and would have been happy if the garbage men had taken them away. Which, technically, she was paying for her garbage to be taken away.

The 3rd man from Chuck's crew was Ivan, who was leaning against the kitchen sink, looking impatient and bored. "What do you think, Ivan? Is that a fair price for that wood?"

Ivan stood up straight and glanced at his boss. "I don't know. Why don't you hit him with a 'Pain in the Butt' surcharge and ask for $10?"

Wanda grinned. Chuck crossed his arms over his chest, as if expecting her to raise the price. "That's very tempting, Ivan. Okay, Chuck, you can have the wood for $5."

"Okay. Good. Now, do you want it in cash, or shall we just deduct it from your bill?"

Was he outraged that I toyed with the idea of raising the price? Was that a dig to remind me I owe him money? But he hadn't wanted to charge me, so why would he want to remind me of what had been a sore spot for me? And he didn't seem outraged. He was simply standing there, arms crossed, a small and rather uncertain smile on his face. "We can apply it to my bill, if I can get a receipt from you to that effect," she told him.

"I don't have a receipt book on me."

"I've got paper and pens in my office," she stated. "Just take a sheet out of my printer."

He immediately started through the living room, asking back over his shoulder, "Can I borrow your garbage cans to get the wood home?" I can drop them off on Monday morning."

Wanda was following him, with the two other men bringing up the rear. "That works. Just leave them in the driveway if I'm not home."

"Dick, Ivan, find the garbage pails and put them in the pickup," he instructed.

"I'll show you where they are," she volunteered and led them out to where two garbage cans stood between the garage doors and the front of her car. "They're heavy," she cautioned them, and then let them get to it.

Chuck emerged from the house with a sheet of paper in his hand. "Here's your receipt," he stated, walking to his truck.

Wanda walked over to look it over. "Good. Thank you, Chuck. I'll see you later, for the game."

He stared at her for a moment, apparently oblivious that his crew members had placed the garbage cans in the back of his pickup, and were now climbing into their usual seats in his cab. Chuck reached out as if to touch one of her braids, as if he'd done it dozens of times before. She grabbed the braid in question and threw it behind her shoulder. "Is something wrong?"

"Did you cut your hair?"

"I got the split ends trimmed," she answered. "Most people don't notice."

"Well, I'll see ya," he stated, and climbed into his cab.

"Bye, Wanda." Dick's simple greetings were getting irritating. *Like he wants my approval for managing to remember my name. Well, it's more than Lyle can be bothered to do.*

"See you at the 4th of July party," Ivan offered.

"No, you won't," she returned with a slight smile.

"Why not?"

"Oh, it's complicated," she returned. "Maybe Chuck can explain it to you." Then she turned and went back into her house.

* * *

5:42 PM

Tommy was the first to show up today, carrying a plastic bag with 7 large tomatoes in it. In his other arm, he carried an oversized bag of candied popcorn, which apparently was his contribution to the game-play goodies, since he lay it on the heating stove.

Wanda admired the flawless tomatoes, even picked one up to sniff. "Oh, these even smell like tomatoes. These will be great, Tommy. Thanks for bringing them." She took them to the kitchen for a quick wash, and showed the lad how to cut the tomatoes into quarters. Then they moved back to the dining room table, where they placed a quartered tomato on each plate. Wanda brought in the bowl of chicken salad from the frig and showed him how to 'stuff' each tomato full of chicken salad.

By then the other kids had arrived, and everything having to do with preparing supper halted when Ella announced, "I've got prints to show off!"

She had brought 4 prints, complete with mat 'frames', and she stood them up across the front of the piano so people could get a look at them. But Wanda had to excuse herself to add the still-frozen corn cobs to the boiling water. "I bought frozen corn on the cob because I thought it might be too early for you to have any from the garden."

"Too early," Tommy agreed.

"Felix, Rusty, could you come in the kitchen, and rearrange the frig, see how much of this pop you can get in it?"

192

"What pop?" Felix asked, and then saw the boxes sitting on the kitchen floor next to the cooler of ice. "Oh, Chuck already dropped it off, did he?" He opened the frig. "Is there anything in here we need for supper? Margarine or ketchup or anything?"

"Butter," Wanda answered. "For the corn. And if somebody wants bread and butter."

"I like bread and butter," Rusty stated. "And some mustard for my tomato." He quickly grabbed those items and took them to the dining table.

"Well, that didn't make a lot of room," Felix stated. "But I think I can combine a couple of these old boxes. We'll just have to be sure that what we grab out is what we actually wanted."

Chuck was admiring Ella's prints when Wanda took a platter full of hot corn on the cob to the table. "Tommy, the salad in the tomatoes looks wonderful. I don't think I could have done any better myself," she told him, and turned to address the others "Felix and Rusty are getting the drinks. If someone would like to get the knives and forks, I think we can get started on supper."

But instead of sitting down, Wanda went to her bedroom and got some money from her wallet. "Tommy, you said $5 for the tomatoes, right?"

"Yeah."

"Here you go." She handed him a 5 dollar bill. "Keep me in mind when you harvest. Especially on a Friday or Saturday, when I can add what you've got to my menu. I was just going to serve chicken salad sandwiches, but the tomatoes make the meal more like an event, don't you think?"

"Looks really good," Chuck stated. "Tommy, your family's coming to the 4th of July party, aren't they?"

The boy seemed stricken, almost, by the simple question, but eventually answered, "Not Pa."

"But your ma and the rest of the kids?"

"Yeah."

Ella pulled her notebook from the sofa. "Do you know what your ma will bring for the pot luck?"

"Veggies," he offered."

"You mean, a vegetable side dish?"

"Veggies," he repeated, and went on. "Tomatoes, radishes, onions, cucumbers, lettuce."

"That's great," Chuck decided. "Think of it, Ella, all the fixings for the hot dogs and hamburgers."

"No," Rusty refuted. "You still need ketchup and mustard."

"You're right. Ella, see if Bob can add those to his list. If not, add them to mine. On 2nd thought, add them to both our lists. And salt and pepper, too."

Rusty had separated his chicken salad from the tomato, and used a couple slices of bread to make a sandwich, and now he was squeezing mustard from the container onto his tomato before he cut it into bite-sized chunks. Wanda watched him eat 2 yellowed bites before she commented. "Rusty, I don't think I've ever seen anyone eat tomatoes and mustard together."

"The mustard gives the tomato more tang than regular salt. My dad likes spicy foods, and this is how he eats tomatoes."

"Well, I'll have to try that sometime, although in my mind, tomatoes are pretty perfect the way they are. I'm just not sure I could handle the added tang too often. I love tomatoes, but if I eat too many, they start to play havoc with my tummy."

"Yellow and white," Tommy muttered.

"What?" Wanda asked.

Felix told her, "He means you should try the yellow and white varieties. The paler the color, the less acid they have."

"And are you growing any yellow and white tomatoes?"

"Some," Tommy answered.

"I would like to try some, when you get some. I don't think I've ever seen any tomatoes that aren't red. Well, except the unripe ones, of course."

"Well, once again, supper was delicious, Wanda," Chuck stated. "Now, who brought dessert? Do I see a cobbler over there on the stove?"

Chapter 24
Wednesday, June 17, 12:40 PM

Wanda entered the tiny post office and opened her mail box. She had paid her bills, so all she anticipated getting were some advertisements from 'local' businesses. Some of them were from as far away as Columbus and Grand Island. That hardly would have been 'local' in Chicago. And then she noticed a post-it note attached to the fliers. It said, 'Please come to the service desk.'

What's this about? I'm pretty sure I paid for 3 months worth of box rent. That won't come due yet. Was there something else I was supposed to do?

The service lobby was empty, but when she opened that door to go in, a little bell rang, and the past-retirement-age post mistress came forward from somewhere in the back. "How may I help you?"

"I'm not sure," Wanda stated, and handed her the note. "This was in my box."

"Oh, yes, your name is Wanda, isn't it? Wanda... now, what was it? Sinclair?"

"That's right." She hadn't gotten her mail box until after Bob had warned her not to use her own name.

"And that was box 122?"

"Yes."

"Have you ever used a different last name?"

"What?"

"I have a package here, a large envelope. It's addressed to a Wanda, but a different last name. And the box number is wrong, too. But the owner of the other box number said it didn't belong to them, and they suggested it might be yours."

"Well, yes." *How do I explain this without revealing every-thing? Weren't Bob and I just talking about this last week?* "I went by Wanda Davis for a while. Sort of a short term marriage." *A lot shorter than I'd ever thought it would be.*

The older woman sniffed. "Well, that's a pretty common last name. We got bunches of 'em right here in Belgrade. Anyway, do you recognize the sender?" She peered at something she held below the countertop level. "Young Lee? From some big fancy company in Chicago."

"Yeung Lee," Wanda stated, pronouncing the name correctly. "Yes,... I met him in college. He was going into finances or business. He called me a few weeks ago and said he'd send me something. When it didn't show up, I kind of forgot about it." She took the overstuffed business envelope that was passed over the counter and checked the return address: Mr Yeung Lee, Fidelity Investments, 1212 South Park Blvd, Chicago... "Thank you for taking the time and making the effort to get it to me."

"Well, it took extra postage for it to get here, so I figured it was important. I'm glad I've solved that little mystery. Thanks for stopping by, Ms Davis. Oh, I'm sorry. Ms Sinclair."

Wanda headed out the softly dinging lobby door with a wave at the old woman and then was on her way home. *Lee said he was sending me a report on Hank's nest egg account. From the looks of this envelope, it's more of a thesis!* Which was, perhaps, a reflection on where she had met him. High schoolers made reports; college kids wrote a thesis.

Still, she couldn't understand what he could say that would take so much paper. She tore open the envelope. Walking at a snail's pace, she tried to make sense of the financial report. But the more she looked at it, the more confused she got. It didn't make any sense. Finally reaching her porch door, she opened it long enough to toss the fliers in on the floor, and then turned right around and headed for the one person in this town who— she hoped—could explain the columns of figures to her.

Bob was wiping down the bar when Wanda entered via the back door. "Hi, Bob."

He looked up in surprise. "Wanda! You're early. Most people wait until they're off work before they come in. I didn't think you stopped working until 5 or so."

"Usually," she agreed, hopping onto a bar stool. She laid the envelope on the bar. It was the reason she had come, but she didn't want to make it that obvious. "I usually stop working about 5 or 5:30. But I can't work until I get some answers."

"Uh oh, that sounds serious," Bob stated. "Is something bothering you?"

No, there's no way to stretch this out and make it seem like I came to see him and oh, yeah, could he explain this paperwork? As soon as I show it to him, it's going to be obvious that that's why I've come. I might as well admit it. She picked up the envelope, looked around to make sure they were alone in the bar. "Bob, a friend of Hank's—a friend of ours—sent me this. Supposedly, it's about Hank's nest egg, which Lee has been investing for us. I guess the stock market went kind of caflooey about the time Hank died. Lee got super busy and I never made the time to touch base with him before I left Chicago. Never gave the nest egg a single thought, if you can believe that. Anyway, he sent this to me, and... I can't make heads or tails of it. I was hoping you could..." She hesitated and gave him a wry smile." Do you think you could translate it for me? Just give me the gist of it?" She pushed the envelope across the bar toward him.

"Well, let me take a look." He took several printed pages out of the envelope and started looking through them. After a moment, his brow furrowed in confusion, and after some time, he nodded and started sorting the papers into 3 piles on his bar. "I get the feeling you've tried to make sense of these, and didn't necessarily keep them in the order they came in."

"I did try," she admitted. "And I'd think I could halfway understand one page, then the next page I looked at seemed to say something very different."

"Okay," he said, and sorted the pages into 3 stacks of papers. Then he folded one stack of papers together, grabbed a pen and circled something on the first page. "This stack is a financial statement from October to December of last year. No need to concern yourself with it. Just file it with your financial records." He returned that stack to the envelope, then organized, folded and circled the date on the 2nd stack. "This is a financial statement from January through March of this year. Still old news, but I can see that he sold some stocks and put the money in other investments. From what I remember of the stock market at that time—and I don't keep an eagle eye on it—it looks to me like he dumped some major stocks that really had their bottom fall out. And he bought small amounts of other stocks that I don't recognize, but which at least held steady in that volatile time. So you lost a little bit of value in your nest egg, but not nearly as bad as it could have been. If you want to look up the stocks he invested in, we could do that next Tuesday."

"I'll think about it," she answered. "Hank usually told him, 'Whatever you think we should do, Lee. You have a head for this stuff, and I trust you.' And I trusted Hank, so I never questioned that arrangement."

"Okay, you think about it and let me know if you want to at least see what you now own a piece of." He slid that group of pages into the envelope, too. "Which leaves this partial financial statement, which is for April through May." He circled the dates on the front page. "Again, he's sold a couple stocks that presumably weren't doing well, and bought a few others. The stocks that he bought last quarter are doing better than the ones they replaced. And this—" He drew a box around a large number near the dates. "—is what is currently in your nest egg."

"That's got to be a mistake," Wanda stated. "It can't be."

"How much was Hank putting away and how often?"

That simple question stopped her whirling brain. *I don't know. I know how much he got paid his first year on the job, and we lived on about half his paycheck, the rest went to the nest egg. When he got bonuses, we went out for dinner and a movie to celebrate. Each time he got a raise, he added a modest $100 a month to our budget. We got by, but I never suspected he was putting away that kind of money.*

"Bob." She barely got the word out, wondered if it was loud enough for him to hear it.

"Yes, Wanda?"

"Could you fix me a sloe gin coke?"

"Yes, Wanda."

When he placed the glass in front of her, she took a sip, remembered the last time she had come in and had a sloe gin coke.
"And a hamburger," she decided. "With french fries."

"Yes, ma'am," he said and made his way to the kitchen.

Wanda picked up the remaining papers and returned them to
the envelope. She wished now she had worn a jacket or a sweater, to have a pocket where she could hide the envelope. She was
certain anybody who saw the envelope would know automatically how much money she had in her investment account in Chicago. "Bob?"

He walked over to show she had his attention.

"Don't tell anybody," she requested.

"Of course not, Wanda. It's nobody's business."

She nodded, and he went back to the grill. *The things I could
do!* Her head swirled with dozens of possibilities. "I could for
sure pay Chuck's bill off," she said aloud.

Bob put her burger and fries in front of her. "He doesn't care
if you pay him or not. But you rather loudly told him you had
limited means. Now you're thinking of paying him off all at
once? People might wonder how much money you have."

"Well, I do. Have some money."

"But do you want everybody to wonder about how much
money you might have? This isn't Chicago, Wanda, with a police man on every corner. All it would take would be one nasty
man—or woman—to decide they need your money more than
you do."

"Do you really think somebody in Belgrade would... do
something like that?"

He hesitated. "Yes. I do. That's why I take a different route
to Fullerton every Monday, and I go to the bank first thing when
I get there."

"That's right, you do," she realized. "When I asked why,
you said something about bandits and indians. I got distracted by
the 'indian' part, and never gave a thought to bandits." She took
a large gulp of her sloe gin coke and shuddered. "Somehow, I
never thought of living in a small town like Belgrade as being
dangerous. Not really."

"It only takes 1 bad apple," he said. "If you want my opinion—and I know you haven't asked for it—I'd just keep paying Chuck the same small amounts you said you'd pay. Like I said before, he doesn't care. And you don't want him thinking he can do whatever he wants, all in the name of doing it for your benefit, and then somehow, you'll find the money to pay him back. No, I wouldn't want him to get started down that path at all."

"You're probably right," she agreed after swallowing her latest bite of hamburger. "He's got to stop and think about the position he's putting a woman in. I know he's mad at his grandmother for not letting him give her house all the latest and greatest do-dads, like an ice maker. But she probably didn't want to feel beholden to him, either, and couldn't afford to pay him."

"Wait a minute. Your refrigerator has an ice maker."

"Yes, but Gram wouldn't let him hook it up to the sink water, so he had to do that after I moved in."

"Gram was a bit set in her ways. She didn't always need the latest and greatest do-dad, as you called them."

Outside the display window, Tommy parked his red wagon. Walking in, he stood for a moment, pulling his sweaty shirt away from his body and soaking up some of the cool AC. Then he walked over and sat at the bar. "Orange," he requested, and put a bill on the bar.

"Watch it, Tommy. That money from working with Chuck seems to be eating a hole in your pocket," Bob said, but never-the-less, he got the boy the desired can of pop and took the money away. "You done hoeing my garden patch already?"

Tommy nodded. "Want 'maters?"

"You know I love tomatoes, but you plant the odd colors on my patch." Bob turned to tell Wanda, "I think he's afraid I'll steal all of them if he plants red tomatoes in my patch."

"I got reds," Tommy revealed.

"From my patch?" Bob asked in surprise.

"Mom's."

"Well, don't just sit there, bring some in so I can buy them."

Tommy went outside, came back with 2 plastic pint cartons. He placed the one piled high with large red tomatoes on the bar for Bob. He pushed the other container—which held a hodge-podge of smaller tomatoes in various colors—down the bar toward Wanda.

Wanda laughed. "I thought it would be a little longer before I got any white and yellow tomatoes."

"Pink and orange, too," Tommy stated. "A little early yet."

"Yes, they are a bit too small for putting in sandwiches, but just the right size for adding to a salad."

"Full grown," he stated.

"Yeah, the odd colors don't get very big," Bob stated. "The pink and orange ones might be a little bigger; that's what happens when white and yellow pollinate with the red ones. Those must be from your mom's garden."

"Yep."

"How much?" Bob asked the youngster.

"Five," Tommy said, pointing to the over-filled pint container of red tomatoes. Then he pointed to the pint container of multi-colored and said, "Four."

Wanda reached for her purse and realized she hadn't brought it. "Oh, no!"

"What's wrong?" Bob asked as he got his wallet out of his back pocket.

"I didn't bring any money!" she told him in alarm. "I was so wrapped up in this letter, I didn't even think about my purse! I can't pay for my supper, nor for these great looking goodies."

"Relax," Bob told her. It's not a big deal."

"It is a big deal!" she declared. "I have to pay my bills."

"Well, just this once—"

"No, don't tell me you're going to pull a Chuck on me and tell me I don't need to pay you. I won't tolerate that behavior from him, and I don't want you starting it, either!"

Bob put his wallet on the counter and waited half a moment. His voice was calm. "Please let me finish, Wanda. I know how you feel about unrequested favors, especially financial ones. I'm only going to offer you the same thing I would offer 90% of my customers, in similar circumstances. That I run a tab for you for what you've purchased today. A short-term tab; you can pay me on Monday. That way you don't have to run home and then run back with the money. It's only a few days, and... maybe you've forgotten, but I know where you live." He waggled his eyebrows at her as if he was trying to be menacing.

Wanda laughed, for he was not menacing in the least. "Run a tab until Monday! And who else do you run a tab for? If you don't mind my asking."

"I run a tab for Chuck every week. Of course, I know I'll get paid, because I'm his bookkeeper, so I just write the check to myself on Mondays. I've also run tabs for Helen, Alice, Val, Robert... Do you want me to name them all? Because I'm not sure I can remember them."

"No, of course not. As long as I'm not getting special treatment, I agree to pay you on Monday. Thank you." She turned her attention to Tommy, and pushed her pint of tomatoes towards him a little bit. "I can pay you when you come to hoe the patch near me. I mean, if you can break a $20 bill for me. I'm pretty sure that's all I've got left in cash. Or I could write you a check."

The youngster hesitated and frowned with uncertainty.

"Let me guess, you forgot to set up a petty cash for making change, right?" Bob asked. Tommy nodded, his face pink. "Okay," Bob said and turned to Wanda. "I haven't quite gotten him to think like a business owner. And up until now, everybody has kept small bills around to pay for whatever they buy from him. Or they write a check, but he's lost 1 or 2 of those before he got them to the bank. So, let's see if we can come to some kind of agreement that everybody can be happy with."

"I'm happy to write a check," Wanda repeated.

"But he's a little leery of losing those. I should have him write a sale slip for what he sells, but he's been a bit reluctant to do that, too. Can't say I blame him. Look here, he'd have to make out 2 sales slips just selling $9 of tomatoes. So, here's what I suggest, for this time only, and it's just a suggestion. If anybody doesn't like it, we'll try to find some other way to solve this dilemma."

"Why do I think you believe I won't like this idea?"

"It's just a suggestion, Wanda."

"Spit it out."

"Since I'm running a tab for you, why don't I pay Tommy for your tomatoes, and you can pay me back on Monday?"

Wanda stared at him, considered how close he had come to pulling a 'Chuck'. Then she smiled. "At least you asked instead of just doing it."

"I'm... not hearing an answer in there," Bob told her.

And he even waits for an answer before he moves forward with the idea! "Yes. I agree. Tommy can have his money, in a form he's comfortable with, and I can have my tomatoes. Which probably won't last longer than tomorrow. But I will pay you, Bob, on Monday."

"Okay. Everybody's happy." He picked up his wallet again. "Nine dollars. If I give you a 10, Tommy, do you have a dollar to make change for me?"

"Sorry."

"Okay, so you need a 5 and 4 ones." He pulled bills from his wallet and counted them out on the bar. Tommy folded them all together and shoved them into his back jeans pocket. When he pulled his hand out, a $5 bill went fluttering to the floor.

"Tommy, you dropped some money," Wanda told him.

"What?" He looked down, bent over and retrieved it.

"Don't you have a wallet?" Wanda asked. The boy shook his head. "Well, you should probably get some way of keeping your money from falling out of your pocket." She turned and finished eating the last of her fries.

"Tommy, you might not get to the big patch near Wanda," Bob stated. "Not today. The clouds have really started to darken up. I think it's going to be a rainy day."

The teen looked out the front windows and sighed. Wanda didn't know if it was a sigh of relief or frustration. "I'll head home."

"Hey, don't forget me the next time you get some red tomatoes ready," Bob told him as he walked out the front door.

Wanda looked at the front windows, and saw a few drops start to splatter on the glass. She heard a low growl of thunder that seemed to go on and on. "I'd better head home, too," she decided. "With my luck, it will drench me on the way."

"I'm thinking it'll be an all night on and off shower," Bob stated "But, what do I know?"

"Thanks for your help, Bob. I think I'll try to get some writing done, now that the mystery of this report is cleared up." She picked up the envelope and headed for the back door. "And don't let me forget to pay you on Monday!"

"Hey, I'm a business, not a bank," he answered, and watched her leave.

Chapter 25
Saturday, June 20, 5:55 PM

Wanda took the last of the 'meatloaf' patties out of the oven and turned it off, then used a spatula to transfer the patties to a plate, which she sent out to the dining table with one of the boys. "How are we coming?" she asked Zita and Rusty, who were helping her get the food to the table.

"The green beans are done," Zita said. "Do you want me to transfer them to a bowl, or just leave them in the pot?"

"The pot," Wanda told her. "How are the potatoes, Rusty?"

"Smashed," he returned. "I can't guarantee there aren't any lumps, and they might be a tad dry."

"Sounds like it's time to eat," Wanda stated. "Take the pots in, I'll bring serving spoons for them."

Ella looked up from studying her notebook when the food came in, tossed the notebook to the sofa. "Chuck isn't here yet."

"He knows what time we eat," Wanda told her. "He's probably taking a hot shower and trying to relax before he comes. He's been working long hours."

"I thought that's what the game was, a chance to relax," Felix stated.

"I've been meaning to ask, Ella, did you send an invitation to the Thompsons for the 4th of July party?"

"I think Chuck did."

"I did what?" Chuck asked, coming from the front porch.

"Sent an invitation to the Thompsons," Ella answered.

"Well, not a written invitation, exactly," Chuck answered. "Eating already? I may have to stop working another 5 minutes early on Saturdays."

"Or don't stop by just to drop off the pop and ice on your way home," Wanda suggested. "My frig is half full of pop."

"Really? I figured we were drinking it all up."

"Not quite, and the extra has been adding up."

"Maybe I should skip bringing any pop next week?"

"I think that would work."

"Chuck, what do you mean you haven't invited the Thompsons?" Ella asked.

"I invited them at your graduation party," he reminded her. "And about a week later, I stopped by Mr Thompson's office to give him a map of how to get to my place. So I reiterated the invitation then. I haven't sent any invites out by mail, if that's what you mean."

"Oh," Wanda said tonelessly. "That's too bad."

"Well, I did mail them an invitation to them for my graduation party, and never heard from them whether or not they'd be there."

"Maybe they didn't know themselves until they actually got in the car and drove to Belgrade," Wanda suggested.

"You think I should send them an invitation?" Chuck asked.

Wanda opened her mouth and then closed it again. "Perhaps I'm just thinking of how it's done in the city," she suggested, and took a bite of her meatloaf burger.

"These burgers have a lot more flavor to them than most burgers," Zita stated. "What did you do to them?"

"I made meatloaf patties," Wanda answered. "That lets me add spices and herbs, for that extra flavor."

"How do they do it in the city?" Chuck queried. "Although Fullerton is not Chicago."

"No, it's not," Wanda agreed. "In the city, it's all a matter of how formal you want to be. Good friends tell each other, 'Come over, let's have a party.' And that's fine. But if you don't know the other people that well—and I gather that feelings are strained between the two families right now—then you formalize your request with a written invite. One that includes time and place, instructions on how to get there in case they don't know, and in the case of pot luck, a clue what's expected of them. A simple line saying, 'This is pot luck, so could you bring a side dish or dessert?' Or whatever you need to even things out. Or if the

Thompsons are known for a specific dish, you can make that one
of your suggestions."

"That's a lot of work," Chuck stated.

"This entire party was started to give the Thompsons a
chance to visit their daughter. It would be a shame for them to
miss that opportunity just because they weren't sure you were
sincere."

"Hmm." Chuck ate green beans, looking thoughtful.

Perhaps now is a good time to change the subject, Wanda
thought.

"Mom usually makes gravy when she makes mashed potatoes," Felix stated.

Wanda gave him a smile. "So do I, but I didn't get any milk
last Monday, and I barely had enough to make the mashed potatoes. Hence, the big tub of butter on the table."

"How are your gardens doing, Tommy?" Zita asked across
the table.

The question seemed to surprise him. "Good," he stated, and
took a drink. "Started harvesting."

"I loved those pale tomatoes you sold me the other day,"
Wanda stated. People finished their meal and moved on to dessert. "Ella, I've been meaning to ask how many conventions
you've lined up to send your prints to," Wanda probed.

"Close to a dozen," Ella answered enthusiastically, and
rolled her eyes in disappointment. "Too late to help me come up
with the money for UNO, most of them. But, mom has a sister
who lives in Omaha, and her daughter is only home for the
summer before she goes back to school in Missouri. So there's a
good chance I'll be able to use her bedroom while I'm at school.
Which is good, because the dorms are enormously expensive!"

"What do you have to do to pay your room and board for
your aunt?" Chuck asked.

Ella chuckled. "The way it was explained to me, pretend to
be their teenage daughter, without the drama of actually being
their teenage daughter. So, the same kind of chores I'm already
doing at home, take care of my own finances, and try not to give
them a reason to ground me. And share a bedroom with their

younger teenage daughter. Anyway, they're coming out for the 4th of July party, so hopefully we'll have some time to spell out details for each other."

"Whoa, wait a minute. How many kids are they bringing? I don't know if I have room for them in my houses."

"Don't worry, Chuck," Ella told him. "It's my mom's sister and family, so they're staying with us."

"Good," Chuck returned. "Because I think the Applegit Motel is pretty well full."

"Not quite, you've only got one bedroom left," Ella told him.

"The what Motel?" Wanda asked.

"The Applegit Motel," Chuck answered. "That's what I call my farmhouse."

"Oh." She blushed. "I don't know why I'm surprised, but I always thought your last name was Davis. Or LaFlamme."

"No, there are no LaFlamme's left in Belgrade," he answered. "And Gram was my mother's mother, so I'm not a Davis, either."

I don't really know anybody's last name, Wanda realized. *Just some relationships.* "What's Bob's last name?"

"Nichols," Chuck answered. "Lyle is a Davis." He licked the last of dessert off his fork. "Now Helen—"

"No, give me time to get these 3 names settled in my brain before you try to teach me anymore. Maybe next Saturday, we could add a couple more names to the family tree that is Belgrade."

"Okay, everybody done with supper? Then let's get things put away and cleaned up so we can play our game. Who helped put supper together, Wanda?"

"Zita and Rusty. Why?"

"Then the rest of us can do the dishes and clean up." He got up and grabbed Zita's and Felix's plates, as well as his own, and headed for the kitchen. "Give me a minute to get some water ready. I'm washing tonight."

Surprised, Wanda turned to Ella and quietly said, "I'm surprised he's actively helping."

"Why?" she returned. "He's always willing to help when mom has him over for a meal. "Of course, she routinely asks him to. He is family."

"I'm supposed to ask him to help?" Wanda asked, while a voice inside said, *he doesn't know I'm family*.

"You do with us," Rusty stated, his brow furrowed. "Whichever one is handy when you need help. If you're going to treat us like family, why not him?"

"That puts me in an uncomfortable position. With him."

"Well, this looks an awful lot like a family meal to me," Zita said.

Which made Wanda uncomfortable and she was eager for the game to start.

Chapter 26
Monday, June 22, 10:09 AM

"No, no pie for me today," Wanda told Uma, the waitress. "Just a glass of iced tea."

Bob sighed. "No pie for me, either. Just coffee."

After the waitress moved off, Bob touched Wanda's hand to get her attention and then whispered, "Thank you."

"For what?"

"For giving me an excuse to forego the piece of pie I've been getting every Monday for the past 5 or 6 years."

She looked confused. "If you want pie..."

"It's a habit. But I also want to drop a few pounds. They've snuck up on me, but now I want to do something about them."

"It must be hard to get any exercise when you're open— what—14 hours a day?"

"Yeah. I work out on Mondays, after I do Chuck's books. He has a machine, but once a week isn't doing the job."

"Maybe you could get up and take a walk before going to work."

"I tried that. Frankly, after being on my feet for14 hours, I don't have the time or energy to go for a walk."

"Well, you open at eleven, right? But most of the afternoon, you don't really have any customers. Maybe you need to walk while the place is empty."

"I can't leave the place unlocked," he protested.

"I didn't mean you should. But walking from the front door to the back door is half a block. Doing that a few times a day would make a good start. Turn on some music and dance."

"Alone?"

"Why not? If you don't have a partner, move to the music. At least you'd be moving." She thought for a moment. "Don't you have a couple boards or a wooden box or something that you keep behind the bar, at the cash register?"

"Yeah, a stepping box, so Helen can get into the register."

"Well, pull that out a ways and do step exercises on it. You can listen to music while you do that, too. Makes it more fun."

"You give me hope," he said with a smile.

"Good. Because you aren't really fat, Bob. You just need toning up."

"And now you've given me some ideas how to work on that, while I'm at work. Thanks."

"Speaking of thanks, I need to repay you for Wednesday. I don't remember how much supper was, but the tomatoes were $4. And I was right, they were all gone by noon on Friday."

He got out his wallet and fished out the guest check he had prepared. "Did you get change at the bank?" he asked. "Because I did, if you want me to break one of those 20s."

She considered that suggestion. "I did get change, and small bills, the better to pay Tommy, now that he's started to harvest. But if you don't mind, I will pay you with a 20 and take the change."

"It's fine with me," he stated, and placed her change on the table between them.

"I haven't brought your checks yet," Uma stated as she set their drinks on the table.

Wanda gave her a bright smile. "We're settling up a bill I charged this past week."

"You selling booze on credit, Bob?" Uma asked.

"I don't make a habit of it," he explained. "But I knew Wanda was good for it. And she just paid me, so I was right."

"Well, that's okay, then," the waitress said, but was shaking her head as she walked away.

"Oh! Look what I found at the general store." Wanda rummaged through her shopping bags and pulled out a purple canvas bag on a belt.

"A fanny pack?" Bob asked.

"More of a belly bag. I keep my wallet and phone in it, a little notebook and a pen. This way, I don't have to carry a purse,

and I can have my hands free. My old one is developing holes."
She started rummaging through her sacks again. "I got another
one to give..." She pulled out a green one.

"Wanda, I'm afraid that would emphasize my belly too
much," Bob stated. "Maybe after I lose some weight..."

"It's not for you!" she said. "I was going to give it to Tommy. See? He could put his checks and larger bills in this back
pocket, closest to his body; a notebook and pen and smaller bills
in the large middle pocket, and any coins he might have in the
front pocket. He could wear it while he was working in the gardens, and be ready to make a sale at a moment's notice. What do
you think?"

"I think it's a wonderful idea." After another moment, "I'm
afraid he might be embarrassed to accept it from you. It might
seem like charity to him."

She sat back in her seat, nonplussed. "I don't see him as
needing charity. You've said his home life isn't beautiful. I haven't pried because it isn't my business, but a lot of us don't
have all roses and cream at home. I admire him for working so
hard, and so I thought... I just meant it as a gift."

"Then you'd better impress upon him that it is strictly a
friendly gesture, made out of admiration for his work ethic."

Wanda opened her mouth to say more, then paused to drink
half of her tea. "Bob, am I... Am I pulling a Chuck here? I see
that Tommy could use a wallet or something to help keep track
of his money, so I've run out and bought this, without consulting
him, and I'm about to try to cram it down his throat. Whether he
wants it or not."

"Are you trying to impress Tommy with your largess?"

"What? No. I don't feel the need to impress him. Besides,
I'd hardly call it largess. I only paid $10 for it."

"You have a generous nature," was Bob's response. "You
do realize that the amount Chuck charged you for those cooling
machines isn't much, to Chuck. Just like $10 isn't much to you.
To Tommy, that's a lot of money. So, tell Tommy you saw this
item, and immediately thought how useful it could be for him,
and you were afraid it wouldn't last long at the store at the price

of only $10, so you bought it, and you hope he'll accept it as a gift. Then be prepared for any number of reactions. If he's ready to realize he should be more business-like with his money, he might accept it. If he isn't, he might say no. Whichever way he goes, you've got to acknowledge and respect his decision. Otherwise, you would be pulling a Chuck."

"Thank you, Bob. I will do my best not to pull a Chuck." She put both belly bags back in her shopping bags. "Say, I saw you talking with Mr Thompson in the bank this morning. I was a little surprised, because I didn't think the Thompsons were very fond of you."

"He thought I was Chuck when he started talking to me. I told him who I was. He seemed a little speechless for a moment. I can't blame them for thinking I'm to blame for Gloria marrying Lyle. Anyway, I said I hoped they could make it to Chuck's party, so they could spend some time with their daughter. After that, he asked about the hours of the party, and if there was something they could bring. I hope they decide to come, and that they get there early enough to spend the entire day with Gloria."

"Does Mrs Thompson have a dish she's known for?"

"She does a fantastic German Chocolate cake. Why?"

"I explained to Ella and Chuck that I thought they should send the Thompsons a written invitation for the party. One that included the hours and a couple suggestions for what they could bring."

His eyebrows rose in surprise. "You did?"

"It was just a suggestion. I explained my reasons, and then I let it drop. I don't know if they'll do it or not."

"Well, at least you didn't pull a Chuck and send it for them."

"I wouldn't!" she declared.

"Glad to hear it." Bob drank the rest of his coffee, and put his payment on the table. "You ready to move on to groceries?"

"Yes," she said, and left some ones on the table.

"That's a hefty tip for a glass of tea," Bob whispered.

"I've been a waitress, and it occurs to me that by not having a piece of pie, I have cut Uma's tip in half. Less than half."

They waved to Uma and left the cafe. "Okay," Bob said. "I

213

guess that makes sense. But next week, let me be the generous one. I don't want to be seen as miserly."

"You? Miserly?"

"I've told you. My reputation isn't good."

Wanda deposited her shopping bags in the back seat of Bob's car and they got in. "Why would the Thompsons blame you for Gloria marrying Lyle?"

Bob grimaced and took his time looking for on-coming traffic before he pulled out of his parking stall. "Because I was dating her when Lyle suddenly swooped in and stole her."

"What?"

He shrugged. "I figured he'd get tired of her in short order, but before that happened, she was pregnant, and they got married."

"Wow." As he drove toward the grocery store, she stated, "I really don't like your cousin Lyle."

"Yeah. Me, neither."

Chapter 27
Wednesday, June 24, 4:49 PM

Wanda gave up trying to think about her book and left her office. The envelope and its contents still lay on the table, almost glistening in a stray sunbeam from the shaded window. She would have been happier if the breeze from the overhead fans had sent it skittering off the table, perhaps to fall behind the heating stove and thereby be 'lost'. *I could claim I remembered getting an envelope, but before I could open it, it disappeared off the table. I could just throw it away. Claim I never got it, if anybody asks. I could... How do I get out of this?*

In a dark mood, she called Paula, several years older than her and able to speak her mind to anyone.

"What do you mean, you don't want to go?" Paula asked after Wanda had explained her problem. "A family reunion sounds like fun. You never did get a chance to meet Hank's family. This is the perfect chance!"

"But I'm not family! I mean, I am, but nobody here knows that I am. Except Bob."

"But they invited you anyway."

"I'm sure they think if I don't go, I'll be bored at home."

"Well, it's a Saturday, not like a weekday. So, if you don't go to the party, what will you do?"

"My usual Saturday stuff."

"When you lived here, that was shopping."

"Well, not that. I shop on Monday's."

"Then what?"

"I don't know. Housework. Reading. Maybe a jigsaw puzzle." She had found a door in the paneling next to the rocker on the front porch, When she opened it, the closet was full of jigsaw puzzles.

"That's all you do on a weekend? Dear, that is the definition of boring!"

"No, that isn't all. Usually on a Saturday, there's a group of people who come over and play dungeons."

"And you won't be doing that on the 4th because...?"

"Because the entire group will be at the party," she admitted softly.

"You said they also invited the Thomkins, or something like that, who aren't any relation to the family having the reunion."

"The Thompsons. Their daughter married one of Hank's cousins, so around here, that makes them family."

"My girl, I don't know why you are fighting the idea so hard. They invited you. Even went so far as to send you a written invitation. Sounds to me like they really want you there. And you have nothing better to do. So just go! Meet the family, have a good time. And if it isn't any fun, then say you have headache, go home and you can make your jigsaw puzzle."

Wanda hesitated for a long minute. "That isn't what I wanted to hear from you, Paula."

"If you expected me to say 'go ahead and stay home', then you haven't been listening to me. Ever since you got married, and Hank took on supporting both of you so you could write full time, you've practically been a hermit. I can't imagine it being any different there, where you hardly know anybody. Get out of the house! Meet the relatives. Mingle. Maybe you'll meet someone special."

"It's too soon to worry about meeting someone."

"Then I guess you won't meet anyone special. Not with an attitude like that. Now, look, I know Hank was all about letting you pursue your dream of writing. I can't say enough good things about him for giving you that support, in all the many ways that he gave it. But writing—even fiction—doesn't take just imagination. You also need a solid base of knowledge, of experience. Go out and get some new experiences for your imagination to use! Do some people watching. And what better place to do that than at a party where you don't already know everybody?"

"But Paula!"

"No buts. You called me for my advice, and I've given it. If you just want to hide in your house and not mingle with the natives, then go ahead and do that. But don't come running to me if your characters start sounding flat and unimaginative."

Wanda sighed, knowing the conversation was as good as over. And Paula was right. Well, except for the 'meeting someone special' remark. "Paula, I don't think you understand how much work going to the party will be. It's pot luck, and they want me to bake bread."

"You like baking bread."

"I like baking a **batch** of bread. I'll have to bake 5 batches to come anywhere close to enough for this large a party."

"What are they serving that they want so much bread?"

The host is serving hamburgers and hot dogs. So I assume somebody is bringing buns for that. I don't think they actually expect me to bring enough bread to feed everybody."

"There, you see? Even that excuse doesn't hold water. Bake a batch of bread. Or two. However far it goes will have to do. They don't expect one person to bring enough cake for everybody, do they?"

"No, they don't," Wanda admitted.

"There you go. Oh, supper's done. I've got to go, Wanda. Call me on the 5th and tell me all about the party!"

Before Wanda could say good-bye, the line went dead. She glared at her phone as she put it on the table, then shifted her glare to the invitation that was still sitting there in plain view. *Well, that didn't go the way I expected! Why do I feel like a wall flower whose mother is trying to convince her to go to the prom and have fun even though she doesn't have a date?*

But she probably is right about one thing. I don't need to bake 4 or 5 batches of bread. 2 batches would be 6 loaves, and that should be plenty for a pot luck party that's serving meat in a bun. Guess I'm going to a party.

She looked out the windows, saw Tommy working in his garden patch. She had meant to give his pint box back to him last Saturday after the game, but had forgotten to. Remembering what Bob had said about how to approach him with her gift, she thought, *No time like the present.*

She got the green belly bag from her bedroom, put a can of cold pop into it, grabbed the pint container and walked out to greet him as he worked. "Tommy, I've brought your pint container for you," she called from the vicinity of his red wagon.

He looked up, got up off his knees and walked over, his hands full of something she couldn't quite make out. When he got closer, she saw he carried several cucumbers. She placed the container in his wagon, opened the belly bag and handed him the can of pop.

"Thanks."

"Tommy, I got this belly bag the other day, thinking you could use it for keeping your money, so that it doesn't fall out of your pockets. It was dirt cheap, and I didn't think it would stay there very long at that price, so I snatched it up, intending to give it to you. If you'd like to have it." She showed him all the pockets, explained how she thought they could be used, and then she waited for him to respond.

He took a deep drink of his pop and considered the belly bag in her hands for a full minute. "Trade?"

Her heart jumped in something akin to triumph. "Trade what?"

He waved his hand at his wagon. "Whatever." Now that she took a good look, she saw that the wagon was full of vegetables; tomatoes, carrots, green onions, radishes, some yellow summer squash, cucumbers and zucchini were all tumbled together in a beautiful hodge-podge of colors.

"Great! Now, the price on the belly bag was $10, so let me know when I reach that, because I didn't bring any money from the house with me." Tommy grinned, and so did she. "Yes, I have a habit of leaving the house without any money, don't I? Well, let's have 5 zucchini and a pint of tomatoes. Red ones, this time." She saw a few of the 'odd colors', as Bob called them, but not enough for a pint. Tommy put 4 or 5 large tomatoes in the pint container, then got a plastic bag and put in 4 zucchini. As he held up the 5th green squash, he asked, "Saturday?"

"Yes, I've got a great side dish in mind," she stated.

He quickly made it 7 zucchini in the plastic bag and held it out to her. Then he pulled a waitress' pad of guest checks from next to his water cooler, and dutifully wrote out 'Pt tomatoes, 7 zucc, traded for belly bag'. He then placed the pad and his pen in the belly bag, and put it on.

Wanda chuckled. "Bob's going to make a business man out of you yet."

"Teaching me bookkeeping," Tommy stated. "Don't know how to input trades yet."

"Well, pay attention. That knowledge can be very important as you go through life."

"Thank you, Wanda."

"And thank you, Tommy. And remember, if you need another can of pop or anything, just come to the house."

As she walked back to the house with her produce, she realized Tommy had actually spoken some full sentences to her. Well, if you didn't count the missing subjects of those sentences. That was a lot better than when she had first moved in!

Chapter 28
Saturday, June 27, 5:58 PM

Chuck walked in the front door a couple minutes before 6, but Wanda and Ella were already putting the food on the table. "Ha!" he declared, sliding into his usual chair opposite Wanda. "I managed to get here in time."

Wanda smiled. "I think there would be enough for you. If you weren't too late."

"Well, we'll never know, because I am not late."

"What is it?" Rusty asked, picking out some of the white-covered noodles with a pasta spoon.

"It's called Fettuccini Alfredo." Wanda tried to pronounce it as the Italian would. "The Fettuccini refers to the thin noodle used; Alfredo is the type of sauce. I don't make it often"

"Is it hard to make?" Zita wondered.

"No, it's fairly simple to make," Wanda answered. "But it's also known as 'heart attack on a platter'. It's made with plenty of cream, butter and cheese, so those with any kind of heart disease probably shouldn't be eating it. I hope that doesn't include anybody here tonight."

"I think we're all safe," Chuck stated. "I eat a lot of burgers, and I haven't landed in the hospital yet."

As they started eating, Zita asked Chuck, "Have you talked to Bob recently?"

"Didn't I just say I eat a lot of burgers? Most evenings, Bob cooks them. So just about every night this week, why?"

"He's been acting weird," she stated. "When we went there on Wednesday, he spent close to an hour pacing between the front door and the back door. I walked past yesterday afternoon on my way to the post office, and he was standing at the end of the bar, taking a step up and a step down. Didn't see what he was

220

stepping on, but he kept going up and down, over and over again."

"Good for him," Wanda stated and claimed another spear of roasted parmesan zucchini for herself.

"Why do I get the idea you know something about this?" Chuck asked.

"He stated that when he works 14 hour days at the bar, he doesn't have time to do any exercise. So we brainstormed about forms of exercise he could do while we was at work, before the crowd comes in for the evening."

"What was he stepping up and down on?" Zita asked.

"The wooden box Helen uses when she needs to get into the cash register. At least, that's what I suggested he use."

"I've told him he can use my exercise machine whenever he wants," Chuck stated.

"He does, on Mondays. But one workout a week isn't enough. And working 14 hours a day only leaves him 10 hours to go home, sleep, and go back to work again."

"Well, there's an answer to that," Chuck declared. "It's called 'Hire another bartender'. I've told him that."

"Maybe he's afraid he'd hire someone like Useless Young," Felix suggested.

Chuck gave the lad a quizzical look. "What do you know about Useless Young?"

"Steve told me he was ready to quit, if you hired Useless again. But then you hired 5 wet-behind-the-ears teenagers, and he nearly quit right then. But he's glad he stuck around, because it turns out we're okay. We aren't idiots and we're not only willing to work, we're willing to learn."

The corner of Chuck's mouth twitched. "He keeps saying things like that, he'll swell your heads up, and then you won't be good for anything," he claimed.

There was relative silence for a moment, and Wanda wondered how to bring up the invitation she had received in the mail on Wednesday. She had put the invitation in her office before anybody could see it, and now she wondered how to bring it up.

"Oh, Chuck, I heard from the Thompsons this week," Ella stated. "You keep me so busy at work, I kept forgetting to mention it. They got your invitation, and they do plan on coming, arriving around 12:30 or 1:00. They're bringing the other 2 kids, too, and a German Chocolate cake."

"Good," Chuck acknowledged, and then paused his eating to look down the table at Wanda, as if he expected her to say something.

So she did. "Ella, I've changed my mind, and I will be at the party. And yes, you can put me down for bread."

If she had had any remaining misgivings about whether or not she was actually wanted at the party, the excited reactions the kids expressed made it abundantly clear that she was. Even Chuck smiled, not with smugness, but with pleasure, and resumed his eating.

And somehow, having made the announcement, she found she was actually looking forward to the party.

Chapter 29
Wednesday, July 1, 5:30 PM

Wanda was answering an email before leaving her office for the day when her phone rang. She tried to finish her thought before she answered it, and missed the call. It was recognized as coming from Bob's Bar, and she thought she could finish the email before she called back. He couldn't be needing a cocktail waitress; the place was usually pretty empty on Wednesdays, except when the kids came in. He could wait a minute or two.

She had just hit the send button when her phone rang again. This time when she picked it up, it identified the caller as Chuck. She answered. "Yes?"

"Wanda? You should be here."

"Where is 'here'?"

"At Bob's Bar. You should come. It wouldn't've happened without you."

There seemed to be a lot of talking on the other end, and his voice sounded rather thick.

"You aren't making sense, Chuck. Are you drinking?"

"Of course I've been drinking! I'm shelebrating!"

"Isn't it early to celebrate the 4th of July." *In college, I knew some guys who would 'celebrate' whatever day of the week it was. Or that they managed to get out of bed that morning.*

"No, not thatsh. Ohh." His voice went distant, as if he pulled the phone away from his face. "I must have drunk that beer too fasht. Here, Bob, you talk to her."

"I'm cooking. I can't do that and be on the phone, too."

"No, I guesh not. Ella! Where are you, Ella?"

"Here, let me have that." And then another masculine voice asked, "Wanda?"

"Yes?"

"This is Steve. Chuck is a little drunk, because he drank an entire beer without coming up for air. Anyway, he wants you here, at Bob's Bar, because he's celebrating, but he wants to tell you all about it when you get here. It's really important to him."

She sighed, wondering what the mystery was all about. "Well, you might tell him for me that I don't really care for drunks. And in the 2nd place, well... give me 5 or 10 minutes to get there."

"Okay, okay. Now he wants to know if you've eaten yet."

That's an idea. If I take some money, I could eat while I'm there. On the other hand, I have food here, and don't need to fritter away my money. "No, I haven't eaten yet." *I'll take some money with me, just in case, but if this doesn't take too long, I'll just come home to eat.*

"Good, good. Then we'll see you in 5?"

"About that long," she agreed, and hung up.

* * *

5:45 PM

Wanda entered Bob's place through the back door, which had become her habit. Chuck, it turned out, was standing behind the bar, where the teens were sitting. Bob was in the tiny kitchen. She said hello to Steve and Ivan as she passed them at the pool table. The rest of Chuck's crew were at a table in the middle of the bar. Wanda slid onto the bar seat next to Tommy. "Okay, I'm here, Chuck. What's up?"

He was drinking from a can of pop, and lowered it so quickly, he spilled some of it down the front of him. "Wanda! We finished the house!"

"What, you mean the house you're building in Fullerton?"

"The exact one!" he agreed with a grin. "We actually finished it 2 days ahead of time! Our deadline was this Friday, and I turned the keys over to Mr Zimmerman at 4 o'clock this afternoon."

"Congratulations," she said. "You could have told me—"

"And it's all because of you."

She wished she could smell the can he was drinking from. She had a sneaky suspicion he was still drinking alcohol. "I

224

didn't have anything to do with it," she denied.

"Yes, you did," he insisted. "If you hadn't moved into town, hadn't hired these kids, I mean, youngsters, to help clean and organize your house, I probably wouldn't have realized how grown up and responsible they've become. They aren't adults, yet, but they are well on their way. You helped me see that, and so I hired them. They worked hard to get us caught up on that house, and I am pleased as all get out that we got 'er done early, because, we got a bonus! And all my crew are getting a bonus, too! Not until Monday, so Bob can make sure the checks are made out right, but you're getting them!"

Bob had come out of the kitchen, handing plates to the kids. "Chuck, either make yourself useful or at least get out of the way."

"Well, that's nice for you and your crew. I'm very happy for you."

"And you would like a sloe gin coke," Chuck guessed.

"No," she returned. "But I will take a lemonade."

Chuck filled a glass and gave it to her. "And what would you like to eat? Do you want to see a menu?"

"Maybe you could give me the lemonade to go?" she asked. "I was just getting ready to fix my supper at home."

"Chuck, you forgot something," Bob stated as he passed by with plates of food for the older members of the crew.

"I did?" Chuck asked, and looked thoughtful for a moment. "Sorry, I've been planning this since 3, and I kind of got ahead of myself. Wanda, my crew and I are celebrating. I am buying them all supper and a drink. I asked you to come here so that I could include you in that celebration. Well, and tell you why we're celebrating, but to include you."

She frowned in incomprehension, and realized the boys— Tommy, Rusty, and Felix—were all trying hard not to giggle. She resisted the urge to tell them not to eat while laughing, lest they choke. Instead, she reminded Chuck, "I'm not part of your crew."

He drew a breath, possibly to keep his temper. "You're the reason why my crew is this big. I need to thank you somehow."

Bob stopped nearby on the way back to the kitchen. "Wanda, I know he said things all out of order, and he babbled quite a bit, but he really wants to thank you." He grinned and added, "It's not like I'm a 5-star restaurant."

"That's an idea!" Chuck declared. "Forget about eating here, Wanda. I'll take you for a steak in Albion!"

She stared at him with wide eyes, almost in a panic.

Bob shook his head. "Chuck, you're hopeless," he said and went back to the kitchen.

"Well, if that's your alternative way of thanking me, then I'll take a grilled cheese."

"With fries?" Bob asked from the kitchen.

"Cauliflower," Wanda answered.

"Give me a minute," he returned.

Chuck leaned on the bar and took her hand. "We could do it tomorrow. Go to Albion for a steak."

She tugged her hand free and quietly told him, "Chuck, I'm not looking for a date."

"Well, how am I supposed to know when you change your mind, if you won't tell me when it happens?"

"What makes you think it will happen?"

Bob emerged from the kitchen with a burger and fries and handed it to him. Chuck came around the end of the counter and sat down next to Wanda. "Hope springs eternal," he muttered. He ate a couple fries and said, "You are a hard nut to crack."

"Maybe I'm not a nut that needs to be cracked," she returned. "Maybe I'm a rock, a perfectly happy pebble without any cracks."

"Chuck," Bob said warningly as he placed another burger and fries next to Chuck. Wanda wondered who that plate was for.

"Okay, okay, I'll shut up," Chuck mumbled to himself.

The bar settled into a quiet broken only by 3 men talking quietly at a table and the occasional click of pool balls hitting each other. After a couple moments, Bob placed Wanda's meal in front of her, then he sat down next to Chuck and began to eat.

"You're included in this celebration, Bob?" Wanda asked.

"I can't leave out my partner," Chuck stated.

"Partner!" Wanda exclaimed.

"I told you about that," Bob stated in confusion.

"You said you're his bookkeeper, and he's your handyman."

"Well, yeah, of course," Chuck agreed. "But we're each a silent partner for the other one."

"Give her a break, you two," Steve called from the pool table. "She's only been in town a month or so. She can't have you two completely figured out in that short a time."

"What's to figure out?" Chuck asked of no one in particular. "I'm Chuck and he's Bob."

"No," Bob disagreed. "I'm Bob and you're Chuck."

"Have you looked in the mirror lately? You are obviously Bob, which makes me Chuck."

"The 2 of you sound like Quince and Yantz," Wanda told them, and popped a piece of deep fried cauliflower into her mouth, hurriedly caught it between her teeth and began mouth breathing, trying to cool it off. Finally, she took a drink of her cold lemonade, which cooled the vegetable enough she could chew it up and swallow.

"Are you okay?" Chuck asked.

She felt her cheeks go red. "Hotter than I thought it was."

"Straight out of the fryer," Bob stated. "I guess you don't know us as well as we thought, because that's what we do when one of us is being pig-headed, and the other wants to make them see it. Eventually the pig-headed one gets the idea."

"Or laughs at the silliness," Chuck added.

"Oh." She thought about that as she took another sip of her drink. "Is that what the Eggers brothers do?"

"Oh, heck, no," Chuck declared. "They do it out of sheer contrariness."

"If one of them were to come around to the same viewpoint of the other, the other wouldn't skip a beat in reversing their opinion, just so they'd be on opposite sides again." Bob added.

Wanda wasn't sure she believed them. She tore a corner off her grilled cheese and wondered if it was cool enough to eat. "I think you're pulling my leg."

"Nope," Chuck asserted. "Legend has it they were like that even before they were born. Can you imagine sharing a womb with a twin you're always bickering with?"

Wanda smiled. "It's hard to imagine." She dared to eat the corner she'd torn off.

Bob told her, "Gram said they couldn't be told apart when they were young. But life hasn't been easy on them. Yanzt got hit on the head, and the swelling never completely went down, so he's got a bump. It's why he almost always wears a cap. And Quince has a scar on his face. If you look close, and if he's shaved in the past week, you can see it. Nobody seems to know how he got it."

Chuck swallowed his latest bite. "Maybe he got it shaving. He doesn't do it enough to be any good at it."

"That's not a nice thing to say," Wanda stated softly.

"Wanda, I swear, that's what Quince told me, over a decade ago, when I asked about the scar. He said he didn't remember, but cutting himself shaving seemed a good possibility, because he'd never been any good at it."

"They'll be at the party this weekend," Bob stated. "They never miss a party. You ask him, Wanda, and see what tall tale he gives you."

"I'd have to figure out which one to ask," she protested. Both men seemed to favor baseball caps.

"Just ask him if he's Quince," Bob told her. "It'd tickle them both pink that somebody still can't tell them apart."

Wanda took a bite of her sandwich while she pondered what to say next. "I don't know, Chuck; you don't seem to know the difference between a nut that needs to be cracked and a pebble that won't crack."

Chuck laughed, and it was a genuine laugh. "I knew inviting you would be worth the effort."

She smiled at his choice of words. "Effort? You made a phone call. And somebody else actually issued the invite."

"Cause I could tell I was screwing it up. And then I was afraid you wouldn't come because I didn't send a written invitation."

"Impromptu parties happen in the Big City, too, Country Boy."

"I'm glad to hear that, City Girl." He cleared his throat and returned to eating. "How about after you finish your supper, we pick a song on the juke box and dance?"

No, no, no, we're veering into territory where I don't want to go. Again. "You're assuming I know how. How about this? We play a game of pool."

"Okay," he agreed. *I hope he knows better than to put his hands all over me.*

The game of pool actually didn't last very long. Chuck kept his hands to himself, but just to be sure, she always chose to play from the opposite side of the table from him. Sometimes, that meant she didn't have any good shots to take, and she'd have to try banking. Her angles were a little off, and the ball never quite went where she wanted it. Before long, she was shaking his hand. "Congratulations, Chuck. I guess I should practice more."

"You know the theory," he agreed with a smile. "Practice is probably all you need to give me a run for my money."

"No, no money involved. I'm not a gambling woman. Well, Chuck, it's been nice being included in your little celebration. Thanks for inviting me. And now I think I'll head home."

"Yeah, everybody's headed out," he agreed. "Thank you for coming, Wanda. It's been... fun."

Wanda waved at the others, who were all gathering their things and getting ready to leave, and then she slipped out the back door.

It was fun. Except for one or two moments that seemed... strained. Or unnecessarily nervous. Chuck doesn't seem to take it serious that I'm not looking for a date.

Chapter 30
Saturday, July 4, 10:33 AM

Ella had asked Wanda to arrive early, citing she would need some help getting things ready for the party. Considering how frequently Ella had helped prepare Saturday suppers, never complaining, Wanda had agreed at once. Besides, if she could help with the preparations, maybe she wouldn't feel so much like an outsider. Felix was coming over to be Wanda's guide to Chuck's home, somewhere west of town.

While she waited for Felix, Wanda wrapped her 9 loaves of homemade bread in clean dish towels, then into grocery sacks, which she placed in her SUV. She felt guilty for only having 9 loaves of bread, even though reason told her she didn't need to feed the entire reunion.

"Hi, Wanda! You ready to go?" Felix called from the front door. Wanda was in her office, having just shut off both her window units, since she wouldn't be there all day, and it would likely be cool, or at least cooler, in the evening.

Wanda grabbed her belly bag and her keys and met him on the porch. "The bread is in the car. Is there anything else I need?"

"A swim suit?" Felix suggested. "People might go swimming in the afternoon."

"What, you mean in the river?" She remembered Chuck's place was supposed to be fairly close to the river, but she wasn't sure she wanted to swim in it.

"No. Chuck's got an indoor swimming pool behind his garage. Sometimes he has pool parties, usually in July or August, when it really gets hot."

"It hasn't already been hot?" she asked.

"It'll get worse," he answered.

"Well, let me find my swimsuit, in case I decide to join them."

"And a towel," Felix offered as she hurried to her bedroom. "It's Bring Your Own Towel."

Wanda grabbed another grocery bag and stuffed it with her swimsuit, a towel, and a pair of jeans, in case the evening got chilly. It wasn't long before they were in her car and on their way. "Turn west at the corner," Felix told her as they exited her driveway.

"Yes, I know that much," she answered. "I just don't know how far to drive, or if there's any other turns to make."

"The next turn is into his driveway, and it's just a little past the railroad tracks. There'll be signs or balloons or something to mark the place. There usually is for a swim party."

"What did you guys do Thursday and Friday, since you got the house in Fullerton done?"

"We did a lot of work on Chuck's houses. Especially the old farmhouse, which sits empty most of the time. You know, creaky floor boards, patching cracks, that sort of thing. Made sure all the lights work, and the plumbing, too. Lit the pilot light on the hot water heater. Washed all the dust away. Made the beds and put out towels and stuff. Ella and Zita spent time making phone calls, trying to drum up new work for us to do."

"Ugh! I would have preferred working on the houses."

"That's what Zita said. Some of the oldsters made fun of them for complaining, so after lunch, Chuck put the girls to work making beds, and had Steve and Dick making phone calls. Don't know if that continued after we left, but Chuck has several places to go on Monday and Tuesday to give price quotes."

"No work to do on Monday?"

"Oh, yeah, we have a roofing job in St Edward for Monday and Tuesday. Steve will be in charge."

"Wait, did he have you kids working more than 4 hours? On Thursday and Friday?"

"No, since we were working on Chuck's houses, he had us youngsters arrive at 9, take a half hour lunch at noon, and then take off at 1:30. And here it is, coming up on the right."

Two houses, a barn and another building stood on the right side of the road. A sign near the rural mail box next to the driveway declared this was 'Chuck's Place' and a number of balloons tied onto the fence were blowing in the breeze. The balloons were red, white, and blue, and there was even some patriotic bunting attached to the fence as well.

"Well, he doesn't want anybody to miss it, does he?" She slowed down to make the turn.

"The bunting is new," Felix stated. "And the balloons are usually all colors. He must have decided on a July 4th theme."

"Well, that would make sense," she said and slowly entered the barn yard. The newer house came first, with a 2-car garage, a long and low porch where the front door was, and then a larger section with windows. There were already half a dozen cars parked, some in front of the house and a couple on the other side of the barn yard, facing the fenced corn field.

"Where should I park?"

"Anywhere," Felix opined. "It probably won't be long before the cars are lined up on both sides, all the way out to the barn, and maybe beyond."

"As many as that?" She pulled in next to the last car in front of the house.

"I wouldn't be surprised."

"Can you help me carry the bread in, Felix?"

"Sure."

It was a surprisingly long way back to the front door. Wanda deduced the house was larger than anything she was used to. She had her own house in Belgrade, which seemed large to her, but this house seemed to dwarf it, and she hadn't even stepped inside yet. As she walked, she noted red tulips and lilies of the valley running riot around the raised porch of the farmhouse, which rested on a small rise. There were also a number of cats of all colors roaming and sitting around the outer farm buildings.

Felix stepped inside the newer house without knocking, and held the door open for her. This central room was a multi-purpose room. In the adjacent right hand corner was a fireplace with a large screen TV on the mantel. Two big sofas at right angles to each other faced the angled fireplace. Straight forward from the door was a triangular island marking the extent of the kitchen. Bob, Ella and Zita were all in that kitchen, so Wanda couldn't really see any details. In the opposite corner from the front door were sliding doors out to a patio. In front of the sliding doors stood a large dining table, although there weren't any chairs in sight.

"Hi, Wanda!" Ella called. "You brought a lot of bread! If there's any left, can I take some home with me?"

"That suits me," Wanda stated. "Where do you want it?"

"Just put it on the island for now. Eventually, we'll clean the island off and use it for the desserts."

"What can I do to help?"

Ella rolled her eyes. "Just pitch in wherever. There's a plastic tablecloth for the table somewhere. We need to get that on the table before we put any food or anything on it. Felix, go outside and see if they took all the tablecloths out there, or if they left one in here someplace. And if they left it in here, where did they leave it?"

"Okay." Felix was out the sliding door in a flash.

Ella grinned. "I knew he wouldn't want to get stuck in the kitchen, but the guys are working just as hard out there."

"What are they doing?"

"Putting up tents. They brought all the tables and chairs from the fire hall and any others they could borrow. They're setting them up, putting table clothes on them. Plus a tub of ice for the soda pop. Setting up trash cans. Believe me, they're busy."

"Who's here so far?"

"Chuck, his crew, Bob, and now you."

Zita moved a large coffee pot to the island, pushing things out of her way so it would sit directly on the island top. "Here it is!" she declared, and pulled a flat bit of plastic from the stack of stuff currently on the island. "The table cloth!"

"Good! Give it here," Wanda suggested. "I think I can put down a tablecloth."

"We should tape the tablecloth down," Bob stated. "Every time somebody opens the patio door, a breeze will go through, and the edges of the cloth could land in anything."

"Good idea," Zita said, and walked over to open the patio door. After an ear-piercing whistle, she called out, "Hey! Could we borrow the tape for a minute?" Without waiting, she walked back into the kitchen and started her next chore.

Wanda tore open the package and took out the red and blue plastic inside, stuck the packaging into her back pocket while she set about unfolding and laying down the plastic cover. Just as she got it straightened out, the sliding doors opened and a breeze sent the plastic sliding along the table top. She made a wild grab to catch it before it fell on the floor.

"Sorry." Chuck stepped in and closed the door behind him. "I should have knocked before I opened the door, since you don't have it taped down yet."

"Happily, I caught it before it got very far."

"Let's get it back in place, and I'll tape it down for you." He taped the corners down tight against the table legs, then taped the center of each side to the bottom of the table.

Wanda was surprised he was using duct tape, and said so.

"It gets the job done."

"But doesn't it leave a sticky residue?"

"It's not so hard to get off if you know how," he answered. He glanced at her for a moment. "If you ever need to, Rusty knows how."

"Thank you. I'll keep that in mind."

He applied a final piece of tape. "Okay, I don't think it's going to escape again."

"If it does, we'll call it Houdini," Wanda quipped.

He smiled as he moved toward the sliding door. "Good to have you here, Wanda."

"Oh, I'm just another mouth to feed," she said as her cheeks went pink.

"It's worth it," he muttered, and then was back outside.

"Is there anything I can put on the table yet?"

"Yes." Ella indicated a batch of grocery sacks sitting on the sofas. "Start with the paper plates and plastic silverware. Arrange it so that people come in the door, get their plates and utensils, go around the table getting food, and then go back out the door. All the seating for eating will be outside."

Wanda placed the plates and utensils on the edge of the table closest to the door. The rest of the grocery sacks held a dozen or more bags of chips. She started to place one bag of each flavor on the table, but even that looked like too many chips.

"Bob, did you bring the chips?" she asked.

"No, the oldsters on Chuck's crew brought them. And more are likely to show up as people start arriving. Take the extra stuff down that hall." He pointed down the hall headed toward the garage. "The last door on the left is the office. We can store some food in there."

She found the office easily enough. It had a sofa along the right wall, a desk in the middle of the room with a couple chairs in front of it, 2 file cabinets in the far corner, and a refrigerator and freezer chest along the left wall. *What does Chuck do in his office that he needs a refrigerator and a chest freezer? Well, none of my business.*

She brought in the rest of the chips and lined them on the couch so that the different flavors could be seen relatively easily, then went back to the grand room to see what else she could do.

A platter of freshly picked and sliced vegetables had appeared on the table, next to the plates. Bob had 2 other platters ready and went past her with one in each hand. "Hey, open the office door for me, will ya?"

"Of course." After she opened the door, he set one platter on the freezer so he could open the refrigerator, where he placed both platters, one on top of the other. "I was wondering what he did with a frig and a freezer in his office," Wanda remarked.

"Mostly, he keeps ice in the freezer," Bob answered. "Sometimes a few steaks. Usually, the frig holds beer, pop and water. The beer is in a cooler today. The pop and water are outside, in a tub full of ice. Along with the pop I brought." He paused halfway to the doorway. "You brought bread, right?"

"Homemade bread," she confirmed.

"Well, I'm done slicing and dicing veggies, at least for now, so I guess I'll slice your bread."

"I'm sorry," she said as they started back. "I should have thought to do that."

"Don't worry about it," he tossed over his shoulder. "Sliced bread tends to dry out faster." Which was true; she knew that.

Now 2 bowls had appeared on the table, one with diced tomatoes and one with sliced tomatoes. In addition, Zita had placed a large dispenser of lemonade on the island next to the coffee pot. The island was beginning to get crowded, so Wanda grabbed 3 of her sacks of bread and took them to the office, where she placed them atop the frig.

When she got back, Ella was moving her notebook and assorted papers to the coffee table, which helped clear the island, although there was still a lot of empty packaging on the thing. Remembering all the bits and pieces of plastic packaging she had stuffed into her back pocket, Wanda picked the scraps off the island and asked, "Where's the waste basket?"

Bob was drying off a cutting board. "Should be a big one right outside the patio door, on the left."

"Thanks." It was getting hot outside, and realizing how cool the house AC was set, she shut the patio door behind her, then emptied her hand and her back pocket into the trash can she found.

She paused to look around. This place was obviously getting ready for a party. The house had 2 wings reaching west from the patio, which had a slatted roof that broke up the sunlight. Big tents had been erected between the wings, with the sides tied back or up, providing shade but allowing any breeze to wander through. She saw any number of tables, long folding tables and card tables, but each with a red, white or blue tablecloth taped to it. A number of cats and kittens wandered through the area, investigating everything but not letting any of the working men (and boys) get too close.

"Time to light the fire, Chuck?" she heard Steve ask.

"Yeah, I think so," he answered.

Wanda turned toward the voices, realized there was a brick cooking pit over to the right, close to the patio, where a plastic toy wading pool held a heaping mountain of ice. Chuck picked up a bag of charcoal and poured it into the body of the pit, then Steve put the grill back in place.

Wanda knew a moment of confusion, then one of fury. But she didn't want to make a big scene and make him regret inviting her. She walked over to the grill as Chuck lit the charcoal. "Hello, Chuck."

He smiled and asked, "Houdini hasn't escaped, has it?"

"No," she returned, with a slight smile. "I'm confused, Chuck."

He cocked his head to one side a smidgeon. "What about?"

"Remember when you bought that wood from me?"

"Woops," Ivan muttered, and walked away.

Chuck's eyelids drooped, and he guardedly said, "I remember doing that."

"You were going to use it to cook hamburgers at today's party," Wanda went on. "And yet, you're using charcoal."

"That's because the wood isn't dry enough," he explained. "But don't worry, it'll be dry in time to use in the fireplace this winter." She wanted to stay mad at him, and yet, she didn't want to ruin the day for everybody by her being mad at him.

A loud whistle got their attention, and Zita hollered, "Come back inside, Wanda! Bob's got a problem with your bread!"

"Oh, no," she groaned and hurried back inside, sure the bread had somehow gotten smashed, or had gone completely dry, or something horrible.

"What is it? What's wrong?" she demanded as she entered the kitchen.

"I can't cut this," Bob told her, and held up her swim suit. "This one, neither." He waved at the rolled up pair of blue jeans.

Wanda felt her face burn. "Oh! Felix told me to bring a swim suit and towel, in case there was swimming this afternoon. And I worried the evening might get chilly, so I brought jeans."

"I'm still not going to slice them up," Bob said with a gentle smile.

"I should hope not!" she declared, and snatched them away.

"You could put your clothes in my bedroom," Chuck suggested from behind her. "Until you need them."

She turned to face him, her clothes and towel hugged to her chest. "I think the office will do fine," she answered. "I have to go there to get the bread anyway."

"Sure, that works," Chuck agreed and stepped back out of her way. Wanda hurried to the office and back, just in time to hear Chuck tell Bob, "Suddenly, I want to open up the pool."

"I never mentioned that possibility," Ella told him. "When I contacted people."

"Well, don't do it on my account," Wanda told him as she handed a bag of bread to Bob. "I was following Felix's advice."

"Well, we'll see how people feel when the afternoon gets hotter," Chuck decided.

"Hello, hello." Wanda didn't recognize any of the people walking in the door. Ella got up and abandoned her notebook and papers to greet them. They were, apparently, her relatives from Omaha. One of the teen girls came forward and held up a covered cake container. "Mom's devil's food cake with chocolate walnut frosting. Where should I put it?"

Zita had just put yet another dispenser—this one of tea—on the island, but she paused to take the cake. "Do you have a name on the container?"

"No, I don't think so. We usually just recognize it when the party's over."

"Oh, this party is too big," Zita stated. "Just a second."

She pulled out a roll of masking tape and a pen. "Just write a name on the tape, we'll put the tape on the container and hopefully we won't have too many labels that say 'Bob', 'Chuck', or 'Alice'. Those are popular names in Belgrade."

"Mom was worried we'd get lost once we left Belgrade, but the decorations at the driveway were a dead giveaway."

"I'm pretty sure that's what Chuck had in mind when he put them up. Or had them put up. We've been working for 2 days to get the place ready. The whole crew has."

"Oh, is this a... ranch?"

"No, Chuck sold the land, except for the farm yard. Chuck has a construction company, and he hired us all to help him get ready for the party."

"He hired his own construction company? To get ready for a party?"

"Seemed only fair, since he needed help, and we were all invited to the party. By the way, my name is Zita Craig."

"Hi. I'm Violet Bosiljevac, Ella's cousin."

"So am I, on her other side. And the man behind me, slicing bread, is Bob, another cousin. And this is Wanda. She's the new girl in town, only been here about a month, so she's probably as nervous about being here as you are."

"Somebody brought homemade bread?" Violet asked.

"It was specifically requested," Wanda stated.

"Helen hasn't arrived yet," Chuck was saying. "She's picking up a young relative who otherwise wouldn't have any transportation, but I expect her shortly. You can come outside and claim a table to sit at, if you want. I need to check the fire, see if it's time to start cooking the meat yet."

"Any chance I could get a slice of that bread?" Violet asked. "I didn't get up in time for breakfast, and I'm starving."

"Ask and you shall receive," Bob stated, and turned around with a plate full of sliced bread, which he handed to Wanda. "Go ahead and put that on the table." He followed her with a large tub of margarine, which he opened and put on the table next to the bread. "Might as well get yourself some vegetables, if you want, and feel free to open a bag of chips. Zita's organizing the drinks. She's got coffee, lemonade and tea. And there's pop and water in a tub of ice out on the patio."

"Is he always that nice?" Vi whispered to Wanda when Bob went back to the kitchen area.

"Bob is always nice," Wanda stated.

"Is he your boy friend?"

Wanda smiled. "No."

"Well, I find him dreamy."

"I understand," Wanda told her, and moved back toward the kitchen as the girl headed outside with her plate of snacks.

More people arrived, and Ella greeted all of them. Zita, Wanda and Bob accepted whatever they brought in the way of food and decided where to put it. Before long, the dining table was strained by a load that included 2 types of potato salad, a carrot salad, an apple salad, a salad that seemed to include coconut and small marshmallows, bowls of pickle relish, pickle chips and olives, a plate with slices of zucchini bread, 2 bean salads and a succotash salad. Meanwhile, every flat surface in the kitchen was taken by any number of cakes, pies, and other desserts. In between arrivals, Bob pulled out bottles of ketchup, mustard and more pickles, which he put on the table.

"Bob, I think we underestimated how much space we need for desserts," Zita complained. "I wanted to put out cups of lemonade and tea, at least, so people wouldn't have to fill one. But as it is, I've only got enough room on the island for about 2 cakes and 1 pie."

"Okay, come with me," Bob told her, and they disappeared down the hallway headed away from the garage.

Wanda checked all the cakes they had received so far; there were 3 chocolate cakes. She took 2 of them to the office and left them on the desk. There were pens, pencils and bits of paper on the desk. She opened the center desk drawer—or tried to— and swept everything into it and out of the way. Then she felt around inside the drawer and found the item that seemed to be sticking up too high for proper functioning was a picture frame.

She pulled it out to fold the stand part down flat, and caught sight of the picture. It was her and Hank, on their wedding day. *How did this get here? Hank said he sent a copy to his grandmother. Oh! Could this be the missing picture of Hank from that frame I took down to put up my artwork? Which, again, how did it get here?* But she didn't have time to sort things out. It had obviously been put out of sight for a reason. *If I ask about it, Chuck will know I know... He'd think I've been snooping! And if he hasn't recognized me by now, he's blind. Oh, this is terrible. He knows who I am, and nobody was supposed to know that!*

She shoved the picture and frame back in the drawer and closed the desk, fearful of being caught rummaging through Chuck's desk. By the time she got back to the kitchen, Bob and Zita had reappeared with a short, long bookcase, which they placed along the wall between the kitchen and the front door.

"That's good," Zita decided. "There should be room for 5 desserts on that, and that will give me room to put out some glasses of lemonade and tea. "Thanks for remembering this bookcase, Bob."

"I just hope Chuck doesn't get stuck doing all the clean-up tomorrow."

"I'll come out and help, if I have to walk," Zita promised.

"I would, but I have to open up," Bob said. "Now, let's get a tablecloth and some tape and get the bookcase covered."

While they worked on that, more people arrived. Wanda took 2 apple pies to the office, and another big bowl of potato salad to the office refrigerator, since the kitchen refrigerator was full of plates of hamburger patties and hot dogs, each plate stacked atop others.

Bob made the tablecloth fit inside the shelves of the bookshelf. He and Zita put 5 cakes along the top of the unit, and put 2 pies, a platter of cookies and a pan of lemon bars on the middle shelf. On the bottom shelf, they placed a stack of smaller paper plates and plastic silverware. While they were busy, Wanda continued accepting food, and running it to the office, since the table, island, kitchen counters, and now the bookcase, were full.

"Gloria, we've been through this," Helen said as she came in the door. "If Lyle doesn't want to come, that's his decision, but we told him weeks ago that we expected you and Sammy to be here, as part of the family."

Bob abruptly stood upright. "Hello, Gloria."

The girl's face turned bright pink, and she mumbled, "Hello, Bob." She turned away to face Ella, who seemed overly excited to have the young woman show up. "I'm Sorry, Ella, I didn't have anything to bring for the pot luck."

Wanda spoke up, "I brought enough to cover for you."

Gloria looked at her and asked, "Why would you do that?"

"Technically, I didn't, but I brought so much, it can easily cover." Wanda turned to Helen. "Helen, it's good to see you."

"You don't come into the bar on the weekends," Helen complained. "I understand you're busy on Saturdays, but Friday is still lively."

With a quick glance at Gloria, Wanda said, "There's just some people I don't care to see, not any night of the week."

Helen nodded. "I understand. We'll talk about that another time. Have you met my husband, Keith? Keith, this is Wanda, the new girl in town."

They were all startled when Bob hollered out the patio door, "Hey! How's that fire coming?" Wanda couldn't make out what the answer was, but Bob hollered back, "I'm bringing out the first batch of meat. People are getting hungry." He hurried to the kitchen refrigerator, took a plate of burgers and dogs outside.

"Gloria, would you and Sammy like to start eating?" Ella asked. "There's salads and vegetables to get started with."

With her face going pink again, Gloria quietly stated, "Sammy only eats hot dogs. So I guess we'll wait."

Ella stooped down onto her knees to talk to the boy, and Helen took advantage of the moment to hand her donation to the pot luck to Zita. "You girls seem to have things organized well."

"Bob's a big help," Zita stated. "Green bean salad, huh?"

"Just put it in the office frig," Helen suggested. "That way it'll be fresh for the supper crowd."

Wanda took charge of the new salad and took it to the office. On her way back, she noticed Ella, Gloria and Sammy were at the table. Gloria was putting little samples of various salads on a paper plate, while Ella took hold of a piece of Wanda's bread and started slathering butter on it. Then she took another paper plate, put the bread on it, and offered it to Sammy.

The patio door opened, Bob stared at the table. "Oh, good grief," he muttered, and hurried out the front door.

While Wanda wondered what had him so upset, Ella pretended nothing unusual had happened. "What would you like to drink, Gloria? We have lemonade and tea in here, water and pop outside in a tub of ice. Your parents and family should be here shortly, and I bet we could find a nice table outside where you could all sit together."

"Um, lemonade," Gloria stated. Zita had a few glasses poured, so Ella was able to just pick one up and then guide the young woman and her son outside to the patio.

Bob came through the front door with a big restaurant-style bag of hamburger buns and several small bags of hot dog buns. He rushed over to the table and frantically began to reorganize, all while muttering to himself.

Wanda hurried over to intercede before he knocked something onto the floor. "Bob." She grabbed his hands to stop him. "Bob!"

He stopped short and looked up, panic in his eyes. "I forgot the buns!"

"No, Bob, you didn't forget. You just now brought them in." Wanda tried to reason with him.

"This isn't enough. This isn't enough." He pulled away from Wanda and stepped to the patio door. "Felix! Rusty!" He came back as if in too much of a hurry to stand still.

"Bob, calm down," Wanda said quietly. "This is what we'll do. I'll put this stack of paper plates atop the kitchen frig, and now you have some room for the buns."

He watched her move the 2nd stack of plates and blurted out, "Wanda, you're a life-saver!" He threw his arms around her and gave her a hug.

The patio door opened, and Chuck stopped short. "Whoa, that was something I wasn't expecting to see."

Bob let go of her and turned to face his cousin. "I'd forgotten the buns."

"So you hugged Wanda?"

"What's up, Bob?" Felix asked as he and Rusty worked their way past Chuck.

"Boys, I've left the buns in my car. There may be some in the trunk, too." He tossed them his car keys. "Bring them all in and put them in the office."

As the boys hurried off, Chuck grabbed a paper plate and returned to the grill.

"If he's sending meat in, we need a place to put it, and he'll need another plate of meat. Wanda, you run out the next plate of meat, and I'll put one of the bean salads in the office."

Chuck was scooping burgers and dogs off the grill and placing them on the paper plate. He looked out of sorts as she placed the fresh meat where he could reach it. "Take the dirty plate in with you," he instructed. "Wash it up so it doesn't cross-contaminate, and then I'll use that to send in the next batch."

"Okay," she agreed, although inside, she bristled at what sounded like orders.

As she turned away, he asked, "How long you been giving Bob hugs?"

She turned back around. "He was in a frenzy trying to find a place for the buns. I solved his dilemma. He hugged me in relief. If you'd come in a second later, I would have been pushing him away. Not that it's any of your business."

"Maybe not," he reluctantly agreed, and sighed. He picked up the last cooked burger and added it to the paper plate. "Thank you for ferrying the meat back and forth. As for the other, I apologize. Old habits die hard."

She bit her tongue before she could say, 'Especially if you make no effort to kill them.' Instead, she picked up the paper plate of meat and the dinner plate that had held raw meat, and headed back inside.

Zita took the dirty plate from her and headed for the kitchen. Bob was just finishing up rearranging the table, and placed the meat in a newly created space next to the bags of buns. "Sorry, Wanda, I wasn't thinking," he stated softly.

"No, you weren't, and that's a side of you I haven't seen before. I don't mind the hug, but some people actually started acting jealous!"

He raised his eye brows for a moment, and then shrugged. "Old habits, I guess."

"Well, I don't appreciate being treated like an old habit." She heard the door open behind her, turned and saw that people were coming in, quite a few of them. After food, no doubt. "We should get out of people's way."

They moved back to the kitchen, where Zita was drying the dinner plate that formerly held raw meat. "Things okay between you?"

"I think so," Bob said.

"Yes," Wanda stated.

"Any other chips?" someone asked.

"Yes," Wanda answered cheerfully. "What flavor?"

"Cheddar, if you have it."

"I'll go check. Be right back." She got back with a bag of cheddar-flavored chips, which she added to the table. She noticed that all the cooked meat was already gone. The influx of diners were grabbing drinks from the island—or not—and filing back outside to find a table.

"Has everybody arrived yet?" Wanda asked.

"Not quite," Ella answered from the coffee table. "The Egger brothers won't show up until supper time. The Thompsons still aren't here. And a couple others from out of town."

A doorbell rang. Ella got up and opened the front door. The Thompsons had arrived. While Ella gushed at the parents, a handsome young man brought a covered cake display to the kitchen. "Mom's German Chocolate cake," he told Zita.

"My favorite flavor of cake," Zita returned, although Wanda could have sworn she had once said her favorite cake was white with chocolate frosting. "How are you doing in college, Ulric?"

"It's going well," he returned. "Another year, and then I'll get to start concentrating on my major. Where are you going in the fall?"

"Columbus," she answered without enthusiasm. "Just get a certificate and get to work somewhere."

"Oh, yeah? What kind of certificate?"

"Automotive."

"I should have known. You always—"

"Ulric!" Mrs Thompson called to him. "We're here to see your sister!"

"Sorry," he whispered, and turned away. "Coming, mom."

Ella lead the Thompsons outside to show them where they could find said daughter, and was back soon, followed by Rusty.

"Chuck says he needs more meat," Rusty declared, and headed straight for the frig. He also grabbed the clean dinner plate, and Bob opened the door to let him out.

"I don't know about you guys, but I'm ready to eat," Bob said, grabbing a paper plate and silverware. Rusty was back in a moment with a dirty dinner plate and a plate of cooked meat. Bob grabbed a burger for his bun and began filling his plate with all sorts of food to go with it.

Bob had gotten half-way around the table when the door opened and the Thompsons entered, Gloria and Sammy in the middle of the group. Bob stopped filling his plate, turned, and headed for the office, his face absolutely white.

"Is he alright?" Wanda whispered to Zita as they filled plastic cups with lemonade and tea.

Zita shrugged. "Not my business. Nor yours."

No, it isn't. Except Bob is a friend, and he certainly looks distressed. Because of Gloria? Nothing I can do to help, if that's his problem. Except sympathy. But some men don't want that.

"Do you want to eat now?" Ella asked as she returned from the coffee table. "Especially you, Wanda. Get yourself something to eat, go outside and mingle. I certainly didn't expect to tie you up all day with organizing the food."

"Are you sure?"

"Yes. I never imagined there would be so many people arriving at almost the same time. If they had spread themselves out a bit more, I could have helped organize. Nice idea about the bookcase for the desserts, Zita."

"It was Bob's idea. I'd completely forgotten it was in the library. I've got to come and help put things right tomorrow, Ella. We dumped all the games off the bookcase to get it out here."

"Zita, don't worry. As soon as they've eaten, the boys will be in the library, playing those games, so Chuck will probably never know about the dumping they got." She turned to Wanda. "I think there's a hamburger left, if you're ready to eat."

Wanda felt her heart beat a little fast. "I guess I'm nervous. I hardly know anybody."

"Well, you know mom. And grandma and Val are out there, too. Hang out with them, and you'll probably soon meet most everybody. Kind of the matriarchs here in Belgrade, since Gram passed. If that's not enough, I'll send Bob out, once he's eaten."

"I'm a little worried about Bob," Wanda admitted. "He's been acting funny."

"He just needs time to... pull himself together. You'll see."

I came to this party to mingle. I can't do it very well by standing here in the kitchen. "Okay, then."

* * *

1:42 PM

Wanda felt a little out of place approaching the matriarchs' table, especially since she had a plate of food, and they didn't, but they gave her a warm welcome. made room for her at the table and introduced her all around. Her ears particularly took note of the other older couple at the table, Robert and Anna Davis. She hadn't met them before, but she recognized the names. They were Hank's parents.

And here I am, pretending to be someone I'm not.

This was awful. She wanted to tell them who she was, but just as the urge began to be unbearable, Bob came out with a cup of coffee and sat down with them. "What are we talking about?"

"I was wondering if it's going to rain before the fireworks get set off," Val stated.

The day was still bright and sunny, but there were some clouds coming in from the west. Wanda mused about those clouds, studied them as if her answer was written on them.

"You seem far away, Wanda," Anna stated.

"What? Oh." She took a drink of her water. "I was originally wondering if I had left any windows open. Which doesn't seem very likely. So then I was wondering if I left my AC on."

Val cackled in amusement. "How pragmatic. Are all you City Girls such worry warts about a little rain?"

"No, in Chicago, my windows were rarely open, so I didn't worry about rain. But let's not forget the night a few weeks back when a big storm came through. All my windows were open, and it took all morning the next day to get the puddles cleaned up. Not to mention getting the water sucked out of the sofa on the porch."

"You're supposed to wake up and close the windows when the storm blows in," Robert stated sensibly.

"I probably would have, but I and my guests were down in the basement, hoping my house wouldn't blow away."

247

"Oh, the night of the tornado," Anna recognized. "Other than some water puddles, was there any damage to Gram's house?"

"I haven't noticed any," Wanda said, and then wondered what kind of damage might have happened that she wouldn't notice.

"You might get the roof looked at," Robert suggested. "As far as I know, that one's getting pretty old."

"No, Chuck's crew redid the roof last fall," Bob stated.

"I thought he was leaving that house for Hank," Alice stated. "Every time someone mentions the house, Chuck's done something more to it."

"What exactly brought you here, Wanda?" Anna asked. "How did you even hear about a house so far from Chicago?"

Wanda quickly stuck a potato chip in her mouth while she tried to figure out what to say. "Well, not so long ago, I lost my roommate of several years, and I couldn't afford the apartment on my own, so I started looking for a cheaper place to live. I wasn't particular where it was, because I work from home. My boss told me about a friend who had a house in the middle of Nebraska. The rent was right, so I packed up and came."

"Sight unseen? Not many are brave enough to do that. The place could have been a wreck."

"Well, when I followed the real estate's instructions on how to get there, the first house I saw was the Egger house. I just about had a heart attack!"

Everybody laughed. "That would do it," Robert agreed. "I don't know how long that house has been condemned, but Quince just won't clean it up and/or tear it down."

Felix appeared in the open-walled tent. "I'm supposed to tell you guys that another batch of meat just went into the house."

"I suppose that means we should go inside and get something to eat," Val stated. The older people got up and headed for the patio.

Bob leaned forward to ask Wanda, "Do you need me to explain that hug to Chuck?"

She blinked in surprise. "No. I already did. And then I told him it was none of his business."

Bob gave her a tight smile. "You don't let him get away with anything, do you?"

"I think he gets away with far too much," she returned. "If I let him have an inch, he'll walk all over me."

"He's not that bad."

"You aren't the one trying to keep him at arm's length."

Bob laughed. "Okay, you've got me there. Are you ready for dessert?"

"Not quite yet," she said, and finished drinking her water. "But I think I will go get a pop."

"Maybe I should go with you. That might put you within reach of Chuck."

They walked over to the grill, which had the tub of ice on one side, and a small patio table on the other. There was a can of pop on the table. Bob tossed out his coffee cup and soon joined Wanda at the drink tub, where he whispered, "Here comes trouble."

Before Wanda could ask what he meant, the patio door opened and a large woman with a rather shrill voice announced, "I insist you fix us steaks, Chuck! None of this plebeian mystery meat you're feeding everybody else!"

Chuck's head slowly turned to face her, his face set in stone. "Queenie," he greeted her coldly. "I haven't got a single steak in the house. Let alone enough for you and your brood."

"Don't be vulgar!" she snapped, apparently objecting to her children being called a brood. "And father always had some steaks in the freezer."

"Well, I am not him. And all I've got in the freezer right now is ice. For drinks."

She stepped out onto the patio and seemed to see Bob for the first time. She walked over and aimed a pasted-on smile at him. "There you are, Robert. Do be a dear and get me a Tom Collins."

"We aren't serving alcohol, Queenie," Chuck told her. "You should have brought your own."

"This is no way to treat your sister," Queenie snapped. Wanda stared in surprise. Queenie looked 20 years older than

Chuck. Her two daughters were probably close to Wanda's age. Her husband—if that's who the tall man was—looked another decade older than Queenie.

"I don't remember inviting you."

"It's a family reunion, isn't it? And I'm family, aren't I?"

"I thought you'd had enough of this town," Chuck returned.

"I've never heard her name," Wanda whispered to Bob.

Queenie turned and stared at Wanda over the top of her glasses. "And who is this woman? I don't recognize her." As if that proved Wanda must be a non-entity.

Chuck sighed. "She's new in town. And my girl friend."

"Chuck!" Wanda yelped in shock and disbelief.

He frowned blackly at the meat cooking on the grill, glanced in her direction. "Or maybe she's Bob's girl. We haven't sorted things out yet."

"What?" Bob was in the same condition as Wanda.

Chuck turned his attention back to Queenie. "All I can offer you is the same hospitality I'm giving all the guests. I know you've had a long drive, so you can stay if you want. But, all my rooms and beds have been spoken for tonight. If you expect to sleep over, you'll have to find someplace else to do it."

It was obvious Queenie didn't care for her options, but after thinking about it, she quietly said, "Agreed," and went inside. Presumably to get something to eat.

Wanda stepped closer to the grill and in a grim tone said, "I could slap you right now."

"Please do," he countered. "Dealing with my sister always leaves me cold and numb."

Bob stepped up beside Wanda and said in a quiet voice, "I'm with Wanda, Chuck. We're never going to put those reputations behind us if even **we** imply there's a rivalry between us."

Chuck nodded slowly, his eyes on the cooking meat. Then he raised his head for a quick look at the patio door and whispered, "She wants me to sell the farmyard, Bob. Says she has a family to feed and she needs the money."

Bob looked stunned. "Well, that's tough," he finally said. "You already paid her for it when you sold the farmland... practically before your father was in the ground."

"She thinks I cheated her, didn't get enough for the farm-land."

"I don't care what she thinks. I know what you did, and you gave her exactly half of what you got for the farm, which was all she was entitled to. Plus you paid her half of what the farmyard and buildings were worth, because you didn't want to sell those. She's gotten all she's entitled to from this farm."

"I know that, and you know that, but she doesn't feel that way."

Bob shook his head. "Look, Chuck, I know she's bullied you her entire life. But you're not a kid any more. Take the bull by the horns and tell her she's not getting another dime, because she's already gotten everything she's entitled to."

"I don't know, Bob."

"The family will be behind you, Chuck. Talk to some of them today and see for yourself."

"Doesn't really matter if she sues me."

"If she does, we'll go to court and let the court go through the records itself. You did everything you were required to do."

Chuck sighed and started to remove the burgers and dogs from the heat. Tommy showed up as he was doing that, with another plate of uncooked meat and a fresh, clean plate for when it was done cooking. He disappeared inside with the hot food.

Wanda studied Chuck's face, uncertain what to say, after the conversation between the two cousins. Chuck seem pale and flushed at the same time. He'd worked all morning getting the place ready, and here it was, almost mid-afternoon.

"Chuck, why don't I bring you a plate of food?"

He stopped transferring burgers from the plate to the grill and turned to gaze at her for a moment. "Thank you, Wanda. I would appreciate that."

She hurried for the patio, afraid she might hear more secrets before she could get away. It wasn't until she was inside, faced with choosing what to put on the plate that she realized she didn't know what dishes he wanted. So she got him one of each type of meat, with buns, and various condiments. When she was loading up the rest of the plate with side dishes, she heard Queenie's husband state, "Quite a nice house, Queenie."

Queenie was helping herself to one of the potato salads, and without looking up, she returned, "Uh huh. Should sell for a pretty penny."

"I don't know," Wanda said. "It's out in the middle of nowhere. How much call is there for a house in Belgrade?"

Queenie looked up and stared at Wanda calculatingly. "Well, you should know; you're the new girl. Which house did you buy, and how much did you pay for it?"

"I didn't buy," Wanda said, "The owner died and the widow didn't know what to do with the place." She was bending the truth ruthlessly, but parts of what she'd said were true.

"Which house?" Queenie demanded.

"Hank's house."

"He never should have inherited that house! It should have been sold and divided up. All I got from Gram's estate was a pair of cheap earrings!" She took a moment to put the spoon back in the potato salad and move further around the table. Then she seemed to remember something Wanda had said. "Hank's dead? Good riddance. Make a note of that, dear; maybe we can sue for part of that estate."

"I don't think so," Wanda told her. "In Illinois, the wife inherits everything."

"That's a common misconception," Queenie said, and she and her family turned for the patio door. "The nerve of that little nobody!" Queenie said as they moved outside.

Wanda found herself shaking, and leaned against the wall to try to calm down. Now she had an idea what Chuck meant about dealing with his sister. Of all the conniving, self-centered—

"You've got to be meaner than that to make an impression on Queenie," Ella stated.

"Bob says she's a bully," Wanda revealed.

"Oh, she bullies everybody," Zita confirmed. "She was a teenager when Chuck arrived, and it was a personal affront to her that her parents had a second child. She was used to being the center of attention, and suddenly, she wasn't."

"Yeah, but my mom says she was a bully even before that, probably because she was an only child."

"Well, that explains a lot," Wanda stated. "Where does she live?"

"Lincoln. The state capitol."

"Is that bigger than Omaha?"

"No, Omaha's the biggest city in the state; Lincoln's the 2nd largest. But even adding them together won't get you anywhere near the size of Chicago."

"That's what I was thinking. And what does Mr Queenie do for a living?"

"Mmm, can't be sure," Zita said. "Some say he's a CPA, but from what I've heard, he acts like a hot-shot lawyer. Always threatening to sue somebody."

"Well, that sounds unfriendly." Wanda put a handful of chips atop everything else already on the plate and claimed a glass of lemonade.

"I thought you'd already eaten," Ella said.

"I did. This is for Chuck."

"Oh, good. That must have been a horrible shock, to have Queenie show up. Remind him I did **not** invite them; I don't know how they found out about the party."

"I will," Wanda promised, and headed outside.

She placed the overloaded plate and silverware on the small table, where Chuck could get to it easily. He quickly moved a potato chip to his mouth. "I could kiss you."

She raised her eyebrows in surprise. "Because I brought you a plate of food?"

"No. Well, yes. I mean, that's part of it, but... Never mind, I'm pretty sure you won't go for it."

If he didn't think she'd go for it, she wasn't sure she wanted to hear about it. On the other hand, if he was still upset by his sister, maybe he needed somebody to talk to. She wasn't his best buddy, but everybody else seemed busy, completely unaware of Chuck's discomfort.

She glimpsed one of Queenie's girls selecting drinks at the ice tub. She didn't realize how loud her voice was when she said,

"You're never going to know until you ask me." As the girl skittered back to her parents, Wanda brought her voice down to its normal level. Chuck wore a confused expression as she claimed one of his chips. "So tell me about it and let me decide." The chip turned out to be a dill pickle flavor, not one of her favorites, but she crunched it into mush and swallowed it while he fiddled with the cooking meat. "Chuck?"

"It's a stupid idea," he mumbled.

"I can't decide that until I hear what it is."

Chuck stopped fussing and turned to the plate on the table, leaned forward to quietly state, "Queenie says she needs more money from her inheritance because she has a family to feed."

"What she thinks she needs doesn't change what she's allowed to get in the eyes of the law."

"She thinks it does." He stabbed a chunk of potato from one of the potato salads and ate it. "I just thought... I mean..."

"Spit it out," she coaxed.

He raised his head and looked straight into her eyes. "If I could convince her, without actually saying it, that I was starting my own family..."

He let it trail off, and Wanda looked around in something of a panic. She caught sight of Queenie glaring at them, surrounded by her family. Chuck was desperate for a way—anyway—to get his sister off his back. No doubt he had thought he was through with her once he had sold the farmland and paid her for half of that and half the farmyard, which he hadn't wanted to sell. But here she was, putting the same kind of squeeze on him with a flimsy excuse. And he was trying to get away from her with an equally flimsy excuse.

"That's why I said you were my girl friend," he finally said. "I know I shouldn't have, but all I could think of was throwing my family against hers. Except I don't have a wife and kids. Yet. And could you please stop eating my potato chips?"

She stared at the chip she held, realized she had another batch of pickle-flavored mush in her mouth. She smiled at him evilly and swallowed. "Oh, you bad boy," she told him, and gave him a playful slap on his arm. "You can't mean that." She pulled on his arm so that he bent down, and she whispered in his ear, "Besides, it won't work. She's too self-centered to care anything about what you might need for a family, even if you already had one." She leaned back, let go of him and asked, "I'm right, aren't I?"

He cleared his throat. "I... believe you are," he agreed.

"See? We can get along just fine when you agree with me. Now, since I ate several of your chips, I'm going back to get some desert. Is there anything you want?"

"Did the Thompson's bring German chocolate cake?"

"Yes."

"Then I'll have that." When she turned, he added, "And a beer. They're in the office, in—"

"I know where they are." She turned back. "But I'm not bringing you one."

"Why not?"

"Because one evening not long ago, you called me after drinking one beer, and you weren't the most reasonable man at the time. I know you don't want to make a scene taking on your sister in the middle of a party, but a beer will only make you more likely to do that. Think about what you want to say to her, practice it in your head. I know you can do it; you had a nice little start at it when you told her you couldn't treat her any differently than any other guest. If you don't want to say it today, then put it in a letter. But stand firm. Don't let her get to you. And that's why I'm not bringing you a beer."

He gave her a lop-sided smile and simply said, "Thanks."

* * *

2:58 PM

Helen and Keith were sitting at the little table next to the grill when Wanda returned with 2 slices of German chocolate cake. There were 2 other chairs also, apparently for her and Chuck. The table wasn't big enough to hold much more than their drinks, but everybody was satisfied to hold their own plate as they ate. Chuck kept an eye on the meat on the grill and sent another platter of cooked food into the house before long. He didn't put any more meat on the grill.

255

"Don't you need to put the fire out, or something?" Wanda asked.

"No," Chuck answered. "I have to start cooking again in about 3 hours."

Wanda checked her watch. "That will be 6 o'clock. Excuse me, how long does this party go?"

"Why? You in a hurry to leave?" Helen asked.

"No, it's just... I'm an introvert, and I'm not used to smiling longer than the 6 hours that Chuck and the kids are at my place on Saturday nights." She laughed like it was a joke, but she was only half joking. Between helping organize the food, and Bob apparently falling apart, and then Chuck doing the same, she felt she had been through enough for one day.

"I wish I'd thought of that," Chuck said when he got back from throwing plates and plasticware away.

"Thought of what?" Keith asked.

"Organized to play our game of dungeons here, this afternoon. Would have given Bob a chance to join us, at least as a guest player."

"Maybe you haven't noticed, Chuck, but all the youngsters, as you've started to call them, have disappeared into the house," Helen stated.

"They're probably playing electronic games," he stated. "Sorry, I'm not sure even dungeons would win that contest."

"Well, what about you, Helen?" Wanda asked. "Shouldn't you be talking with your sister while she's here?"

"She's staying through most of tomorrow, so we can settle the arrangements with Ella's input. Since she's been so busy acting as hostess."

"And doing a fine job," Chuck affirmed.

"Anyway, Patty and her husband brought cards and they're playing pitch with anybody who will play with them. They'd probably be fine until dawn, if it doesn't rain."

Chuck grinned. "Maybe I should go look for some lanterns for them."

"No, now don't encourage her! She's an addict, I tell you."

"Everybody needs a hobby," Keith stated.

"You know, I'm sure it's been mentioned at some point, but I don't remember what kind of job he's got there in Omaha."

"He's a firefighter," Helen explained. "And Patty's a crime lab supervisor for the police department, so there have been times when their schedules have been really skewed. To hear her tell it, it's a wonder they even had any kids."

"As I remember, starting a kid doesn't usually take long," Keith teased.

"Don't talk like that!" Helen told him. "You'll have Wanda thinking you're a dirty old man!"

"Has she met Lyle?"

"Yes. You know that."

"Then I think I'm safe."

Wanda gave a short bout of laughter and said, "Nobody's as bad as Lyle."

"Yeah, she's met him," Keith acknowledged.

Wanda noticed a middle-aged man approaching. It took her a moment to recognize him so she could greet him. "Hello, Mr Thompson."

Caught by surprise, Chuck stood up and faced him, offered his hand. "Glad you and your family made it, Mr Thompson."

"Thank you, Mr, um, Davis?"

"I'm a Davis on my mother's side, but I grew up an Applegit. You can call me Chuck, if you want."

"I wanted to check on how late this party goes on. I thought it might be a typo that the invite said 'sometime after 9 pm'."

"No, not a typo," Chuck told him. I've got some fireworks to set off, starting about 8:45 or 9:00, depending how soon it gets dark. Of course, if the clouds keep getting darker, we might set off the fireworks earlier. But everybody is welcome to stay until after the fireworks. And about 6, we'll start cooking more hamburgers and hot dogs, get the rest of the side dishes and desserts out, so you won't starve waiting for the fireworks."

Mr Thompson's mouth tightened for half a second. "Speaking of food, Sammy keeps asking for 'bed and brudder'. Gloria thinks he means 'bread and butter'. But when I looked inside, all the food has been put away."

"We can't have Sammy going hungry," Chuck said, and turned to Wanda. "Wanda, the girls are probably in the library, playing games with the rest of the youngsters. Could you help Mr Thompson find some of your delicious bread and butter?"

"I'd be happy to," she stated, got up and headed for the patio door.

Not all of the food had been put away, it turned out. There were still 2 partial packages of chips on the table, folded over to keep them from going stale. She went to the kitchen to look for the sliced bread, but couldn't find any, not even in the refrigerator. She got the butter out and went looking for the library by following the voices she heard.

The library door was open. There was quite a crowd of teens sprawled on the sofa and across the floor, watching those on the sofa play a game on the large TV.

Wanda knocked on the door jamb. "Ella? Don't get up. Just tell me where to find the bread that Bob sliced this morning."

"There isn't any left, that's sliced," she answered. "He said he'd come in and slice some more for supper."

"Okay, so the bread's in the office. Thank you!" As she passed through the great room, she told Mr Thompson, "I have to get another loaf to slice. I'll be right back."

She was surprised when she turned away from getting a sack of bread from atop the office frig to find Mr Thompson had followed her. "I wondered where you were going to find bread."

"Oh, well, I like the kitchen, but it doesn't have a lot of space to store party supplies, so we confiscated Chuck's office as a pantry for the day."

"This is Chuck's office?" He stood in the doorway and looked around. "Nice and clean. Well organized."

She started forward, and he stepped into the hallway. "I can't vouch for how it looks during the work week," she stated as they started back for the kitchen. "This is my first time here, so I can't vouch for anything. Just give me half a moment, and I'll have a slice of bread ready for Sammy." She got out a cutting board and knife and started slicing off the heel. "Is there anything else your family would like this afternoon? Some chips?

Dessert?" There were still several desserts on the makeshift dessert stand, all covered either with a lid or with plastic, but she'd seen several more desserts waiting in the office.

"Are you sure no one would mind?"

"No, we won't," Ella said from the north hallway. "When Chuck throws a party, he wants people to be happy. We have plenty of chips, and desserts, and even salads, if that's what you'd like. I think we even have a cold hamburger or hot dog that I could throw in the microwave." She claimed the 2nd slice of bread and started buttering it.

"You both are so kind. Hard to believe you're in the same family as Lyle."

Ella grimaced. "Mr Thompson, none of my family approves of Lyle's behavior. We thought, that possibly he was changing. Unfortunately, if he has changed, it's for the worse. If Gloria wants out of the situation she's in, all she has to do is tell my mother, and we'd all rally behind her, not Lyle."

Wanda cleared her throat and turned from slicing bread, began buttering the heel for herself. "While I'm not one of the family, and I hardly know your daughter—or Lyle, for that matter—I totally agree with what Ella said."

The front door opened and the Egger brothers came in, each with a bag of chips. "Ho! Thought we'd sneak in when no one was looking," one of them said.

"Told you there'd be people in the house," the other said.

"Well, you're both right," Ella told them. Wanda and Mr Thompson came in to get a snack for Sammy. Other than that, only kids are in the house, and we are all in the library, playing games, and never would have known anybody came in."

"That can be dangerous, not being aware of somebody coming into the house. So where's everybody else?"

"In the back, nibbling and talking. Aunt Patty's here, playing pitch, if you want to get in on that."

"Oh, yeah, we'll join that in just a minute. But first we'll need a snack to tide us over until supper. What time is supper?"

"Chuck will start grilling again about 6," Wanda answered.

"That looks like homemade bread," one brother said, pointing at the stack of bread Wanda had just sliced.

"Bread and butter would just about hit the spot," said one brother. "And maybe a piece of pie."

"Not pie," said the other. "Cake! Pie's too heavy if you want to eat in less than 3 hours. Is there coffee in that pot?"

Wanda glanced at the glass tube above the spigot. "Looks like it's about half full."

"That's one thing about Chuck; he knows how to have a party. Even when it's pot luck." The brothers set about getting themselves plates, buttering bread, pouring themselves coffee and helping themselves to the remaining desserts.

Ella got a plate and put Sammy's bread and butter on it, then the last lemon bar, and handed it to Mr Thompson. "Tell your family if there's anything else they'd like, just come right in. We'd be happy to help them find a little something."

"Well, one of those half bags of chips," he suggested.

"Of course," Ella agreed. "Let's see, we've got corn chips and cheese-flavored potato chips. Oh, tell you what, take both of them. We have plenty more bags in the office."

"Thank you again, girls. I wasn't sure what to do. It almost seems like Sammy hasn't eaten in a week!" It didn't quite sound like a joke.

Ella stiffened for half a moment, then smiled. She opened the door for Mr Thompson and let him out with a smile and a wave, then stepped aside for the Egger brothers to go out.

Wanda had poured herself a glass of tea. Her slice of bread half eaten, she eyed what was left of the desserts, took the lemon bar pan and its serving spatula to the sink and began running some water.

"How are the rest of the desserts?" Ella asked.

"I was about ready to get another slice of German chocolate cake, if Quince left any."

"How do you know it was Quince that wanted cake?"

"I don't. I just use one of their names and figure I have a 50% chance of being right."

Ella laughed. "Over the years, I've noticed little differences in how they behave. I can't tell you what they are, but sometimes

I know which one I'm talking to."

"I'll have to pay close attention so I can figure it out," Wanda said. "In a decade or so." She raised the lid of the cake pan. "No, it's empty." She carried it to the sink.

"Is there anything else nearly gone? We could put it on plates with some plastic wrap and wash the containers. The machine only needs another couple of things, I think."

"Machine?" Wanda asked, and then realized there was a dish washer built in under the stationary cutting board. "I guess I never thought of Chuck having a dish washer."

"Anything that would make life easier for his folks, he put it in. And then he lost his mother as soon as he got this house done. I doubt if this machine gets used, unless he has a party."

"The cookies are almost gone," Wanda said. "I'll just finish them off. There's really only one piece of chocolate-chocolate cake, and either 1 large piece of apple pie or 2 small pieces."

"Cut it into 2 pieces. People will be reluctant to take a large piece. I'll get the plastic wrap."

Wanda busied herself with the desserts, and before long, someone cleared their throat. "Excuse me?"

She turned around and found Gloria standing between the dining table and the kitchen. "How can I help you, Gloria?"

"I wonder if I could have another slice of bread and butter?"

"Oh, my, he is hungry, isn't he?" She got a smaller plate from the dessert station and took it to the kitchen, put a slice of bread on it and said, "The butter is right here. Would you like to butter it for him?"

"Would you... could I please have 2 slices? I don't think I've ever had homemade bread, and I seem to have an appetite today, myself."

Which reminded Wanda that when she'd first seen Gloria, she thought the girl looked half starved. And her son didn't look any better. Wanda put a 2nd slice of bread on the small plate, and Gloria started buttering them. "Is there anything else you'd like, Gloria? We're trying to clean up the lunch desserts, to make room for the rest of them. We've got chocolate cake, apple or cherry pie. And don't forget something to drink."

"Are you sure it's okay?"

"Of course it is, Gloria," Ella piped up, reappearing. "It's a party, eat your fill. Mom always said us kids had a growth spurt after an Applegit party, because we ate so much. So have the cake. Or the pie, or both. We have plenty more desserts, right, Wanda?"

"Oh, at least 10 more," Wanda confirmed. "And there's the bowl of jello that has both carrots and marshmallows in it."

Ella chuckled. "Old Mrs Andresen always brings that. Sometimes it's served as a salad, sometimes as a dessert." She leaned forward and lowered her voice. "Technically, she's not family, but she's the oldest woman in Belgrade, now that Gram's passed, and nobody would think of not having her here."

"I will have cake," Gloria decided. "Apple pie. And tea."

"Good," Ella pronounced and got the goodies while Wanda poured the tea. "Wanda, can you let us out the door? I'll help Gloria carry these things."

Afterwards, Wanda rinsed off what baking pans and serving spatulas she could fit in the dish washer. Just as she got the machine started, Felix and Rusty appeared. "Wanda, has any more of your bread been cut?"

She smiled, got a plate from the cupboard, put the remainder of the sliced loaf on it and handed it to Felix. "Put it on the table and take yours." She handed the butter to Rusty. "Ditto."

"Thanks, Wanda!" they told her almost in unison, and then a trail of youngsters came from the north hall, each wanting a slice of bread. Seeing how many there were, Wanda got another loaf from the bag and started slicing it, too. There was still another bag of 3 loaves in the office.

Before the kids were done claiming a slice of bread each, other people were coming in from outside, looking for a 'little something'. Ella brought in Mrs Andresen's bowl of jello for the table, and a bag of chips to go with the 2 bags the Egger brothers had brought. Then another platter of cookies for the dessert station, and a couple of the salads left over from lunch.

"I knew this would happen," Ella told Wanda as people came and went. "See, people are used to eating well—and often—when it's an Applegit party."

"Even if it's not a pot-luck party?"

"An Applegit party is always a pot-luck party. It's the way things are."

"I don't know if I will ever understand the rules of Belgrade," Wanda stated. "No matter how long I live here."

"Any more corn chips?" someone asked.

"I think so. Let me check," Wanda said to the room in general and headed for the office.

By the time she returned to the dining room, Ella was headed for the office, and came back with a bowl of carrot salad and a platter of finger vegetables; carrots, radishes and cucumber slices. Before long, the 'rush' for snacks was over. A few more came in, singles or couples, but soon Wanda and Ella were putting food away so it didn't spoil.

Wanda was ready to take the vegetable platter when Bob came in. "Leave that," he told her. "The chef-o-matic is back."

"The what?"

"He slices, he dices, he... does not make julienne fries. What is a julienne fry, anyway?" He picked up the vegetable platter and took it to the kitchen.

Wanda answered, "I've never heard the term before."

"You obviously don't watch TV in the wee hours of the night," he surmised, and headed for the north hallway.

The dish washer dinged and Wanda opened it, backed away from the cloud of heat and steam. Bob came back around the corner with a grocery sack of vegetables, which he placed on the cutting board. "Okay, first we dry dishes." He opened an upper cupboard and pulled out 2 dish towels, handed one to Wanda."

"I thought the dish washer was supposed to dry the dishes," Wanda complained.

"Supposed to, but seldom gets all the water gone. Careful, the dishes are hot, but just give each one a quick dry, match the top & bottom, if it has that configuration, tell Ella the name on it and place it on the dining room table."

With two of them working, they soon had the machine empty, and Bob set about putting the few items that hadn't fit in that load in to be washed. "What's this?" Bob asked. "I see I didn't slice enough bread this morning." He got a dishrag and started wiping bread crumbs off the cutting board.

"I'm sorry, Bob," Wanda told him. "Sammy wanted bread and butter, and then the teens wanted some, so I sliced up 2 loaves. I got so busy, I forgot to clean up after myself."

"Easy to do," he said and smiled. "How much bread did you bring? Or put another way, how much do we have left?"

"There's about half a loaf on the table," Ella answered. "And I put another loaf in the pantry." She stepped out onto the patio.

"And there's another sack with 3 loaves in the office," Wanda added. "Wait, there's a pantry? Why did we confiscate the office?"

"Habit," Bob returned. "We tried using the pantry the first time or 2, back when Chuck's dad was still alive, but it doesn't have a refrigerator, so we'd put stuff in the office anyway. Plus, that corner gets busy once the kids start playing games in the library. So we developed the system where we put the extra food in the office, and only put the stuff I'll be cutting in the pantry."

"More rules for living in Belgrade," Wanda muttered to herself. She heard Chuck bellowing outside, but couldn't quite make out what he was saying. It might have been a list of names. Or recipe ingredients, she just couldn't tell.

"You looked like you were having fun with Chuck," Bob observed.

"He managed not to irritate me too badly. Today." But it was more than that. *He revealed he's a human being, with fears and desires all his own. I still don't understand him, but maybe this knowledge will make it easier to be patient with him. Maybe.*

"Why don't you go back outside and enjoy yourself?" Bob suggested. "It'll be another hour before I send any meat out for Chuck to cook."

She considered that for a moment, decided to be truthful. "Because I'm afraid I might gravitate to Chuck again, to see if he's doing any better than he was. And that might lead people to think what he said earlier was right."

"So you're choosing to stay inside with me, which might lead people to think the 2nd part of what he said might be true."

She grimaced. "I suppose he didn't mean to, but he's tied me into a bind. What should I do, stay away from both of you? You 2 and the teens are the best friends I've got in Belgrade."

He turned from slicing vegetables to give her a long look. "You're counting Chuck as a friend?"

She thought about that for a long moment, too. "He's made it plain that if I need help, he'll be there for me. It's only when he rams that help down my throat that he irritates me." Bob nodded and went back to the vegetables.

Ella came in from outside, followed by a number of people who picked up their pans, cake containers and utensils from the table and took them out the front door. When the 3rd person disappeared out the door, Ella told Wanda, "The easiest way to keep the people's dishes from getting lost is to send them to their owner's car. They'll be back in a moment, relieved to know they didn't lose their property."

Wanda almost muttered something about 'Belgrade rules' again, but it made sense. Especially with a pot luck with this many people in attendance.

* * *

5:45 PM

"Wanda." She turned from organizing food on the table, to see Bob in the kitchen with a plate of raw meat in his hands. "Would you please take this plate of meat out to Chuck?"

"Is it 6 o'clock already?" she asked.

"Close enough," Bob said. "Those clouds are getting darker. The fireworks will go off early, to beat the rain." As she approached to take the plate, he added quietly, "This gives you a reason to go towards Chuck, to see how he's holding up."

"What about a plate for the cooked meat?"

He took a dinner plate from the cupboard and handed it to her as well. "Ella and I can handle this in here, and Zita's close by, so go ahead and mingle."

She stepped onto the patio wondering if that was an order or a suggestion. If it had been Chuck, she would have taken it as an

265

order. But since it was Bob, she assumed it was a suggestion.

It almost seemed like twilight already, the clouds had gotten so thick and so low. As she approached the grill area, she realized it was Queenie Chuck was talking to. "We need to talk!" Queenie said forcefully."

"I can't talk to you today," Chuck responded evenly. "I have nearly 200 guests, and it's time to cook again. I can't ignore the ones I did invite just because you showed up uninvited. If you want to talk to me, try calling. But do it during the evening; I work during the day."

"I've been calling you, and it seems like you don't ever answer your phone. Even on Saturdays!"

"Well, until today, I've been working Saturdays too. We got behind on a project, and had to go to a 6-day work week." He turned to take the 2 plates from Wanda. "Thank you, City Girl. Could you get me a beer? I mean, a root beer? There should be some in the tub."

"If you'd just answer your phone when I call, we could get this settled quickly and you could go back to being the big construction boss! Talk about putting on airs! You're nothing but a handyman, and everybody knows it!"

Chuck gave a slow nod. "Most of the time, it is odd jobs we do, stuff the customer can't or doesn't want to do themselves. But my team of handymen just finished building the biggest house in Fullerton. And stop putting down my chosen profession, Queenie; I don't say a word about yours. This year, I have doubled the size of my work crew, and that makes me the biggest business in Belgrade. Probably puts me in the top 10 in the county!"

"Oh, who cares about a tiny village in a middle-of-nowhere county?"

Wanda found a can of root beer and walked back with it.

"Well, I suppose everybody living in that tiny village and in that middle-of-nowhere county," was Chuck's answer. "Possibly everybody else at this party, Queenie. Go back to your mansion in Lincoln. And since you insist on talking, and that's what we've been doing, here's your answer. You're not getting another red cent from me, because I've already paid you your half of the inheritance. Now, stay and have supper, or go home, but leave me alone!"

He took the can of pop from Wanda, who thought it only fair to wipe the icy water coating her hand onto his t-shirt. "Whoa!" he said, and quickly grabbed her hand in his big, callused but very warm hand. "Your hand is cold!"

"The water in the tub is like an icy slush."

"Good. I wasn't sure we put enough ice in it this morning."

Since the tub had been a veritable mountain of ice, bottles of water and cans of pop, Wanda didn't see how he could have put more ice into it, but she didn't say anything, just wondered when he was going to let go of her hand.

"We'll see about that!" Queenie threatened, and turned for the patio. Her husband and 2 daughters abruptly left their table and hurried after her.

Chuck took a deep, shuddering breath and let go of Wanda's hand to start putting the meat on the grill. "Well, now she's going to sue me for sure," he muttered.

"I thought that was pretty much a given," Wanda stated. "But you did a fine job of telling her off."

"Actually, most of it was stuff people said to me this afternoon."

"Then I'm glad you listened to them."

"It took you a long time to slice and butter some bread," he commented.

"It turned out a lot of people wanted bread, so I sliced 2 loaves, and then we started cleaning up, washing the empty bowls and pans. I kept busy."

"People out here wanted to spend time with you. They hardly ever see you. That makes it tough to get to know you."

"I don't like to go to Bob's on Friday or Saturday for fear of running into Lyle again."

"Bob is open other days of the week. There's not as many people there, but there are some."

"I'll think about it," she relented. "I didn't realize until I came outside how dark it was getting. Are you going to start the fireworks early?"

"Quite a bit early. Keith and Melvin are getting them set up, while the fire brigade is getting the garden hoses ready. They'll all be eating first, then we'll set off the fireworks while the others are eating. With luck, we'll get everything done before the rain gets too bad."

She could see men out in the distance of the back yard, which, she realized was newly mowed, right up to the corn field beyond. The corn wasn't very tall yet, but it looked taller than what Tommy had planted near her home. *Would Tommy's corn have time to grow ears? Maybe it had been too late...* Chuck had said something, and she hadn't heard it. "What?"

"I said, I'd appreciate it if you could sit with Robert and Anna Davis while you have supper tonight. Their youngest was Hank, the oldest of us 4 Cousins, and it's his house you're living in, so they'd like to get to know you a little."

"I haven't seen them until today," she stated, remembering the couple. "Do they live out of town?"

He nodded. "They live in Columbus. They own the end of the block from your place, where I mow the grass from time to time. Their back yard was where Popper had his garden for many years. They're happy to see Tommy make use of it."

"I'll look them up when I get my food," she promised.

"They'll like that. Now, why don't you either mingle or go back inside, before my reputation catches up to you."

There it is, the same sort of statement as Bob had made. It didn't sound like an order. More like a warning.

Wanda moved away from the grill area, moved from table to table, exchanging a few words with far more people than she had realized she knew. At one point, she came to Steve and Ivan and their significant others, and pulled over an empty chair.

"So, Chuck blurted out your secret in front of everyone, huh?" asked Fran, Steve's girl friend.

Wanda frowned in confusion. "What secret?"

"That you and he are an item."

"Oh, that." She waved the idea away. "He was unnerved by his sister's arrival. Especially since he hadn't invited her." To squash the idea, she added, "We are not an item."

"Then you prefer Bob?"

Wanda heaved a great sigh. *I'm so tired of this subject. When is it ever going to die?* "Bob is a friend, not a boy friend. Chuck is... well, most of the time, Chuck is an irritant."

"I can vouch for that," Steve said.

Ivan nodded. "I'm beginning to think he doesn't know a thing about women."

"Well, he knows how to charm them," Fran stated. "Or at least, he did back in high school."

"Whoa, whoa, when did you find that out?" Steve wanted to know. "When did you date the cousins?"

"I didn't," Fran assured him. "I was 3 years behind them. None of them looked at girls that far behind. All we could do was watch in wonder as they charmed their way through all the girls their own age, and a few a year younger. They were all charmers then. Then Hank got married, and Lyle became a drunken idiot. I wonder how the other 2 managed to forget how it's done. Charming a girl, I mean."

"I think Bob had his heart broken," said the other woman at the table. Ivan's wife's name was Irene. "Or he just got tired of playing games. He was always the most serious of them."

"Serious! He dated 2 or 3 girls at a time!" Ivan protested.

"Yes, he did," Ilene agreed. "Girls the others had cast off. He scooped them up, showed them a good time, tried to make them feel special... right up until they broke up with him. I don't remember Bob ever breaking up with a girl, do you, Fran?"

"Not specifically," Fran answered slowly. "Although I'm not sure what happened between him and Gloria."

"From what I've gathered, Lyle decided he wanted Gloria. Then she got pregnant, and somebody convinced Lyle to marry her." Ivan cleared his throat, as if this line of gossip was uncomfortable for him.

"Well, whatever," Wanda summed up. "Chuck said a couple things without thinking, and Bob and I both objected. And now, I really must keep moving on if I'm going to try to at least greet everybody here. See you later."

6:20 PM

Wanda emerged from the house onto the patio and paused to see where Robert and Anna Davis were sitting. They were sitting at the table Queenie and her brood had monopolized all day. Wanda took her plate of food and glass of tea over to them. "Do you mind if I join you?"

"No, not at all," Robert answered. There was already a younger couple sitting at the table, but they scooted closer around the table so that she could sit. Thankfully, there was an empty chair nearby that she could pull over. The younger couple was their son, Edward (who bore a striking resemblance to Robert), and his wife, Virginia.

After introductions, Wanda cleared her throat and dove in. "Chuck said that because I'm living in the house that Gram left to your son, you'd like to know more about me. Well, I promise I haven't made any big changes to the house, but I have moved some furniture around."

"I thought I saw some air conditioners in a couple windows as I drove by," Edward stated. "Good idea."

"Oh, those. And a couple ceiling fans in the living room. As it happens, Chuck and I had a big go-around about those."

Anna's brow puckered. "He didn't want you to install them?"

Wanda looked up in surprise. "He and his crew came over and installed them without talking to me about it. Like I needed his charity. I made him present an invoice, and I'm making payments." *Very miniscule payments, but so what? He doesn't even care if I pay him.*

"Didn't you pass that invoice on to Hank's wife?" Robert asked. "That's usually something the landlord takes care of."

Oh, good grief, my lies are coming home to trip me up. I handled the situation as if I were the owner, because I am. But I should have handled it as a tenant. What do I say? "If I thought she could deal with it, I would have." *Now I have to tell more lies to hide the ones I've already told.* "A mutual friend knew I was looking for a place to live, and where wasn't important, because I work from home. But she seemed to be in heavy grief, could hardly keep her mind on working up an agreement. It was basically this mutual friend and I hashing out the details. Perhaps, in a few months, I'll broach the subject with her." *What else have I been doing like an owner and not like a tenant?*

What am I doing, telling all these lies? And why? Bob knows the truth. I have reason to believe that Chuck does too, because of that picture in his desk. What if Hank's parents got a wedding photo from Hank? They might know the truth as well, and wonder why I'm lying to them!

"What kind of work do you do?" Anna asked.

The change of subject threw her for a loop. "What?"

"You said you work from home. I wondered what kind of work you do."

"Oh. I'm a writer." *That's safe; I've been saying it for years. It isn't specific. As a writer, I could be a copy writer, a freelance writer, a journalist... If I say I'm a novelist, they'd want more details, like what I've written. Then the disappointment when they learn I write fantasy. Sometimes, I wonder if I could garner more respect by saying I write romances.*

Conversation became more difficult as the fireworks started. It wasn't full dark yet, and the clouds had settled very low, but the colors and brightness could still be seen. All the teens came out to watch, and a couple of them sat at the next table; the boy bore a striking resemblance to Edward. Further introductions confirmed that the boy and girl were Edward's and Virginia's children.

After the fireworks, everybody took their plates to the closest of several metal trash bins. And then they started folding up the tables and chairs they had been using. "Well, this is interesting," Wanda commented. "Why are we doing this?"

"The rain that's coming could have some wind with it, which could play havoc with the tents, tables, and chairs," Robert stated. "So before we leave, we'll at least put the table and chairs in the garage, where the wind can't get to them."

"That way, it'll be easier to talk Chuck into doing this again. Maybe next year," Anna added.

"That makes sense." Wanda hoisted 2 folded chairs herself. "I know he and his crew worked hard to get ready for this."

"He's a little bit of a show-off," Anna stated. "He wants people to have a good time, so he wants things to be perfect."

Lights came on at the corners of the south wing of the house, and Wanda followed the others around the south wing and to the front, where Steve opened one side of the 2-car garage. "Just stack them up against anything except the car," he instructed. "And thank you for your help."

As they exited the garage, Anna said, "I need to go inside and see if my pan is ready to go yet. Do you want me to look for yours, Ginny?"

"I'm going to get my travel mug from the car and get some coffee," Robert decided.

"Me, too." Edward said.

"Well, I might as well go get my own bowl," Ginny said.

"Are you guys going to take long?" her daughter asked. "I don't want to sit in the car all night waiting for you to finish talking to people."

"Oh, don't get in a tailspin," Anna told her. "We've had all day to talk to people, and I'm just about talked out. Besides, everybody will be busy either feeding people or trying to get them gone before it starts raining."

"Exactly," Edward agreed. "And I'd just as soon get going before it starts raining."

Wanda, Anna and Virginia walked in the front door, saw people loading up plates with food and heading outside to eat their supper. Ella was chatting with the Thompsons, while Gloria sat on one of the sofas, her son asleep and sprawled across her. Zita and Bob were in the kitchen, dispersing drinks and washing bowls and platters and such by hand.

"I think I see my pie tin," Anna stated, and walked over to the 2nd sofa to free it from the rest of the pans and bowls.

Wanda followed Ginny to the kitchen area. Bob looked up from opening the dish washer, grabbed a bowl and a dish towel, gave it a few swipes and handed it to Ginny. "Oh! You could have just rinsed it out," Ginny told them.

"No, we might want some coconut marshmallow salad again next time," Bob replied.

"Will there be a next time, do you think?" Ginny asked.

"I hope so. It's been a great day off for me."

"You spent most of the day in here, working! How is that a day off?"

"I got to see a lot of people I don't see that often," he replied with a broad smile. "Plus, I didn't have to eat my own cooking!"

A faint rumble of thunder reminded everybody that rain was on its way. The Thompson's left, nearly waking little Sammy as they hugged and kissed Gloria. Robert and Edward came in, went to the kitchen island and filled their travel mugs. With final good-byes to everybody in the house, they left also.

"Is there anything I can do to help?" Wanda asked.

Bob opened a lower island cabinet and pulled out a box of sandwich bags and a dozen small containers. "Time to put the leftovers away so that we can wash the dishes."

"Has everybody eaten?"

"I think so. They said Chuck was spraying down the ashes in the grill. That's a sure sign he isn't going to cook anymore."

"What is Chuck going to do with all these leftovers?" Wanda wondered.

"Oh, they'll get eaten at the after-party."

"Oh," she said, and marveled that after working all morning to get ready for this party, eating 2 big meals as part of this party, now there would be an after-party? *Bob said there was some beer in a cooler in the office; would that be brought out for the after party? Personally, although it's still early in the evening, I'm tired and I'll probably leave before too much longer.*

More people came in through the front door to claim their pans and say good-bye. Some grabbed a final dessert or a cup of coffee before they left. Ella was there to say a fond farewell to all of them. Whenever someone said they hoped they could do this again, Ella would smile and say, "I'll keep you informed."

Helen came in, looking a little damp, and asked Gloria if she was ready to leave. At Gloria's nod, Helen went over to the kitchen and handed Bob a set of keys. "Give this to Chuck. He's loaned me his truck to take Gloria home, in case the road turns to muck before I get back to town. Ella, bring my bowl home, okay? Either tonight or tomorrow, doesn't matter."

"These are your car keys," Bob remarked.

"Exactly. Chuck loaned me his truck. It's only polite that I leave my keys, in case he needs to use my car."

"But he has a car," Bob reminded her.

"I know that! I'll come out in the morning to swap vehicles. I know he'll want his truck back for the after-party."

"He'll put you to work," Bob warned her.

She smirked. "I think I remember how. Come on, Gloria, let's get you home before it really starts raining."

Wanda continued emptying salads and veggies into sandwich baggies or containers. Zita grabbed the bowls and platters to wash them. Bob tossed the leftovers into the refrigerator and dried the washed dishes as quickly as he could. Ella continued saying good-bye to people as they came in to claim their pans and bowls. Between them, they got the table cleaned off, and then the bowls and platters were laid out on the table. There were 3 partial bags of chips on the table, and when everything was washed and dried, Wanda started snacking on one of them.

"Good idea." Zita picked one of the others to snack on.

Fran, Irene and a couple other ladies came in from the patio and helped themselves to some of the desserts that were still out. "Oh, good grief," Wanda moaned, and when the ladies took seats on the available sofa, she started transferring the leftover desserts to small paper plates.

"Wanda?" Fran called to her.

"What?"

"Will we see you tomorrow?"

She looked up from transferring half a cherry pie. "Why would you see me tomorrow?"

"For the after party," she answered. "You've pretty much been working all day, you might as well get something for it."

Wanda shook her head. "No, I don't know anything about the after party." *So, apparently, the after party is the day after the official party. Not the way it works in Chicago, but then, those attendees aren't expected to work at the party. Is everybody as tired as I am?*

"Oh. I just assumed..."

Ella spoke up. "The after party is for those who worked at the party and their significant others, if applicable. It starts about 8, when Chuck makes waffles. The men will take down the tables, chairs and tents and take them home. The women make sure the insides of the house are tidy; run the vacuum, wash any towels that got used, stuff like that. It ends with trying to eat all the leftovers and watching a comedy on TV. You can come if you want, Wanda, but as tired as you look, I kind of assumed you'd want a quiet day at home."

"I am tired," she agreed. "And a quiet day sounds good." Part of her tiredness, she knew, was spending so much time around so many people, when she was used to being alone most of the time. The biggest group she was used to, anymore, was 6 assorted characters trying to work their way through her dungeon on Saturday nights. *Although, she thought after a glance at her watch, I've only been among a lot of people for about 8 hours. Only a few years ago, I routinely spent 8 hours a day as a busy waitress, and I refused to let that get me down.*

In some ways, Hank spoiled me.

The patio door opened, and Chuck walked in, carrying cans of pop, which he deposited on the table. Wanda was glad there was a plastic tablecloth, or the moisture from the cans would leave water stains. He left again, leaving the patio door open.

Significant others. But I'm not Chuck's significant other. And the way I feel, I might just sleep half of tomorrow away.

She heard a spattering of rain on the patio, gone as quickly as it had started. "Look, I'm beat, and it's starting to rain. If it's okay, I'm going to steal this bag of chips and a can of pop and head home. I assume Felix can get a ride?"

"Oh, the boys are sleeping over," Ella stated. "They usually sleep on the sofas. So go ahead, Wanda. I'm sorry for working you so hard today, but you were a great help. Thank you so much. Maybe you should give yourself a break and just make cold sandwiches for supper next Saturday."

"Oh, I haven't even thought about next Saturday yet." *Last week, they took a turn I didn't expect, and now I've got to plot out an entire new section for them to explore. Unless I just let them keep running into dead ends until they have to turn back to a section I've already plotted out.*

She gathered her selected bag of chips and can of pop and headed for the front door. "It was a lot of fun, Ella. I'm glad I came."

"We're glad you came, too," Bob said. "Like Ella said, you were a ton of help today. Do you want a piece of pie to take home?"

"No, thanks, I'm just going to go home and read a little before I go to bed."

"Wanda," Chuck called from the dining room table, where he deposited more cans of pop. When she turned, he paused for half a moment. "Thanks for coming. People were happy to meet you. And those who already knew you were happy you were here. I'm glad you came."

"Yes, I—thank you for the invite. Good night."

It was sprinkling when Wanda stepped off the front porch. She hurried to her car and drove home. It was sprinkling even heavier when she unlocked her front door.

Had they really wanted to invite her to the after party? Nobody had mentioned it before Bob had let it slip as I was packaging up leftovers. Then Fran asked if I'd be there, which prompted Ella to explain what it was, and to extend a late invite. But had she really meant it?

Chapter 31
Sunday, July 5, 7:49 AM

Wanda groaned, rolled out of her bed and staggered to the living room to answer her cell phone, which she had left on the table. "Hello?"

"I wasn't sure you'd answer your phone this time, either."

She thought it was Chuck. Or maybe Bob. She hadn't looked at the screen to see who it was, and without visuals, the voices were pretty close to each other. She couldn't stifle a huge yawn. "How many times did you call? I was sleeping."

"I'm sorry for waking you. I guess the party really wore you out yesterday."

"Well, I'm not used to being on my feet for hours at a time," she explained. "Not anymore."

"I was hoping I could talk you into coming for waffles."

It was probably Chuck, then. "Don't you have enough people there for your after-party?"

"Oh, they'll get the work done, but without Ella, I don't know how long it will take the ladies to get organized."

"Why isn't Ella there?" She sat down, because her feet were still sore from the day before.

"One, she has out-of-town visitors with whom she needs to work out details for going to college, and 2, she has worked very hard being my hostess, up to and including yesterday. So I excused her from the after-party."

Wanda yawned again. "Good. So tell the ladies what needs to be done, and let them have at it."

"I really can't entice you here with a waffle? Or 2?"

"It sounds good; I remember how great your waffles are. But I'm not done sleeping."

"Are you so completely exhausted from the party?"

"Well, not by itself. When I came home last night, I started reading, to unwind. I got so engrossed, it was 2 or 3 o'clock before I finally went to bed. And the phone ringing drug me out of a deep dream, so it's all I can do not to fall back asleep while I sit here. Even if I came out—and I don't think driving would be a good idea—I'd probably just curl up somewhere and fall asleep again."

She heard a heavy sigh. "Alright. I owe you a waffle breakfast. When I invited you to the party, I had no intention of making you work it."

"Everybody keeps saying that. Nobody made me work the party. I simply pitched in."

"I should have seen that you were ensconced in the most comfortable chair, and had others tend to your every whim."

She gave a short laugh. "As I remember it, all the chairs were the folding type, so not a lot of comfort to be had."

"Well, that's true," he conceded. "Still, isn't it the thought that counts?"

"If I acknowledge that as true, you'd completely run roughshod over me." She planted her elbow on the table to prop up her head.

"That isn't what I want to do with you."

Her eyes had been nearly closed, but somehow, what he had just said forced her to wake up. A bit. "What?"

"Don't you remember? I want to take you to Albion for a steak dinner."

And follow up the next morning with waffles at his place, her mind finished, sending alarms echoing through her body. "Don't hold your breath," she told him coldly, and then, in a slightly warmer tone, she said, "Good bye." She hung up, turned the phone off, and went back to bed.

When is he going to get the message? But she fell asleep before she could really give the question much thought.

Chapter 32
Saturday, July 11, 5:35 PM

Ella was all smiles when Wanda let the girls in; Zita looked more somber. "Everything's set!" Ella announced almost before she stepped into the porch. "I get to go to college in Omaha!"

"Wonderful! I assume you got some financial assistance from the college?"

"Oh, I haven't heard back from them, yet. But I've got enough money put away to pay tuition and fees. I'll be staying with Aunt Patty, so I won't have any room and board to pay for. So all I need to come up with now is money for incidentals, books, supplies and gas for my car. If Chuck keeps me on until school starts, I should be set."

"If you can find out what books you'll need, maybe you can find them cheaper online," Zita suggested.

"That's what I'm trying to do. I've already emailed all my teachers for the fall, asking about what books I'll need. I understand that next to tuition, books are the most expensive part of going to school."

"Oh, I think room and board usually comes in there somewhere," Wanda stated as they sat at the table.

Zita placed a cake pan on the stove. "What are we cooking for supper, Wanda?"

"Actually, it's all done," she stated. "Somebody suggested I serve cold sandwiches tonight, so I am. I have ham slices and tuna salad, with potato chips, 2 types of dip and sliced tomatoes. It's all in the refrigerator, waiting for people to arrive."

"Well, if we set the table, then the boys will have to wash the dishes." Ella's enthusiasm got both girls up, and soon, the table was adorned with plates, forks and glasses. They sat down again and waited for the others to arrive.

Chuck arrived at about the same time as the boys came up the sidewalk. Looking out across the front porch, Wanda saw Chuck get out of a low-slung sports car, and recognized the car that had been in his garage during his party. Such a change from the double-cab pickup he used for work.

Between the four males, they carried in chips, candy, 3 boxes of pop, and a bag of ice in a small cooler.

"No cooking tonight?" Chuck walked toward the kitchen.

"Not tonight," Wanda stated, and followed him. "Let me get the food out of the frig before you guys try to put any pop in."

Soon they were eating, with no complaints about it being a cold supper. Wanda swallowed her latest bite of her ham sandwich and spoke up. "As you remember, I won't be able to dungeon master next Saturday. I'll be in Denver on assignment for my publisher." All the kids frowned and groaned in disappointment, and she went on. "If one of you wants to try your hand at DM-ing, I can give you a small module that the rest of you can probably get through in 5 or 6 hours. I'll even throw in a lesson on how to DM before I leave." She looked across the table at Chuck.

"Don't look at me," he told her. "I'm headed out for a long weekend."

"Oh. I didn't realize that was the same weekend."

"Strange that it worked out that way, but it has. What about you, Ella?"

"I don't think it's fair to everybody else. I mean, I'll be leaving for Omaha in a few weeks, and I doubt I'll have the money to come home on weekends. Bad enough they have to lose a character from the party, without also losing their back-up Dungeon Master. Zita could do it."

Surprised, Zita quickly turned it down. "Sorry. I've got a lot on my mind, trying to figure out how I'm going to get everything I need so I can go to school this fall. I mean, I guess I need a car, but if I get a car, I'm not sure I can afford to go to school."

"Have you tried asking Uncle Robert?" Chuck asked.

"You mean your Uncle Robert?" she asked. "I know he works at a dealership, but I for sure can't afford a new car."

"There are used cars on the dealer's lot, too," Chuck told her. "Plus, he has friends at just about every used car lot in Columbus. Tell him what your budget is, and he'll find you something."

"That's just it, I don't have a budget for a car! I've been putting all my paychecks in my college fund, and I still don't know if I have enough. And I kind of have to get a car, because I can't get to the school without one." She heaved a heavy sigh. "Maybe I'll just have to put it off for a year, and continue to work for you, Chuck,"

"I knew I'd be losing Ella once school starts, but I didn't realize I'd be losing you, too."

"I just don't know! I don't know what to do!"

Chuck was sitting next to her, and put his hand over her balled fist. "I can see this has you tied in knots. If I'd known about this last weekend, I could have had you and your parents talk to Uncle Robert during the party. But never mind. You were probably tied up in knots and didn't think of anything like that. Let's just set the whole thing aside for tonight and enjoy ourselves. If you can set the problem aside and relax, sometimes that helps you see a solution you couldn't think of before. And I'll tell you what. I'll come over and help you go through all the data on going to school. Together, we should be able to figure it out. And if you have to put off school for a year, I'd be glad to have you continue to work for me. Full time, if you want."

"Full time? Really?"

"If you decide that's what you want to do. Now, can you set it aside for the night and try to have some fun?"

After a momentary hesitation, she gave a determined nod. "I'll give it my best try."

"That's the way. Don't let a problem get you down. We'll beat it in the end." He turned back to the rest of the table and picked up one of the chips on his plate. "Looks like that back-up dungeon master will be one of the boys."

"Not me," Tommy said. "Busy." Indeed, Wanda suspected he had spent the entire day in his gardens; she hadn't seen him leave his Big Patch until almost 5.

281

"I'd probably try to put everything on a computer," Felix stated. "Even though I don't know enough programming to know how to do that."

"I guess that leaves me," Rusty said. "So, okay, Wanda, when do you want to get together for that lesson?"

"Well, any time tomorrow afternoon, or Monday evening about 6 or 7? It shouldn't take much more than an hour, if that. Depends on how easily you pick it up."

"Yeah, no promises," he said with a wry smile. "How about 2 tomorrow afternoon? That way, if I get hopelessly confused, we can get together Monday evening, and you can try again."

"That sounds okay, but I'm sure you're going to do fine."

* * *

9:09 PM

They typically took a short break around 9, when the kids all lined up to use the bathroom and get a fresh drink from the refrigerator. Hardly had the kids left the living room before Chuck moved down the table into Ella's normal chair.

"Wanda, I wanted to ask if I said something last Sunday that upset you." he asked quietly.

"Why would you think that?"

"Because you said good-bye, hung up, and wouldn't answer your phone after that."

She tried to brush his concern away. "I told you I was half asleep. Falling asleep, actually. So after I said good-bye, I turned off my phone and went back to bed. I didn't get up until almost noon. I forgot I'd turned off my phone until I went to call my publisher, about supper time."

"Okay. I just... I don't want you mad at me, Wanda. I thought maybe the comment about taking you for a steak dinner might have riled you."

"I was too asleep to get riled. But since we're on the subject, I don't want you to bring that up again. To me, it sounds like a date. Waffles at your place with a lot of other people there is one thing, but just the 2 of us sounds like a date. And I'm not ready to date. Anyone. I'd appreciate it if you'd remember that."

282

He nodded, looking somber. "I'll try. So... it's okay for us to get together and... do stuff, as long as we're with others?"

She felt like this could be a trap. She didn't want to make any promises. "Chuck, it depends on the circumstances."

"What do you mean?"

"Going out with Steve and Fran to see a movie or have dinner or... anything, would be too much like a double date. It needs to be a bigger group than that, so that I'm not automatically paired with you. Or anybody."

"Well, now I'm confused," he returned. "You go to the Dew Drop Inn every Monday with Bob."

And now he's jealous, on top of everything! Well, I suppose, given his history... "Bob and I each pay our own bill there. We meet up when we've finished our errands, except for groceries. It gives us a chance to sit down for a few minutes. And besides that, we're just friends, there's no date aspect to it at all."

He nodded again. "This puts me in a position I've never really been in before. I might make mistakes, but I'm going to try. To do things the way you want to."

That's all I can ask. Wait, what 'things'? But she couldn't ask because the kids were coming back from the kitchen, ready to open up the 'goodies' waiting on the heating stove.

Chuck stood up, took his own glass and hers to the kitchen, came back with fresh ice and a couple cans of pop. "Oh, Wanda, did you leave some clothes at my place last weekend?"

She froze at the sudden memory. "I did. Swimsuit, jeans and a towel."

"I thought so. Fran found them as she was cleaning the office. Nobody claimed them. And then I remembered you had brought a swimsuit. So I thought it might be your stuff. If it's okay, I'll bring it by tomorrow on my way to Zita's house."

"Yes, that sounds fine," she stated, and took a drink of her pop. "Okay, everybody ready? You were ready to search the bedroom of the Grand Poohba of the goblins. Remember how I described it? Okay, Ella, exactly what will you do?"

Chapter 33
Thursday, July 16, 7:19 AM

Wanda locked her front door and put her 2nd suitcase in the back of her car. She was getting a little later start than she'd hoped, and wondered if she'd be able to make up any time on the road. The convention didn't start until the next day, but it was likely some convention staff members would be there tonight. She was hoping to slip in and claim her hotel room without any of the convention staff realizing she had arrived alone. This weekend was going to be tough enough without trying to explain that.

As she came up the cross street toward Belgrade's main drag, she saw a red sports car headed south, probably out of town. It was Chuck, and he seemed to be in a hurry. Eager to get into those Colorado mountains for his vacation, she decided.

As she turned south onto the main street, she saw the sports car turn left at the edge of town, to start up the Big Hill. By the time she reached the top of the Big Hill, the sports car was out of sight, possibly just over the next rolling hill, but she didn't see it again. It looked like Chuck's car. *He sure is flying low for someone who's just headed out for some sightseeing. Hope he doesn't drive like that in the mountains.*

She put that thought away, determined not to bring any Belgrade problems with her to Denver. Denver would present her with enough problems.

Chapter 34
Friday, July 17, 9:41 AM

Wanda rode the elevator down to the hotel lobby and looked around for the registration table for the convention. The lobby seemed unusually busy for so early on the first day of a convention, but maybe people were checking out.

The concierge sent her down a side hallway. She felt like she'd walked half a mile before she found the convention registration table. They didn't seem to have themselves pulled together yet.

"Can I help you?" One woman finally asked.

"I'm Wanda Davis."

"Did you pre-register?"

"I should have a complimentary badge. I provided transportation for Linda Sinclair."

"Oh, Linda has arrived? People have been worried." She glanced at her watch. "They might be calling her room right now, to see if she wants breakfast."

"Oh, Linda won't answer the phone. She had breakfast in the hotel cafe earlier, and charged it to the room. But she's in the middle of writing her next book, and probably won't leave her room much more than she has to. Um, could I get our badges?"

"Oh! Of course." She turned to the other people trying to make sense of boxes of supplies. "Does anybody know where the Guest badges are?" It took a couple minutes, but eventually, the woman had a manila envelope in her hand. She squeezed it and gently bent it. "Yep, that feels like it's got 2 program books in it. Check inside and see if it has both badges."

Wanda pulled out 2 badges, pinned the one that said "Wanda Davis" on her t-shirt. "Thanks," she told the registration people, and added, "I'll go up and make sure Linda knows when she has to be where." She turned to begin the long walk back to the elevators.

"Hey, Wanda!"

The voice sounded familiar, but out of place. She looked up and saw Paula's assistant pushing a luggage cart full of boxes down the hallway. "Hey, Debby. So you're the lucky one manning the table, are you?"

"Aren't I always? Good to see you found your way here."

"Yeah, well, Linda wasn't much help as a navigator, but I managed."

"Well, since we ran into each other, you want to help me set up the table? The dealer's room opens at noon, and I need to get something to eat before that."

"Sure, I can help for a while. Let's find your table and I'll get started while you go eat."

"No," Debbie returned. "That won't work. Paula's changed the whole table arrangement, and I'm not sure my notes will make sense to anybody but me."

"Wasn't it just last year she had the 'perfect' table arrangement, and she was never going to change it?"

"Yep. This time she's got me building a pyramid atop the table to display the books, with the apex books at eye level. Oh, here's my table. Let's just get all these boxes shoved under the table, and then I'll move behind and get started."

"Okay. I'll take the luggage cart back to the lobby and get you something to eat. What do you want?"

Debbie stopped to think. "Oh, just go to the hotel shop and load me up with candy, a couple cans of soda, some kind of sandwich, and a cake, if they've got any. With a pyramid as tall as Paula wants, I'll probably have to stand all day long, in order to see over it." She handed Wanda 2 twenty dollar bills. "Try not to get anything that might spoil before I get around to eating it, which might not be today."

"I know, the usual convention fare. I'll be back shortly."

Wanda returned the luggage cart to the lobby and headed for the hotel shop. As she crossed the lobby floor, she heard somebody ask, "Has anybody seen Charlie?"

"I think he was headed for the con suite," someone answered.

"Oh. Okay."

Wanda wondered that the convention didn't have radios or some other form of communication so they could find staff members when they needed them. Even a list of people's cell phone numbers would be better than nothing.

About 10 minutes later, as she was headed back for the dealer's room, she heard the same voice ask, "Does anybody know where Charlie is?"

"Con suite."

"No, he's not there."

"Well, try the art show."

"That's who's looking for him!"

Wanda smiled, having seen and heard similar conversations at other science fiction conventions she had attended over the years. Some problems, it seemed, were universal and perennial.

When she got back to the dealer's room, the man at the door wouldn't let her in, because she wasn't a dealer, and the room wasn't open yet. She managed to get Debbie's attention, and gave her the sack of snacks. "Do you know when the panels begin?"

"It's either 2 or 3," Debbie answered. "Opening ceremonies is at 6."

"And the art show?"

"Not until 7. But it's open until 10."

"I really want to see it this evening. In case I don't, if you get to the art show, keep your eyes open for prints by a new kid, Ella Swanson. She's got a cute sense of humor in her paintings. And now, I'd better go up, check the schedule and make sure Linda's ready for her panels."

"Don't let her forget Opening Ceremonies."

"Yeah, she's not going to like that, but it's part of what she signed up for. See you later, Debbie."

"Stop by and see the pyramid, if you get a chance, Wanda." Wanda nodded and started to go. "Oh, Wanda, we're taking advance orders for 'Footsteps in the Moonlight', starting today."

Wanda's heart leapt. That was her 3rd book, and wasn't due out until November, in time for the Christmas rush. It was the one she had worked so hard to get rewritten just after moving to Belgrade. "Well, that will get her attention," she said, and laughed.

Wanda went up to her room and checked the schedule. It turned out Linda didn't have any place to be until 6 PM, when she would be involved with the opening ceremonies. Wanda opened up her laptop and started working on her next book.

At 11:30, she ordered room service, which arrived surprisingly quickly, so by 12:30, she put the tray outside her door and went down to check out the dealer's room. She wondered if Debbie had gotten her pyramid finished yet.

The pyramid was constructed of boxes that Wanda recognized as shipping boxes that held 2 dozen books each. On top of each box was a book in a bookstand, facing the customers. Debbie had filled the rest of the table with books laying down flat. "I have to admit," Wanda said as she approached, "the pyramid looks good. Is it sturdy enough to get through the weekend?"

"It has been so far. This is the 4th convention I've used it at. It's time consuming to get it put together, but I use enough giant binder clips to hold it together. Unless somebody gives the table a shove, then the books go flying everywhere."

Wanda looked over the arrangement. "I didn't realize Paula had published so many books."

Debbie leaned closer and whispered, "Look again. Some books on the pyramid are also laying flat on the table."

"Oh! You're right." The other 2 'footsteps' books—sitting atop the pyramid—were also among those laying down. She couldn't remember any other time when her books had appeared more than once on her publisher's table at a convention.

"She sent a lot of Linda's books to this convention, expecting to sell a lot."

"Well, I'll see that Linda does everything expected of her," Wanda said, and hoped Paula's dreams of big sales weren't disappointed. "You seem to have things in order, so I'll take a look around the dealer's room."

* * *

5:10 PM

Wanda finished combing her brown hair and put it in a ponytail at the nape of her neck, letting it flow down her back almost to her waist. Her 2nd suitcase rested on the luggage rack, and she got out her 'Linda' makeup. First some pale foundation. Normally, it was a couple shades lighter than her own skin tone, but this time, it seemed to be 3 shades light. She must have gotten out into the sun more since moving to Nebraska.

After foundation, she put on purple eye shadow, eyeliner and mascara, blush and some purple lipstick. She put on her black wig, anchored it down and made sure it didn't look too disheveled. Then she got out the black slacks, purple shirt and black jacket and put them on. The wig was a long page style, coming down to her shoulders, so between that and her collared shirt, no one would see her real hair. Then came a pair of knee-high hose and her black slip-on shoes. Then she slipped on a pair of glasses with a purple frame. She looked in the mirror.

There. Now I'm Linda Sinclair.

She got into the manila envelope from the registration desk and got out the badge that said 'Linda Sinclair, Author Guest of Honor.' It made a really nice touch on her jacket lapel.

She got a purple felt pen from Linda's suitcase and put "Linda S" on the cover of the program book, then started going through the schedule and putting an L at every panel or event that she was supposed to be at this weekend.

There was a knock at the door. She slipped the purple pen in her jacket pocket and went to answer it. A handsome young man stood in the hallway. "Hi, I'm Eddie. I've been assigned to be your handler this weekend, and I'm here to take you to the Opening Ceremony."

"Oh, wonderful. Let me get my room key." She went back to the dresser, picked up the room key, and slipped it into her other jacket pocket. As she headed for the door, she paused to rap on the bathroom door. "Wanda, I'm leaving now." She pretended to listen for an answer, and then left the room, making sure the door closed tightly behind her.

289

Her heart was beating rapidly as they rode down in the elevator. She had never done this before without Hank at her side. And this time, she was part of the 'main dish' of the convention, as Hank used to say. She hoped she didn't make too many mistakes.

She was given a seat in the front row before the stage, and Eddie faded out of sight. She was surprised when someone approached and asked her to autograph her first book, 'Footsteps in the Snow', but she pulled out her purple pen and autographed it.

Others started to come forward, books in hand, but a middle-aged woman got up on stage and took the microphone. "Could we all sit down, please? I see people asking our guests for autographs, and I'd like to point out that each guest has 2 autograph sessions, on Saturday and Sunday, so you should be able to get your autographs at those times. Right now, I'd like to go through some last-minute changes and the rules of the convention, as well as a few other things."

As far as opening ceremonies go, this one was relatively painless. There were few last-minute changes to the schedule, and the obligatory convention rules that wouldn't be needed if people treated each other with respect and common sense. But some of the less mature hadn't figured out how to do that yet, so the rules were usually posted inside the program book, as well as enumerated during the opening ceremony. Linda wondered if it did any good, other than reassure the ones who did behave.

This convention, in order to make things less boring, had worked out a skit, or a series of skits, so that somebody wandered across the stage, doing exactly what the speaker had said would not be allowed. The speaker then called for "Security!", where upon 2 people wearing Star Trek red tunics came on stage and dragged the misbehaving person away. After the 2nd skit, the audience began calling for security before the speaker could. It was fun and filled the audience with camaraderie.

After the speaker got done and urged the audience to 'go out and have fun!', Linda asked Eddie to take her to the art show. It was a good-sized art show, and she started through it methodically, admiring the talent and hard work of the various artists.

When she found the 4 prints from Ella, she studied them closely, trying to decide which one to bid on. Unable to decide, she put an opening bid on each one, Using 'Wanda Davis', and then continued to the rest of the artwork.

"Charlie?" somebody asked.

"We lost him at 7," one of the staff stated. "Try the party rooms. He might be looking for Mildred."

This Charlie character sure is a popular guy here.

Eddie reappeared before she finished viewing the art show and asked if she was ready to visit the party rooms. This was the least favorite part of a convention, for her, and doubly so now, without Hank's strong presence to keep the drunks from bothering her, as well as making sure her drinks were non-alcoholic. But the convention expected her to attend at least some room parties, so she sighed and agreed.

The party rooms were on the opposite end of the floor from her own room. As they approached that section of the hall, which seemed over-flowing with people, she told Eddie, "I will look in on a maximum of 5 party rooms and the con suite. The party rooms should be odd numbered."

"Why odd numbered?"

"It's my method of being fair. Tomorrow, I'll visit even numbered party rooms."

"Why only 5 rooms?"

"Because I'm an introvert and being in a crowd quickly drives me crazy. So if you can, find me party rooms that have interesting conversation or entertainment, and not just people getting drunk."

"But drinking is half the fun."

"Not for me," she answered.

He led her into an odd-numbered room. She got as far as the dresser and turned around and left without greeting anybody. She had seen a keg in the bathroom, and there were no fewer than 3 pitchers sitting around the room, some fairly empty. Nobody seemed very stable on their feet, or like they knew how to speak without slurring.

"That was room 1," she told Eddie when he came out to see

where she had gone. "Now I'll pick the rooms myself." And stepped down the corridor to the next odd-numbered room.

This room had the TV on, playing a very old B-rated movie that she'd seen many times. There were cans of pop in the bathtub, interspersed with ice, and a few bottles of liquor that seemed to be under the control of a middle-aged man who was alert and articulate as he conversed with the people in the room. No one seemed to be watching the TV, but nearly everybody was engaged in the conversation.

"Eddie, would you get me a coke, please?" she asked as she took a seat next to another woman on the edge of the bed.

"And here is our lovely and talented Author Guest," said the man presiding over the liquor. "Good evening, Ms Sinclair."

"Please call me Linda," she returned.

"I shall, and my name is John and you may call me... John."

"Good evening, John. And what is the topic under discussion tonight?"

"We were pondering how many more tomes there might be in your 'Footsteps' series. I personally have no problem with you continuing it without end, but Shirley, the woman you're sitting next to, feels the characters must be getting tired of adventure, and want to settle down at some point."

"That's a very good point, Shirley," she stated to the woman. "I thought 'Footsteps in the Moonlight' was going to be a stand-alone book, and so I hinted at the end of it that everybody lived happily ever after. But my publisher wanted to break it into 2 books, which we did, and that's how 'Footsteps in the Twilight' came about, but by then, after I'd done the rewrite to break it in two, I'd started thinking of another book, so I couldn't have everybody living happily ever after."

"There are more 'Footsteps' books coming?" Shirley asked.

"Oh, yes," Linda answered, wondering how long Eddie was going to take to get a can of pop from the bathroom. "The 3rd book is called 'Footsteps in the Moonlight. I'm currently working on book #4, 'Footsteps in the Sand'. I don't have a title for the next book, yet. After that, maybe I'll let these characters settle into middle age while I explore another world with another set of characters. But you have a point, John, I can think of many more titles to continue the 'Footsteps' series. I just haven't thought up stories to fit the titles yet."

"So, if I understand you correctly," John wanted to sum it up, "both Shirley and I get to have things our way."

"Yes, I guess that is one way of looking at it." Eddie finally handed her a can of coke, already opened. When she raised it to take a drink, she could smell some kind of alcohol in it. She lowered it without drinking as Shirley asked a question.

"Do you know when your next book will come out?"

"I do. 'Footsteps in the Moonlight' will be released in November. And if you go downstairs to the MoonPhaze dealer's table, they are taking pre-orders for it this weekend."

That elicited some excitement among the people in the room, and she stood up, offered to shake hands with Shirley, and then with John. "Thank you for allowing me to monopolize the conversation, but I have other parties to visit this evening." She turned to address the room at large. "Thank you for having me as a guest. I appreciate each and every one of you who have enjoyed my books, and I hope you continue to enjoy them. Good night." Most of the party-goers waved good-bye, one or two wanted to shake her hand, but she got out of that room with little difficulty. On to the next one.

She paused in the open-doored bathroom of the next room to dump her alcohol-laced coke down the sink. Leaving the can on the bathroom counter, she got her own can from the bathtub, and then looked to see what was going on in this room.

There were small groups of people talking together at various places around the room, with a bowl of chips on the dresser. She opened her can of pop, grabbed a couple chips and slowly made her way around the room, inserting a comment when she could think of something to say. Some people got tongue-tied when they realized who she was, but most of them welcomed her into their conversation, however briefly. It took her about 15 minutes to make her way around the room and then she moved on to the next room. And after another 20 minutes or so, she moved on to the last party for the night.

At long last, she entered the con suite, which was also having a party. Here she got herself a bowl of popcorn while she looked around. There were several people here wearing 'staff' t-shirts. She made her way to the closest one and asked, "Of all the people on the convention staff who are here this evening, who is the furthest up the ladder?"

The young woman seemed confused for a moment, then looked around, and abruptly pointed to a middle-aged woman standing behind the bar. "Yvette."

"Okay, and what is her title?"

"She's con chair."

"Oh, good. Excellent. Thank you." She walked over and asked if she could speak with Yvette.

"What can I do for you, Ms Sinclair?"

"Please, call me Linda," was the first response, and then she went on. "I am releasing Eddie as my handler. I assume you can find other work for him to do for the rest of the weekend."

Yvette glanced behind Linda, presumably at the young man in question. "What did he do?"

Linda grimaced. "I don't want to get into details in such a public setting. Shall we discuss this by email after the convention?"

"Would you come with me, please?" Yvette asked, and unlocked the door to the adjoining room. Which was full of soda pop, bags of chips and other goodies. There was hardly room to step in, but they made it, and Yvette closed the door. "I can't find a new handler for you if I don't know what this one did wrong."

Linda sighed, wondering how to be tactful. "I'm sure I—I mean, Paula must have told you I'm not one who drinks alcohol; it isn't the image I want. And while parties are outside my comfort zone, me being an introvert, I can manage as long as the majority of the attendees are not drunk."

Yvette's face burned, either from embarrassment or anger. "Let me guess; he took you to rooms that were mostly drunks."

"He only took me to one of those, because after that, I chose which rooms I would visit."

"I'm so sorry, Linda. I told him what the rules were, and he assured me he would follow them. I feared he was too young to be trusted. Seems I was right."

"He also brought me a can of pop that I'm sure had alcohol in it. I could smell it."

Yvette apologized again. "If that boy still lived at home, I'd ground him for a year or two. Well, at least I can ground him until he goes back to school."

"Oh, he's your son! I don't know whether to be relieved or mortified!"

"No need to be mortified. He's my son, and I thought I had raised him better than that. Well, never mind, I'll pick a handler with more sense for the rest of the convention."

"Oh, I'm not sure that's necessary," Linda said. "The map in the program book makes sense; I'm sure I could find my own way around."

"Maybe, but the convention will double in size tomorrow," Yvette revealed. We did some extra advertising this year, and a mass of people who have never attended before are coming on Saturday. So it's going to be crowded, and I'm guessing you'll need somebody to keep your autograph line under control. That won't be completely left to your handler, but if your handler can get you through the crowds, so much the better."

"But really—"

"We promised you a personal handler. I've got a guy in mind. He's a hard worker, no matter what the job that needs done. He's mature enough to have a brain in his head, and he's often said you were his favorite author. I think it's time he got to do something fun at the convention, after all the work he's put in, year after year. You see how he does tomorrow, and if he doesn't work out, I'll assign my own husband! And I don't say that lightly, because he's the head of our security."

"Well, if you're sure it won't take this paragon away from more important duties."

"He's already helped us set up. He's usually a roamer until we start closing down on Sunday. No, that's what I'm going to do. I'll ask him to be your handler. People are beginning to take him for granted, and I think it's time to recognize him for all he's done for us."

With yet another apology, Yvette opened the door and they exited.

After half an hour of browsing through the goodies offered at the con suite, 'Linda' decided she was tired and went back to her room.

Chapter 35
Saturday, July 18, 8:08 AM

Wanda yawned as she opened the door to the pool and exercise area. She'd been late getting to bed, and she's had real trouble getting up this morning. But she and Hank had never missed using the hot tub at the hotel when they were at a convention, and she saw no reason to give up that pleasure now.

The pool area was empty at this time of day, but she was certain someone was in the exercise room. The glass between the two areas was fogged over, so she couldn't really see them.

She got a towel from a rack and placed it and her room key on a table, then turned on the jets for the hot tub and got in. It wasn't until then that she realize how tense she was, being at a convention without Hank. She leaned back, closed her eyes and let the heat and bubbles massage her whole body.

After some time, another person got into the hot tub also. The water level rose, and she sat up straighter to keep her mouth above the surface. She opened her eyes and stared at the person sitting opposite her. "Chuck!"

"It is you," he stated, as if he'd had his doubts. "What are you doing here?"

Without thinking, she said, "I'm here for the convention. What are you doing here? You're supposed to be driving through the mountains."

He grimaced and admitted, "I've never been sure how people back home would react if they knew I spent a weekend at a sci fi convention. So I lie about where I'm going."

And here I've been feeling guilty for my lies! "Do you make a habit of lying to friends and family?"

"No," he answered firmly. "It's one week-end a year, and it's the closest thing to a vacation that I get. What about you?"

"What about me?"

"You told people you were coming here as a journalist, to cover some kind of business convention."

"No, I did not," she refuted. "I said I was coming to Denver on an assignment from my publisher. If people assumed I was attending a business convention, that's their problem, not my doing."

"Maybe. So what kind of assignment are you on, then?"

"My publisher is also the publisher for Linda Sinclair, who doesn't drive. So I got her here and I'll get her home."

"And what do you get out of it?"

"I get to attend the convention, when I'm not baby-sitting Linda. And I do mean baby-sitting, because she brought her laptop and would rather be working on her next book."

"You took several days off from writing your book to do this assignment?"

"No. I'm plotting out what comes next in my story. Once I get home, the words will flow as fast as I can type." *Another lie.*

"Yeah, when I get home, it'll be right back to work for me, too," he agreed. "Sometimes I get home in time for Steve to brief me on how things went while I was gone."

"Is it worth it?" She thought of a day driving here, and a day driving back, and only 3 days of actually doing anything fun.

"Usually, yes. But, this year..." He sighed. "I have to admit, I'm worried about the kids."

"Well, today's Saturday, you could call one of them and see how things are going. By the way, I thought they were youngsters these days, not kids."

"When I worry about them, they're kids. But you're right, I left the dangerous jobs for after I get back."

"Dangerous? Like what?"

"Roofing jobs. If somebody looses their footing and falls off, that can be nasty. I try to keep my crew wearing a safety harness, but if there's nothing handy to attach to..."

A cold shiver went through her, despite the heat of the water. "Ugh! I don't want to think of any of you being up on somebody's roof."

"Well, roofs need to be replaced from time to time, and somebody has to do it." He frowned at the bubbling water for a time. "I try to keep the kids on the ground. At least for now. They can send up supplies and drinks for the oldsters, whatever else I can dream up for them to do."

He really is worried about the kids. "That reminds me. You were going to get together with Zita and her parents last Sunday. Did you get anything figured out?"

"I at least got her settled down some. This weekend, she and her father are going to go to Uncle Robert in Columbus and see if he can find her a car. I pointed out she doesn't have to pay for both years at once, so she has some money to spend on a car, and with her father's help, she should be able to keep it running. He's a shade-tree mechanic, just like she is. But she wants to go to school and get her mechanics certificate, see if she can't have an easier time getting a job. Her classes will only take half her day, so she should be able to work some hours for me, and that will help her replenish her funds for the 2nd year of classes."

"I saw how panicked she was, and you make it sound so simple."

"She was panicking," he agreed. "And it took all of us time to realize she didn't have to pay for both years of classes before she could start any of them. Even better, this gives her a chance to apply for financial aid for her 2nd year."

"You have this habit of solving everybody's problems for them," she remarked.

"Something I picked up when Mom was so sick, the last couple years of her life. Dad alternated between denial and despair. So if I wasn't trying to help her figure out how to do something she wanted to do, I was trying to find a way to cheer him up."

"Well, I have to give you points for having good intentions, even if you also tend to run rough-shod over the people you want to help."

His face went pink, and she was pretty sure it wasn't from the water's heat. "I'm trying to break that habit."

"Good."

A companionable silence settled over them for a few minutes, and then Chuck said, "Maybe I should install a hot tub in my house, in the corner of my pool room."

I've often dreamed of having my own hot tub. "Why?"

"Well, we've spent the past 2 months getting mad, being mad, or getting over being mad with each other. Now, just a few minutes shared in the hot tub, and we're getting along just fine. One could almost believe we're friends."

Wanda chuckled. "I'm not sure we've gotten there yet, although we do seem to be getting closer to the possibility. I'm not sure the hot tub has much to do with it, though. Maybe we're just tired of fighting, so we're willing to talk instead."

"So, have you eaten, yet?"

"Yes, I have. Why?"

"I was thinking maybe we could have breakfast together. Dutch, of course."

"Sorry, not today. "

"Tomorrow?"

"Maybe. I don't know when I'll get up. If Linda gets home by midnight, then I might be up for it. As in, being awake."

"Oh, is Linda a party animal?"

"The reverse, actually. But she agreed to attend 5 room parties and the con suite on both Friday and Saturday night, and I don't know how long that will take her. I seem to remember she has a panel this evening, and I'm not sure how late that takes place."

"Well, then I'll hope it's not too late. Shall I call you in the morning and see if you're up yet?"

"Okay, but not before 8. That will still give us time for breakfast, won't it?"

"It should. The convention doesn't get started very early."

She glanced at the clock on the wall. "Oh! I've been in here far longer than I should have been. Don't they recommend 20 minutes or less?" She started to climb out of the tub.

"And I need to go get breakfast," he stated, standing up.

"Charlie!" called a female voice. "I thought you'd be here!"

"Yeah, here I am," Chuck answered with no enthusiasm.

Wanda hesitated on her way to get her towel and room key. *Charlie? Chuck was the Charlie everybody was trying to find yesterday? Probably*, she decided, and continued on her way, sure it was none of her business.

A young woman with brassy red hair approached, her bikini leaving next to nothing to be imagined. "Oh, I got here just in time to relax in the hot tub. Come on, Charlie, let's get in."

Wanda did a quick wipe down with her towel and wrapped it around herself.

"I've already been in the hot tub, Mildred. I'm ready for breakfast."

"Oh, come on, Charlie! I have a headache, and you're so good at massaging my shoulders."

"Sorry, Mildred. I have things to do, and Vet wants to see me first thing this morning. But the hot tub should do you some good. If not, go to the con suite and have some orange juice. I hear it's good for hangovers."

Wanda headed for the exit, trying not to hear their private conversation. But the woman's voice was bordering on shrill.

"Charlie, you promised!"

"I said if you got up in time, then we could have breakfast together. As soon as I get dressed, I'm going to breakfast. You go ahead and enjoy the hot tub."

"But Charlie!"

Wanda reached the door and was through it. A brief glance back revealed Chuck putting on a t-shirt and shoes. The pouting redhead hadn't made any move towards the hot tub.

* * *

10:39 AM

Linda's Saturday outfit consisted of gray slacks and vest and a dark purple shirt with long, 4-button cuffs. Everything else was the same, except today she carried a notebook-sized purse. She put her room key and several of her purple pens in the purse; it was entirely possible she wouldn't get back before it was time for her autograph session. After checking the schedule again, she sat on her bed and waited impatiently for her new 'handler' to show up.

She had a panel with some other authors on writing at 11, the autograph session at 2, a panel on creating characters for a series of books at 7, and a panel on creating sexual tension at 9. That one would get over at 10, so she should be able to get through the party rooms and the con suite in time to get to bed by midnight. It didn't leave her much time for writing today, though. Still, that was mostly an excuse for why she didn't spend time roaming through the convention. Especially if Yvette was right about the crowds they expected today. She tucked the program book into her purse, and made sure she had the correct badge attached to her vest.

A knock at her door startled her. She got up and answered it, wondering who they had found to be her handler this time.

"Hello. My name is Charlie, and the con chair asked me to be your handler today, Ms Sinclair."

Linda swallowed a sudden lump in her throat and forced herself to stop staring at him. She hadn't even thought of this possibility this morning when she discovered Chuck was at the same convention. *Is my disguise good enough? Or does Chuck know me well enough to see right through it?*

"Umm, we should probably get going," he stated.

She nodded, pulled her voice down into her throat a little and told the empty room, "Wanda, I'm taking off." Then she hurriedly stepped into the hall and closed her door. "I was told the convention was expecting a lot of people to show up today."

"And they are jammed at registration. So if we are lucky, we might get to your first panel without too much trouble. After that... I don't know." He led her to the elevators, and they got on the first one that stopped, even though it was already crowded. It seemed people on lower floors were traveling up in order to go down. It happened at these conventions.

Once they reached the lobby, Chuck led her around and between pockets of people and down a hallway to one of the panel rooms. "Here we go, with a couple minutes to spare," he told her, and opened the door.

They stood in the back not because there weren't any seats available, but because in just a minute or two, this panel would end, and Linda would need to go forward and claim her position at the table.

When that time came, she was surprised when Chuck followed her forward. She started to take her usual seat at the end of the table, thought better of it—*I am, after all, the Author Guest of Honor*—and sat in the very middle of the table. "How many panelists are there?" she wondered, and pulled her program book from her purse.

"Five, I believe," Chuck answered. "Timothy Hightower is moderator." He poured her a glass of water from the pitcher, started going through a stack of folded name tents.

Linda bit her bottom lip for a moment. The name sounded familiar, but "I don't know him."

"He's a local author, finally beginning to get some notice outside of Colorado."

"My ears are burning," said a man walking up the central aisle. "Charlie, are you telling tales about me?"

"I was just telling Ms Sinclair who you were; she said she didn't know you."

"No, we've never met," Timothy stated, and held out his hand to Linda. "Hello, Ms Sinclair. I am this panel's moderator, Timothy Hightower."

"It's always nice to meet new people," she returned, shaking his hand. "Especially when we share a common interest, like writing."

"I am quite jealous of your popularity," Timothy went on as Chuck handed him a name tent. "Here I've been coming to this convention for many years, and I've never been asked to be a guest."

Linda smiled in understanding. "I've never been a guest in Chicago. I was blown away when I got the invite from Denver. I'll try to put in a good word for you in Chicago, shall I?"

"Oh, indeed. Tell the Chicago people I held the audience absolutely spell-bound with my oratory skills." Charlie put a name tent in front of Linda and handed some to 3 more people approaching the table on the small stage. "Ah, here are the rest of our panelists," Timothy stated and conducted introductions.

Charlie had disappeared. Or else, Linda simply couldn't see him in the crowd. And the room was crowded. All the chairs were full, people were standing against the back and side walls, and a few even ventured to sit down between the chairs and the small stage. So far as Linda could see, both sets of double doors to the hallway were open, and those who couldn't get into the room were standing just outside the doorjamb, listening.

It was enough to give her stage fright, combined with a hint of claustrophobia. This was something that hadn't happened to her since her first few conventions, and she did the same thing now as she did then; concentrate on listening to her co-panelists and try to add something pertinent. It helped that Timothy was a good moderator and made sure everybody got to say their piece.

And then, Charlie was there, gently forcing his way through the nearest doorway, avoiding walking on those sitting on the floor, and stepping up on the stage to take hold of the nearest microphone.

"I'm sorry, but this panel is done. We can't let it go late, as the next panel needs to get started. Now, please, stand up—if you aren't already—and leave the room in an orderly fashion."

People did stand up, but many tried to make their way toward the stage, so Charlie went on: "I'm sorry, but these panelists do not have time to do autographs right now. They all have autograph sessions scheduled later today. Those will be held outside, in the hallway, at the tables. If you want an autograph from Ms Sinclair, she will be at the last table on the north end at 2 this afternoon." He put the microphone down, grabbed Linda's name tent and waved her towards the end of the stage. "Let's go find something to eat." He put one hand on her shoulder, and the other hand out in front of them, as if he would force their way through the crowd, but it seemed the crowd moved with them.

The crowd became a muddled mass as they entered the hallway. He turned Linda toward the front of the hotel. When he realized a number of people were following them, he turned his head and reminded them that Linda would be giving autographs at 2 o'clock. It was uncertain if the crowd behind them diminished any or not.

There was a long line sticking out of the entrance to the hotel restaurant. "Oh, that doesn't look good," Charlie stated.

"The con suite?" Linda asked.

"They serve hoagies for Saturday lunch, which is very popular with the regular attendees. I don't know if any of the new ones know about it."

"Excuse me, where's the con suite?" asked one of the women behind them.

"Room 1401," Charlie answered. Slowly, the crowd behind them seemed to break up as people headed for the elevators.

Charlie grinned. "It worked. Now we have to find something to eat. We'd never get through the restaurant in time."

"Let's try the hotel shop," Linda suggested. "Sometimes they have sandwiches."

"Good idea." They hurried across the lobby and around the corner to the hotel shop. They both found something to eat and drink, charging them to their rooms. Then they sat down at the closest table in the hallway to eat.

"Well, Yvette told me last night they were expecting a big crowd today, about twice what they usually have," Linda stated as they watched people pass by.

"At least twice," Charlie agreed. "Maybe more. Twice was based on the number of pre-registered they got."

As Linda neared the end of her banana and her pop, she glanced down toward the opposite end of the hallway. "I'm thinking the next thing I should do is start giving autographs."

"That's not scheduled until 2."

"Look down there," she returned. "It's only about 12:30, and people are already getting into line for an autograph. I don't have anything else to do, so I might as well make them happy. Who knows, it's possible the only reason they are here is to get an autograph."

Charlie studied the half dozen people standing in line at the northernmost table. Three more joined them. He sighed and pulled a cell phone from his back pocket, dialed a number. "Hey, Vet, people are already lining up for Linda's autograph. She's inclined to go ahead and get started with that."

305

"And go until 4 pm or when the line is done," Linda added.

"Did you hear that?" Charlie asked. "Yeah. Okay, send some people down with painter's tape so we can try to get some organization to this." Linda wondered how they were going to organize with painter's tape, but apparently 'Vet' understood what he meant. "Yeah. I thought the Fire Marshall would show up and shut that panel down. I was sweating bullets. Okay, we'll get started." He hung up and turned to face her. "Do you need a rest room first?"

"Not yet. I might before we get done, if most of the new people are really here because of me."

"Well, sing out when you get to that point, and we'll try to hold the line together while you're gone. Are you ready?"

She finished her banana, and her pop and threw her trash in the closest trash bin. "Let's go."

The good thing about starting her autograph session early was that it gave her something to do. If she had gone back to her room for an hour, she probably would have started working on her story, and then it would have been a jolt to come back down and get into 'convention' mode again.

Wanda sat down at the very northernmost chair and pulled her purple pens from her purse. Charlie stood her name tent just to the south of where she would be signing, and then addressed those who had gathered early. "Ms Sinclair has decided to start her autograph session early so that you can then find something entertaining to do and not have to stand here so long."

"Really?" one of them asked. "I have friends who are coming back at 2."

"That's okay," Linda told him. "They can come at 2. I will be here until 4 or whenever the line gets done, whichever comes last."

By the time Linda had given two people 2 autographs each, more people had arrived. The line now stretched across the hallway. About that time, two other people in 'Staff' t-shirts arrived with rolls of blue tape, and Charlie organized them at laying down lines on the carpet to indicate where people should stand while they awaited their turn.

A group of attendees came in through the door from the parking lot. "Oh, look, Linda Sinclair is already autographing!" And they joined the line.

"Thanks, Ms Sinclair. I can't wait for your next book to come out!"

"My next book is called 'Footsteps in the Moonlight'. It's due out in November, and if you go to the MoonPhaze table in the dealer's room, they are taking pre-orders for it."

"Thanks!" and that young man took off at a jog to find the dealer's room.

Done putting tape on the floor at Charlie's direction, the other two staff members left, leaving a roll of blue tape with Charlie.

Charlie came around the long end of the table and sat in the other chair, pulling it next to Linda without crowding her. He watched her autograph books. "You're a leftie?"

"Yes, why?"

"I don't know. I just never thought you'd be left-handed. Come to think of it, I always thought of you having brown hair."

Linda gave him a nervous glance; he was far too close to the truth. "I'm sorry if I don't fit your preconceived notions."

"No, don't be. Preconceived notions are seldom right. I mean, how can you know somebody until you've met them?"

"That's right," Linda agreed, and continued with her autographs.

* * *

10:11 PM

Linda and Charlie got off the elevator on the 14th floor and headed for the party rooms. "I went to odd-numbered party rooms last night," Linda said as they walked. "So tonight I'll do even-numbered rooms and the con suite."

"5 party rooms," Charlie stated, showing he'd been informed. "You're looking for parties that aren't just a bunch of drunks. You don't drink alcohol. And if you ask for a soda, you want the can brought to you un-opened."

"Is that going to put a damper on you enjoying yourself?" she asked.

307

"Nope. I long ago decided I didn't like hangovers, so I never... well, hardly ever... drink more than one."

"Well, if we're being completely honest, I do occasionally drink a little alcohol, but it didn't take me long to decide that conventions are not the place where I want to do it."

"You don't have to explain anything to me. You don't want any alcohol. That's all I need to know."

Room 1412 had flyers up saying it was a party room, but the door was closed, so maybe they hadn't started yet. 1410 was too crowded; they couldn't get in.

1408 was crowded, but they got in. Timothy Hightower was conducting some kind of game. He would read a 5-line limerick, and people were supposed to name the character and the book or series of books that character was in. Those who first called out the right answer got a piece of candy tossed to them. Or thrown at them, depending on how far away from Timothy they were.

Some of the riddles were about Linda's books, and she kept her mouth shut. A few weren't answered by anyone, and one or two were met with silence. Then there came a riddle that Linda could answer; "George, from the Hound & Horses series!"

"Aha! Linda! I was afraid I had put you on the spot earlier, since I wasn't sure you had read any of my stuff, but you obviously have!" He tossed her a piece of candy.

"Oh, malted milk balls! I love these!" Linda said. "I have to admit, I only discovered your work a couple months ago. But I do like your work."

"Folks, Linda is this week-end's Author Guest of Honor, Linda Sinclair. Now, I understand you have another book coming out later this year."

"Yes," and Linda gave the particulars again. The party attendees clapped. "And when do you have another book coming out, Timothy? I don't want to miss it."

Timothy smiled. "My book comes out in October. It's called 'Call Off the Hounds'. You can ask about pre-orders at the Pikes Peak Publishing table in the dealer's room." More applause, and then it looked like Timothy was getting ready to read another riddle, so Linda waved good-bye and moved on.

11:43 PM

In order to attend 5 even-numbered parties, they had to go back to room 1412, which was just getting started at their 2nd arrival, and didn't yet have many people there. Linda spoke with those who were there, and Charlie brought her an unopened can of pop. She munched a couple of chips, and they left, working their way up the sardine-packed hallway toward the con suite, which was nearly as full as the hall.

There didn't appear to be anything resembling actual 'food' this late at night. When they had gone to the hotel shop looking for something for supper, the shop had been out of sandwiches, and they had made do with candy and pop, which was lots of empty calories. Linda was definitely hungry for something more substantial, but wasn't finding it. So she got herself a bowl of popcorn, a few corn chips and a brownie as she visited with a number of people. It was nearly midnight when she tracked down Charlie, who seemed to be having a serious discussion with Mildred, the redhead.

"Excuse me, Charlie," Linda broke in timidly.

He immediately turned. "What can I do for you, Linda?"

"Oh, nothing, really. I just wanted to let you know I'm going to my room."

"Oh, let me see you there," he said, stepping forward.

"You don't have to," she assured him. "I know where it is; I can get there on my own."

"The costume contest is over, and the hall is going to be even more crowded, so I'll get you through the crowd."

"Charlie!" the redhead protested.

"This is my assignment, Mildred," he replied coldly, and turned Linda around, guided her to the doorway with a hand on her back.

He walked her all the way to the elevators. After those, the hall was nearly empty. "I can get there from here," she stated, and offered him her hand. "Thank you, Charlie. You did a wonderful job today of keeping the crowds from tearing me limb from limb. Now, if you don't mind, it's been a long day."

He took her hand instead of shaking it. "I was just going to suggest we grab a taxi and find something to eat."

"Oh, no, I'm too tired. I'm just going to go to sleep and order room service when I get up." She pulled her hand out of his. "Good night, Charlie." She was relieved when he made no move to stop her.

When she closed and locked the hotel room door, she wondered what Chuck had meant, suddenly suggesting they go out this late in search of food. It sounded too much like a date, and she—well, Wanda wasn't ready to date again. Linda had never had to face the question before.

Chapter 36
Sunday, July 19, 7:54 AM

Wanda opened her eyes to stare sullenly at the bright sunlight trying to stream in between the curtains. Her cell phone rang, and she rolled over to answer it. "Hello?"

"Did you want to get some breakfast this morning?"

Chuck! She'd forgotten about having breakfast together. "Yes," she blurted out, and quickly added, "On 2 conditions."

"What conditions?"

"I just woke up, so you'll have to give me 15 minutes to get dressed and down to the lobby."

"Okay. What else?"

"We're going Dutch, right?"

"At the prices they charge here, you may regret that idea, but okay, if that's what you want."

"Great. I'll be down as soon as I can."

* * *

8:13 AM

Wanda stepped off the elevator and turned to hurry across the lobby to the restaurant. "Wanda!" She turned at the shout, to see Chuck standing between the banks of elevators. "I didn't want to miss you," he explained as he walked toward her.

She grimaced. "I had trouble finding one of my shoes, and I was afraid you'd start without me. I'm starved!"

He caught up to her and they started for the restaurant. "In that case, you might want to consider the omelet buffet. For $21, you get omelets made to order, plus everything on their breakfast buffet. It also includes coffee, tea, juice and milk."

"Sounds wonderful. Do we wait to be seated?"

"Not for breakfast. Come on, I see a nice table in a corner." As they made their way across the floor, a number of people called out to 'Charlie'. He paused as they passed one table to greet the people sitting there. Wanda waited rather impatiently, then was surprised when Chuck told the group, "Wanda is not only my neighbor from home, she's also Linda Sinclair's chauffeur for the trip here." He then proceeded to introduce her to Timothy Hightower and all the others at that table. Wanda had to pretend she had never met any of them before. Hank would never have done that to her, but then, she and Hank had attended the Chicago conventions for a few years before 'Linda' made her appearance. It had been hard to remember who she had met as Linda and who she hadn't, so Hank had handled introductions. Linda was not good with names, he would say.

After a little chitchat, they continued on their way to a booth in the back of the room. Placing their orders, they went to the buffet and ordered omelets, then got some fresh fruit and French toast from the buffet before returning to their booth.

"Are you enjoying the convention?" Chuck asked as they sat down again.

"I am," she stated firmly. "I was surprised by how busy Linda is here. You took her for her first panel yesterday, and she didn't come back until midnight."

"Well, she spent 4 hours or more giving autographs," he stated as a partial explanation."

"Did she? No wonder she groused about how tired her hand was."

He watched her lift a piece of fruit to her mouth. "You're right handed?"

"Always have been," she stated. "Now you're going to say Linda and I look a lot alike, and that's true, we do. Like you and Bob, we're cousins." This lie rolled off her tongue easily, she had said it so many times since Linda had made her first appearance. And come to think of it, it had been Hank who had suggested the 'relationship'. Their omelets arrived, and Wanda began to eat her protein.

"Wanda, I want to talk to you, ask you for a favor."

She looked up. He hadn't yet touched his omelet, and he seemed very serious. Almost as serious as he'd been when his sister arrived uninvited to his 4th of July party. "Is something wrong?"

"No. Well, yes, or I wouldn't be asking for a favor. Fact is, I'm in a mess, and nothing I've tried has gotten me out of it. I'm getting desperate. If I can't figure something out, I may not come back to this convention next year, and that seems like cutting my nose off to spite my face. I suppose I can find some other convention to go to, but I like this one! Except for this... problem."

"Well, don't keep me in suspense. What's the problem?"

Chuck's mouth went taut, and he viciously cut his omelet. "Her name is Mildred," he revealed.

The redhead with the semi-shrill voice. "How is she a problem?"

"She won't leave me alone," he answered. "From the moment I get here until the moment I leave, it seems like I can't take a step without bumping into her."

So he's got a girlfriend in Denver. But they only see each other once a year? That doesn't sound very serious. "How long has this been going on?"

"Since the first time I came here, 4 years ago."

"What did you do that made her notice you?" *Wouldn't have taken much. 'Show up' and almost any woman would notice him.*

"Well, okay, I flirted with her. But that year, I flirted with all the women, some of them twice my age! It was so good to be away from Belgrade, where everybody expects the worst of me. So I flirted, and I kissed a couple of them, but that was it. Not enough time for more than that."

"And do you still flirt while you're here?"

"Only very lightly. More of a friendly chatter, really. And even that is likely to get me a black look from Mildred. I don't know why she thinks she has some kind of claim on me! Yesterday, she even had the audacity to suggest I move to Denver and get a construction job here!"

"You mean, shut down the company you've worked so hard to build?"

"Exactly!"

"Well, that is a problem," she agreed. "People in Belgrade are depending on you to find work for them and provide them with a paycheck."

"I have no desire to move to Denver. Everything I have is in Belgrade. My home, my business, friends, family, co-workers... Everything!"

"What are you expecting me to do about it?" Wanda asked, and finished her hot tea.

"I know you aren't looking for a boy friend, aren't interested in dating, but I thought maybe, since you're here, you might..." He stopped, seemed unable to continue.

"I might what?"

He looked around, leaned forward and whispered, "Pretend to be my girl friend." Wanda raised her eyebrows in surprise, and he hurriedly went on, "Just for this last day here! Just to get Mildred off my case!"

Wanda lowered her voice, too. "We went over this before, when Queenie showed up just a couple weeks ago."

"I know, but I wouldn't expect you to, to do much. If you catch her flirting with me, which she does at every chance, pretend to get mad at me for supposedly encouraging her. Something along those lines."

"When am I supposed to see her do that? I've been here 2 and a half days, and I've only seen you once before this morning. It's not like you've been hanging out with me at this convention. Which people might think you'd have done, if we're supposed to be a couple!"

"There you are!"

"Damn!" Chuck swore under his breath. "Please, Wanda—"

The redhead slid into the booth next to him. He slid over all the way to the wall, and she just kept following, until she was practically sitting in his lap. "I assume you're staying over until tomorrow, lover boy?" Mildred's finger slid down his jaw line.

"Yes, as usual. It's a long drive home."

"Well, my friends are checking out today," Mildred told him. "But I could stay over with you, and we could have a lot of fun after the convention finally shuts down. Just you and me. In

314

your room. All alone."

Chuck cast a glance at Wanda, who watched the redhead speculatively. *Would it even matter to Mildred if Chuck had a girl friend? How about something more than that?*

"What are you looking at?" Mildred asked her testily.

Wanda stabbed her last bite of French toast. "Actually, I'm waiting to see how he reacts to that suggestion. I have a friend who would be very interested in hearing how he responds."

"Wanda—" Chuck started.

"Don't talk to me. She's the one who asked the question. I didn't come here to spy on you, or to carry tales of misbehavior back home to your wife, Chuck. But Elizabeth is my best friend, and as much as I know such tales will hurt her, I have to tell her the truth. If the roles were reversed, I'd want somebody to tell me my husband was making time with women in another city while supposedly on a business trip."

"Wife?" Mildred repeated.

"But Wanda—"

"I wasn't happy to hear her asking you for a massage yesterday, but now to hear you having her stay in your hotel room tonight, before you return home to Elizabeth... That I can't turn a blind eye to, Chuck. So you had better make up your mind who is more important to you; this woman or your wife and son. Because unless I hear you break it off with this woman, I'll go home with plenty to say, and not to Elizabeth! By the time I'm done, your name will be mud in Belgrade!" The look on Chuck's face was half confusion and half shock. *Almost as if he thinks I really would tell everybody about his Denver paramour.* "Well? I'm waiting for you to respond to this woman."

Chuck pulled his arm out of Mildred's grasp. "Well, that's it, Mildred. It was fun while it lasted, but it's over now."

She grabbed his arm again and leaned against him. "No! I'm not going to give you up! You don't need to go back to... wherever. Stay here with me, get a job with a local company, or the state roads department. You can divorce your wife, and we can be together, just like we've talked about!"

Chuck gently pushed her away and shook his head. "No. We

haven't talked about it. **You've** talked about it. I didn't talk about it because... I don't want to divorce my wife. I can't give up my son. Nor the baby that's due next month. Wanda's right. I've been a cad and heel to have led you on all these years when I knew perfectly well it couldn't possibly lead to anything meaningful."

"No, Charlie, don't..."

"I have to, Mildred. Now let me out of this booth."

Mildred stared at him in shock and despair for a long moment, then she suddenly whirled and ran from the restaurant. Wanda saw her head for the elevators.

"Do you think that worked?" Wanda asked.

"I hope so. It was a rough way to let her down, but I just wasn't interested, and she wasn't taking any hints." He signaled the waiter for their checks. "Unfortunately, now everybody will think I have a wife and 2 kids back home."

"You're the one who added the 2nd kid," she reminded him.

"Presumably, I would have been the one who added the first kid, too," he said with a smile. The waiter brought their checks. Chuck charged his breakfast; Wanda used her credit card. "It would've have been easier to say you were my girl friend."

"I don't do cat fights," Wanda answered.

"What?"

"Mildred thought she was your girl friend. She would have felt she had just as much claim to you as any other girl friend you might have."

"But if I preferred you..."

"No, that might have made her more determined to have you. But a wife has a legal standing, a legal relationship with you. And even that, by itself, wasn't quite enough to make her give you up. Not until you made it plain you preferred your old life, with your wife and kids, rather than a new life with her."

The waiter was back again, and they each signed their receipts. "There are times when I wish I had a wife," Chuck said with a touch of whimsy. Then firmly, "But her name wouldn't be Elizabeth."

"No?" *Did I stumble across the name of someone he hates?*

316

"No, because the only Elizabeth I know is Ella."

Wanda froze for a moment as she put her credit card away. *Ella! Prints!* "When does the art show open this morning?" She got up to leave.

He looked surprised by the change of subject. "Uh, about 10. But only for people to pick up what they bought, and for artists to pick up what didn't sell."

Wanda bit her bottom lip. "I bid on Ella's prints, got busy and didn't get to the art auction last night to defend my bids. So I don't know if I need to go pick up any artwork." She glanced at her watch; it was going on 9:30, and she didn't know when Linda's first Sunday event was. "I don't know if I've got time to check before I have to get Linda ready for her first panel."

"Linda's first panel is at noon," Chuck told her.

"You seem pretty sure of that."

"I've been asked to be her handler again today, so I've memorized her schedule for the day."

"Good, because she won't know what it is."

"Come on, the art show is this way," he told her. "You know, you've made a couple remarks about Linda's lack of intelligence, and I've found her quite intelligent and sensible."

"Hmm. Old habits, I suppose. I don't mean to say she isn't intelligent, just that she spends most of her time distracted. I couldn't understand it when we were growing up. Now I recognize it for spending time with her books' characters."

They came to a meeting room whose door was closed. Chuck knocked. "Not yet!" came a muffled call from inside.

"It's Charlie," Chuck called back.

The door opened and a blue-haired woman looked out. "Did you bid on something, Charlie?"

"I did, but I was number 3, and I didn't get to the art auction to defend it, so I don't imagine I got it. What I'm checking on is the bids placed by this woman. She placed a bid on one of Ella Swanson's prints..."

"All of them," Wanda corrected. "I put opening bids on all of Ella's pieces. And like Charlie, I didn't get to the art auction."

"Well, that's easy," the blue-haired woman answered. "All

of Ella Swanson's pieces went to auction with multiple bids and sold for quite a bit of money, especially for a newcomer. So if that's all you bid on, there's nothing to pick up."

"Bad news for you," Chuck summed up.

"But good news for Ella," Wanda returned.

"Hey, Charlie," asked a younger blond boy from the middle of the art show room. "What's this I've heard about you not being able to help us tear down today?"

"Oh, I've been asked to handle Linda today, get her where she needs to be when she needs to be there."

"I knew Eddie would blow it," the blond said.

"So we do it all ourselves," blue-hair said. "I know it doesn't sound hard, Charlie, but we don't have your muscles."

"Or your tools," the blond boy added.

"Well, do you need help now?" Chuck asked.

"I always need help on Sunday mornings," blue hair replied. "Most of the staff is too hung over to be of any use."

Chuck checked his watch. "I can help for 2 hours, then I'll have to get Linda to her panel. Then she has an autograph session. At that point, I could maybe sneak back."

"I'll take anything I can get, Charlie."

"Do you mind, Wanda?"

"No, not at all."

* * *

11:43 AM

Linda glanced at the clock on her laptop and knew she wouldn't be able to concentrate on her book any more. She had expected Charlie to show up before this. She got up from the desk and began pacing back and forth.

Today she wore a pair of loosely flowing trousers in plum, an ivory blouse with lace sleeves and an eggplant-colored camisole. She regretted that she hadn't ordered any breakfast from room service. Breakfast had been delicious and plentiful, but she was already beginning to get hungry again.

At the knock on her door, she grabbed her grey purse and answered it. "Are you running late?"

"I think we can make it," Charlie stated. "As long as we

318

don't have yesterday's crowds."

The elevators were slow and crowded with quiet, out-of-focus people who mumbled and winced at each unexpected noise. Charlie forced his way onto one that didn't look like it would hold any more, and pulled Linda on with him. They rode all the way to the lobby with his arms around her protectively. Once they reached the lobby, he gently pushed her out of the machine, grabbed her hand, and hurried down the long hall. He finally pulled her into a large panel room that was nearly full of people waiting, and continued to hurry her to the stage. He poured her a glass of water, found her name tent and set it up before her, then grabbed one of the microphones.

"Sorry we're late, the elevator insisted on going all the way to the top floor, and then stop on every floor from there to the lobby. But we are here now, so without anymore waiting, please welcome our Author Guest of Honor, Linda Sinclair!"

A loud round of applause broke out as Charlie stepped off the stage. Confused, Linda never-the-less smiled and pulled a microphone close to ask, "Charlie, where are the rest of the panelists?"

As the applause faded, Charlie put the microphone to his mouth again."Now, Linda, when I said you should check your schedule, I didn't mean you should just make note of what times you had something going on. This isn't a panel, it's a Question & Answer hour. The audience gets to ask questions, which you then answer. But first, do you have anything you want to say? About yourself or your work?"

"Yes, just a few words," she started, uncertain how well a Q&A session would work. She'd been answering questions, it seemed, at every party room she had visited! "I am Linda Sinclair, and I write fantasy novels. I attended college in Evans, Illinois, and I've been writing ever since I graduated. Well, actually, I've pretty much been writing my entire life, but it's only since college that I've written anything worth publishing. But that's good; I've learned a lot in the first 2 decades of my life, about writing and how to make it interesting for people to read.

"I think that's about all I have to say about that. How do

they get their questions to me? How does that work?"

"Something like this," Charlie answered, and turned to face the audience. "Who has a question for Linda? Raise your hands!" Several hands went up. He called on a young man from the middle of the crowd, and took his microphone down the aisle to meet the lad. Then he announced, "Elliot from here in Denver. Go ahead, Elliot, ask your question.

Elliot got a little too close to the microphone, but Linda could make out his question. "I, um, know your publisher is based in Chicago, do you, um, live in Chicago?"

Great, more lies, Linda thought. "Yes. I mean, no. Let me explain. When I got out of college, I had a job in one of the suburbs of Chicago, so that's where I lived up until fairly recently, when my mother became ill. She's doing better now, but it was a big scare, and I don't know if I'll go back to Chicago any time soon. You don't have to live in Chicago to work with a Chicago publisher, if that was your question. And if your question was, where do you live? Let's just say a small town in central Nebraska, and leave it at that. Any other questions?"

The majority of the questions she could answer (mostly) truthfully. People wanted to talk about what they perceived as inconsistencies in her books, or her plans for the 'Footsteps' series, or why did she pair this character with that one, instead of with somebody else?

But she was surprised when Charlie told the audience, "That's all the time we have. Linda will be giving autographs at the opposite end of the other hallway, starting as soon as I can get her there. Linda, do you have any closing comments"

"What, is our hour up already? Yes, I do have a few words. Thank you to each and every one of you for coming to ask your questions. It's been a pleasure to be here this weekend, and a real delight to find so many fans in one place!"

Charlie was putting his microphone back on the table, urging her to hurry. She stood up with her purse, started for the stairs off the stage and stopped to use the last microphone. "Oh, one last thing. Charlie, how long am I signing autographs?"

"Until 3."

"Okay, I will be signing autographs until 3, or whenever the line is complete."

"Closing ceremonies is at 5," Charlie pointed out.

"I might have to take time off for the closing ceremony," Linda said into the microphone, and hurried off the stage.

"Are you up for that?" Charlie asked as they made their way out the door with the rest of the crowd. "You signed for a solid 4 hours yesterday."

"I don't think the crowd is as large as it was yesterday."

"It's still larger than it usually is on Sunday." The crowd thinned a bit, and they began walking faster, passing those who didn't know yet what event they wanted to attend next. When they got to her autograph table, there were already a handful of people waiting. Linda sat down thankfully, tried to catch her breath. She was dismayed to see the blue tape was no longer on the floor, but when she turned her head to mention it to Charlie, he was on his phone. She smiled at the first person in line and beckoned them forward. "What's your name?" she asked, digging her purple pens from her purse.

The next time she looked up, Charlie was gone. Two women wearing 'staff' t-shirts were repeating the pattern on the floor in blue tape, cajoling the fans to use it as a guide. Nobody seemed to fight the idea.

And then Charlie was back, his arms full. He put down a bottle of cola and a small bag of chips for her, then asked, "Roast beef or ham?"

"Ham."

A pre-packaged sandwich joined the other items. He opened his own drink and took a long swallow. "Now, are you okay? Carol—" he pointed at one of the staff ladies, and she waved her hand in the air, "will stick around, in case you need anything, but the art show is falling behind and I need to go."

"No, I'm fine. Go ahead." She turned to the next person wanting an autograph, gasped when she realized she not only had both of her books, but the 3 magazines that had started her career by publishing her short stories. "I don't get many requests to sign the magazines," she explained to the young lady who owned them.

* * *

6:18 PM

Wanda stopped typing on her laptop when a knock on the hotel room door startled her. *Who can that be? I haven't ordered supper yet, and I should do that soon.* She got up to answer it.

"Hey, Wanda."

"Chuck. What are you doing here?"

"I've been sent to bring Linda to the Dead Dog Party. Did she forget it?"

Damn. I forgot. And here I am, having removed my makeup and packed all my costumes. "Uh, yeah, I think she did. She's been working on her book, and she's taking a bath right now."

"Oh. This is the chance for the convention staff to interact with the guests for a while. Vet—Yvette said it was mentioned to you when you were ironing out the details."

"Yes, I remember that. But it slipped my mind. Both of our minds. Tell you what, let me rouse her from the tub, give her time to get dressed, and I'll send her down. Where is the party?"

"In the con suite."

"I'm sure she can find that. It's the other end of the hallway, isn't it?"

"Yes. She's been there before."

"I'll hurry her as fast as I can, but it might take her 20 minutes or so. She doesn't leave the room without her full makeup on."

"Tell her if she doesn't hurry up, there might not be any chili left. And it's almost as good as yours, Wanda."

"I will hurry her as much as I can."

"You can come, too, Wanda. You made it possible for Linda to be here."

"Oh, that's sweet. But I'm not anybody. And I've got a long drive home tomorrow, so I was going to turn in early."

"It's barely past 6."

"Yes, but I need to veg out for a while before I go to bed. My body is tired, I just need to convince my brain that it is, too."

"Are you sure you don't want to come for a little while?

We've been known to have some interesting conversations at the Dead Dog."

"Now, see, that would get my brain firing on all cylinders, and then I'd have a dilly of a time falling asleep. No, you go ahead. I'll help Linda get ready and send her down, and then I can find something on the TV and start vegging out."

He didn't seem eager to let her bow out, but he conceded and walked off. Wanda tore open her purple suitcase and started becoming Linda once again.

Linda could hear Charlie's voice through the open door as she approached the con suite. "She was working on her next book, and time got away from her. She'll be here."

"You were there," somebody else said. "Why didn't you just bring her back with you?"

"She was in the bathroom. I chatted with her cousin for a couple minutes, but Linda didn't come out, so Wanda said she'd get her sent down as soon as she could."

"And here I am," Linda stated as she walked into the con suite. "Sorry I'm late, the words were flowing. Wanda usually gives me a heads up when I need to be somewhere, but I think she's starting to droop already this evening."

"Welcome," Yvette told her. "That's okay, as long as you come down and help us eat leftovers. I think there's a bowl or two of chili left, and some pepperoni pizza, and then, of course, whatever chips, candy and other goodies are still scattered around the room. Charlie, get her a drink, since you abandoned her so callously this afternoon."

"The art show needed help," Charlie said defensively, but he got up and disappeared into the open bathroom, returned with 2 cans of cola, one for himself. For very close to 3 hours, Linda chatted with convention staff members about the convention, her books, other books, and many other subjects that seemed to come up at random.

At one point, Mildred walked in, got herself a can of pop, glared at Charlie, who was facing the balcony and didn't see her. Then she walked out.

"Charlie, what did you do to Mildred?"

Charlie turned red, sat up straight and looked around the room.

"You missed her," Yvette told him. "She's been in a foul mood all day, and when she left just now, well, if looks could kill, then you would be dead about 10 times."

Charlie took a big drink of his pop and then shoved himself deep into the sofa cushions. "I told her we can't be together."

"You dumped her?" exclaimed blue-hair from the art show.

"I knew she was playing with fire," Yvette muttered.

"I never really wanted to get together with anybody here in Denver. My flirting that first year didn't mean anything. But nothing I've said the last couple years could convince her I wasn't going to move to Denver and get some construction job somewhere."

"That girl doesn't listen to anybody," Yvette stated. "Even I know it isn't just a job you have back in Nebraska; you own the company."

"Me, too," said blue-hair. "How did you finally get through to her?"

Still blushing, Charlie couldn't look up. "I told her I have a wife and kids back home, and I chose them instead of her."

Yvette winced. "Ouch."

"No doubt it was an ouch for Mildred," blue-hair agreed. "But there comes a time when a person can no longer put up with someone else making plans for them. Especially if the plans are for something that person doesn't want."

"Well, it'd gotten so bad, I wasn't sure I should come back next year."

"And that's where it becomes 'ouch' for us," Yvette stated.

"And me," Charlie added. "I like this convention, or I wouldn't have been back these last 3 years. So, I've got your number in my phone, Vet, so I'll call you next summer and see what you think about my coming back. You know, if she's managed to get over me, or what."

"I probably won't be con chair next year, but I can speak to him or her and see what they think."

From somewhere behind her, Linda heard someone whisper,

"I never heard him talk about a wife and kids."

Several people got drinks or some more snacks. As people began settling down again, someone asked, "What do people think NASA should do? Go back to the moon, or head for Mars?" and the conversation of this 'party' got started again.

Chapter 37
Monday, July 20, 8:36 AM

Wanda entered her room for the last time. She was still a little tired, since 'Linda' hadn't gotten back until after 10, at which time the purple suitcase had to be repacked. 6 had arrived damned early this morning, but the alarm had gone off only moments before room service arrived with her breakfast. She had watched TV while she ate, got dressed and made sure everything was packed, then took her 2 suitcases to her car and came back for her laptop. After one last look to make sure she had everything, she opened her room door and stepped out.

"Good morning."

She looked around, saw an unshaven Chuck in the doorway opposite hers. "I didn't realize we were neighbors here, too."

"Obviously, I did," he stated. "Going down for breakfast?"

"No, I've already eaten. I'm going to check out and leave."

"Where's Linda?"

More lies! "Already in the car, settling in for a nap. I think she stayed up half the night, writing."

"Drive safe. I'll only be an hour or 2 behind you. "I'm meeting Vet—the con chair—for a heart-to-heart. Thanks for the help yesterday. Though it wasn't what I expected."

"The question is, did it work?"

"I think so. Mildred hates me now, but..." He shrugged.

"Well, I'll see you back in Belgrade."

"Sure. See ya."

* * *

8:40 PM

It seemed like the whole town of Belgrade was in shadow as Wanda made the sharp right turn at the bottom of the Big Hill. The sun was almost setting, and between the buildings and the trees along the main drag, she felt like she was in a semi-dark tunnel.

She reached the main corner, and there was Bob's Bar. Of course it wasn't open, because Bob didn't open on Mondays. She wished she could stop in for a cheeseburger, but she couldn't, so she turned the corner and headed home. She'd find something at home to eat.

What a day it had been. She just wanted to eat something and then crawl into bed.

For that matter, what a weekend it had been! Half starved on Saturday, and her left arm was still sore from all the autographs she had given. This had been so much easier in Chicago, when her handler knew the duality of her existence and could help her cover her tracks.

She pulled into her driveway and got out with her laptop. *Leave the suitcases where they are; I can get them in the morning.* She got out her keys and got ready to unlock her front door when she heard the squeal of a car's tires making a sudden turn. Looking around, she saw a red sports car zip into her driveway and screech to a stop.

Chuck got out and demanded, "Where have you been?"

She didn't like his tone, and wasn't in the mood for his attitude. "Driving home from Denver."

"It doesn't take 13 hours to drive that!" he declared. "Even if you had to stop somewhere and drop off Linda!"

"Maybe I don't drive like a demon, like some people! In any case, it's none of your business where I was or what I was doing!"

"You just about drove me crazy with worry! I was afraid you'd been in an accident, had car trouble, any number of things could have happened to you!"

"Well, I'm here, so obviously they didn't!" she shot back

"Please don't argue."

They both stopped, dumb-founded at the soft request. Turning, Wanda saw Gloria standing on her porch, talking through the door's screen. "What are you doing here?"

"Please come in and I'll explain," Gloria stated, and unlocked the door. "Please do it quickly; the whole neighborhood would have heard you arguing, and I'm not supposed to be here."

"Well, she's right about that," Chuck stated, and followed Wanda into the house.

The shades were all pulled down, the ceiling fans blowing furiously, but the house was still a little warmer than Wanda liked it. She went into her office and turned her AC unit to a cold temperature.

Sammy sat at the dining room table with half a glass of milk and a chocolate chip cookie in each hand. A plate of more cookies sat on the table.

"Okay, Gloria," Wanda said, trying to keep her voice friendly. "What are you doing in my house, and how did you get in?"

"I've left Lyle," Gloria answered, sitting down at the table. Since Sammy was sitting at the end near the heating stove, she sat next to him. Chuck took his usual chair at the other end, and Wanda sat between Chuck and Gloria. "I left him Saturday, walked into town with Sammy. The only things open were the 2 bars, so I chose Bob's, because... at least I know him. He was surprised to see me. And nervous about me being there. I explained that I was looking for a ride home—to my parent's house. He said he'd be glad to drive me, but he couldn't leave right then. Then he pointed out that my parent's place would be the first place Lyle would look for me. He gave me a key and told me to come here, but leave it looking unoccupied, because the new owner was out of town. I guess that's you." She turned to Wanda.

"Yeah, I guess," Wanda agreed. "But... He sent you to stay here and surprise me when I got home?"

"Oh, no! Not at all! He said when he went to Fullerton on Monday, he'd see my dad and the sheriff, let them know what was going on, and they'd figure out how to keep me safe. That I should go ahead and eat whatever we needed to eat, and he'd pay you back, Wanda. But I'm not much of a cook, and about all we've eaten has been TV dinners. And I've used up all your cookie dough."

"In that case, would you hand me one of those cookies?"

Gloria handed her one, and then went on. "I've been expecting Bob all day; he said he'd be here by noon at the latest. But he never has shown up, and now you're here, and... I just don't know what to say. I'm sorry I invaded your home and ate your food—" She started to cry.

"No, now don't be sorry," Wanda told her soothingly. "It's for a good cause and I don't begrudge it one bit. I just don't understand why Bob didn't show up when he said he would."

Chuck was frowning. "He hasn't been to my house today, either. He usually comes out on Monday afternoons to do my bookkeeping," he added for Gloria's benefit. "But the checks weren't there this evening; Steve left a note about it." He pulled out his cell phone and made a call.

"I'm sure there's a good explanation," Wanda told Gloria, and gave her hand a gentle squeeze on the table.

"Hey, Aunt Val. This is Chuck. Is Bob sick or something? He didn't get to my place to—" He listened intently for a time. "How bad is it?" He ran his free hand through his hair, leaving it standing up in spikes. He finally breathed in relief. "Yeah, no, it's past visiting hours now, so I'll go see him tomorrow. Uhh, I've got to go, Val, I've got to call Steve, make some kind of arrangements for work for tomorrow. I won't be able to, and I suppose the kids won't, either. I'll call you tomorrow, maybe somebody will know more by then." He hung up, took a deep breath and told them, "Bob's in the Fullerton Hospital, unconscious. He had a car accident on the way to Fullerton this morning, ran off the road."

"Oh, no!" Wanda exclaimed. Gloria looked horrified.

"She says he doesn't seem too badly hurt, mostly bruises, but he did hit his head, and he's been out all day." He turned his attention to Gloria. "So he hasn't explained anything about your situation to anybody. That's why nobody has come to get you."

Gloria seemed uncertainly relieved. "I had all sorts of nasty thoughts going through my mind, but this explains everything, although I certainly wish it hadn't happened. He always seemed like a careful driver when... when we were dating."

"He is," Chuck agreed. "I can't imagine what happened."

I can't believe I came home and immediately started telling Chuck more lies That's not the kind of person I want to be.
"Chuck, I—" Wanda was interrupted by several loud 'woops' by the town's siren, a version of the sound that she hadn't heard before. Before the 3rd 'woop' faded into something tolerable, Chuck was answering his cell phone.

"Yeah. I'm in Belgrade, I'll be right there." He bolted from his chair, headed for the door.

Wanda jumped up and caught his arm. "What is it? What's wrong?"

"That's the fire alarm," he answered.

"So?"

"I'm on the fire department, I've got to go."

She followed him out onto the porch. "Come back when that's over, okay? I have something I want to say to you."

"It can wait."

"No, I don't want to wait. I need to get it said."

"It could be very late."

"I don't care. Wake me up if you have to. I... I had a terrible day, and I want to explain something to you. It won't take long, if you'll just... come back as quickly as you can."

He paused in the open door. "No matter how late?"

"Yes."

"Okay, but... don't wait up."

"Not sure I could," she answered, and he was gone, sprinting for his car.

Wanda watched him pull out of her drive and head for the fire station. She locked the porch door, turned on the porch internal light, and locked the house door as she re-entered the living room. The room was going dark, and she turned on the lights.

"I need something to drink," she muttered as she went to the kitchen. When she opened the frig, both the lemonade and the ice tea were gone. She settled for an orange soda, and started looking around for something quick and easy to fix to eat. "Gloria, I'm going to fix myself a grilled cheese. Do you and Sammy want any?"

Gloria appeared in the doorway from the living room. "I don't know if Sammy likes it, so maybe we could share one?"

"Sounds like a plan," Wanda said with a smile, and got out the margarine and cheese.

"Do you mind if I watch?" Gloria asked.

She did say she's a terrible cook. Looks like she's interested in learning. "Not at all. First, could you get down a couple of the small plates?"

In short order, she had 2 grilled cheese sandwiches cooked, and they rejoined Sammy at the dining table. Gloria tore off a piece of her sandwich, blew on it to cool it off, and offered it to Sammy. It wasn't long before the two of them had finished the sandwich, and Wanda had already finished hers.

Gloria offered to wash the dishes, but Wanda put her off. "To tell you the truth, Gloria, I am just about ready to fall asleep. Just leave the dishes, and we'll wash them after breakfast in the morning."

"Could I... impose on you even more by asking you to drive me to Fullerton tomorrow?"

"That will not be a problem, as I need to go in, anyway. To check on Bob, of course. So I will happily drive you to your parents and help you explain what's been going on."

"You are so kind."

"I am simply treating you the same way I would want to be treated, if I were in a similar situation," Wanda told her. "Now, I assume you've been sleeping in the bed? That's fine, go ahead and sleep there again tonight. Let's keep things as consistent as possible for Sammy. I will sleep on the couch, and hopefully you won't be woke up when Chuck comes back."

"It must be something very important you want to tell him."

"I hope so. I mean, I think it is, so I hope he does, too."

"You look so tired."

"The day started out pretty good this morning, but it got all messed up somewhere between Kearney and Grand Island, and it's been going downhill ever since. It could take a few days for me to crawl back to something that resembles normalcy. So... what time do you 2 usually go to bed?"

Gloria looked at the clock on the wall. "Oh! Before this, actually. Sammy, go potty. It's time for bed."

In fact, Sammy looked like he was on the verge of falling asleep sitting up, but he opened his eyes, nodded in agreement, and padded off for the bathroom. After a moment, he called out, "Mama," and Gloria took off to see what he needed.

Wanda munched on another cookie and finished her pop waiting for them to come back. It was all she could do to keep her eyes open, but on the other hand, she was worried about Bob. *How could he have lost control of his car? We occasionally slid around corners on the gravel roads, but Bob never showed any trepidation about it. If he'd driven off one of those gravel roads, how long before somebody stumbled across his car and got help for him? It might have been hours. It could—*

Someone cleared her throat. She looked up to find Gloria and Sammy standing near-by, holding hands. Looking very serious, Sammy said, "I'm Sammy, and this is Mama."

Wanda smiled. "Hello, Sammy. My name is Wanda, and this is my house, which I am happy to share with you while you and your mother need a place to stay."

"Does Bob live here, too?"

Wanda blinked in surprise. "No, he has his own house."

Sammy looked up at his mother. "What's a hopital?"

"Hospital," Gloria corrected slowly, and repeated it at normal speed. "That is a building where people who are very sick go so that doctors can make them better."

"Bob doesn't live at the hopsital?"

"Hospital," Gloria corrected again. "No, he doesn't. He has been hurt, so he was taken to the hospital so he can get better."

The little tyke nodded again, let go of his mother's hand, and headed for the bedroom.

"Good night, Wanda," Gloria said, and followed her son.

"Good night," Wanda returned, and kicked off her shoes. She went to the bathroom, left the wash room light on as a night light on her way to the living room. She turned the fans to a slower speed, turned off the lights and stretched out on the sofa.

She thought it might take her some time to fall asleep, after the 'adventure' she'd had today, and the news of Bob's accident. She wished she could call someone and find out exactly what had happened, but it didn't sound as if anyone knew.

Having Bob in the hospital after a car accident was far too reminiscent of having Hank in the hospital after his car accident. The very thought brought tears to her eyes, and she wore herself out far beyond exhaustion as she silently cried into the night.

* * *

11:59 PM

A noise woke Wanda, but as tired as she was, she couldn't remember what the noise was. *Was it a knock at the front door? Chuck said he'd come back.*

She rolled off the sofa, stood and staggered for the front door to let him in. She stopped, frozen, as she looked through the window of the door to the porch. Lyle was stepping inside!

He grinned when he saw her just inside the door. "Let me in, Wendy. It's time we have some fun."

She made sure this door was closed, and leaned against it to put emphasis to her words when she told him, "Go away. I want nothing to do with you."

"That's not very friendly," he returned. "I hear you're all friendly with everybody else. I'm just here for my share of friendliness."

"We aren't friends. Now, go away."

He shook his head. "I'm not going away until I get what I've come for." He raised his fist. It had some cloth wrapped around it, and she realized he meant to break this window in order to get in.

She reached for her phone, realized she'd left it on the table, and lunged in that direction. Behind her, glass shattered. She got 911 dialed before Lyle grabbed her and sent the phone flying across the room.

Lyle forced her to the floor and started pulling her t-shirt up. When she tried to push him off, he punched her. She tasted blood and her mind went cottony; nothing made any sense. "That's better," someone said, and laughed. She felt someone unfastening her jeans.

333

Her mind came back to her. *Rape. I'm being raped!* "Help!" She called out, hoping the phone was active. "Help me! Rape!"

"That's an ugly word," he said. "But if that's how you want it..." He punched her again.

She was aware of him atop her, trying to force her jeans down over her hips, but she couldn't think, couldn't do anything to stop him. And then he landed flat atop her.

She heard a woman's voice, quiet and calm, tell somebody to send the police and an ambulance. The woman finished with the statement, "My husband just tried to rape my friend."

Things faded into darkness, interspersed with bits of knowledge of things happening. Lyle's weight rolled off her and she could breathe again. She coughed as she tried to get her lungs full.

She tried to move, to get away. A woman said, "Just lay there. The ambulance should be here soon."

* * *

"Go back to bed, Sammy. Daddy had an accident."

Someone was fussing with her clothes; she tried to stop them. "No, I'm trying to get you dressed. Nobody needs to see you half undressed."

* * *

She heard something crunching, voices speaking quietly.

A pungent stench assaulted her nose, bringing all the scattered pieces of her mind together in one place, and she reached up to batter it away. She choked and coughed as she tried to breathe without dragging any more of the stench into her lungs.

"That's better," said a familiar voice. "Can you hear me, Wanda?"

"Yes," she muttered, swallowed and said more loudly, "Yes." Her eyelids fluttered, and she found herself staring into a familiar face. "Hank?" she whispered. He waved something under her nose, and the stench was back. She pushed it away. "Stop that, Chuck."

"She's awake, deputy, but I don't know how alert she is."

An unfamiliar woman's voice. "I suppose getting her statement might wait until morning, if she can get herself to the station in Fullerton. But we're supposed to try to get a statement while we're on the scene."

"You got one from Gloria. Won't that do?"

"She's not the victim, Chuck. And not exactly an innocent by-stander, either."

"I couldn't let him do to her what he's done to me." That was Gloria.

"Somebody help me up," Wanda requested

Chuck used his considerable strength to get her onto her feet, and then urged her to sit down on the sofa, next to the young woman in a deputy's uniform.

"You need a statement?" Wanda asked the young officer. The side of her face hurt.

"Whatever you can remember," was the answer.

Lyle, Wanda realized, was mostly under the table, his hands behind his back. He appeared to be unconscious. Strangely, her cast iron skillet was sitting on the table, her cell phone next to it. She drug her mind back to what had happened, tried to formulate it succinctly, but with all the important bits intact.

"I was asleep here on the sofa when I woke up, but I wasn't sure why. I got up and went to the door—the internal door—and saw Lyle stepping onto the porch. I could see him because I'd left the light on out there. I don't know how he got in that far. He said he wanted to have fun. I told him to go away. He raised his fist to break the window, and I got my phone, called 911. He knocked it away, forced me to the floor, was trying to undress me, hit me a couple times... I don't remember much past that."

"I should take you to Fullerton for an examination, see just how far he got before Gloria got to him."

"He didn't get me undressed enough. And I'd rather stay here and sleep. If I can. This has been the absolute worst ending to an already dreadful day."

"Let me tend her face wounds, okay, Gibson?"

"Sure, go ahead. I never said you couldn't."

Chuck pulled a large tool chest closer to the couch, sat down and began cleaning Wanda's face with alcohol wipes. She jerked away when he touched a sore spot on her lip. "Ow!"

"Yes, he managed to cut your lip," Chuck told her quietly. "You may have a scar after this." After cleaning her face, he got up and disappeared into the kitchen. A moment later, he came back with a bag of frozen peas, which he gently laid against the side of her face. "You're going to have a big black eye, plus another bruise stretching from your cheekbone to your jaw. Hold those peas there for a while."

"You're awfully familiar with her household, Chuck," Gibson remarked. "You been here much?"

"Saturday evenings," he answered. "A few other times."

"Didn't realize you had started dating again."

"I haven't," he responded. "The teens and I come over on Saturdays to play dungeons. I've done some work for her at other times, as a handyman. What does that have to do with Lyle's attempt to rape her?"

"Nothing. Just thought if you were dating again, I might get gussied up from time to time." Gibson turned her attention to Gloria. "What about you, Gloria? How did you get here? Did you come with Lyle?"

"No, I left Lyle," she answered at once. "I left him Saturday and walked into town. Went to Bob's place, because I didn't know the owner of the other bar. He convinced me to come here and hide for a couple days. But he apparently had an accident going to Fullerton this morning, so nobody came to get me, because nobody knew I was here."

"So there's no chance Lyle came here to drag you home, and got distracted by Wanda?"

"I have no idea if he even knows I've left," she answered. "He wasn't home when I left, and I had no idea when to expect him. Bob never would have told him where I was, even if Lyle showed up in Belgrade."

"Gibson." Chuck was frowning. "When the call for an ambulance came, we had just finished fighting a fire at the old Jessup place."

"Why is that important?" Gibson asked.

"That's where we've been living," Gloria stated.

Chuck grimaced and looked at Gloria. "It burnt to the

ground. We've got a call in for the state fire marshal's office to investigate it tomorrow." *What is he leaving unsaid?*

"Did you check the rubble for corpses?" Gibson asked. "I mean, for all you knew, Gloria and her son might have been caught in that fire."

"No, we didn't," Chuck answered, and looked to Gloria. "I knew they were okay, because I knew they were here."

"How?"

"Wanda was out of town for the weekend, and when she got home, I came over to see how her trip had been. Gloria met us both at the door, explained why she was here."

"I did have car trouble," Wanda blurted out. "Plus, I got lost."

Chuck turned his attention to her, gently pressed the peas back against her face. "Car trouble, okay. But, how did you get lost?"

"I broke my fan belt somewhere between Kearney and Grand Island. I limped it to the next exit. Happily, the gas station did repairs, but I had to wait for what seemed like forever before the new belt got brought to them. I was so stressed out, I missed the Grand Island exit I needed, and by the time I realized it, the next road going north was highway 81, which took me to Columbus, waaay out of my way, but at least I figured out how to get home from there. It's a good thing I carry a road atlas in my car."

"That's why you were so late getting home?"

"Yes. But I didn't want you to think I was a helpless female."

"That's not the way I think of you," Chuck responded. "You are so put together, it makes it hard to think of things I can do to make your life easier."

"So much for getting gussied up," Gibson muttered.

"Deputy, can I sweep up the broken glass?" Gloria asked. "Wanda isn't wearing any shoes."

"Yes," Gibson told her, and closed her little notebook, put it and her pen away. "I've taken pictures of both doors, enough to prove it was breaking and entering. I am asking both of you ladies to come to the sheriff's office tomorrow, to sign your statements. The sheriff might have more questions for you. But you, Wanda, shouldn't drive until a doctor checks you out. Don't get me wrong, Chuck's fine for first aid, but he's only a paramedic."

"How can I get us to Fullerton if I can't drive?" Wanda wondered.

"I'll get you there," Chuck volunteered.

Wanda smirked. "In your sports car? Or your pickup?"

"Either one," he answered. "Although I don't have a car seat for Sammy."

"He never has had one," Gloria stated, returning with a broom and dustpan.

"Holy cow," someone said outside. Everybody turned to look at the porch door, and soon Steve was walking in. "What happened?"

"Lyle happened," Chuck answered.

"Oh." That seemed to be enough explanation to suit him. "Is everybody okay?"

"Wanda's got some bruises, but Lyle got the frying pan," Gibson answered, and stood up. "Gloria crowned him."

"Should have done it years ago," Gloria muttered, and started sweeping broken glass into a pile.

"Can you gentlemen help me carry Lyle out to my patrol car?" Gibson asked. "I'll get him checked out at the hospital and see that he's properly booked."

"You're arresting him?" Gloria seemed relieved.

"Oh, yes. There's a warrant out for his arrest even without tonight's shenanigans. Bob woke up this evening and asked for the sheriff. Told him Lyle had started following him Monday morning on his way to Fullerton. Following too close and all sorts of things. Bob lost control and ran off the road. Even then, Lyle stopped, searched Bob's car, and left again. It wasn't until another driver came along, saw Bob's car off the road and called it in. So he's already being charged with attempted murder and robbery. Tonight, we'll be adding breaking and entering and attempted rape."

"And possibly arson," Chuck stated grimly.

"Well, we'll see what the state fire investigator has to say," Gibson said.

"Is he safe to move?" Steve asked.

"Well, he's cuffed," Gibson stated.

"I checked him over," Chuck added. "He's got a big egg on his head, but I didn't find anything broken. The only thing is, if he wakes up, he might kick."

"Well, let's get him in the patrol car before he wakes up, then," Steve said. He and Chuck drug Lyle out from under the table, carried him out to the patrol car.

Gloria continued sweeping, suddenly stopped. "Gibson, can you call my parents and tell them I'm okay? Tell them that I'll see them tomorrow."

"I will do that." The deputy handed a business card to Wanda. "If you need any help, you call me, okay?"

"Thank you, Officer Gibson."

"Try to get some sleep," Gibson suggested, and turned to leave. "You, too, Gloria."

"Thank you, Gibson."

Wanda thought longingly about laying back down, decided against it. *Not until plans are made for tomorrow.* "I'm sorry you had to do that to Lyle, Gloria," she stated. "On the other hand, I'm glad somebody was here to stop him."

"He had it coming," Gloria muttered.

Chuck and Steve came through the porch. "Well, this has been a hell of a day," Steve stated. "Chuck, how do you want to handle tomorrow? Or, later today. I'm not sure what time it is."

"Take whoever shows up and go to the porch job in Cedar Rapids. I don't know if any of the youngsters will show up. If they do, try to keep them busy. I need to drive Wanda and Gloria to Fullerton. I don't know how long that will take. Wanda?"

She opened her eyes, realized they hadn't been open. "What?"

"Steve and the team need my pickup to get to work tomorrow. Gloria won't be very comfortable in the back seat of my car. Is it okay if we use your car?"

She started to nod, thought better of it as her bruised face

339

rubbed against the bag of frozen peas. "Yes."

"Good. Gloria, let me finish sweeping up the glass. You look almost as exhausted as Wanda. I suspect the adrenaline rush is fading. For both of you."

Gloria handed over the broom, but sat down at the table instead of heading for the bedroom. "All the cool air will get out that broken window," she complained, and seemed on the verge of tears.

Chuck automatically took charge. "Steve, there's a closet on the porch. In among all the jigsaw puzzles, there's a glass insert for the outer door. Could you find it and put it in the door? I'll take the screen in and get it fixed tomorrow, too."

"I'm on it," Steve agreed, and went to the porch.

"There, the cool air will not all escape," Chuck told Gloria. Now why don't you go back to bed? Lyle's going to jail and you're safe now."

"Yes," Gloria agreed. "I've still got Sammy to care for."

"Wanda?"

"Yeah?" She opened her eyes again. It was harder this time.

"If it's okay with you, I'm going to sleep on the porch tonight. What's left of tonight. That way, if you need anything, I'll be here."

"Okay," Wanda agreed, and laid down, her eyes closing of their own accord.

Somebody gently put the bag of peas back on her face. "Good night, sweetheart."

It was a comforting sound.

The End

Dear Reader;

<u>Hank's Widow</u>, which you have just read, in the first of my Small Town Happiness series with the Location of Belgrade, Nebraska. I hope you enjoyed it. I would be delighted if you want to read more of my work.

There is prequel to <u>Hank's Widow</u>, a short story called 'The Game', which should have come to you as a bundle when you purchased this e-book. If something happened and you did not get 'The Game' for any reason, you can still get it. Just let us know at MoonPhaze.com, and we will send you a copy. Sorry, but it only comes as an e-book.

There is another book coming in the Small Town Happiness series with the Location of Belgrade. Bob gets his chance.

The title is <u>Waiting for Glori</u>, and I expect it to be available right around the New Year of 2022. Gloria finally makes her escape from Lyle's abuse and neglect, and is surprised at how much help and love come her way from the rest of his family. Including finding part-time jobs to help her support herself and her son. The part-time jobs morph into a full-time job, and a stint at the local community college as she works to make up for lost time. Little did she realize that finding herself would mean finding love as well.

I hope you will enjoy that book. Other books set in other small towns will be forthcoming, but I'm not sure when. You can sign up to receive our monthly newsletter, MoonPhrazes, by visiting www.MoonPhaze.com. The newsletter will keep you informed on upcoming books by all of the MoonPhaze authors, sales, special events and personal appearances.

I hope to see you enjoying my other books!

Linda (NMI) Joy

Books by Linda (NMI) Joy

The Secret in Morris Valley - (currently available only in print, from MoonPhaze.com.) Ondrea is sent to Morris Valley to study the wolves, but Barry Morris won't let her out of the house without a heavily armed guard. He has plans for Ondrea. So do the wolves. (60 pages.)

The Game - In the tiny town of Belgrade, 4 cousins have been raised more like brothers, each trying to out-do the others all the way through high school. One night when the eldest is back in town, visiting from college, their relationship is torn apart by revelations made by two of them. (24 pages.)

Hank's Widow - (Available in July 2021) She wanted a quiet place to pursue her writing. He's loved her since he first saw her photo. Will her grief prevent him from claiming her heart? (340 pages)

Waiting for Glori - (Tentatively scheduled for January 2022.) She finally escaped her husband. Now she must grow up and become self-sustaining. How long will it take her to realize love is still available?

Books by Trudy V Myers

The Atlans; The Truth/The Legend - The Atlans claim to be descended from Gods. The legend isn't far from the truth. (E-book only.)

The Woman on the Dock - When an Atlan warrior finds a woman tied to the dock as a direct provocation, she must decide how best to react. (E-book only.)

The Cave - A cave can supply shelter from a coming storm, or danger from creatures that have also sought shelter. This cave, it turns out, offers much more. (E-book only.)

Hero - Herotio grew up hearing tales of the adventures of various heroes of old. He finds out early that being a hero isn't as easy as it sounds. (E-book only.)

Cali - (currently available only in print, from MoonPhaze.com.) Cali has been left for dead—twice—by a gang of men who also killed 2 children left in her care. Sidek tags along as she searches for those men, wondering if there'll be any pieces to pick up if she finds them again. (240 pages)

Science Fiction by John Lars Shoberg

The Stone Builders - An accident in the forest uncovers a hidden underground city left by previous colonists. Everything in the city is built of stone. Can the scientists discover what chased these previous colonists away before the same thing happens to them? (273 pages.)

The Waste Gun - Dr Von Scorio has developed a way to permanently dispose of radioactive waste. Others see it as a threat to the Earth. (247 pages.)

De-Evolution - Two colony children lost in a violent storm leads to first contact with a sentient native race, and a mystery that must be solved if the colony is to survive.

The Stone Ship - The military finds a derelict piece of a spaceship made of stone and reassemble the team that studied the stone artifacts before (The Stone Builders). Can they figure out what happened before the ship currently bearing down on them gets there? Is it the Stone Builders? Or whatever race cut the stone ship in half? (263 pages.)